KU-342-646

Penelope Farmer was born in Kent in 1939, and attended St Anne's College, Oxford, where she graduated with a BA in modern history. She taught for a while then trained as a social worker, but, since the birth of her first child in 1964, she has concentrated on her writing. She is married to a doctor and lives near Hammersmith in London.

Her first book, a collection of short stories, was accepted for publication when she was nineteen, and was subsequently published in 1960. *The Summer Birds* (1963) was her first book for children and was shortlisted for the Carnegie Medal. Her best known books for children, *Charlotte Sometimes* (1969) and *A Castle of Bone* (1972), have just been reissued to great critical acclaim. *Charlotte Sometimes* inspired a song of the same name by the rock group The Cure. A more recent ghost story for children, *Thicker Than Water*, was published in 1989. She has also written one non-fiction book: *Beginnings: Creation Myths of the World* (1978). Her first novel for adults was *Standing in the Shadows* (1984), followed by *Eve: Her Story* (1985), *Away from Home* (1987) and *Glasshouses* (1988).

Snakes and Ladders

PENELOPE FARMER

An *Abacus* Book

First published in Great Britain in 1993
by Little, Brown and Company

This edition published by Abacus in 1994

Copyright © 1993 by Penelope Farmer

The moral right of the author has been asserted.

*All characters in this publication are fictitious and
any resemblance to real persons, living or dead,
is purely coincidental.*

Every effort has been made by the publisher
to clear permissions in this book.

All rights reserved.
No part of this publication may be reproduced,
stored in a retrieval system or transmitted, in any
form or by any means, without the prior
permission in writing of the publisher, nor be
otherwise circulated in any form of binding or
cover other than that in which it is published and
without a similar condition including this
condition being imposed on the subsequent purchaser.

A CIP catalogue record for this book is
available from the British Library.

ISBN 0 349 10505 7

Printed in England by Clays Ltd, St Ives plc

Abacus
A Division of
Little, Brown and Company (UK) Limited
Brettenham House
Lancaster Place
London WC2 7EN

*To the memory of the real social scientist,
my twin, Judith*

1939–1991

ACKNOWLEDGMENTS

I am grateful to the Author's Fund for the grant which gave me the means and the time to research and write this book. I am also grateful, in particular, to Judith and John Roberts for the use of their house in Somerset, to complete the first draft; to Sarah Hayes for her detailed comments on an early draft; and to Victoria Nelson for advice on a later one. Many people in the pharmaceutical industry and the medical profession have put up with my pestering them for advice and information; to all of them many thanks. Above all I want to thank Russell Ellison, who gave me far more of his time than he could spare or I deserved, and also, last but not least, my husband, Simon, for helping this not always humble, let alone grateful, non-scientist to get it right (or at least not too hopelessly wrong).

Contents

Long have I looked for the truth about the life
  of people together
That life is criss-crossed, tangled, and difficult
  to understand.
I have worked hard to understand it and when
  I had done so
I told the truth as I found it.

Bertolt Brecht

There was a project, there were patients, there is a pharmaceutical company out there somewhere. The rest is as near fiction as anything ever can be.

BOOK 1
Setting Up

Chapter One

Anna Kern first heard of the project which was going to take up large tracts of the life of many people, including hers, and in some cases transform them, while lying in a large bed in Marin County, north of San Francisco, in early September 1985. On a shelf over her head, rather perilously in her view, this was an earthquake zone, stood a row of kachina dolls, reflecting, she supposed, like the Navaho rug displayed on the wall opposite, her friend Nikki's claims to native American blood. In the bed next to her lay the naked body of Nikki herself. This had no sexual connotation as far as Anna knew; the alternative in Nikki's very small house, for one or other of them, was the floor (the camp bed had been commandeered by Anna's fourteen-year-old son Benjamin, currently asleep downstairs).

'You can trust me not to grope, hon,' said red-haired Nikki, the night before, while stripping off without embarrassment to reveal pubic hair as red as the other; she was nothing if not direct in these matters (in most matters so far as Anna was concerned, Nikki came as a one-woman culture shock; this was one of the reasons she liked her so much; the reverse was also true; her Englishness was one reason Nikki liked Anna, Nikki said). 'Old hat I may be, but it's men I'm into that way, not women. Or rather' (here she giggled) 'let's be vulgar, *men* who are into *me*. And I mean to keep it that way; why else do you think I spent all that money having my face lifted?' (She was the only woman the neurologist's

3

wife knew who would have considered for one minute having her face lifted; *and* she's an academic, Anna thought.) What she had been less direct about was the fact she snored. The neurologist's wife, already jet lagged, hardly had a wink of sleep till dawn, and then, having dozed off, was woken almost at once, or so it seemed to her, by the insistent single ring of Nikki's phone.

'Answer it, hon, will you. If it's for me I'm still asleep,' mumbled Nikki. Pulling the mock leopard-spotted duvet firmly over her head, she started snoring again to prove it.

But it wasn't anyone for Nikki Anna found when she had managed to extract the receiver from the forests of little bottles and jars on Nikki's bedside table – vitamin pills, cod-liver oil capsules and so forth; it was David Kern, the neurologist, for his wife. At six o'clock in the evening in Jerusalem, Israel, well over seven thousand miles away, he was not sleepy in the least; he sounded excited rather; from the middle of a big medical conference on epilepsy, he spoke so fast, by his standards, the still dazed Anna could hardly understand a word he said.

'You sound half asleep,' he said at last. 'I left it as late as I could bear to. I didn't want to wake you up.'

'Well you did wake me,' she said. 'Now start again, will you. What is this all about?'

So he told her over again his story about a Canadian drug company executive who'd set up a meeting with him – a marvellous lunatic, he said – you'll really like him, Anna – about a research project into epilepsy he was proposing, about Africa and Ecuador, and an Ecuadorian neurologist called Gomez. About the Canadian's suggestion that he, David, should take charge of the medical side of the project. Everything about it excited him, from the medicine to the travelling involved. If the travelling sounded the most exciting aspect to his wife, that was because neither of them could have guessed how much more closely it would all involve her in due course. 'Can I come too, sometimes?' she asked him at some point. 'Of course. I hope you will, Anna. But you'll have to pay for

4

yourself,' he said. And then on he went about more scientific matters – he still sometimes forgot, she noticed, she wasn't a scientist – they'd known each other barely a year. But she wasn't a scientist. And what he left her with, for now, for all his talk of projects and trials, of patients and treatments, had nothing to do with science and medicine; nothing to do with protocols, methodologies, questionnaires, disease, the matters that would perplex and involve her so thoroughly later. It was that one word: Ecuador.

That word, that place, that association, no other, had her, an hour or so later, all of them crammed round a tiny table eating bagels and croissants and drinking coffee out of green French cups, quoting pieces of a half-remembered poem. Nikki, however, her ripe flesh now covered, more or less, by a brilliantly striped, rather short bathrobe, was too occupied with the vagaries of her expresso machine to be much interested; besides, if Nikki's literary taste was eclectic, it was not quite eclectic enough to have taken in English, Georgian, poets.

As for Anna's son Benjamin, he kept groaning loudly; all he wanted was to get in Nikki's car and drive down the coast to San Francisco.

'When I was thirteen or so I went into a golden land . . .' Anna quoted. 'Cotopaxi, Chimborazo . . . (or was it Chimborazo, Cotopaxi?) have stolen my heart away. . .'

'Ever my romantic friend,' said Nikki. 'Hasn't getting married to a scientist had any effect on you whatever, Anna?'

'Mum,' wailed Benjamin. '*Mum*. It's the Golden *Gate* I'm interested in. I want to be there before the middle of next week.' Since, at the same time, he was staring rather too hard for Anna's liking at the gap between the edges of Nikki's not very well-tied bathrobe, she kicked him hard under the table, missed and got Nikki instead – after one indignant look, Nikki summed up the situation precisely. She laughed uproariously, winked at both Anna and Anna's son, tightened her bathrobe, but could not do anything about its shortness; Ben went on staring; Anna herself grew more irritated by the minute, but then Nikki often had that effect on her. As for Nikki – 'You're so adorable, Anna,' she was always saying. 'You're so naïve.'

At that time, 1985, Anna knew as much about pharmaceuticals and the pharmaceutical industry as any vaguely socialist, sixties-reared, *Guardian*-reading child of her generation with a – relatively recent – medical husband would be likely to know. Apart from the fact that this industry was, undeniably, responsible for substances for which she herself had been grateful in her time, and without which her husband could not treat the majority of, if not quite all, his patients, this knowledge could, mostly, be summed up as what Carter Jacoman would call 'bad, bad, bad' (adverse drug reactions – scandals about the behaviour of sales reps etc. – lavish, all expenses paid trips to Venice, for doctors, etc.), no need for reflection, thereafter, not even on the contradictions inherent in this position.

It all changed afterwards, of course; to the extent of obsession; to the extent of a notebook full of relevant observations and quotations. For instance – to take a sample at random:

1. (Sigmund Freud.) 'Life as we find it is too hard for us; it entails too much pain, too many disappointments, impossible tasks. We cannot do without palliative remedies.'
2. (Corneille.) 'What destroys one man preserves another.'
3. (*The Epic of Gilgamesh*.) 'There is a plant growing in the sea. It has a prickle sharp as a thorn and sharper that will hurt your hands mightily, but if you can endure the pain of seizing it and eat you will live for ever. . .'
4. (Ad from the *British Medical Journal*, c. 1988.) LENYTOL – FOR THE EFFECTIVE CONTROL OF EPILEPSY. (Side effects; in small very small print.) 'Dizziness and diplopia, less frequently dry mouth, nausea and vomiting. Generalised erythematous rash, disappearing on cessation of therapy, isolated reports of oedema, hyponotraemia, exfoliative dermatitis, leucopenia,

thrombocytopenia, agranulocytosis, aplastic anaemia, cholestatic jaundice and acute renal failure . . .'

5. (Thomas Mann. *The Magic Mountain*. Last read aged 18! All I remembered was Peeperkorn, nothing and no one else;) 'The truth was, Peeperkorn said . . . the truth was in the world of matter, that all substances were the vehicle of both life and death, all of them were medicinal and all poisonous, in fact therapeutics and toxicology were one and the same, man could be cured by poison, and substances known to be bearers of life could kill at a thrust, in a single second of time . . .'

6. (The Book of Genesis; annotated.) 'God permitted Adam and Eve his wife to eat fruit from every tree in Eden except the tree of Knowledge . . . The serpent cried, "God has deceived you. Its fruit does not bring death, it only confers wisdom . . ."'

7. (Piet; drug co. executive, friend.) 'Let's get it clear, we have to admit firstly we're in the business of selling poisons. That doesn't mean we shouldn't sell them.'

8. (Answers to my own questionnaires, circa 1987.) Q. 'What do you think this treatment will do for you, apart from preventing seizures?' A. 'I'll get married – go to school – get my brain back – stop having headaches/ stomach aches/depression . . . my husband will come back – I'll have a happy life . . .' Q. 'How much would you be prepared to pay for such a treatment?' A. 'What it costs. Life is more precious than money.'

There are, of course, many other beginnings to this story. One might be Anna Owers' meeting with David Kern – some called their marriage five months later over hasty; what can such a pair have in common? they said. (Especially, Anna suspected David's older sister Sonia of saying it; David's ex-wife was also rumoured to have given the marriage five years, at best.) The epilepsy project was the first major test of such gloomy predictions in all events. Not that either husband or wife saw it that way at the start; far from it.

Another beginning, of course, might be a patient; patient 037, Beatrice, for instance, whom Anna Kern only met twice, but never forgot thereafter. Patients are more important than anything in this story; without

7

them there would be no project. So let us get ahead of ourselves here and now, to Kenya, April 1987. Let us have a:

Digression.

A very small, very thin woman, Beatrice wore a torn blue dress and a dirty white headscarf at her first meeting with Anna. The neurologist's wife, on her second visit to Kenya at this time, noted that she had a bad burn scar on a narrow arm, also that her face was pinched, her eyes bloodshot. Her age was hard to tell – so small and slight, she looked fifteen one minute, the next fifty. She was, in fact, it said so on her file, thirty-seven years old, older than her English interrogator. The reason she and Anna, another small, thin woman, with cropped hair, a burnt nose and, for today, very dark glasses, were sitting on a bench together, neither at all at ease, was that every now and then – several times a week, sometimes, though not in the presence of the neurologist's wife who only knew it from Beatrice's notes and from the fact she was included in the project – she would suddenly fall down and jerk and shake; once she had fallen on a cooking fire, hence the burn scar on her arm. (Her affliction is sometimes called the burn disease in this part of the world for obvious reasons. Beatrice herself called these episodes 'kifafas'.)

Beatrice had come to the hospital to be checked up, to be given her anti-epileptic drug, to be asked otherwise impertinent questions, at the moment by the project's anthropologist, who happened to be the neurologist's wife. She was a patient in Dr Carter Jacoman's project, one of those wretched people whose lives it was the proclaimed mission of that unstoppable Canadian to change – for the better, of course.

'You do think big, Carter, don't you?' the more cautious neurologist teased him now and then. 'Why not?' answered the Canadian. As for the neurologist's wife, Anna, acolyte as she was, or had been, experience had made her less certain. Listening to the young health worker's, Peter's, translations of what Beatrice said, or rather whispered to him, eyeing the bowed head, the stains on the once-white kerchief that covered it, she could see that changes *were* needed in Beatrice's life. She wanted her husband back, she wanted a job, to send her children to school out of her own resources, not paid for by the government as now, to live somewhere better than she did. She was one of the poorest of all the patients, Peter told Anna, looking concerned. But whether such changes could be achieved by the administration of little white pills was another matter.

They were sitting in a row, Peter in the middle, on the benches outside the hospital, where patients waited for their appointments. It was a good hospital by local standards; the president of the country lived nearby, that was why it was good, why a corrugated iron roof had been raised to shelter the patients from sun and rain. The sky above was brilliant, the trodden earth red mud after a downpour. Anna had to shade her eyes to see Beatrice, who did not look at her once all the time they were talking, at least not until the very last minute. Her husband had asthma, he couldn't work because of that, in any case they had split up because of her epilepsy. This started just after her marriage. Did she know why it started? Anna asked. The woman crouched further down on her seat, further from Anna, began speaking, very hurriedly, and in a whisper. Peter translated. 'She said – before marriage, she had a lover. When she said she was going to marry another man, he said, "Then you will see what you will see." Two days after that she fell down in her first fit.'

'You mean she thinks it was witchcraft, Peter?' asked Anna, feeling for once like a real anthropologist, instead of a not very experienced sociologist posing as an anthropologist. But when she glanced up from her notebook, she saw that Beatrice was looking at her at last, the wretchedness in her eyes so intolerable Anna could not look away. Neither woman looked away, not even when Beatrice spoke very urgently. Peter translated.

'She asks for two shillings for her bus fare,' he said, nodding when Anna handed the money over.

Two weeks later they went to visit Beatrice in her home; Peter insisted on it – he was not a good-looking boy, like some of the others, nor did he smile like them; he was very serious always, very concerned, too nice for his own good, thought Anna. Walking down the street bending his head towards her, he confided that he himself came from a poor family, not as poor as Beatrice's; but he understood how it was for her. He made Anna buy sugar and biscuits for Beatrice. Walking through the market, skirting trodden cabbage leaves, crates, dogs, dust, Anna stopped at a stall and added bananas and oranges to the sugar and biscuits she herself would never have chosen, thinking of the children's teeth.

How difficult it all was. Anthropologists, for instance, were meant to detach themselves like doctors; they were meant to be scientific and precise, and when they wrote up their field notes leave out what Galileo called secondary impressions, that is anything you couldn't measure or weigh or count – the smell of fruit in the market, for instance, rotten and ripe; the grind of dust and cabbage stalks underfoot; the sound of four women singing in four part harmony from a doorway just below the market which suddenly filled her with such ecstasy on such a morning. After days of this and that, homesickness, frustration, stomach ache, loneliness, ecstasy was what Anna felt, suddenly; pure joy you could say; Africa someone else told her, at least Africa on good days. But how could you measure that? She recorded it anyway, scientific or not, together with the boys in woollen hats, selling solitary packets of fruit gums or shoelaces or single biscuits out of open packs or lone bananas, who pursued them as far as the bus station. Here, she recorded her discomfort at herself, the white woman, Lady Bountiful, with her bag of goodies, being awarded, unquestioningly, the honoured place at the front of the matatu that lurched through the streets thereafter to its final halt outside the Day and Nite Club, at the far end of a line of single story shops and businesses; transitory, pioneer constructions, arcaded at the front; Dodge City minus cowboys.

The sky was brilliant blue over the scattered ram-shackle shanties beyond, over the distant red cliffs of the Rift Valley. The red earth was turning to dust beneath their feet – this indication the rains were failing ought to have sobered Anna a little; it did not – or only briefly.

Beatrice lived in two square, leaky huts, behind a barbed wire fence that had to be climbed through; there did not appear to be a gate. Flies buzzed in the doorway of the stinking latrine hut. None of the villages the neurologist's wife had visited had stunk of ordure – on the contrary – but Beatrice's compound did. Though the hut Anna was led into was like others in some respects, with its dirt floor and roughly woven walls, it was also the poorest she had seen by a long way. There were two wooden beds covered in ragged dirty blankets and set at right angles to each other; two rickety stools at once allotted to herself and Peter; a battered dustbin lid for a fireplace; three wooden shelves holding a few dented tin pots, nothing else to speak of. The walls around the door were papered with sheets of old newspaper and faded pictures of filmstars cut out of other newspapers – Raquel Welch she saw, Clint Eastwood, even Doris Day – white Americans, every one.

Only a daughter, a pretty girl of twelve or so, in a dress so ragged and old you couldn't tell its colour, was at home when they arrived. But almost at once two small boys detached themselves from the throng of children who'd followed the visitors as far as the fence, calling 'Hullo,' 'Goodbye,' and trotted after them into the hut to sit on the bed nearest Anna, reaching out to touch her but never quite doing so, tittering behind their hands whenever she looked at them. The daughter disappeared briefly, reappeared in a brilliantly clean red dress with white spots. Beatrice herself entered twenty minutes or so later, a load of vegetables on her back. She was a different woman entirely. She smiled at Anna, though shyly, looking away again quickly. She even sang as she worked, quickly, deftly, separating the vegetables – bunches of carrots, cabbages, potatoes – into smaller bundles to resell at the market. This was how she made her living, Peter told Anna. The songs were hymns, he added, but they did not sound like Praise My Soul or Onward Christian Soldiers, the kind of hymns Anna had grown up singing; apart from the lack of harmonies, they sounded more like the songs the women were singing in the doorway, back in the town. She did not stop even when a man came into the hut, screwing up his eyes in the dim light, and sat down on the bed beside the little boys. A small, thin, mild-looking man, his hair quite grey already, dust on his clothes and on his skin, he smiled at Anna, but did not speak, just sat looking at his wife, singing at her work. Anna assumed this *was* Beatrice's husband, despite the separation Beatrice had told her of last time they met. She assumed right; after a while, still smiling, he got up and went out, and Peter whispered to Anna that this last week, since Beatrice was better, her husband had come back to live with her again. He still couldn't work because of his asthma. Anna wondered if he and Beatrice blamed that on his rival's witchcraft along with Beatrice's epilepsy.

Twice then Beatrice did stop singing; the first time she instructed her daughter to light a fire in the dustbin lid and boil up milk for cocoa. The second time she went to the bed at the back of the hut, pulling out a little bottle of pills from under its mattress which she handed to Anna. Peter explained. 'She wants you to count them; to show she is taking the pills. She is very happy. She had only one seizure this week, that is all.'

'I can see she's happy, at this moment,' Anna said. But then she was happy herself – this was also worth recording in her view, secondary impression or not, because here they both were in this wretched hut, thousands of miles from home as far as Anna was concerned, guest and host, in perfect harmony, giving and receiving without fuss or bother. Reciprocity, anthropologists would call it, that was one thing they did have a word for. Anna's gifts of sugar and fruit had been accepted without comment, almost without acknowledgment, like any other transaction between equals. Just as Anna herself took the mug she was offered and the bread

12

buttered with margarine from a huge can, dismissing thoughts of the not very clean hands of the girl who'd done the buttering, of her own previously upset stomach; happiness making her hungry.

Outside, a thin thread of smoke from the fire climbed upwards to the sky. Sitting on her stool looking out at it, at the girl tending the cocoa in her dazzlingly clean red dress – how could you get things so clean in such a place – Anna took a gulp from a mug filled for the third time, before she could stop it, and contemplated the likely incompetence of herself and her kind in conditions most of them would describe as 'backward' or 'primitive' or at the very least 'poverty-stricken' – for of the poverty there could be no doubt. She could see sky through the roof and the walls of this insubstantial dwelling; it did not, for sure, keep out the rain; it could not keep out anything or anyone – the large padlock on the open door seemed a poignant but useless gesture of defiance. This family, moreover, did not have the smallest, meanest plot of earth, a shamba, from which to feed itself. All it had was bare trodden earth inside a barbed wire fence, two leaky huts, a stinking latrine. Yet Beatrice, of whom she had known nothing previously, except her ragged clothes, her seizures, the misery in her bloodshot eyes, of whom she knew little more now except the grace with which she and her daughter did their work and entertained their guests, for today just kept on singing. Whatever word could be found to describe this, it was not 'backward'. Or 'primitive'. Or even 'poverty-stricken'. Though it was in all obvious senses.

Anna had experienced such contentment before sitting in African huts, surrounded by animals and children; she had not expected to have such feelings today; feelings of ease, so intense, so grateful, so utterly unequivocal, that they did not, at that moment, admit anything as dubious as pity.

When Anna and Peter took their leave at last, reluctantly, Beatrice insisted on accompanying them to the matatu stop, outside the Day and Nite Club, along the pioneer arcade. Halfway down the track, she left them, briefly, went across to a stall and came back holding something in her hand, Anna could not see what. There was a matatu waiting. Once again Anna was ushered into the front seat, alongside Peter. As soon as they were installed, Beatrice reached over them towards the driver. Anna had forgotten the two shillings Beatrice had begged from her. But Beatrice had not forgotten. What she gave the driver, what she had been holding in her hand, was two shillings for Anna's fare.

('Surely you didn't accept it?' said the neurologist when told this story, back in England. 'From a poor woman like that?'

'Of course I accepted it,' said Anna. 'She knew a lot more about giving us that than I did,' she said, ashamed. 'Can't you see, it meant both her dignity and mine?' The neurologist just looked at her and said nothing. She was not sure if he saw or not. Working together was not proving very easy at that point; partly because he was, in effect, her boss.)

Whatever else could be said about this encounter, it was, certainly for Anna, along with the time in Ecuador, high up in the Altiplano, in a cold white room, when a woman blamed her husband's epilepsy on *'pena y suffri-miento'* – 'trouble and woe' it was, truly, a turning point; a point at which for her the project ceased to be, if in her case it ever had been, just a good excuse for travel; just protocols and methodology, questionnaires and blood counts, ceased to be lists of names; became a human problem with eyes, nose, mouth, limbs and torso, just like her own; or Ben's, more accurately.

Chapter Two

So much for Beatrice; just one piece of evidence among many, if Anna only knew, and at the same time material for what a good journalist does – a good novelist come to that; stirs your feelings with a good human story, of which neither she nor her readers can ever know the true ending, then punches up the facts. And the facts, of course, are the real story. Time, therefore, for a little digression on the disease in question; even though the disease in question, it should be made clear here and now, is not necessarily the chief, let alone the only priority of medical research projects. Anna found that out very early.

'Oh come on Anna, don't be so naïve,' said her husband. 'What about money, kudos; what about commercial considerations, for God's sake? Do you think this company would be doing this project if it didn't make an anti-epileptic drug? What about politics? What about the simple fact a research project is expected to be done? What about you wanting to see Chimborazo – Cotapaxi – what about my jumping at the chance to see epilepsy in its untreated state? What about Carter Jacoman wanting to make his mark in public health? That's what it's all about.'

'Not for the patients it isn't,' said Anna. (A year or so later she'd have added; 'Not for Beatrice.')

She took her notebook and wrote a digression on epilepsy. It was not difficult for her; even before this she knew rather more about epilepsy than she'd ever let on to her husband; when sometimes, inadvertently, she let her presumed ignorance slip, she wondered why he continued to suspect nothing.

And here it is.

A short digression on epilepsy by Anna Kern:

Let's start by looking at names – there are any number, apart from epilepsy itself which means 'seized' in Greek (seized by a god or a devil – take your pick). This is the official name, the one used by doctors, by drug companies, and by Hippocrates who wrote the first treatise on it around 400 BC, which he called after one of the other names for epilepsy, 'On the Sacred Disease'. It is also – for obvious reasons – the falling sickness, also the burn disease, also kifafas; its manifestations can be kifafas, fits, seizures, accidentes, attaques; take your pick.

The kind of seizures which make you fall down and shake, the way Beatrice did, for instance, is a generalised or *grand mal* seizure. Of course it is not the only kind of epileptic fit, but I'll confine myself to this most dramatic of its manifestations for the moment, first because the study mainly does, and second because these are the manifestations most stigmatised and feared, and also the most common. Fifty per cent of all epileptics suffer from *grand mal* seizures; hence 'the falling sickness'. This is what it means to have a *grand mal* fit.

A neurologist calls it a 'tonic clonic seizure' and describes it thus. (I quote).

'An attack may be heralded by a cry, the patient will fall, stiffen (the tonic phase) and may injure himself in the fall. He will lie rigid and during this stage of tonic convulsion may become cyanosed due to spasms of respiration. This stage is succeeded by the clonic phase, during which convulsive movements (usually of all four limbs) will occur, breathing may be stertorous and saliva (sometimes blood-stained due to tongue-biting) may froth from the mouth. Incontinence may have occurred during the attack.'

Or to put it more bluntly, from a patient's eye view (I can vouch for it) you fall down rigid and senseless, banging your head usually or worse, remain stiff for a while, jerk, turn blue in the face, bite your tongue, froth at the mouth (the froth may be bloody because of the

16

tongue-biting). After a bit your arms and legs start twitching, sometimes in the course of all this you piss yourself or shit yourself. Usually you end up confused; very often you have to sleep it off.

To that list add aches in your limbs and stomach and head; nausea; possibly injuries from your fall. Sometimes the post hoc symptoms continue for days afterwards, plus weakness and inertia, confusion, forgetfulness, unwillingness to do anything much (laziness, unsympathetic onlookers may call it). To that add uncertainty – you never know when another fit is coming, it is like a bomb planted who knows where and when waiting to go off, or an unseen manhole in a dark street, or a thunderbolt out of a clear sky. And if you are unlucky enough to have had your attack in public, add embarrassment, shame, people thinking you are drunk, possibly, or mad, or possessed by devils, or retarded or ineducable or incapable of work, or unfit to marry, let alone have children.

There have been rather more romantic not to say holy images of epilepsy, of course. The Greeks didn't call it the sacred disease for nothing. Hear this, epileptic, if you're not a madman then you must be a prophet or even a genius. Prophets, too, have been known to fall down and shake. Some of the most famous have actually been rumoured to be epileptic; Mohammed, for instance, though you have to be careful where you make that point. There was once an expatriate drug company executive in Pakistan particularly well-informed, or so he thought, who hoped to improve the image of the falling disease locally by mentioning Mohammed's affliction in a company newsletter. He was deported next day. He could be said to have escaped lightly.

Then, of course, there are the geniuses (who was it said 'the epileptoid nature of genius'?); leaving aside Napoleon and Richard Burton, Dostoyevsky, for instance. In a famous passage in *The Idiot*, Prince Myshkin meditates as follows:

'. . . that in his epileptic condition, there was one phase before the attack itself (provided the attack came during waking hours) when suddenly in the midst of sadness, mental darkness, oppression, his brain momentarily was as if set on fire and all his vital forces strained themselves at once, in an unusual outburst. His consciousness and feeling of being alive became almost tenfold during these moments, which repeated themselves like lightning. His mind, his heart were illuminated with an unusual light; all excitement, all doubts, all troubles were at once as if at peace, full of intelligence and final reason. Yet these moments, these flashes were nothing but the presentiment of that final second (never more than a second) with which the attack itself started. This second was, of course, unbearable.'

This moment of presentiment is not just a literary conceit; it is a recognised pathological phenomena, known technically as 'the aura'. My neurologist husband has encountered something similar in some of his patients; nevertheless he doubts that many of them, let alone those who are not granted this moment of insight, would also ask, as Myshkin does, 'What about its being a disease?. . . if the result itself, if the moment of sensation as remembered and considered in the healthy state, proves in the highest degree harmonious, beautiful, gives an unheard of and hitherto unthought of feeling of completeness, measure, conciliation and rapturous and gracious fusion with the very highest synthesis of life?. . .'

Nor, in my experience, would such a question occur to those who find themselves witnessing an epileptic attack; far from it. A German Protestant pastor defined it as a basic ontological terror of disintegration and chaos. 'A journey through madness into death,' someone else – a psychiatrist – called it. Another – William James – wrote that one patient worse affected than most – he was an idiot – represented 'the path of insecurity beneath the surface of life . . . *That shape am I, I felt potentially*' . . . that's much more like it.

For our bodies are, of course, the central image of our humanity; on and in our bodies the drama of our existence is symbolically and actually worked out; life, death, God, man, good, evil, belief, disbelief, reverence, irreverence, law, anarchy, tyranny, democracy, order, disorder, hope, despair. That's why medical issues, the doctor's role, arouse more passion and anxiety than almost any other. That's why, I'm beginning to realise, pharmaceutical companies, whose products in some way alter our bodily state, are more suspected, even vilified than any others; as if no one had the right to be in the business of buying and selling, making a profit out of the primary physiological and symbolic facts of our existence.

Thus when the epileptic falls and shakes and foams at the mouth, it is as if a hole opens in the world; he threatens, at levels deeper than most of us care to know, our not to be taken for granted ability to contain in our minds and bodies the vast mystery of the universe about us, to preserve it and ourselves from dissolution.

('Aren't you being a bit superficial?' the neurologist asked Anna, when he read this bit. 'Isn't it obvious that what everyone's afraid of is seeing any illness? Isn't it just more immediate in epilepsy than most?'

'It might be obvious to you,' said his wife, 'you're a doctor. It's not so obvious to most people, let alone anyone who runs away when they see someone having a *grand mal* fit. Or the ones who laugh, for that matter.'

'No one laughs when they see an epileptic having a fit. It's much too frightening.'

Given her reasons for not agreeing with this statement, experience not least, Anna phrased her response to this as cautiously, as formally, as possible.

'Lots of epileptics say they do. Their families say they do. You'd expect it. Don't people often laugh when they can't handle something? Bergson said that all situations provoking laughter involve humans behaving mechanically in some way. What's more mechanical looking in fleshly terms than an epileptic fit?'

'I suppose you could say that,' said the neurologist.)

Most people don't laugh when they see an epileptic fit, my husband says; and if people do, it's because they don't know any better. But if they do know a little better, though not much, they may attempt, for the best of motives, to ease the shaking body before them, to protect the tongue in the foaming mouth, by thrusting something hard between the poor wretch's jaws. This is another of the less publicised problems of epilepsy; jaws broken in such ways, as it happens, take longer to heal than bitten tongues.

This is why, presumably, six centuries ago, Hippocrates set out to dispel some of the superstitions, both social and magical, surrounding the epileptic, by showing his disease to be as natural as any other; and why 'On the Sacred Disease' still keeps on having to be updated; and not just in the so-called backward parts of the world.

Ask any sufferer. Ask the girl the teacher training college principal declared to be unsuitable; or the mother thrown out of a taxi with her small children, while having a seizure; or the woman forbidden to marry not so long ago, in one of the Southern American states, (who, incidentally, dared turn up at a medical conference on epilepsy, recently, and had delegates visibly squirming with embarrassment: what, a *patient* at a medical conference?) Ask anyone who here, now, today, does his best to conceal his affliction from the world. (As Richard Burton did, for instance.)

Ask Beatrice.
Ask Don Manuel Padilla
. . . Grace Ojuko
. . . Simon Mugambe
. . . Elisa Sanchez
. . . Senora Amada Simhalla
Ask Beatrice

(This last paragraph and its coda were in fact scratched out – though not sufficiently to hide what Anna had written. JOURNALISM! TOO RHETORICAL BY HALF!! was scrawled underneath.)

What she'd also added – this too was scratched out – was:
Ask Ben
Ask Anna

Chapter Three

Before coming to California Anna could only guess what kind of things Nikki surrounded herself with. If she'd thought about it – she hadn't, much – she'd have guessed right, in most respects; not least she'd have expected the many books, though not perhaps the eclecticism they revealed. On the shelves which took up almost all the wall space downstairs, and quite a lot upstairs also, literary criticism from Walter Benjamin onwards – some of it esoteric – sat alongside Wallace Stevens, John Ashbery, Ted Hughes, Auden, Amy Clampitt, alongside Kafka, Henry James, Thomas Mann, Willa Cather, Moby Dick, Conrad, *Rabbit is Rich*, John Cheever's selected stories, *The Natural, The Color Purple, Gone with the Wind*, Colleen McCulloch and Agatha Christie; movie biographies of such as Marilyn Monroe, Joan Crawford, Orson Welles, nudged biographies of Sylvia Plath and D. H. Lawrence. Tatty copies of *Ladies Home Journal* and *Cosmopolitan* were interspaced with equally tatty copies of West Coast literary journals and East Coast academic ones. On one top shelf, Anna was quite touched by this, remembering Nikki's reports of her upbringing – she thought only the English were nostalgic about childhood – were Louisa May Alcott, *Little House on the Prairie*, the Bobbsie Twins; also a shabby, leatherbound copy of the Bible.

The whole house, though, was more eclectic than Anna had expected. She might have predicted the Indian artefacts, the rugs, the kachina dolls, even the mock leopard skin duvet cover; but not the Minnie Mouse flanking one kachina, nor the Scots doll in a kilt next to two healer dolls from Peru. Likewise, on one of the few walls not taken up by books, a print of a Fra Angelico Annunciation and a lurid evocation of the Book of Revelations – this had to relate, Anna thought, to Nikki's grandmother in Alabama, the central figure in Nikki's best-known book – kept company with Andy Warhol's soup cans, a Georgia O'Keefe lily, a more than usually blurred and sentimental Renoir woman, Greta Garbo as Ninotchka and a Tarot chart.

Yet, on reflection, all of it, except perhaps the children's books, were of a piece with what Anna knew about her friend. She could still recall from their very first meeting the precise note in Nikki's voice, its real frisson, when, quoting Conrad, she had intoned 'the horror, the horror'. As she could also recall her surprise and delight, when Nikki had followed up her dissection of the *Heart of Darkness* with a precise description of a wonderful meal she'd had yesterday, and an equally precise description of a frightful one the day before; proceeding from there to theories of God as Mother, to Lévi-Strauss – 'that monumental inkblot' she called him (a quote Anna discovered later; Nikki liked quotes – she even threatened to write a novel one day made up of quotes entirely – Walter Benjamin, she said had suggested such a thing, but never got round to it; nor had Nikki, as yet) and back to the darling little pair of gold boots she'd seen in Harrods. Anna was drunk enough to say at last: 'This is a very Russian conversation, Nikki.'

'What do you mean?' said Nikki, getting closer than ever; English ideas of personal space were not something Nikki appeared to have heard of.

'I mean that Russians are supposed to mix up metaphysics and –' Anna was about to say 'trivia' but amended it '– domestic details, their stomachs and so forth. I like it,' she said. 'It's not just the way Russians talk,' objected Nikki. 'It's the way women do.' It was after this they'd exchanged addresses and phone numbers; it was on this note their friendship began and continued.

22

It was this note also that Anna identified in Nikki's place. David who preferred things simpler, altogether more linear, would have called it clutter. His wife found it comfortable in most respects; on the other hand she registered dissonance of some kind; dissonance only partly explained by her sense that, altogether, this visit was not turning out as she had expected.

One of Nikki's kachina dolls, for instance, the one with wings sprouting from its head, had a blank triangle where the other dolls had faces. Nikki herself could not explain it. When Anna asked her, she said that this particular kachina always was like that; she'd ask one of her colleagues who was more into these things why, if Anna liked. But what it meant to her was the kind of creative darkness in the mind, the kind that sucked you in; you were staring at nothing and everything. Terrifying, hon. Best not to think about it too long – it was like what Henry James' psychologist brother called the insecurity beneath the surface of life – or some such thing; and gee, she must be psychic, wasn't he talking about seeing an epileptic when he said that? She herself certainly needed an upper or downer if she looked at the thing too long. She gave Anna a hug. 'Don't you look at it too long neither, hon. Just don't.' But still Anna found her eye continually drawn to the figure with the winged head, the blank triangle of a face.

All the same this conversation was the only point in the three days they'd spent in California so far that Anna felt she and Nikki weren't fundamentally at odds; that for all the increased intimacy of their shared bed they weren't more at a distance mentally and emotionally than last time they met.

Of course everything appeared normal and friendly enough; by now Nikki was what she called 'showing them around'. This meant Anna and Ben being driven by her in her old Plymouth – no nonsense with Nikki about small or imported cars; no Chevy Chevette or Renault for her, no throwaway car of any kind – this car was not vintage exactly but certainly venerable, finned back and front, like something out of an old movie; with the remains of red trim on its battered silver doors, and an imitation wood dashboard. The covers of the sagging seats, rubbed, full of holes, were – even smelled faintly of – leather. The great tank of a vehicle was not, Anna knew from previous visits, the least reliable. Luckily Nikki had a tame mechanic who'd fetch up obligingly, not quite at the drop of a hat, but soon enough. Anna suspected Nikki of supplying him with other than financial favours. He was a handsome lad, if taciturn, from what you could see beneath the lime-green baseball cap pulled down well over his eyebrows. She could have fancied him herself if it wasn't for David; if she'd known how to set about seducing him, come to that; she'd need to take lessons from Nikki, she thought, with a bitchiness that surprised her. Nikki had never made her feel bitchy before.

The car was working well enough today, however; a little tour up the coast had landed them around teatime at a pretty village without superstores or gas stations, just what called itself a village store under a wooden arcade, and so on. 'Home for rich freaks,' said Nikki, 'Drop-outs with private incomes, or good jobs they don't let on about, something in the arts or ecology. Or else some little private business; vegetarian foodie stuff, for instance – eighties enterprise, hippy version, all very ecological, all very expensive, all, it goes without saying, very profitable. Real Estate's worth one hell of a lot of bucks around here. And it's exclusive, that also goes without saying. They don't like to let on about this place, either, they don't like anyone even coming here, in case someone shoves up a housing development or feeds in a tourist bus. They take down the signs, soon as the highway department puts one up. That's what it's like here.'

It's true there were no city suits to be seen; sneakers, long hair, jeans, featured on both sexes. Nikki herself wore sneakers and had her red hair loose on her shoulders; she wore shocking pink baggy pants and a wonderful pink, purple and orange tunic, that Anna had coveted as soon as she set eyes on it, knowing, however, it was much too vivid to suit her. Though she didn't, for all her efforts, look as young as she'd clearly like to, she made it appear almost desirable to be on the wrong side of forty; there was no trace of the rather touching defiance, not to say valour, concerning her age and appearance, that Anna had been aware of on this trip for the first time (maybe it was something to do with the face-lift; or maybe not). As she and Anna sat eating blueberry muffins on the wooden steps of the – famous, Nikki said – bake shop, opposite the Village Store, waiting for Benjamin who'd gone off to explore and buy coke, almost everyone nodded at her, Anna noticed. Nodded suspiciously – but nodded. One man, wearing black trainer pants, an embroidered Moroccan waistcoat and a shoe string tie, his straggly grey hair tied back by a bootlace, said, 'Hi, you guys, how are you?'

Sitting in the warm sun, shoulder to shoulder with Nikki, amid the smell of new baking – this village really was a parody of itself – Anna felt more at ease in her company than since she had arrived. So indeed did Nikki judging by the way she reached out and almost tenderly removed a crumb of blueberry muffin from the corner of Anna's mouth. Maybe it was Ben not being there for once. Maybe the new constraint, not to say awkwardness between them, had been due to the presence of Benjamin. She hoped it was; but she was by no means sure. The little scene with Benjamin and the bathrobe, for instance, the deliberate attempt to rile her, had been more of an indicator than she had realised at the time. Apart from incidents such as that one, there'd been the series of niggling, not to say itchy, queries about her married life – 'What do you give David for breakfast?' for instance, or, 'What side of the bed does David like to sleep?' or, more disturbingly, Ben almost in earshot, 'How does David handle having a teenage stepson?' – all of them accompanied by a somehow defiant look and manner, most unusual in the normally brash, what she herself'd call upfront, Nikki. Twice Nikki had even asked, not put off, seemingly, the first time by Anna's stony response – this was still a vexed, far from resolved

25

question – 'Are you and David planning a family?'

Anna was beginning to wonder if it was her marriage to David that had so altered things between them; it was their first meeting since that event, seven months before. She was beginning to wonder if she knew her friend as well as she thought she did; if Nikki, independent, cheerful, seemingly content with her life was not only more vulnerable, more frightened than she'd suspected; but also if she mightn't be jealous.

She couldn't ask her outright if she was jealous, as she might ask her more seemingly introverted friends in England. Despite their intimacy, despite Nikki's uninhibited descriptions of her consultations with her analyst, of her love life, and so forth, Anna had learned early on in their friendship that some things were better not mentioned. She was unsure if this came into that category – but she thought it might; Nikki's being jealous – if she was – was obviously a sensitive issue. But of whom was she jealous, if this *was* so? – of David, her husband? – or of herself, Anna, for having found herself a husband, after all these years of neither actually saying they wouldn't remarry, but both mocking, telling hilarious, in Nikki's case often indecent, stories concerning the efforts of would-be suitors? She did not know; either way found it disconcerting and unlikely.

For all its literary beginnings, theirs was such a peculiarly female, non-intellectual, almost sisterly friendship, she thought, removing a strand of Nikki's hair which had blown across her cheek when Nikki raised her hand to acknowledge the man's greeting; pinned down by such dear, cute little domestic nails, Nikki had claimed once; (most such nails, it was true, were hammered in by her). Much of it was, by necessity, over the telephone; you could say that what made their friendship possible was the fact that Nikki, as writer and teacher, not only earned good money but was prepared to spend it on cross-Atlantic phonecalls – discussing their love lives, what they were currently wearing, the state of Nikki's womb, her face-lift, her massage – all relayed with a degree of self-mockery Anna found invigorating. Sometimes Nikki even rang to discuss what she should wear to some function or other, seemingly unbothered by the fact Anna could not see the alternatives, only offer advice from Nikki's detailed descriptions. Things had marched along so easily, so cosily, in some respects, Anna had taken it all quite for granted. This was the first time she had suspected for one minute – especially given the fact of Nikki having been her chief confidant throughout the courtship – that marriage to David could affect it one jot. But now she wondered how she could have been so stupid; David himself was always telling her she was obtuse in regard to such things. Of course it must make a difference.

For instance it was probably significant that right up to this moment Nikki had not wanted to know anything about the neurologist's epilepsy project; whenever Anna had tried to lay the facts of it before her, the same way each of them had laid their lives before each other over the years, in a sisterly way, she had always, very pointedly, changed the subject. But she did not change the subject now; she herself raised it. Admittedly she contrived to fit in a reference to the marriage, almost immediately, the ambiguous tone of voice in which she did so confirming Anna's suspicions somewhat. She wished it didn't. She really preferred the Nikki she had thought till this week that she knew.

'Did he really say he'd be glad for you to come along?' Nikki was asking. 'Gee, anyone can see that guy's not been married long, that he's still got it badly. Aren't you the lucky one, Anna.'

'As far as I can see,' Anna replied carefully, ignoring this part of the question – the neurologist had called her again the day before, and been slightly more coherent, so there was plenty she could say – 'As far as I can see, this company makes an anti-epileptic drug, the Canadian doctor who works for them is setting up projects in Ecuador and maybe Kenya and maybe some other countries later, to see if it's possible to treat people in countries like that, who live out of the way, in places where the medical services are limited. I mean they'll treat people for a year with this drug of theirs and see how they get on. The thing is, he says, it's much more difficult to treat people with chronic diseases, because it's hard to persuade them to go on taking drugs when they feel better.'

'Nor can they afford them,' said Nikki.

'Well exactly. David's not sure it can work. He's not sure this drug company guy isn't crazy. But he says he really likes him, and that I would too. He wants to meet me.'

'Maybe there's a job going for a sociologist,' said Nikki. 'Though I'd watch that, Anna. Husbands and wives working together can be trouble every which way. And how.'

'Oh come on, Nikki, I'm years out of date. Anyway you'd need an anthropologist really.' (In her heart, though, Anna could not imagine her and David working together causing trouble. After eight months of marriage, she could not imagine anything more to be desired. Nikki's opinion could be put down to her view of her marriage, she thought, entirely.)

'What's David got to do with it, then?'

'They need a neurologist and a research group to design the study, to get the science right. Doctors do that sort of thing, work with drug companies, I mean. What worries him this time is that it isn't a straightforward drug trial; that this time they're only really interested in pushing their epilepsy drug; so that basically, in the end, all he is is a super salesman.'

'So?' said Nikki. 'If it's a good drug? I see nothing wrong with that, Anna. Why are you so picky? It's better than selling cigarettes isn't it? Aw, come on. You're so English, look at you. Doesn't he use the drug all the time in his own practice, if it's any good? Aw, come on.'

Benjamin arrived back then with cans of Coke for himself and Nikki, root beer for Anna, because Nikki had screamed when she said she'd never tried it, and insisted it was time she did. Supping out of the cans as they went – Anna ditched the root beer as soon as she decently could in a brilliantly painted litter bin which announced

'Trash here, folks, *I'm* environmentally friendly even if *you're* not' – they walked up and leaned over the rail that faced onto the water. This was not the Pacific Ocean itself, just over a headland, merely an inlet, its opposite bank a flat expanse of marshland, where the small white shapes of egrets scissored their long legs, and bending their necks dipped their long beaks in rush-fringed pools that mirrored the sky. In the waters of the harbour, anchored yachts and dinghies bobbed in the slight swell. It was the quiet time of early evening. Between her son and her friend Anna felt entirely contented for the first time since she had arrived, taking in everything about her and nothing.

'The name on that dinghy there, what's it mean?' asked Ben, pointing. Looking vaguely in the direction he indicated, Anna saw a shabby rowing boat, bobbing about, the oars still in it. On its stern painted very clean and boldly – the only clean, new looking thing about it – was the dinghy's name; *Smegma.*

'*Smegma*,' repeated Benjamin. 'What weird kind of a name is that?'

Before Anna could open her mouth, Nikki said cheerfully, 'Smegma's the little cheesy white bits which get caught between your penis and foreskin – which you need to clean out if you're not circumcised. Are you circumcised, Ben?'

Ben turned scarlet; choked; giggled; marched off in the other direction.

Nikki said, 'Did I say something? Did I upset him? Do you mean the English never get to mention such things?'

'Maybe he does with *his* friends, I just don't think he's used to discussing it with *mine*,' said Anna, irritation sweeping away contentment. On Nikki's face she again saw that defiant mockery. She could live with it for herself she thought, but not if it upset Benjamin. Ben was enough of a problem to her at this moment anyway. (When Nikki had asked Anna how he got along with David, his stepfather, she'd replied, 'Oh he gets on with *him*, all right; it's *me* he doesn't get on with' – indeed she was beginning to wonder if this holiday alone with him, this attempt at reconciliation, wasn't a mistake. Certainly it had been a mistake ending up at Nikki's). 'I'm not sure anyway,' she added, 'you'd get away with a boat called that in England. You'd probably get done for offending public order or something.'

'I guess there's not too many places in this country you'd get away with a boat called that,' said Nikki.

'Well then,' said Anna.

'What do you mean, hon, well then?' asked Nikki, dangerously.

'I mean we all have things, words we don't like to use publicly. It's just different in different places. I don't know anyone in England who squats under a bush the way you do, out walking, and announces that what they're doing is going to the bathroom. It's comic. What's wrong with the word pee?'

'Sex or defecation. You choose your poison, I'll choose mine. *Did* you have Ben circumcised?' asked Nikki, cheerfully, as if getting Anna irritated had been her only intention.

The status of her son's penis was, Anna considered, none of Nikki's business. 'What's it got to do with you?' she said, making her voice as neutral as she could manage. Remembering with a shock, in this unlikely place, the mare's nest stirred up – though not by her – after Ben was born, the torment of violent feelings and opinions – words like mutilation, superstition – concerning a matter to which she had never previously given a single thought, let alone regarded as a significant issue. This at least she did explain to her friend.

'Why are you so surprised? Aren't people more sensitive about the body, interfering with nature, than anything?' said Nikki, the tone of – self-righteousness was it? – in her voice so goading Anna Kern that she said, 'Christ, Nikki. What about your face-lift for God's sake?'

What am I doing, she thought, having an argument about my son's circumcision, looking at a boat called *Smegma*, and an environmentally friendly litter-bin, in the middle of California? What are *we* doing? – but it was

30

more than an argument now; quite suddenly – Nikki was not prepared to take the gibe about her face-lift, at the very least it gave her the excuse to let out everything that had made her so picky and itchy – her terms – since Anna arrived – quite suddenly it was a full-blown screaming row. Why did Anna have to be so fucking smart-assed, so superior, so fucking British for Chrissake – what was it Henry James said about Brits – 'an inexpressive and speechless race; perpendicular and unsociable? – did he just get it right. Apart from which: had she no tact, no sensitivity to anyone's feelings except her own; what had got into her, all she could think about, talk about, these days was medicine, her bloody husband, and so on, couldn't she see how it diminished her, playing little woman the way she was doing, being so coy about it all, so damn smug, Anna, you should see the look on your face sometimes, Anna, and so on.

Anna, taken aback, shocked even, lost her temper too, almost at once; letting out in her turn all her doubts, her wounded feelings, her fury at Nikki's sheer capriciousness, at her prurient – at this moment Anna called it prurient, maybe it was – curiosity about her marriage, her jealousy, if that was what it was. She hadn't realised before how she'd come to rely on, take for granted, Nikki, this friendship; maybe it had been an illusion all along, they'd never, after all, spent more than a day or two together before, maybe their friendship wasn't as soundly based as she'd thought; that doubt fuelled her voice most of all; sooner rage than grief she thought, she was damned if she was going to weep over the lost friendship if it was so, not in front of her friend, anyway. Staring dry-eyed into Nikki's face, her fists clenched in front of her, she first hissed, then shouted, how fed up *she* was with Nikki; yes, she bloody was picky, she bloody was itchy, if she hadn't wanted her and Ben to come why hadn't she said so in the first place; it was her insisted they stayed five days, she, Anna'd always said it might be too much given Nikki's small living space. Why didn't bloody Yanks ever say what they thought, always so open so jolly, and then bang, for no reason it was as if a door slammed in your face. And, by the way, what was she doing, much worse, flaunting her bloody body, sexually teasing a fourteen year old boy? It was outrageous. How *dare* she?

Nikki had her by the wrists now. Anna was almost too wrapped up to notice at first – the rage was like those conjurors' handkerchiefs, the more you pulled out, the more came; she'd no idea she'd been so upset, so angry. Suddenly aware of the pressure on her wrists, she fought it off; felt it relax suddenly, but her eyes shut, did not see at first the almost casual, not to say ironic way Nikki was looking at her, now; as if her rage had abated as suddenly as it arose.

'My, Anna,' she said, as Anna paused for breath. 'My, Anna. Just look at you flailing your tiny fists. It does make you look cute.' After a minute she went on. 'Why don't you look at me, Anna, while you're shouting at me?' But there was no animosity in it any longer. As Nikki's enquiries went, it was almost benign.

'Don't be so bloody patronising, Nikki,' said Anna. But this time she did look at Nikki; and she didn't shout either; how could she, she was not far off laughing suddenly – Nikki was definitely laughing now. 'And what the hell are you doing with a plastic Scots doll, anyway? You haven't even been to Scotland,' Anna enquired. At which point – whatever had started all this, for goodness sake? – Nikki let go of Anna's wrists, they both started laughing and crying together, hugging each other; when Anna's dark glasses caught on Nikki's hair, were dragged off by it, Nikki tore the glasses out of her hair with such violence she must have hurt herself and flung them to the ground. Shrieking with mirth and contrition – and pain presumably – she hugged Anna again, rocked her to and fro so enthusiastically they almost coincided with the environmental litter bin. At which she stilled completely; laid her cheek against Anna's, murmuring 'What are we thinking of, Anna? But wasn't that fun all the same? I never saw you angry before.' Such a tender scene caused Ben, reappearing, to take one look and go rushing off again.

'Now look what you've done. At the very least he'll think we're gay,' said Anna, before setting off after him. 'And the way you go on, Nikki, he might have a point. You're insufferable, like I said.'

She did not hear Nikki's reply, if any. And the first thing Nikki said, when she reappeared, Ben tagging awkwardly, some way behind, was, 'Is that Canadian drug company guy married, by the way?' She'd cleaned up her face, while Anna was gone; rearranged her tangled hair. Newly brushed it floated, glowing, about her face in the light of the by now close to setting sun. 'Oh and by the way, *are* you and David planning on having children?' she added. Ben was in earshot once more; Anna felt like slaughtering her all over again. But this time she kept her feelings to herself, did not even protest when Nikki tucked a friendly arm inside her own, for their walk back to the waiting Plymouth.

My name is Carter Jacoman. Let's start at the beginning.

Let's start with the concept – my concept. It was to be a freak through medical school. That was it; that was the whole of it. And if you want to know why be a freak in medical school, not law school or business school, or whatever, well, medicine was another concept I stuck to, I come from a family of Jewish physicians, at least on my mother's side; in a way my mother, I guess, would rather I'd broken out from the rest of them, and gone off and been a writer or playwright or something; but neither of my brothers wanted to be doctors, the eldest became an antique dealer, the next settled for being a dentist; that wasn't good enough, she wanted one of us to follow the family trail more directly than that; in the end that left me. Because in my family there was this thing we all had to take note of. A cousin of mine said once it was like that scene in *Death of a Salesman* where all the boys are ganging up on Willy Loman and Linda suddenly turns round and says, 'Attention must be paid'.

And that's it, that's the concern in my family. 'Attention must be paid.' Meaning you've got to think beyond your regular education and your immediate social milieu

– you've got to pay your dues to the world. Not necessarily to the poor or the disadvantaged or the blacks or whatever, directly. It's just the broader issues. And that gets translated down the line with everything and everyone.

So I went to medical school. The freak. But the freaky bit came from my family too. There was this uncle of mine, he was a very famous Freudian analyst, based in New York, in Greenwich village, his name was Stan. He was a really emotional guy, and very wild. I was an uptight, conformist kid, right up till sixteen, until this guy comes to town; he turns up wearing a shirt made up of about ten different shirts. This was in the fifties, and we were in Vancouver, I want you to know. He shows up from Manhatten in this brand new shopping mall – real high class stuff – one of the first we had in Vancouver – you're talking late fifties profanity here – cars with fins in the parking lot. And he walks through the grocery department in this amazing shirt, singing 'Ooh, Mow, Mow,' at the top of his lungs. And everyone was looking at him, he was disrupting the whole place.

Did it just give me a feeling of freedom; that you could get away with this far-out ontological crime? I guess if it had been my father, I'd have been embarrassed. But with Stan, I was just liberated. It all went on from there.

And what I wanted was to stay the way I was and still go to medical school. By which I don't mean I wanted be in medical school and then a physician, as a drug-crazed freak, highly dangerous to society. I wanted to show you could be a drug-crazed freak in Canadian society and still be a good physician. That wasn't so obvious in Canada at the time. Physicians were supposed to be models of probity, pillars of the community, that sort of thing. You know like Jews, Jews always had to be moral examples – that's the point of Israel, there you could be a prostitute or a bandit or a petty crook, and no one would say, 'What's with you, you're a Jew, you're supposed to be better than anyone else.' Well I wanted to do that for doctors; show you could be human, and it was all right, you could still do a good job.

So off I went to medical school, and it was fine. I had this rule with myself, if I passed an exam at more than seventy per cent I was working too hard. So I stayed between sixty and seventy per cent, that gave me time for the adequate amount of debauch and so forth. Though I have to say it meant that for the last two years of medical school I was sleeping about two hours a night and no more.

We did lots of wonderful things. We once smuggled in chickens and balloons and a helium tank into the Post Office – very early in the morning, at dawn. It was a great tall building in the middle of town with a helicopter pad on top. And we blew up those balloons from the helium tank and tied them to the chickens and we set them free, wafting over downtown at seven o'clock in the morning, all over the traffic, all over the middle of Vancouver – simply delightful for everyone.

('Except for the chickens,' murmured Anna, when Jacoman told her and David this story, in the middle of the night, in Ecuador was it? Or one of the times he stayed with them in London? 'Everyone says that, funnily enough,' replied Jacoman. 'But think of this – just imagine the life of a chicken. Mostly they just lay eggs and get their heads chopped off. But these chickens got to go somewhere for the day. They got press coverage. A lot of people say "poor chickens"; but we were good men in our way – we were *serious*. And we did a lot of other things too, with umbrellas and cabbages . . .' Wherever it was, though, it was getting late. The neurologist was yawning as well as laughing. He and Anna never did get to hear what exactly Jacoman did with the umbrellas and the cabbages.)

Before I graduated from medical school I went off on an elective to Papua New Guinea – I was into deserts and jungles and other extreme situations. I found someone in the Public Health Department and I went and put my beard on his desk and said I'd like to go to a jungle or a desert. And he happened to .know someone in New Guinea, but when I showed up in Port Moresby the guy there was shocked, he didn't know what to do with me.

In the end I was sent up to the Easter Highlands to be a freelance survey worker, that's basically the guy who goes into the bush with questionnaires for other people's studies. You know, do you have headaches, how many times last year did someone in your family get malaria, how many rooms in your hut, how many people in your family; that kind of thing.

I had a very nice time doing that. And I learned a lot; especially I learned about how development meddles with what works perfectly well if you leave it alone, even if it doesn't seem to do things the way we'd like. Which means I have to tell you the story of the Irish nuns. I was working in this little district hospital for a while, and women kept on coming in out of the bush with obstructed labour. But you couldn't do a Caesarean Section on them, because if you did, next time there was a baby they wouldn't come back, they'd just stay out there in the bush and die.

So instead we did this very rural operation called a symphyseotomy, we cut the pubic symphysis, and sucked out the baby with a vacuum pump. With most women this would cripple their pelvises for life – but these women were pretty good, we'd keep them in bed for a couple of weeks and off they'd go. If they were Western women, of course, they'd probably get all kinds of uterine prolapses when they were fifty or sixty, but nobody lives that long in New Guinea.

But all this was very bizarre to me; I mean it was only since the Australians came there was anyone to do this operation. How come anyone ever got born before, how come there was a population left at all? At this point I convinced the District Medical Officer to let me take a look at the British medical system in the colonies, he sent me out to some of the villages and what did I happen on there but a whole lot of Irish nuns, who were out doing maternal and child health. And in the course of this they were changing the food chain. Before they came the oldest man was at the top of the chain getting the best food, and the pregnant women were at the bottom. That way you get malnourished women having malnourished

36

babies; no problem; baby fits pelvic girdle, out it comes. Of course the babies died very often, they were so underweight. But the women lived, mostly.

But now here the Irish nuns were ably convincing the men (by which I mean to say they came in and beat them up if they didn't listen, didn't do what they were told) that if they let the pregnant women have the food, they'd have many more kids to grow up and work in the fields.

So then you got well-nourished babies, malnourished mothers, no way they were going to get out of the space available without those terrible operations. Not that the nuns minded. They had all these pictures of healthy babies to send back to their convent in Ireland to show what a good job they were doing. That was what they really wanted, nothing to do with the people really. What development worker ever really does want something to do with the people? I mean there I was doing my elective, there's the anthropologist having a nice time in the jungle doing his Ph.D., there's the journalist making his name with an in-depth report ('Just like you, Anna,' Jacoman said, looking at her sourly, 'Just like you.') there's the coffee trader looking for his bag of beans, the priest for his souls, the nuns for their pictures of healthy babies; who gives a shit for women with beat-up pelvises who aren't going to live beyond fifty and sixty anyway?

So that's what I learned. That's where I got to be suspicious of development workers, Unicef, War on Want, Africa Aid, you name it. What do these workers really want? It isn't clear. That's what I like about the pharmaceutical industry. At least it's honest. At least it says it's in it for the money. No nonsense about doing good in some way. Doing good for whom, I want to know?

I'll tell you another story. It's famous – by which I mean it's not my story; but it sums it all up in my view.

It's about a malaria spraying programme in the Pacific, or was it the Solomon Islands? – it doesn't matter. This was when they went round spraying the grass huts for malaria, because the mosquitoes sit on the walls all evening then come out and start biting them and their kids. Well, they spray the walls with insecticide and of course the mosquitoes die, that's why they do it, the bugs soak up the DDT and fall to the ground and then the chickens eat them. And then the chickens die. So this is what the villagers see. They see the development workers spraying their walls and then three days later they see their chickens die.

So next time the sprayers come, they won't let them in. And the workers say, 'How can you not let us in? If we don't kill the mosquitoes, your children will keep on getting malaria and keep on dying.'

And you know what those villagers answer? They answer. 'Children is easier. Chickens are harder to replace.' And you know, they mean it. And you know, in their terms, they have a point.

To continue. Anna Kern's notebook: A Short History of the Pharmaceutical Trade.

Easily enough done; the history is *very* short. Of course the history of the human desire for medicines – elixirs of life – philosopher's stones – is a great deal longer; you *could* say (see above) that the very first pharmaceuticals were to be found in the garden of Eden; immortality and understanding, the fruits of the trees of life and knowledge, are the same twin poles of human longing and aspiration which lie behind pharmaceutical company profits. Complete with side effects.

Time for a little Bible story, perhaps. Scene: the Garden of Eden; the trees of life and knowledge; ripe fruit hanging from them. The fruit didn't smell particularly nice. The serpent said that wasn't the point. It was what fruit did for you that was the point. The serpent was a good salesman, the first pharmaceutical detail man you could say; very well-trained, very glib and skilful. He'd brought Eve presents of other – not forbidden – fruits, to show his good intentions. He had a bag full of papers all demonstrating, he said, just how well-trained he was, what wonderful fruits he was selling. He brought some out to show Eve. Though Eve couldn't read yet, she could see that some of the writing was in very large letters and some of it in very small; 'that's side effects,' the serpent said; 'Not significant in this case – well, not fatal; you don't have to bother your pretty little head about these.'

38

There was also a picture of a woman just like Eve looking extremely happy, surrounded by books and globes and telescopes and microscopes, and all kinds of other equipment – not that any of it meant anything to Eve.

But she could see how happy the woman looked. She could also see the two little copies, one of herself and one of Adam, she was holding in either hand. 'Her children,' said the serpent helpfully.

'Would I have – children – if I ate your fruit?'

'Of course,' said the serpent. Eve was tempted then – life in the Garden was all very well, but what was outside it? Jehovah knew everything – why should she and Adam not know everything there was to know just like Jehovah? (As well as living for ever, whatever that meant. If you were alive, weren't you alive for ever?) In particular she would like to know how to make little copies of herself and Adam. What a charming idea! As for this little word, what was it? – death, that the serpent muttered under his breath; what did that mean?

'Death, of course,' the serpent, was saying, 'That's a very mild reaction, compared to the dangers of ignorance; and only likely to affect two per cent of sufferers, our trials show.' He failed to hear Eve's repeated question, 'But what is death exactly?' Instead he whipped out a large picture of the human skull, complete with cerebellum, grey matter, lobes, hemispheres, etc., all in technicolour detail. With a pointer he demonstrated to his bemused customer exactly where and how the paths of knowledge would go. He put that chart away only to produce an even larger chart of male and female reproductive organs, proceeding to demonstrate the working of each with his little pointer. Though Eve understood very little, it was all too much for her finally. Surely someone who knew as much as the serpent just had to be believed. She seized the rosy fruit he was holding out to her and took a bite.

Of this, of course, everyone knows the result. The serpent and Eve got blamed, of course, and duly punished. As for the serpent's managing director, Jehovah – who, in the heretical versions, almost certainly meant the bait to be swallowed – he was not only not the last manufacturer of such double-edged substances to blame the salesman for being over-enthusiastic. ('Such methods are not official company policy; they will be looked at in the future.') He was also by no means the last to blame the victim – 'a rather hysterical woman,' he suggested at the time – for not reading the small print before swallowing the bait. Oh no, certainly not. 'On your head be it,' he bellowed as the Archangel Michael lifted his flaming sword and drove Eve and her husband out of the gates of Eden. 'Know what you know, copulate all you like, give birth to as many children as you need to satisfy your maternal instincts. But remember, I have my share-holders to consider; don't complain to me when it hurts.'

And so it goes on; and on; and on; mankind, womankind, having opted through Adam and Eve for a life which is nasty, brutish and short, that is mortal, as opposed to immortal, have refused, persistently, ever since, to accept such a verdict. Just as they have refused to believe the sages and priests and gurus who tell them suffering is holy; instead they hunt the world over for potions and lotions, for simples and infusions, for pills, for tablets, for elixirs of life and love, to ease pain and grief and tendencies to fall down and shake; to make them beautiful, wise and happy; to attract fine men and beautiful women; to banish death for ever, before death banishes them. Everyone has always wanted medicine. The disease it's meant to cure is called life: a disease many have profited from over the years, it must be said. Magicians and alchemists, white witches and black, apothecaries and physicians, quacks and charlatans of all kinds with their elixirs and potions and promises have done very nicely for themselves – and why not? You couldn't expect them not to try and profit from the substances they brewed and peddled, could you? Selling dreams is a business like any other. This query, why should these tradesmen and women, unlike others, be expected to be saints, has been around a long time. Viz: Mandeville on Passion. c. 1730.

'Pray tell me what Grocer, Druggist, Linen or Woollen Draper, Goldsmith or other Tradesman of the most reputable Employment would you put that Confidence in, that he would sell you as much of his commodity as he thought you wanted? They have a whole Shop full of Medicines of which too many are in danger of being spoil'd and would you imagine they won't dispose of them and vend as many as they can? Ought not everybody to promote his Trade?'

Naturally, not all were successful at promoting their trade even so. Maybe most weren't; maybe, in those days, Shakespeare's poor apothecary was much more typical.

('Meagre were his looks/Sharp misery had worn him to the bones:/ And in his needy shop a tortoise hung/ An alligator stuffed and other skins/ Of ill-shaped fishes; and about his shelves/ A beggarly account of empty boxes,/ Green earthern pots and musty seeds,/ remnants of packthread, and old cakes of roses,/ were thinly scattered, to make up a show.' *Romeo and Juliet*, Act V.)

Certainly, selling medicines wasn't big, that is enormous business, till the twentieth century; the second half of the twentieth century to be exact. It was a matter of science, really; though science has a far longer history than the pharmaceutical industry, it took a long time to get round to serious pharmacology; largely because pharmacology needs so many other sciences to bring it about.

Alchemy you could say was the beginning; it fused the longing and the science – mystic aspiration on the one hand, practical equipment, beakers, burners, retorts upon the other. What alchemy led to, in the end, was chemistry, which doesn't believe in mystical aspirations any longer, merely in what all science does, weighing and counting and measuring. Pharmacologically speaking this has its uses; medicines, by necessity, as life-saving poisons, are measured in microgrammes; in minims.

The biologists came along later; like all scientists they had reason to be grateful to Galileo, he was the first to grind glass into lenses, to examine mysteries very far off, and close at hand. Latterly it's the work of physicists that has been more significant; first X-Rays, then radio isotopes, now ever-more sophisticated scanning processes – magnetic resonance imagers (MRI) among the most recent – my husband has great hopes of it in his work – have taken over from microscopes in the case of the human body, making it possible to track precisely the effects of drugs on the functioning human organism. Along with the discovery of penicillin, and in due course all the other antibiotics, it has been the machines developed by physicists that have enabled the pharmaceutical industry to become big business; the history of the pharmaceutical industry is short, like I said.

The neurologist, David Kern, first encountered the name Carter Jacoman in a letter from the medical director of the English subsidiary of Jacomans's pharmaceutical employers. It was a very revealing letter in its way; of its writer David thought at first, inasmuch as he did think about it – he was used to being addressed cautiously by such English contacts, particularly if they were on the medical side of the business and not directly trying to sell him anything. It was Anna who pointed out, two years later, when rummaging through David's files for purposes of the book Jacoman wanted her to write about him she came upon the letter, how very revealing it was of Carter Jacoman himself. Dr Jacoman did seem rather vague about what he was proposing, the writer said. Also for some reason he insisted on telephoning, rather than writing. He hoped Dr Kern would not object to his giving Dr Jacoman his phone number. He could expect to be contacted shortly. In fact Dr Jacoman rang that very evening, and spoke for nearly an hour, the forerunner of many interminable conversations.

'And was he vague?' asked Anna, who knew nothing about this at the time. Even at home David was frequently and at length on the telephone to someone or other; rarely if ever did he tell her what it was about; his professional life remained a mystery to her – how much of a mystery she was then only beginning to comprehend. More recently, of course, having realised the extent to which his work enveloped him, she'd attempted to penetrate the mystery, somewhat; or at least to involve herself in it. It may have been one reason she was glad to be sucked into the epilepsy project as soon as she was; why David encouraged her to be – working apart from his wife was one thing, travelling without her was quite another. Did her own professional life appear as much a mystery to him, she wondered? If so he seemed to have no desire or need to penetrate it, the way she wanted to penetrate his. Indeed, on a practical level at least, he reacted sometimes, to her fury, as if her profession was an alibi, rather than an identity. But then maybe it was nothing to do with the different nature of their respective professions; maybe it was their different genders. Maybe it was just them.

'How should I know?' said David. 'That was three years ago, Anna, just one call among hundreds. How should I know?' Then he relented a little. 'But I daresay he was. He was always vague until he'd picked your brains long enough to know what he was talking about.'

'And did you think he was as nuts as the man who wrote the letter clearly did?'

'If I did,' said David, 'it might have been a recommendation if anything.'

'You mean you were intrigued by his being nuts?'

'I was intrigued by what he was proposing,' – in this way, as usual, Anna's husband circumnavigated the question.

Yet he had been intrigued by Carter Jacoman's eccentricities; and knew that she knew he had been all along. As she knew he would have been insulted if she had not recognised it; much of their mutual attraction lay, after all, in such things. What he objected to was her stating, defining such recognitions; where she, much more tentative in her judgments, needed to state in order to explore, he only stated what was concrete, provable; in effect scientific; in other words that which was, indisputably, available to the senses, as opposed to the intuition. (Encountering Galileo's statement of this, with some relief, she thought 'David. Precisely.') This did not mean he did not like mysteries, things hard for people – for him – to decipher. He had difficulty in deciphering the music manuscripts he collected, for instance, though he had taught himself to read music years ago for just that purpose. He said he liked the sheer mysteriousness of the notes, it soothed him, trying to work them out. Nor did it mean he rejected the power of intuition. Far from it. He trusted it more than she did, as Anna even then suspected.

At the time though, she just said, 'Why is it that all

43

the people you really like talk too much? Is it just because it gives you the excuse to complain all the time they talk too much? Or rather say too much?'

David, as usual, did not answer. Except to say much later, apropos of nothing, 'No point in telling Carter he talks too much. You might as well save your breath.'

Ben had been seven years old when he had his first seizure. Anna had been warned it might happen, from the time, aged a year or so, he'd escaped her in the bedroom, fallen downstairs and cracked his skull; not very severely it is true; still he had cracked it. It had maybe been the final blow to his parents' marriage; on top of his other, still larger, resentment her husband had always blamed Anna for leaving the stair gate off, briefly. Both he and Anna had been present when the charming little boy, who'd been standing there screaming – their deep marital dissension expressed itself in him at that time in temper tantrums – suddenly keeled over, lay rigid on the floor before them. Then, foaming at the mouth, urine running out of the jeans Anna had only just bought him – afterwards his having wet his new jeans was what Ben harped on most – he began to twitch, madly. How long had it lasted – Anna hardly knew; all she did know was that it had been the worst moment of her whole life; her whole life had as if in those minutes disintegrated before her.

Ben had been lucky, as it turned out. These days, deep in patient records, Anna was more aware of that than ever. He'd had one more seizure a month after the first; Anna and possibly Ben also, though he didn't say, and she was not going to put the idea into his head if it was not there already, had spent that whole month expecting it to happen any minute. Eventually it did. Whereupon the GP had put him on medication – Lenytol, ironically enough, Bader-Kleitz' anti-convulsant. From that day he had been clear of seizures. And for the last few years, since well before Anna met David, clear of medication also. He had never, therefore, had to see a neurologist; they could, almost, forget the whole thing had ever happened; of course they didn't. Though the fear of Ben's having seizures eased somewhat over the years, it never left Anna entirely; she did not know whether or not it left Ben. Ben rarely mentioned his epilepsy – and usually only then to warn her not to tell someone about it, the whole thing still so embarrassed him, seemingly. As soon as he learned of David's profession, for instance, he begged Anna not to tell him, in particular, about 'what happened to me.' Ben always talked about 'what happened' or 'when I fainted', he never used the word 'epilepsy'. Anna used it to him, deliberately, telling him there was no stigma attached. But Ben had seen a stigma, whether she liked it or not – that his second attack occurred in his school classroom, in front of all his friends had been by far the worst of it for him; he'd become so unhappy at school, she'd had to move him. Many years later, quite recently in fact, he'd admitted that the other kids had taken to calling him Pissbum, because, yet again, apart from jerking and biting his tongue he'd wet his jeans. He would not wear those jeans thereafter; Anna contemplated sending them to Oxfam. In the end, guiltily, astonished at herself, she'd made a bonfire and burnt them.

Where they met, finally, David Sachs and Carter Jacoman, was appropriate enough – as Carter pointed out, not David; David was much less inclined to make anything of his Jewishness, out loud, at least. 'Not next year, this year in Jerusalem,' Jacoman said and laughed, or rather guffawed, very loudly. David sensed that at this first meeting Carter was, by his standards, nervous.

The occasion was the sixteenth Epilepsy Congress, which they were attending in their professional capacities; David as neurologist, Carter as drug company executive. They had set up a formal dinner meeting, with two other colleagues of Jacoman's, for the second night of the congress. But quite by chance they'd bumped into each other in the Old City, before the congress even started. David and his companions (one of his research assistants, the research assistant's Portuguese wife, and a neuro-physiologist from David's Institute whom they

45

had met in the hotel lobby on their way out) had already visited the Wailing Wall and the Temple Mount and were now navigating the uneven steps and paving stones of the Via Dolorosa.

It was much too hot to be comfortable; the conference had been convened somewhat earlier in the year than usual, so as not to coincide with the Jewish New Year. Around the corner just ahead, singing lustily to the accompaniment of two guitars and a tin whistle, straggled a procession of various ages and ethnicity and both genders, almost all long-haired apart from the two women in grey cotton skirts, grey t-shirts and the grey head dresses of nuns. Though the voices were thin and the words indistinct, though the tune to which they sang was more reminiscent of the Beatles than religion, the message was plain for all to see, Jews, Arabs, Christians, Buddhists alike. The young man wore jeans and earrings, his hair was in a pony tail; the thin girl's Indian kurta shirt, topped a droopy Indian skirt; each, inexplicably, carried a half dead Madonna lily in their spare hand, and laboured together under the weight of a not very substantial-looking wooden cross.

'Jesus lives,' said David, *sotto voce*, to his research assistant.

'And dies, circa 1965,' returned a voice in front of him, a little further down the same broken steps. 'Give me the Wailing Wall, any day.'

Two heads then turned and looked up at them; the dark one that of a pharmaceutical company rep whom David had met several times at conferences like this; the fairish, and somewhat loftier one belonging to a man with a long, almost parchment-coloured face, a smile that showed one broken tooth and others leaning every which way, and eyes – the colour of daiquiri was how David described him to Anna – Baltic eyes her definition, not his – who was promptly introduced as Dr Carter Jacoman.

Jacoman walked to the King David gate with them; he and David agreed to meet for a drink that evening, back at the conference hotel, a bland tower on one of the hills that surrounded the city, some way from the centre.

Their respective rooms were paid for, as was common at such events, by different pharmaceutical companies; for obvious reasons in Jacoman's case; in David's case, not much less commonly, because he was a speaker at a symposium on the subject of prognosis taking place the day before the Congress proper opened, funded by that company. They had offered to pay for Anna too, at least for her shared bed and room, if not her air ticket. Anna had declined the offer, owing to her American trip rather than to any disinclination to accept pharmaceutical company hospitality; she had hardly taken in the fact it was that. Much less cynical and suspicious than Giselle Jacoman, Jacoman's wife, for all her vaguely radical opinions – her journalism did not deal with political issues – she'd failed as yet fully to comprehend the symbiosis of David's profession and Carter Jacoman's.

She had attended another such gathering, in this case a purely European event, earlier in the year, in Denmark, not long after she and David married. There, though she had noted the presence of the pharmaceutical industry, not least the way drug company logos were emblazoned on everything, from pencils to tote bags, what had disturbed her much more was seeing, for the first time, how his profession swallowed up her husband.

Even as they were checking in at their hotel, three people, all wearing conference name tags and clutching the briefcases full of the material supplied to delegates – this too was stamped with the logo of the pharmaceutical company that had sponsored it – had descended upon him. All of them wanted professional discussions, either at that very moment or at some time to be arranged. Though David attempted, for her sake, to lie low – that evening, for instance they had room service instead of eating in the restaurant – mostly he let himself be swallowed up.

'It looks like I'll have to make an appointment if I want to see you,' she said, sourly, at last.

'You can see me in bed,' said David. 'No one else does that.' And then, turning to look at her – up to that point

47

he'd been rummaging distractedly among his papers, he said, 'I don't believe it, Anna; you're jealous.'

'Of course I'm jealous. It's absurd,' she said, laughing. 'You should be flattered.'

'I haven't time to be flattered, I'm too busy,' said David. For so he was.

Anna was proud of him, on one level. She had not realised how influential he was, in this world of his. (It was the reason, of course, why Jacoman sought him out.) Too recently married, however, to find it easy being so publicly peripheral, she had lavished some of what she quite conceded was petty – not to say enjoyable – pique on a funny piece about the alternative attractions, the hairdressing demonstrations, shopping trips, sight-seeing, and so on, offered to medical wives (called 'accompanying persons' these days, but still mostly wives) at such conferences – for the woman's page of a national newspaper. David did not think it was funny, naturally. It caused a coolness between them – the first such coolness between them – for about a week. Though that was now several months back neither, perhaps, was entirely sorry that Anna's trip to see Nikki coincided with the big epilepsy congress.

One constant feature of such conferences was the interpolation of local culture into medical business by one means or another. The last big epilepsy congress in Germany, for instance, had opened with musical intermezzi from the Winterhude String Quartet, followed by a presidential oration on 'Epilepsy from a metaphysical point of view: an interpretation of Raphael's transfiguration'. The next, in Delhi, would offer sitar music and a fire lit? blessed? by a Hindu priest. The Jerusalem Congress, however, eschewed both music and metaphysics; *its* invited speaker, according to the conference programme, was to open the proceedings with a peroration on 'Epilepsy in Jewish Law and Religion.'

'I guess that means we'll get the Talmud,' groaned Carter Jacoman when he and David Kern met in the hotel bar as arranged.

48

It was already after sunset. The lobby of the hotel had thrown off its Sabbath torpor; it was full of people arriving, others pinning up conference announcements, others just standing and talking, most in holiday clothes – you could tell the Americans by their Bermuda shorts and tartan jackets. David as usual when not having to play doctors wore jeans, Carter Jacoman on the other hand had changed into a pair of khaki trousers and a blazer, a garment David always claimed much beloved of international executives. From his brief glimpse of Carter, he had not, though, expected it of him.

Not that Dr Jacoman looked like an international executive even clad in such things. Whereas David Kern had the capacity to subdue the brightest colours into himself (the most unconventional clothes, Anna thought – were he to wear them – would be undermined, if not defeated, by his habits of concealment) the fury of Jacoman could not be disguised even by sober ones. It was not the subdued glint of his little gold-rimmed John Lennon spectacles, nor the more sober glint of the gold buttons on his altogether unlikely navy blue blazer. He seemed, even wary, even settled into a leather armchair in the corner of the bar of the Jerusalem hotel, across a low glass-topped table from David Kern, to be possessed of some furious energy that was wholly of himself. The glints of metal might almost have been picking up light from within him, rather than without; the same light that sparked coolly out of his ice-coloured eyes. It was not a hot enthusiasm. Any more than his colouring was hot; he was washed out looking, his hair, his clothes, his skin were washed out. In all the time he knew Carter Jacoman, David Kern not only never saw so much as a flush on his cheek, he never saw him in bright colours. But what spilled out from him became bright, blazed, if coldly. It was as if he turned the air in front of him, or even his listener into a prism from whom, to whom, the phrases poured in, white, sprang out crude, subtle, lively, any colour he liked; the bland enthusiasms of the company man transformed to a not quite manic but unmistakable absolute. It made David not only wonder but fear for him; as he would fear for anyone, in particular anyone in his position, in his job, who could lay themselves quite so open, in certain respects.

How long can he last? he asked himself. At the same time, maybe, he envied Jacoman's openness; but such understanding he did not acknowledge even to himself. What came to the consciousness of this skilful but obstinate diagnostician was, for the moment, only what he needed – quite simple observations: the man's clever; the man's crude; the man's subtle. He talks too much. His fingernails aren't clean. He's mad. He's clever. I like him. If I'm not careful, he'll drive me round the bend.

Meanwhile Jacoman devoured handfuls of peanuts, knocked back tomato juice – he was on his third now – this one had vodka in it – summoning the thickset waiter with a lordly hand that made David think he gloried in some way in being thus, here, in being an international executive with a healthy salary and an even healthier expense account; a man so sure of the services provided, he did not even have to look at the person providing them. There was a growing pile of Marlboro stubs in the ashtray in front of him. He offered David a cigarette each time he took one. Each time, David refused.

And all the time, imprecise as were his gestures – he kept dropping peanuts on the bar carpet, and occasionally, when he flourished a hand too wildly, cigarette ash – he drew from David exactly what he wanted; let David's observations on the difficulties of what he was proposing, the logistical drawbacks, the medical necessities, drop into him as into a funnel; from which he then produced schemes of sorts; which he refined according to the comments he drew from David.

'For instance,' David said, very early on, 'For instance, you have to decide how to find these patients; who's going to diagnose them – and that depends on your resources in the field. You have to decide what types of epilepsy you're going to include. It's much easier to diagnose *grand mal* than *petit mal*, as you've pointed out already. And what about hysterical seizures? How are you going to weed them out? You'll have to have very careful diagnostic criteria. And some very careful cross checking of diagnoses; otherwise you'll spend a lot of money for shit.'

(It would *not* be true to say that Jacoman had not thought of any of this. It *would* be true to say that he had not fully considered the implications of what he thought. Mostly it was because he did not consider it his job; it was for this he consulted people like David.)

They had been together for over an hour already; much longer than either had envisaged. Both running late for other appointments, they'd gone in turn to the lobby telephone to defer them. The bar, dimly-lit both by day and night against the brilliance of this sun-persecuted country, was filling not with the groups of conspirators nor with those intent on the kind of illicit dalliance that might equally be attracted by such shadowed corners, such deep chairs, such discreet opulence, but with groups of doctors – and in some cases doctors' wives – greeting each other loudly in many different languages, none of them the language of the country. Dutch, David heard, German, Swedish possibly, American English, of course. Watches were glanced at; dinner dates looked out for. If the conference had not yet started it was clearly about to. Despite the odd stranger sitting apart, despite the local Saturday night family in one corner sipping cokes, by now the place belonged to medicine entirely.

David had seen several people that he knew, from various countries. Several he fended off – some, more persistent than others, failed, unless prompted, to catch the air of tête-à-tête or even to notice Carter who, too intent to acknowledge such interruptions, drummed his fingers on the table while he waited for David to finish arranging meetings with other people. Once, as he put his diary away, David thought of Anna; how annoyed she would be at these interruptions, no more likely to hide her annoyance than Carter. All the same he was aware, almost guiltily, that with Anna he would have brushed interruptions away less insistently than now. But then he was married to Anna. And this was the first time he

51

had met Carter. And he was, definitely, enjoying himself. He had eaten at least half the peanuts, if more neatly than Jacoman; he'd ordered a third daiquiri – a drink for which he had a weakness; he had become almost talkative, for him.

He and Carter did not just talk epilepsy, of course. They talked of their medical education – or rather Carter told David about his. They talked about their tour of Jerusalem – and thereby, obliquely in David's case, of their Jewishness; both acknowledged the sense of threat from their black-clad co-religionists bobbing and chanting at the Wailing Wall and their opposing religionists on the Temple Mount, the women veiled in duster coats and chadors from head to foot. Both were secularists, or so declared themselves, though both admitted to being bar mitzvah'd in their youth.

'I guess we're bound to get the Talmud,' complained Carter for the second time. 'What does Judaism say about epilepsy by the way? As if we're not going to be told tomorrow. If you brief me now, though, maybe I'll give it a miss.'

'I never asked,' said David. 'The rabbi who bar mitzvah'd me never brought the subject up. He was too busy trying to teach me to sing.'

'I liked the singing. I guess I liked the performing. It was the first time anyone let me, the first time I ever dared,' said Jacoman, '*and* the last.'

A Swedish neurologist greeted Dr Kern now. Things having moved on, there was no reason for David to dismiss him as firmly as he had the earlier interruptions. But he did, for some reason. At once the thickset waiter – too brash to be unobtrusive, nor the least deferential – even after twenty four hours this seemed to David typical of the country – replaced Carter's overflowing ashtray with a clean one, wiped the glass-topped table over. Setting down their drinks he took the empty bowls and laid out olives this time, as well as nuts. They could not talk while he was working, not unless they talked to him, his expression and gestures suggested. Also he muttered to himself as he worked, flipping the napkin about regardless. His wrists were very hairy. He seemed to have violated the intimacy that had grown between them, even to have destroyed it. Yet in the silence he left behind him, in the light of the low lamp, shaded by the same smoky glass as topped the table, the black olives, the golden nuts in their glass bowls freshly set out upon it assumed once more an almost sacramental air. The lamp not only gave the two men their own space of light among the shadows, it picked out the features of the smaller and younger of them. They were emphatic features for such a retiring man; indeed David's whole face seemed somehow too big for his spare body. He had dark, heavy-lidded eyes and surprisingly long and thick eyelashes, as much as you could see them behind the thick spectacles he now wore; the dust in the streets of the Old City had forced him to remove his contact lenses. Tall Jacoman's head, on the other hand, seemed almost too small for his body. Being taller his face was the more shadowed, despite the glints on his John Lennon glasses.

By now they were talking about India, Jacoman congratulating himself out loud, not only had he found an epilepsy whizz kid to do his study – having not yet agreed to do it, David felt a flicker of irritation – his unerring instinct had led him to a man who knew the Third World. This irritated David still further. He said so, very obliquely, making a joke of it. Jacoman got the joke at once, he threw back his head and laughed very loudly. In his pleasure that Jacoman picked him up so quickly each time – Anna often had to have her husband's jokes pointed out – David almost forgave him. He almost decided there and then that he would do the study; just the same when he left Jacoman, he told him he'd sleep on it.

Not that he slept much; it was Jacoman's fault partly; it was Jacoman's fault that he'd had to eat so late, for one thing, as well as Jacoman's plans that kept his head turning. What was not Jacoman's fault was the continual grinding of trucks up the hill outside the hotel – the night before, Sabbath Eve, there had been complete silence. When the reason for this occurred to him, belatedly, secular Jew as he was, David rolled over in bed and missed Anna, fiercely. In the morning, early, came the sounds of building work; chinks and thuds and the clatter of machinery. He got up at last and looked out. The hillside was mostly still bare on this side of the hotel, except for rocks and red earth and dusty pine trees. There were little brown doves in the trees immediately below him. There were Arabs with red and white keffiyehs pushing wheelbarrows full of bleached stones towards the building works beyond them.

Yet again, in his head, he heard Jacoman's voice as they'd walked back to King David's Gate, passing heaps of stones, half-demolished buildings, even a donkey once with panniers full of rubble. 'Didn't they ever stop building this city since Solomon?' he'd asked. How come, David wondered, how come a man from Vancouver sounded so much more like a man from Brooklyn, when he got excited? And what had Jacoman done to him that he kept on hearing Jacoman's voice in his head, whether or not he wanted?

At their scheduled dinner the following night, Jacoman showed another face entirely. David had been aware throughout their previous meeting of a slight holding back, almost a kind of deference in Jacoman's probing, for all the brashness of his manner. Carter, he realised, had been feeling his way, no less than he had.

This evening, on the other hand, Jacoman made clear who was in charge; and on this occasion it wasn't David. He had brought two colleagues with him, a rather indeterminate looking but pleasant Scotsman (like a teddy bear Anna was to say when she met him later), the medical director in Kenya of the company's African subsidiary, and an American epidemiologist, with small eyes and a fat belly who ate steak and drank beer and said very little unless asked to, and even then grunted as much as spoke. But in general no one spoke much that evening, apart from Carter Jacoman. He arrived with a sheath of papers that he handed round, that contained, David saw at a brief glance, a neat résumé of everything he, David, had pointed out, the basis of a plan which, judging by what he'd had to say earlier, Jacoman would have been incapable of formulating before he'd picked the meat from David's brains. On this plan he proceeded to expound, with authority. David admired the cheek of it, quite as much as he was furious; the cheek not least of the fact that Jacoman was assuming his participation, before he'd even offered it, congratulating himself again for having recruited him. He wondered if Jacoman always did this, absorbed other people's ideas and then presented them as if they were his entirely. Wondered, if so, how Jacoman was liked in Switzerland, in Bader-Kleitz, if he set people's backs up there also. He certainly seemed to have set the back up of the man from Kenya, who glowered all this time, inasmuch as a man so patently amiable – also hungry judging by the way he ate – could glower over a surprisingly good dinner. Jacoman ate steak like the American. David and the Scotsman, both, as if to register a protest, settled for fish. Meanwhile, through his steak, Jacoman regaled them all with the story of the Pakistani doctor, he was to tell Anna much later; upon which one anecdote, David learned with amazement, not yet knowing Jacoman, Carter Jacoman despite all his talk of the need for scientific rigour, of budgetry caution, and so on, had based his conviction, his plans for spending large sums of company money; virtually the entire project.

They would go up to his room after dinner, Carter announced, and start getting down to details. David who didn't like staying up too late and could see this session extending into the small hours unless he could find some way of corralling Jacoman, wondered why they couldn't get down to them *now*. Yet still, by the end of the evening – it was, as he'd feared, very late – surrounded by papers and diagrams scrawled by Jacoman, by ashtrays full of Marlboro stubs, his throat full of smoke, his head aching, David was almost as sure as Jacoman – but damned if this evening he would tell him – that they could work together, that this was one project in which he'd like to involve his research group. By the next evening, he still hadn't spoken to Carter; he suspected he didn't need to, Carter knew his mind already – the arrogant sod. All the same he phoned Anna in Mill Valley, Marin County, to tell her he was going to do it.

Chapter Four

Another digression; May 1987. Ecuador. Patient 188. Another marriage. Don Manuel Padilla lives in a village in the Val de Chota, Province of Imbaburra, Northern Ecuador, the deepest valley within the Andean high plain – the Altiplano. Just up from a town called Ibarra, and some little way down from San Raphael, where the epilepsy project was based, it is one of the few places among the Andes proper from which, looking up, you begin to conceive quite how high – and mighty – these mountains are.

Of course you are never exactly warm, up on the Altiplano. The people of this equatorial country walk heads bent, huddled into hats and ponchos, you always feel if you don't always see that it is high country. But to anyone who has ever marvelled at the more obvious grandeur of the Himalayas, or the Alps even, it won't do exactly. There are the volcanos, of course, in other parts of Ecuador; Cotopaxi, Chimborazo, perfect snow-capped cones like the Hokusai prints of Mount Fuji; you can marvel at them. But round San Gabriel, up near the Colombian border, are only little humped green hills, rather a livid green, in fact, reaching in every direction, squared with maize and potato fields, and punctuated by trees that at such latitude know no season, shed their leaves, discreetly, all the year round. Beyond them, where you can't see, the land falls steeply, equally unimaginably, straight down to the Amazon basin.

The Chota, the other part of the study area, is a different matter entirely. It is not green and wet, it is hot and rocky. Leaving aside climate and geography, it is also quite different in human terms. Up on the Alto Plano the population is mostly mestizo, that is people of mixed American–Indian and Spanish blood. Halfway down into the Chota you begin to see black faces. Along the floor of the valley live almost one hundred per cent black communities, the descendants of slaves, possibly, no one knows quite how or why or when they came. They brought with them, into a tropical environment quite unlike the bleak and damp one on the Andean plateau, a social order that still remains more Afro/Carribean than Andean in certain respects, yet has long since incorporated within it the full panoply of Andean – that is American–Indian – culture and beliefs, hardly different from that of the mestizo population above them.

This valley profoundly affected the day's work, on the peripatetic days at least. On such days the three were on the move from six o'clock in the morning till ten o'clock at night, crammed into the front seat of the four-wheel drive truck; the three being Lastenia, the sociologist from Quito, a short, stocky, smooth-faced woman of thirty-five or so, not only part American–Indian but proud of it, unlike many middle-class Ecuadorians; Antonio, the local driver, a wiry and cheerful family man, who laughed a lot, showing off a mouthful of gold teeth; finally Anna Kern, the anthropologist, suffering from altitude problems (headaches, sleeplessness, inability to eat, depression, and worst of all – it was not usually a problem for her – acute homesickness).

Anna Kern's journal. June 1987.

Today was mindblowing. How can I ever get my bearings? We started by going up to 14,000 feet – it's the highest point of the study, Lastenia says – two and half hours or so on awful roads. Had to walk the last bit, very short of breath, because most of the village, including the patient, was out spraying potatoes on a vertical slope. Potatoes are the only crop that will grow at this altitude. Low cloud obscuring the crests above us, and sometimes extending its dank tentacles down as far as us; a smell of smoke from burning off scrub in the wood alongside us; cold; damp; a kind of doggedness about everything, from the crop to the trees to the mountainside to the people working on it, wrapped up in sweaters and ponchos and woollen hats.

The woman we had come to see was a youngish, sweet-faced woman, not Indian-looking at all – I kept thinking that she looked like someone I could have been at school with. She wore a scarlet sweater and green pants; had brought a dog with her which slept at our feet while we talked and occasionally rolled over, or twitched or scratched itself.

Lastenia made me ask the questions, she had to interpret my Spanish usually, and interpret the woman's to me. She said she hadn't had epilepsy long, only for a year or so since her pregnancy by a man she wasn't then married to but now was.

'What do you think caused your epilepsy, Señora?'

'*Nervios; pena y suffrimiento.*' Nerves, trouble and suffering, the usual story. It's easy to believe it up here in the cold, in a place with no seasons; how can you live in a cold place with no seasons? It might just be tolerable in a warmer one.

It also turned out that she had run out of drugs the week before, when the health worker failed to turn up. She'd walked all the way down to Monte Olivio to get some more – two hours down and three hours back – so much for all those doctors who've never thought it worth bothering to treat people like her because they claim they're too stupid to realise you have to keep on taking the drugs, let alone bother to get more when the supply runs out. (And what, they say, anyway, does the odd fit matter to a poor peasant who only works in the fields? I'm not sure I mightn't have said the same myself, once.)

We could see Monte Olivio on the way down – a small white town, miles below us in a shadowed valley; very cold looking. We'd picked up the sun again by then, the whole thing was a crash course in climatic geography (what kind of climate do you need to grow maize, beans, tomatoes, avocados, and lower still, sugar cane, some or all of it, like the potatoes, spaced out on seemingly vertical slopes?) and shedding layers of clothing and trying not to look at the occasional dizzying drops, marvelling at the multiple mountain landscapes laying themselves open to our eyes in ever-changing patterns of green and grey and brown, of crop and rockface, slope and valley, the transient patterns of cloud and sun fleeing across it. Amazing.

At the bottom we hit the main, metalled road, drove along it ten kilometres or so – it was very hot now, we were all in shirt-sleeves, the windows open – turned right, descended a bit more and, what do you know, we were in the tropics, everything steaming from a rain storm that missed us; bumping precariously along a narrow, deeply rutted and very muddy red track surrounded by banana groves. Shirtless blacks with machetes over their shoulders sauntered past, giving us curious glances and the van the odd clap on the side as they went.

No wonder I've got a headache all the time, no wonder I can't eat; those interminable diversions for lunch (two hours today, four courses) are completely wasted on me.

At five o'clock, towards sunset, we went to see a man with three wives and thirty-three children, Don Manuel Padilla; the dust underfoot was glowing literally – it hadn't been raining here. We had to walk right to the end of the village and climb down a perilously steep slope to a stream which I suppose is the village water supply, God help us, it's full of pigs. Don Manuel's wife appeared to be pulling up her pants on the far side, 'going to the bathroom' Nikki would put it no doubt; she giggled and waved at us. Don Manuel's wife is lovely, she needs to be, being married to him. She has a deep voice and an even deeper throaty laugh, like a cross between a thin Ella Fitzgerald and a black Elaine Stritch.

The house was the usual thing; very African looking –

roofed with sugar-cane stalks, dirt-walled,
dirt-floored, windowless, goats and chickens wandering
outside and occasionally inside, but it was the only one
I've visited so far not to have electricity. I don't know
why – the rest of the village was wreathed in wire, like
all the others; the Ecuadorians seem keener on
electricity than clean water. There was enough light
left to show that the main room was as neat and clean
as it was possible for it be in such conditions. Outside,
a goat silhouetted against the sky at the top of the
bank was feeding two butting kids. Inside, a fat girl
holding a fat, naked, male baby turned out to be one of
Don Manuel's many daughters.

'That man's a *macho cabrio* – a billy goat,' said Ella
Stritch/Elaine Fitzgerald, still laughing. She was
dandling her naked grandson on her knee, tickling
him. Making the motion of touching countless little
heads, she said, '*Macho cabrios* have many children.
That's the trouble with being a *muriego* (womaniser).'
And laughed again.

Don Manuel himself came in just before the light
died altogether. A big but gentle and wrinkled man of
fifty-eight or so in a check shirt and gumboots, he
didn't look the least like a *macho cabrio*. He sat down
on the bed and told us, smiling all the time – his wife
in her blue kerchief kept laughing and looking for
candles – how he blamed his epilepsy on yet another
woman; she had put a spell on him, after he'd thrown
her over. When he went to the local *brujo* to find a
cure, the *brujo* had gone as far as he could go, he had
used candles, hens' eggs and a guinea pig – they cure
people by rubbing guinea-pigs on their stomachs in this
part of the world, it doesn't do the guinea-pig much
good – after it was done he had seen the face of his
scorned lover in a mirror and knew it was her put a
spell on him.

As spells go, though, it wasn't too bad. He only had
fits at night; so no one but his wife – this wife, his
first, his favourite by the look of it, no wonder – had
ever seen him having one. He says she rubs his head

61

with cologne to ease him. He also says – we all started laughing then, but he didn't seem to mind, his wife was practically killing herself by now – that the worst thing about having fits was that for about two weeks after each attack he lost his virility ('*potencia para los mulieres*' he called it); in other words he couldn't fuck.

Of course he was happy now. He had been on treatment for six months and hadn't had a single fit. I bet he's happy. I don't know about his wife. But when Lastenia started reading out the questionnaire, with difficulty, there was still only the one candle, they answered between them, interrupting each other, contradicting, amending, augmenting; it felt like a long, tolerant and affectionate marital dialogue, *macho cabrio* not withstanding.

Anna Kern's notebook.

In the mountains of Ecuador, between 1986 and 1987, the following were suggested to me as remedies for epilepsy; pulling the patient's middle finger; rubbing an egg on his/her stomach; whipping him/her with a special herb from the mountains of Columbia 'to bring out the germs' (I have experience of this); removing hormones from the patient by hypodermic syringe. Not a lot of faith, incidentally, was shown in any of these remedies, except by one healer who claimed to heal virgins – in particular by the removal of hormones (it's possible he did heal some cases of hysterical epilepsy by this means or others). But the fact was, no treatment was available for most non-hysterical sufferers; all the above was hope and nothing else.

But then, till recently, the whole history of treatment of epilepsy has been hope and not much else; alternately it's been the history of no treatment; that is no effective treatment; there were plenty of remedies on offer, as above, based on what people thought epilepsy was, aetiologically speaking. Masturbation seriously suggested as a cause in some eighteenth-century cases, the remedy suggested was castration, what else; or in the case of a woman clitoredectomy; a matter of the remedy being worse than or at least as bad as the disease. With epilepsy, till recently, it usually was, so far as I can tell.

For instance; quite early on it was understood that epilepsy had something to do with the brain, though of course this understanding was expressed in terms of humoral medicine – according to which, epilepsy, being related to the phlegmatic humour, is a wet, moist disease, requiring hot, dry remedies. (How satisfactory such oppositions are, incidentally; you can see why they survived so long, they still exist, locally, in Ecuador not least. Given how Levi-Strauss and Co's binary oppositions – raw/cooked, natural/cultural – beguile *me* why should I mock? I don't.) Anyway. Galen (the great Galen, Greek physician, 2nd century BC) said it was a result of phlegm blocking the central ventricles of the brain; this did millions of poor wretches no good at all, since he and his successors also thought this excess of phlegm likely to be driven out by cupping and bleeding, and worse, much worse, by primitive brain surgery; skulls were trepanned – literally had holes drilled in them; the holes so drilled were cauterised, with hot irons and so forth. One set of instructions read as follows: 'Incisions to be made in the skull of Greek letter x. Circumscript cauterization of the head leading to desquamation of the bone.' etc. (All this sans benefit of anaesthetic, it goes without saying.)

Apart from surgical remedies there were:

1) natural remedies advocated by physicians, (in fact, since there were no recognised means of testing them out, empirically speaking, medicines that weren't simply herbal, such as cardamum, mustard, and later, valerian, differed very little from magical remedies).

For example, (advocated by classical physicians):
Blood of the tortoise or flatfish
Genitals of seals
Testicles of the hippopotamus (first catch your seal or your hippopotamus).
Faeces of land crocodile
Lichen of horses or mules
Human bones burnt and ground up
Stomach and blood of a weasel
Hare's rennet, ass's liver, liver of he-goat
Stomach of swallow at the waxing moon

Blood of the land turtle
Stork's dung.

For example; (advocated by the mediaeval, *female*, physician, St Hildegard): The blood of a mole, the beak of a duck, and the nails of a goose. 'For because the mole sometimes shows itself, sometimes keeps out of sight, and because it is wont to dig the earth its blood resists the disease which is at times felt, but at others, hidden.' And so forth; this beguiling explanation is called medicine by analogy; and related in that sense to alchemical medicine; Paracelsus, for instance, chemist, alchemist, philosopher, physician, advocated mistletoe because it will separate the 'epileptic conjunctions' of Venus and Moon, etc. He also advocated chemical remedies; vitriol, coral.

For example (17th century – 19th century) more chemical remedies:
oxide of zinc
nux vomica
turpentine
belladonna (poisonous)
silver nitrate (still more poisonous)
bromide.

(This last remedy, first used circa 1850, was the first known substance actually effective as an anti-convulsant; but that did not mean it was any less nasty. An American physician described a fourteen-year-old boy he was treating as follows 'As you see he is broken down in appearance, has large abscesses in his neck, and is altogether in a bad condition. But this is better than to have epilepsy.' I wonder whether he ever asked the boy if it was?)

2) Remedies of diet and regime, also advocated by physicians: (Keep the patient quiet, in other words see he sleeps properly, leads an ordered life, avoids strong emotion, eats/doesn't eat particular foods, and so on.) But such long-term regimes were only for the rich, the poor were more likely to demand and get a quick, cheap fix, often disgusting; ('Let the person who first saw him fall urinate into his own shoe, stir the urine and give it to the patient to drink.' And so on.)

3) Magical remedies, involving purification very often,

(epilepsy being seen as pollution, by association, if it was not literally pollution by evil spirits). Purification by amulets, by mistletoe, by ground-up bones, above all by blood – human blood especially – Pliny described epileptics drinking the blood of gladiators. Also all kinds of sympathetic magic; (the goat is the animal most prone to epilepsy therefore avoid the goat – alternately, innoculate yourself by eating a he-goat's liver).

4) Religious remedies: the Greeks called on Aesclapius, mediaeval healers, for some reason, called on the three wise men. ('Invoke the names of the magi, Balthasar, Melchior, Caspar, put gold frankincense and myrrh into a box . . .' and so on.) Also they advised paternosters, candles, Ave Marias; and so on.

Here are some modern remedies for epilepsy: benefits – cessation of seizures, (it is hoped); costs – various; see below. (Note, particularly, numbers 1 and 4; these are the two drugs which will be compared in Carter Jacoman's study.)

1) Phenobarbitone. Barbiturate. Marketed since 1912. Side effects: drowsiness, slowing down of mental activity, lethargy, irritability, sexual impotence (in some cases). Hyperactivity (in children). Rapid withdrawal dangerous; leading to possible status epilepticus; that is prolonged seizures – these can kill. (This is the drug most commonly used as an anti-convulsant in the Third World because it is cheap, and has been, if informally, recommended for use as such by the World Health Organisation. Western neurologists are very dubious about this, because of the drug's sedative effects. 'Does using phenobarbitone mean you are putting a hierarchy on Third World brains, Dr Jacoman?' asked one, very senior American practitioner, when Jacoman came to get backing for his study from a neurological committee.)

2) Phenytoin. Hyantoin. Marketed 1938. Side effects: gastric problems, skin allergies, twitching, gum problems, thickening of facial features. Occasionally hepatitis.

3) Primidone (1955) desoxybarbiturate. Side effects: drowsiness; lethargy. 'Syndrome of the first tablet' – can mean insomnia, hallucinations; etc.

4) Carbamazepine 1964. Imenostylbene derivative. Side effects: diplopia (disturbed vision). Psychotic reactions (in some – in others it is suggested by the pharmaceutical company – behaviour improves). Fatigue. Diarrhoea. Liver problems. Kidney – urolological problems. Skin problems. Its most commonly used form is that sold by Bader-Kleitz as 'Lenytol'. *(The very drug, though Anna didn't say, used to treat her son, Ben. It did indeed, to his embarrassment, affect his skin.)*

5) Sodium Valproate (1978) Side effects: thinning of hair, increase in appetite, weight gain. Depression, aggression, psychosis. Liver damage.

All the above side effects are least apparent on lower doses; these days therefore, doses are kept as low as possible, also one drug tends to be prescribed rather than a mixture as before. Though, as a result, fewer patients than used to be are chronically doped, not to say poisoned, some still prefer to keep having fits rather than take medicine; this is their right. We met one patient in Ecuador who manipulated his dose so his fits came only at night. It's called self-titration – who, prescribed some drug or other, doesn't self-titrate at times? Doctors call it failure of compliance. Patients call it making up their own minds. And so on.

Finally, more and more brain surgery is being practised on those epileptic patients, including those of Doctor Kern, where the cause of their epilepsy is specifically, recognisably, sited in their brains. The descendant of trepanning, it is, of course, much more effective (and much less painful) in the right patient; the right patient meaning the one who will still be able to speak, move, think, etc., when the relevant bit of his brain has been removed. These days this can be tested for in advance. Formerly it was a matter of luck as to whether the patient having been cured of epilepsy was left with a problem just as bad, if not worse.

Chapter Five

It was Anna Kern more than her husband who got to hear the story of Carter Jacoman's life. He was very different from her husband; David never talked about himself – sometimes listening to Jacoman, she regretted that. Indeed at times she came to feel she knew more about Carter than she knew about her husband. More than once Carter Jacoman said to her, 'It's so good talking to you, Anna. It must be the journalist in you makes you such a good listener.' (Meaning Giselle isn't a good listener, she wondered. This was a little before Carter started using her as what David called a freelance Marriage Guidance counsellor.) More than once her husband said to her, suspiciously, 'You and Carter are very hand in glove, these days? What do you find to talk about?' 'Him, mostly,' Anna said.

Once Jacoman said to her – there was enough innocence in his glee, to make the statement tolerable, just about – 'I'm a doctor. I like changing lives.'

'So what are you doing in a drug company then?' Anna asked him. Jacoman was in a strange mood that day; even jumpier than usual, he stubbed out his cigarettes half-smoked, instantly lit up another; he'd been talking at, rather than to, her. Some of the things she'd said in her turn, he hadn't even heard. But he heard this; he looked at her this time. He said, his voice pained, as if she really hurt him, really cut him to the quick; or alternatively she was just plain stupid. 'How can you say that, Anna? Look at how your life's changed, and I wasn't even intending that. Look at the patients, look what's happening to them; look at all the people working on the thing out there in Kenya and Ecuador, Turkey and Pakistan. If I stayed a doctor I'd have changed a few lives, but not on that scale, not on that scale. Look at it, Anna,' he almost pleaded. 'Can't you see?'

'Did you know that when you joined Bader-Kleitz?' Anna asked him. 'Is that why you joined?' 'You have to believe it,' said Jacoman angrily. And there and then he proceeded to tell her the story – or rather one version of the story – of how he had came to find himself in Basel, 'a freak in a drug company' he put it. But Anna observed how, as he got into the swing of his narrative, he forgot, or maybe just discreetly set aside, the thesis that his joining Bader-Kleitz followed on from his hope of changing lives. Indeed, after a while, he began claiming that he was telling her all this simply as material for the book he wanted her to write about him, about the project. (Had she read Tracy Kidder's *The Soul of the New Machine*? he enquired. That was a good example of the kind of thing he was thinking of. Anna said she hadn't read it. And repeated what she had said before, that writing a book about this project, about Carter, was quite an idea. She'd have to see.)

There are, of course, many other versions of the story Jacoman told that day. Jacoman himself gave other versions; so did some of his friends and colleagues. In particular there was the one given to Anna and David by Denis Taylor, the man who became and remained Jacoman's boss; the man who in his version of the tale 'groomed', trained, turned the still untried, and, by Swiss standards, uncouth Canadian, with his verbosity, his chain-smoking, his not one hundred per cent pristine fingernails, into a pharmaceutical company executive. For though it was all very well Jacoman being a freak in Medical School, if he was, at heart, a freak in a Swiss pharmaceutical company – and there is some disagreement as to whether he was that – he had better make sure he did not look like one. As for the rest – 'The man's schizoid,' someone said looking at Jacoman's handwriting.

'I need at least one schizoid on my team,' said Dr Taylor. With his broad shoulders and thick neck, his gym-honed body, Taylor himself, crammed into an expensive suit, looked not unlike a boxer, even just possibly a hit man, dressed, literally to kill; he didn't look like a pharmaceutical executive; not at first sight, anyway. 'Action man,' Jacoman's wife Giselle dubbed him, disgustedly, from the start.

Jacoman, on the other hand, was quite as fascinated by Taylor as repelled; in some weird way, Taylor might have been his alter ego. None of this would have happened – no one's lives would have been changed the way they were – had it not been the case. In the context of this story, as of the project itself, Taylor, and Taylor's being what he was, mattered at least as much as Jacoman being schizoid; (which he wasn't, in fact, except in a manner of speaking – as one of his other colleagues, Piet, once said to Anna, he was just such an unconventional as these kinds of companies employ to generate new ideas and so forth when profits are holding up. And on whom they cut down when they are not.)

'And what about Giselle?' asked Anna. 'Were you married by this time? What did Giselle think?'

Jacoman's voice took on the weary, ironic tone, stranded somewhere between sympathy and exasperation, that almost from the beginning any mention of his wife evoked. 'Look, Anna,' he said, 'let *me* tell *you* the story, will you? This was 1979, we'd been married more than two years by then; didn't I tell you how I married her? Well perhaps I'd better get that over first; it all fits. I went travelling straight after the time we got together; so I continued courting her by long distance phonecalls, at midnight mostly, her time; finally I persuaded her to meet me in Morocco. She got a boat from Gibraltar; when I met her on the dockside at Tangier I was wearing a white hat and a white suit, like something out of Paul Bowles, but still with my beard and my long hair, and waving a marriage certificate. That was news to her, all right, but she didn't take much persuading; I got us a black taxi and we headed for the Canadian Embassy where I had it all fixed up. And if you want to know how I fixed it up, how I persuaded her? I mean apart from the fact I was crazy about her – just crazy – I don't think she was crazy about me – well she wasn't saying, anyway; Giselle's not the sort of woman tells people she's crazy about them. But if you want my honest opinion, I think that what she was doing, marrying this Jewish hobo in Morocco, without a word of warning, was punishing her dad. Giselle's into punishing people. Her father's a posh Englishman you know, emigrated, married a beautiful French Canadian before he knew better, I mean before he knew the way people like him in Canada ought to look down on French Canadians. So he took off and married the right kind of Wasp – took Giselle with him, her mother went crazy, not surprisingly, and Giselle punished him ever after by making much of her Frenchness; calling soup 'potage', converting to Catholicism, you know the sort of thing. And then by getting off with me, an Estonian Jew and a degenerate pot-smoking hippy to boot. Like I said, Giselle's into punishment; it makes her feel good.'

Jacoman wasn't bad at punishment either, Anna reflected, hearing him recount, thereafter, how he'd proceeded to drag his new wife round various parts of the world, living on nothing, in the backends of nowhere, in bug-ridden flea-ridden hovels more often than not; ending up in Iran; where Jacoman, ever more scornful of Aid Agencies, got a job running the medical system for American expatriate military advisers. What he got out of this was: the understanding that he could work alongside uncongenial people (in this case mostly gung-ho ex-Vietnam veterans, delighted to be bolstering up the Shah and, with the Shah, his secret police); that he actually liked administration; that he liked what he, picking up the jargon as usual, called the interface between medicine, planning and administration, patients, doctors and administrators; that he enjoyed having a lot of other people's money to spend – and that he liked earning it.

'I walked out of that job, Anna,' he said, 'with around

eighty thousand bucks.'

'And what did Giselle get out of it?' asked Anna.

Jacoman looked gloomy here. 'You put your finger on it, Anna,' he said. 'She didn't get a lot. I mean what could she get out of it?' – this Anna could see all too well, from her own knowledge of Giselle Jacoman, as well as Jacoman's descriptions of her. A woman in an Islamic society, a sixties 'make peace not war' flowerchild – the polite, not to say inhibited Canadian version – among US military red necks, a miniaturist painter of exquisite if disconcerting trifles, confined in a strange land to a room full of cockroaches – for the money didn't come in at once; what was there in it for her? 'She upped and left after six months and went to London to stay with her English grandmother,' said Jacoman. 'As a matter of fact, Anna, I couldn't blame her, even if it was me she was punishing this time instead of her father. Taking her to Iran was a big mistake.'

'You mean you didn't ask her if she wanted to go to Iran?' said Anna.

'Oh I *asked* her. Sure I *asked* her. But I don't think I listened to her answer. I'm not even sure she gave me an answer. Giselle very often doesn't. That's just the way she is,' said Jacoman, grimacing, stubbing out yet another cigarette. Anna discreetly put the ashtray on the floor and replaced it with a clean one.

She didn't ask Jacoman here if he loved his wife. It was obvious he loved – or at least had loved her – a lot. For instance he indicated that it was Giselle's being in London (painting by day, waiting on tables at night, waitressing she called it, using her grandmother's English idioms to get at Jacoman, as she had used her mother's French ones to get at her father) quite as much as his new interest in medical adminstration and Public Health, that led him to applying to do a course in Public Health at the London School of Tropical Medicine and Hygiene. More than applying – bludgeoning himself into it, phoning secretaries and professors alike from Teheran at all hours until the school, on the strength of his cheek, his Canadian MB, his 'amazing record in Iran' (his

71

words) and a very brief interview, agreed to admit him. Of course he had to pay his own fees. This took up so much of the 80,000 dollars Jacoman had brought out of Iran, that he and Giselle had to live in a flat loaned to them by her grandmother at the top of her own house eating lentils and rice for a whole year. But it was worth it, he said.

He'd laid very low at first in London, he said. He'd been on his best behaviour *vis-à-vis* Giselle on the one hand, the London School of Tropical Medicine and Hygiene on the other. This was, after all, London, and he was still in some respects a Vancouver lad. At his first meeting with Giselle's grandmother, at a family lunch, he had not once opened his mouth. (Admittedly – this Jacoman did not tell Anna, Giselle told her at some point – Jacoman's mother was also present on a short visit, and Jacoman's mother rarely shut hers.) 'What a quiet man,' thought Giselle's grandmother, an assessment Jacoman recounted now, with loud guffaws.

During his year in London, still, Jacoman's thoughts of his future had been a long way from the commercial world. What he wanted was to get back to India. But the old India hands were no longer in charge at the School. It was old Africa hands now, one of them liked Carter, took an interest in him. When an executive from a subsidiary of the pharmaceutical company came to pick his brains concerning some public health scheme in Sudan, or possibly Somalia, the old Africa hand recommended Jacoman as consultant on this project. On the strength of which Jacoman was invited to company headquarters in Basel to discuss it.

Even then, years later, retailing the story to Anna, Jacoman remained quite clear in his mind what the invitation to Basel implied. 'I was going to Basel to talk about a consultancy, just that. The idea of a permanent career in Bader-Kleitz never entered my head. My view of the pharmaceutical industry, then, Anna, for pretty much the same reasons, was pretty much yours, Anna, yours and David's. As for Giselle, my so much as considering a consultancy on just one project appalled her; let alone anything else.'

Denis Taylor, however, gave quite a different version of Jacoman's invitation to Basel. His part of the company, he said, wasn't yet in the habit of employing outside consultants in such matters. Given the brief of the subsidiary company whom Jacoman thought he was going to see, it was possible they could make use of a consultant, but by no means certain. What *was* certain was that on the basis of the information they had of Jacoman, based on the recommendation of the old Africa hand, and the CV for which they had subsequently asked him, he seemed worth looking at as a potential executive, and it was for that purpose he was invited, all unwitting, to bring himself along.

This confusion explains why Jacoman found himself in Basel, going here, there and everywhere, up and down in elevators, in and out of company vehicles, eating large and expensive meals with a succession of executives, 'gonefs all' – he called them – none of whom seemed to know what he was doing there, or anything of the project on which he had thought he was there to be consulted; nor did any of them appear to know what anyone else he saw was thinking. This was not Jacoman's idea of a large, efficient, multinational company. On the other hand, it was, in an odd sort of way reassuring. First, because, if the company was much less monolithic than he'd assumed, he might not feel quite such an outsider as he'd assumed. Second, because it was already clear to him that he was at least as clever, if not cleverer than most of them. (Apart from the fact they were interviewing him, wining and dining him, for reasons that, if Denis Taylor was right, he was at no point canny enough to uncover.)

When he did at last meet the man in charge of the project – something to do with contraceptives and population control – he did not find him reassuring. The project he decided, almost at once, was crap. He'd had enough of Basel by this time.

'Look, Anna,' he said, taking another swig of coffee, lighting yet another cigarette. 'Look, Anna. We were dirt poor in London, we lived on nothing. So forty-eight hours of gobbling down large quantitites of fat and protein, not to mention large amounts of alcohol, not to mention smoking big cigars rather than roll-ups, you can imagine what it did to my digestion. My breath would have flattened a camel. I felt overhung, bloated; I couldn't sleep. Giselle was right, I decided, this business wasn't for me.'

'I see your stomach has adjusted, Carter,' said Anna, thinking of the steak and chips, the cheesecake she'd just watched him devouring; not to mention the two Bloody Marys with which he'd washed it down; this was also his third cup of coffee. Jacoman, however, ignored her.

'"But wait," they said,' he went on. '"There's one more person you must see, Dr Jacoman, before you go." I was too exhausted by this time to say no; which was just as well, as the person I didn't refuse to see was Denis Taylor; he was already Medical Director, Developing World.' (At this point it became clear where the story was leading.)

Denis Taylor, Jacoman continued, also thought the Sudanese – or Somalian – project was crap, he was the first person Jacoman met in Basel who seemed to him to talk sense. This meant, Jacoman said, he was the more disposed to listen when, after they'd agreed the original consultancy idea was not worth pursuing, Taylor suggested that Jacoman might consider working in his department; they had a vacancy based in East Africa, for Medical Director, Africa. Of course it wasn't all cut and dried, there would have to be consultations, Jacoman would have to demonstrate his suitability to other guys apart from himself – along with the boxer look and a ready-to-wear tan, Taylor, whose career in the past ten years had taken him everywhere but England had a distinctly mid-atlantic turn of phrase, multinational executive speak, you could call it (Giselle Jacoman certainly did). Along with that went what Giselle later dubbed Taylor's Euro shrug, a contortion that was, in his attempts to entice Jacoman into his pharmaceutical fold, drawing up his eyebrows, making his broad shoulders appear ready to burst out of his jacket that very minute.

Yet Jacoman always insisted that Taylor was clever; certainly they got on well, these total opposites, from the start. Jacoman, beardless by the time he arrived in Basel and shorter haired than he had been since he was fifteen, but still by no means groomed, by no means tidy; against Taylor with his striped tie from St Mary's Hospital Medical School, London, with his waft of aftershave and his hair cut by professionals, not like Jacoman's, by his wife.

After so many years of living rough, of not just rice and lentils, but cockroaches, mosquitoes, bed bugs, in out of the way places, there was more of an attraction in this for Jacoman than he'd expected. Taylor had a smell of power about him; at the very least of power to man-oeuvre; not to mention having his, Jacoman's career now, this minute, in the palm of his hand. Taylor he realised, with his as yet minimal staff, was relatively small fry in company terms. But having seen in the course of his pointless lunches how loosely the company seemed to function at this level, having heard Taylor discuss how he proposed to develop his department, knowing what freedom Taylor had now, this minute, to hire, if not subsequently fire him, he could see the possibilities of making an empire, of some kind, within this loose yet tight federation of commercial states; that is if you played your cards right. Dimly he saw it. Certainly he saw money to do what he wanted, more money than an Aid Agency handled in a whole ten years.

To his own surprise, to Giselle's horror, he arrived home, toxic from the food and drink and cigar, his breath smelling vile, his head aching, seriously considering Taylor's suggestion.

Two weeks later Taylor rang from Basel; he was coming to London; he'd like to invite both Jacoman and his wife for lunch.

Of this encounter there are three versions; Jacoman's and Giselle's are not dissimilar, except in some subtle respects; Taylor's on the other hand might have been of another occasion altogether – this was hardly surprising, the essence of Jacoman and Giselle's accounts being her total, maybe excessive loathing of Taylor; of what he stood for.

Taylor, for instance, congratulated himself on his acumen, of having done his research into Jacoman's CV, into the whole file that was building up on Jacoman; he even knew that his wife was a painter of miniatures. He had invited them to meet him, therefore, not in any French or Italian restaurant, but in an Indian restaurant called the Madras, at the back of Charlotte Street. There, he said, over what his version called an 'interesting' meal – Taylor himself preferred French or American cooking – he'd put it to Giselle straight down the line; he thought she'd been impressed, that it had brought her round to a less prejudiced way of thinking. After that it was up to Carter, she was his wife; and no man was a good executive who couldn't manage his job and his wife, both.

In Jacoman's and Giselle's version, Taylor hadn't been nearly so clever. His Indian restaurant was all wrong for a start; the nearest its Bangladeshi cooks had got to Madras being Dakar, judging by the look of the menu, and by the blown-up photo of the Taj Mahal that covered one wall. But if there was one thing Giselle knew – she'd inherited from her French forebears a liking for food and cooking – it was what constituted good cooking of any ethnic origin; Taylor's enthusiasm as he surveyed the unpromising list of bhajis and kormas, insisted the two of them advised him what to eat, put her back up right away. She picked out four dishes at random – one very hot – this was intentionally malicious, Jacoman suspected – she did not warn Taylor – and left it at that.

Jacoman glancing at her, made a brief calculation of likely outcomes, and said, 'You'd better watch out for the Madras curry, Denis. It's fierce.'

'Giselle likes it hot, does she?' said Taylor, smiling. 'Good for her; well I'm game, I'll have a go.' Even by this Jacoman's back was not put up exactly; at least not the way Giselle's was. His capacity for ripping apart the smallest of foolish pretension, was equalled by his capacity for not recognising them, or at least for excusing them, if he'd decided to like the person, if the person was likely to be of use to himself. This was especially true if they were freaky, his definition of which had expanded since his student days. Oh what an asshole, he remarked of Taylor after this meal was over; and made it sound like a compliment, almost.

The gear Taylor was wearing on this occasion did not help. The expatriate's parody of Englishness – open-necked shirt with a silk scarf tucked into it, brass-buttoned blazer, cavalry twills, chukka boots – looked even more out of place on his neat but chunky body-builder's form, below his foxy eyebrows, his full head of red hair, than his suit and tie had done, the first time Jacoman met him. Nor did he do himself any favours, in the eyes of either Jacoman, self-deprecating Euro-shrugs not withstanding, by spending the first quarter of an hour talking entirely about himself; meetings he had chaired, well-known personages in the field of international Public Health he had button-holed, at some risk to his professional reputation, but who had congratulated him on his open mind for a pharmaceutical company executive; and so forth. His voice was soft – like a dentist, said Giselle – rather monotonous – like a robotic dentist, Giselle said. Though the accent was at base minor public school standard English (not that either Jacoman or Giselle, even after a year in London, were much up in the English class distinctions contained within vowel sounds), it was at the same time overlaid with a tendency to flatten a's, to call them 'you guys', to invite them to share his thoughts; at times he addressed them as if they were a board meeting; at other times he talked in a palpably Swiss accent.

'I submit to you,' he said, when he had at last moved from the exploits and deeds of Taylor – script by Taylor, credits by Taylor – oh! – the food had arrived by this time, they were all indifferently spooning up rice and indeterminate curries, all, vegetable, fish or meat, having roughly the same flavour, if not the same intensity of heat. Taylor took one discreet forkful of the hottest, choked – disguising this as best he could by turning it into a cough – mopped his brow, and failed to finish his sentence. Giselle did not so much as taste the Madras curry, Jacoman noted; for a moment, seeing her faint but definite smirk at Taylor's discomfiture, a surge of the atavistic rage she could arouse in him even then prevented him from hearing Taylor, now rather red in the face, but otherwise master of himself, resume his peroration. 'I submit to you that Giselle thinks drug company executives are crazy, foolish, out for what they can get.'

'I did have a few ideas like that,' agreed Giselle, ironically; tall and thin, with long dark hair, she was wearing jeans and a waistcoat, both richly embroidered by herself, over a white silk shirt. But Taylor didn't seem to be listening to the words, let alone the irony. 'In a way, of course, she would be right,' he went on; 'Who would work in such an enterprise if they weren't crazy, foolish, out for what they can get?' If he thought he was going to disarm Giselle by such admissions, he had only to look at her to know they'd had the opposite effect. But he did not look at her, except in passing. He looked at the knives and forks, at the half-empty curry dishes on their metal warmer, at the plastic freesias in a yellow plastic vase; he even addressed the hovering Bangladeshi waiter – the restaurant was by no means full. He threw a suspicious eye at the dangerous curry, on which Jacoman was now, dubiously, embarking.

'But I will also submit to you that most of us wouldn't work there if it was just like that; I submit that we in Bader-Kleitz are all ethical beings, that we wouldn't want to work in any company that we thought was basically doing more harm than good. Of course, Giselle, we have made our mistakes. In particular we have made our mistakes in developing countries. Let me share with you the thought that as a democratic company, believing in local autonomy, we cannot keep too tight a rein on the guys running our enterprises, locally, nor should we. On the other hand, in the light of new criticisms, changing attitudes, in the light of a, let me put it, new "*weltanschauung*," we have, as from now, to start changing attitudes from the centre. That's why I'm sending really smart and principled guys like Carter here to work in the field. I told *him*, now I'm telling *you*, Giselle, I think he believed me, I hope you are going to, it's because I want his ideals, his principles, I'm sending him. I'm not trying to undermine them, the company's not trying to undermine them in any way. Sure he has to understand a few basic commercial realities, but that's not to say he has to compromise his own views in any way; we in Bader-Kleitz want him in those countries to be Carter Jacoman, himself, in all the best senses, to find out what's best medically for those countries, that is all.'

He'd intended to continue – his hand was up to check any interruption – a practised committee man, Carter was noting. Giselle on the other hand felt she'd had more than enough. She got to her feet – her husband suddenly realised that she was crying – Taylor did not seem to notice this, either – 'I have to go to the Ladies,' she said, and ran, pursued by curious looks from the waiters. She was gone for ten minutes at least. Having told Jacoman at some length what a pretty girl she was, what a lovely figure, what a lucky man he was to have her, Taylor's tone of voice altered completely; he reverted to being the mildly inflated maybe, but sensible enough medical businessman Jacoman had respected in spite of everything; not the company apologist he had made himself out to be, no big noise, just a man with a department consisting, presently, of his own big desk, two assistants, and some good ideas, not least of putting people like Carter himself on the ground in various parts of the world; his hype might have been hype, but was not entirely beside the point, as Jacoman knew, even if Giselle didn't. Jacoman was amused, in a way, by this total distance between his wife and his potential boss; by the contradiction that he himself liked them both – whoever thought he was schizoid might, at that moment, have been right.

When Giselle reappeared, she did not retake her seat. Jacoman could still see traces of tears on her face. She said, 'I don't feel well. I think I have to go home now.'

Though Taylor was all concern, he still kept her standing there while he concluded his carefully planned agenda. This part of it involved Giselle herself, her painting. He had heard she did miniatures. His eyebrows disappeared into his hairline, he claimed to be so impressed, so eager to see them; he assumed they were for sale. And so forth.

'It's a shame I hadn't brought any of my paintings with me,' said Giselle, later. 'The way he went on, he'd have felt obliged to buy one. I could have charged him God knows what.' She had stopped crying at last. When they emerged from the restaurant Jacoman had taken one look at her and called a taxi. But she'd still cried all the way home, with rage, she said, and shame, at having eaten a meal in the company of such a man. And what a meal!

Jacoman laughed. 'All the same don't underestimate him,' he said. 'He's smarter that guy than you think. He's not just an asshole.'

'I think he's just an asshole. I think he's the pits,' said Giselle. 'What's more my grandmother would call him common, if you really want to know. If you're going to spend the rest of your life working for – creatures – like him, you'd better count me out.'

Brave words. But not to be fulfilled as promised; not for a long time anyway. Even then Giselle herself must have known or suspected already, what Jacoman, for the moment, was far too busy to notice – among other things he was finishing his thesis. ('Congratulations, Carter on your kiddy study,' had been Taylor's parting shot before leaving London, 'but what I'm looking for is an executive who can formulate policy, set it into action and ensure completion.') At the same time Jacoman was picking every brain he could think of, trying to make a definite decision on his future. He was still by no means certain that the pharmaceutical job was the right answer. Ironically, what made up his mind for him on this was the news relayed to him two weeks later that also determined the immediate fate of Giselle herself.

Two and a half Jacomans left for Africa in November. Their first child, a boy, called Louis after Giselle's maternal grandfather, was born the following April. The family remained in East Africa four and a half years altogether, before being summoned back to Europe, to Basel. Denis Taylor, considering that he'd tamed Carter by now sufficiently to work among the Swiss, had created a job for him with the title, devised by Jacoman and Taylor between them, 'Director of Disease Control Projects'. There were five Jacomans altogether, by this time. Two and a half years after the birth of her son, Louis, Giselle had given birth to twin girls, whom she insisted on calling Chantal and Suzette. Jacoman didn't argue. He was much too proud of them all. For a time, precariously, as they set up house in Basel, as he helped Giselle with the twins, more dead than alive what with the sleepless nights, what with his daily struggles to plot a role for himself to fit his resounding title, he was almost happy.

One effect of his struggles emerged a few months later when the neurologist was given Jacoman's name in the letter from his English colleague – but failed to mention it to his wife. Why should he mention it? He often got such letters; more often than not they came to nothing. And besides, he and Anna had other things on their minds just then.

What they had on their minds – this was five months or so after their marriage – two months before David Kern met Jacoman in Jerusalem – was whether or not *they* should have a baby, if so when. Both were ambivalent, though for different reasons; Anna, in particular, was surprised at herself, not least for finding at this point, so many years on, that she did not trust herself not to let another baby fall downstairs; or something like that; causing another child to have seizures, anyway. This was not something she could tell David, absurd as such a fear was (for a start, David still did not know anything about Ben's epilepsy). One effect of Jacoman's proposals, not an effect he, of course, either recognised or intended, was that it delayed the moment of decision on this vexed question; how could Anna go running round the world with David if she was pregnant, let alone had a baby in tow? And David had made up his mind he wanted her to go running round the world with him, so far as the work allowed. Thus, though they did not stop talking about babies, though neither said so in so many words, they stopped feeling any obligation for the moment to come to a decision.

Anna Kern's notebook.

Get very irritated sometimes with medical terminology. Here's some random pickings from a medical dictionary; everyone of them with a perfectly good English equivalent. eg:

Anastasis – convalescence. Accona – elbow. Aposia – absence of thirst. Apostema – an abscess. Oedema – swelling. Apyretic – no fever. Odontalgia – toothache. Dyschia – painful shitting. Neonate – newborn. Idiopathic – spontaneous/causeless. Cardia – the heart. Oculus – eye. Ailurophobia – a morbid fear of cats. Bioscopy – an examination of the body to see if life is extinct. Aprosopia – a partial or complete absence of the face (ugh!) Aproctia – absence of the anus (ditto). Temulence – Drunkenness.

Even David didn't know all of these. And of course lots of terms don't have a lay language – while others have become lay language – eg, adolescence, carcinogenic. D. also says that I should do a list of anthropological/sociological jargon, sometime; it's not only his profession hides behind language. And so I will when I've time to get round to it. The trouble is, when it is your own jargon you take it for granted, forget that it's meaningless to anyone else.

A small digression on the history of two companies: HOW THEY BECAME ONE, HOW THEY EXPERIENCED SOME MARITAL PROBLEMS.

Once upon a time, in a mountainous country called Switzerland, in a town alongside a big river, one Johann Erich Rudolf set up as a chemist and druggist. He did not grow fat on it, not fat enough anyway, for the reasons I have already said. At any rate his sons and grandsons started making dyes instead. A century later, in that same town in Switzerland, the other side of our company, not a family business, but a group of like-minded businessmen, good Protestants all and with an interest in missionary work overseas, started off, also making dyes and chemicals. Though the first pharmaceutical products made by this group were exhibited at the Paris Exhibition of 1889, though before 1945 both companies produced medical drugs of some kinds, dyes and chemicals remained the source of their success; pharmaceuticals were still not big business.

For before 1945, all medicine had to offer most people, apart from surgery and aspirins, was reassurance and good advice. After 1945, with the development of anti-biotics, magic wands began waving, disease demons crumbled at the onslaught. There seemed no end to the possibilities of progress – and pharmaceutical profits.

But, alas, the demons were still lurking – lurking what's more within the same magic potions. Some women, for instance, relieved of morning sickness by one little pill gave birth to babies without arms and legs, (not something to be remedied by other pills). Governments began looking more closely at the business of pharma-ceuticals, controls were put on, committees set up, rule books lengthened all round the world; the business of researching and developing new drugs became ever more expensive, the risks of failure even greater. New magic potions, moreover, were ever more difficult to find; more and more time was spent re-developing or mimicking old ones.

Alongside the river in Switzerland, our two companies, makers of dyes, chemicals and pharmaceuticals, agro-chemicals, plastics and additives, photochemicals, electronics, opted for a not quite shot-gun marriage, risking the possible incompatibility of the parties; the different cultures of the companies, in particular, posed certain problems.

Kleitz was Swiss-bourgeois according to Jacoman; its offices shabby, cosy, contained as well as desks, armchairs with anti-macassars, almost. Bader, on the other hand, was a corporation; there were no cosy armchairs in the offices of its directors, only eighteenth century sideboards and portraits of Basel worthies. These differences in style were reflected in commercial habits also. Kleitz was paternalistic to its employees, Bader hierarchical. Communications within Kleitz were very open. Bader, on the other hand, told its employees nothing – its company magazines were full of articles about holiday destinations and collecting antiques, whereas Kleitz put out news sheets informing its employees exactly who was who, who was doing what, no matter how contentious. Yet Bader, unlike Kleitz, believed in being open to the outside world; its PR department was the best, the most informative, in Basel. Kleitz didn't have a PR department. Kleitz believed in fixed procedures for decision making, responsibilities were precisely defined. Bader procedures were much more flexible altogether – decision-making did not go through clearly defined channels; good managers could always manipulate the system – Kleitz executives shook their heads over this. (Some were still shaking them in 1989, eighteen years later.)

In 1972, optimism, however, for their joint future, swept all such cultural problems aside. In 1973, unfortunately, the optimism – and it was much too late to retreat now, and anyway merger was more essential than ever – met world crises on one side (little matters of oil and wars and terrorism) more drug side-effects on the other, and all at a time when the people who swallowed the pills, the consumers, were getting noisier and noisier in defence of their right not to be poisoned by substances meant to cure their ills.

Some illnesses are big business – cancer and cardiac problems, the diseases of rich men, for instance. Some are not; most tropical diseases, suffered from by the poor, for instance. Diarrhoea and arthritis are both big business; rich and poor alike get diarrhoea – not so many have arthritis, but since it's chronic, they keep on taking pain relief, provided they can afford to do so. It was claimed that one of the company's pharmaceutical best sellers, a pill to cure diarrhoea, had paralysed a few people – mostly Japanese; though for years the company denied that their drug had any such effect they were forced in the early eighties to withdraw this most profitable of products. Not much later they were also forced to withdraw an anti-arthritic drug. This was not to mention a cornucopia of other scandals; in the underdeveloped world our company, along with many others, was accused of exploitation, dumping dubious products on unfortunate peasants, bribing doctors with dancing girls and so forth. The Third World (though, in total, less than a quarter of its business) was more important to this company than most – in pharmaceuticals they'd even set up a separate company to sell drugs in these countries. From the late seventies onwards, faced with all these pressures, they set out to improve their commercial and political standing both in the developed and the underdeveloped parts of the world.

This is where Jacoman fits in. This is his version of the story, taped by Anna during one of their many ongoing conversations.

Carter Jacoman.
Everyone sees drug companies as out to screw the poor patient, feed him poisons, just so long as it makes a profit. In particular screw all the poor buggers in the Third World; dump lethal substances on them they're not allowed to peddle in the west, stuff them with date-expired antibiotics, get them feeding babies milk out of a tin instead of good mother's milk, and so on, when what all those countries want is clean water, enough to eat, and the odd aspirin, da, da, da. You get the picture.

OK. So that's exaggerating. But don't tell me Anna that isn't how you and even your dear husband see us somewhat. It ain't surprising, though, is it? People who sell dreams are bound to get a bad press when the dreams turn sour. And they were dreams, in the beginning, between 1945 and, say, 1960. Wonder drugs. Magic bullets. Steroids, antibiotics, anti-ulcers, NSAIDs, boy they were, oh boy, Anna. TB. Zap. Smallpox. Zap. Any number of lethal infections, zap, zap, zap. Pregnancy sickness, zap, headache, zap, colitis, zap, next year cancer zap, zap, zap. No more pain, no more sorrow, if we gave the drug companies their heads they'd abolish death any minute, they'd restore Eden, the end of history'd be courtesy Hoffman la Roche, Bader-Kleitz, Ciba Geigy; not Marx or Hegel; let alone Jehovah.

Then along comes the worm in the apple. A few deformed babies here. Some bleeding ulcers there. Then Hoffman la Roche, Bader-Kleitz, and so on aren't angels any more, they're devils. They've got horns and teeth, they're international destroyers, international villains.

But I tell you this, Anna. You still need them. Yes you do. Didn't Ben get earache sometimes? Don't you see he might be dead now, if it wasn't for antibiotics? Mightn't you be dead, if it wasn't for one drug company or another? No? Never mind, you might be glad of a little pink pill some day, Anna. All of us might be. And I tell you, a lot of your dear husband's patients wouldn't be where they are without his little magic markers; *my* company's magic markers; you ask him. (No, Carter, ask Ben, ask me, thought Anna. What does David know, compared to us?)

And I tell you something else. Drug company executives aren't heroes. But they aren't villains either. Sure they're out to make money. Sure, there's some substance in all the accusations made against them. But they're collections of individuals just like you and me, dear. They're different groups of individuals in different places, who don't always communicate too well with other groups; that's true sometimes in the best regulated organisations. You ask them. Sure there are mistakes and problems. Sometimes quite bad ones. But not one of those individuals wants to go home in the evening thinking I've done harm to someone. Not ordinary Herr Doktor this, not nice Mademoiselle that. Not me, for sure. Not me, Anna. I'm only in this business because I think I can do some good.

'Change people?' murmured Anna.

Yes change people, Anna, and what's the harm in that if their lives are rotten, they're sick, it needs changing. Yes, I know what you're thinking. No one should make a profit out of it. That's an attitude that's always bedevilled medicine in this country and North America. That there's something just a mite indecent about making money out of other people's misery. It's an Anglo-Saxon hang-up, I tell you. Europeans don't think like that. The Swiss don't for one thing. A guy gets dirty, he needs soap, you sell him some. A guy gets a headache, he needs a headache pill, you sell him one. He gets cancer even, you've got a product cures cancer, you sell it to him. What's wrong with that? It's all needs; food; warmth; entertainment; health. The kindest of old herbalists used to sell her simples, how could she live if she didn't? Tell me that, Anna.

I'm not saying there haven't been problems. My company had more than its fair share in the early eighties. And that's one reason I'm here and why you are, Anna, and your dear husband, come to that. If people can learn from their mistakes, so can companies, they have to. That's not only good ethical sense, it's good business. There's no reason good ethics and good business can't go together, that's for sure. That's what my job is based on.

Well in the seventies, like I said, we had great big problems. And we had worse problems because we had more business in the Third World than anyone else. And it's true some companies have had the view that what the Western eye doesn't see . . . Anna, I don't dispute it. And we had these particular problems, we had this diarrhoeal drug, this anti-arthritis drug, we had to take off the market. And that made trouble. Our name was shit. Our business suffered too, those were big sellers, there weren't too many new drugs coming along any more, the research had slowed badly. And what we needed was to sell the drugs we still had better. And get our name out of the shit. And so we set about it. We set up a pharma policy group for one thing, to look at all these things, political problems of selling drugs, adverse drug reactions and so forth. We wanted to pick up problems proactively before they happened; not reactively, that means not shutting the stable door too late, after it happened.

Well that one was one part of it. And the other was people like me. 'Director Disease Control programmes, Developing World.' And I had a desk with my name on it and that great big title, and a part time secretary and backing of Dr Taylor; and that was it. I had no brief, no budget, nothing; I have to write my own brief; then propose and get a budget. I had to invent my own job. That's the way we do it in this company. And that's power, Anna. You should read up about organisations a bit, you should really. One of the ideas now is that where power lies in an organisation it's not in titles, in formal hierarchies; you know, Green bosses Smith who bosses Jones and so on da, da, da, down to the cleaner. It's that power lies in the areas of uncertainty. You invent your own job; that's the ultimate uncertainty. And if you do it right, that's the ultimate power game. And while you make your job, the next thing's making your private contacts inside the business, and, if you can, getting a rich godfather higher in the business. I didn't need to do that so much, I had Taylor, right on top. The clever asshole. I let him do the rest. It was his job, he was good at it. My power was in my freedom; working out the plan I wanted. And I got it. I got all that money, Anna. That's power, that really is.

Right: so I was sitting in my office with a blank piece of paper. Writing a list of diseases that needed controlling in the developing world. The controlling of which would be good for the company's reputation and its bank balance at one and the same time. Mainly I'd been thinking in terms of tropical diseases. While I was still in Kenya I'd thought up a whole concept for controlling bilharzia and river blindness, both. A truly wonderful concept, all calculated in terms of disease dynamics. The trouble was none of it bore any relation to reality whatsoever. Not least the company didn't have any good available drugs against tropical diseases. And that's the first rule, a drug company's not a charity; kudos are fine, in fact necessary, but there's got to be a bit more than kudos in it for them.

So then I had this other list. And at the bottom of it was epilepsy. Which I didn't take seriously. I mean there it was, a chronic disease, had to be treated longterm, needed neurologists to oversee it. It wasn't like TB. It wasn't like leprosy. It wasn't like smallpox. In other words it wasn't a mass short-term problem that governments could get to grip with. You might be able to treat such a disease, but because you couldn't eradicate it, it wasn't politically interesting, no one was going to get credit for tackling a problem most people didn't even know existed. Epileptics don't rush into the street and say, 'Hey look at me, I've got epilepsy.' (Too right; thought Anna. I haven't even told my husband about Ben.) Their families are ashamed of them; they're hidden away. (Am I ashamed? she wondered. Could I be? But she was ashamed; she still thought it her fault.) So epilepsy went in at the bottom of the list; almost as an afterthought. Don't look at me like that, Anna. You mean you didn't know it wasn't need got patients treated? Didn't realise that it's a whole lot of other things, politics and economics not least? That what sick people want also comes bottom of the list?

'I'm learning,' murmured Anna, unhappily.

Then all kinds of things started happening. Business is like that. Serendipity. Coincidence. People nudge things along a bit, but without the rest of it, you don't get very far. It's like life. Not like logic. There was a lot of serendipity in this. And a lot of coincidence. For instance at this very time there was an executive in Pakistan who looked at the sales of Lenytol and looked at the likely numbers of epileptics and worked out there was a hell of a lot of patients not getting treated, and in particular not getting treated with our drug. And no one in Basel took any notice, till his figures landed on Taylor's desk. And Taylor took a look and handed them on to me. And then I went and looked up the other anti-epileptic drugs and what their sales were, and in the course of that I discovered no one in our company knew that Phenobarbitone was used as an anti-convulsant because it was on the tranquilliser list, not on the anti-convulsant list. And I discovered that round the world where poor epileptics were getting treated, including the USA I might say, they were being treated with Phenobarbitone. In other words, there was the major competitor for our drug, a shitty one what's more that really wipes people out mentally. And we weren't competing, we weren't pointing out the shittiness because we didn't even know it was a competitor. Get that, Anna. That's another example companies like ours aren't quite the monoliths you think they are.

So that was one thing. Another was what was going on in the World Health Organisation. Now this is something else you have to understand, my dear, how things were changing around then; the early to mid eighties. The consumerists may have run riot in the seventies, but in the eighties there was Reaganomics. The magic of the marketplace. In other words Capitalism hits back. And one way it hit back was by being suspicious of all those non-governmental organisations running round the world throwing international aid money around, and by making governments suspicious of them too. In particular making the American government suspicious. So there was a lot of doubt about funding in those organisations. Which meant they had to look for cash elsewhere, they had to fight in the market place like everyone else. So where you'd used to get organisations like the WHO sniffing and moving their skirts away at the faintest whiff of anything commercial, in particular multinational commercial, now suddenly they were running after us for money.

And as it happened, quite coincidentally, they were setting up an epilepsy project in various places and one of the guys they were working with, in Ecuador, a neurologist called Gomez, got to hear from our commercial manager in Ecuador that I was interested in epilepsy, so, guess what, Gomez sends me a telex inviting me to a meeting in Geneva with him and some guys from the WHO. And it turns out the WHO project is useless, all it's going to do is treat people with phenobarbitone, and a lot of neurologists everywhere, including your husband, Anna, were making a fuss about it, because they thought phenobarb such a shitty drug. So what with one thing and another, that project all fell through. But it meant the WHO were sympathetic and interested.

Which was good for us, because if organisations like the WHO need our money, businesses like ours can do with the kind of respectability your whiter than white NGO's can give, this being the crazy mixed-up hypocritical world it is. And it also meant I had Ecuador lined up for starters, as one possible base for a study. By which time I also had Kenya to go on with, because I'd been there, I'd appointed the new medical director there, I could fix it.

The net result was epilepsy skipped from the bottom of my list to the top. And stayed there. And that was where your husband came in, Anna, that's where I realised I needed a neurologist and I got his name from all over, so in the end I called him up. And that's where you came in, also.

'And where I went out, too, you could say,' murmured Anna.

Chapter Six

Phone conversation between Anna Kern and Nikki Kaufton: October 1985.

(The rather prickly relations between these two during the five days of Anna's stay in California did not seem to have diminished Nikki's desire for telephone contact. On the contrary.)

'I hate to think what that woman's phone bill must be,' said an irritated David after the third call in ten days, two of which at least took place while he – he claimed – was waiting for urgent medical communications. The first came within twenty-four hours of Anna's return home; Nikki wanted to know – in detail – how Anna and Benjamin's trip home had been, demanded if David had been pleased to see them, made mysterious hints about some new relationship she was embarking on with an Indian novelist ten years younger than herself – and only in Berkeley for a year, which didn't sound promising to Anna.

Anna had little to say about this; there was little *to* say – when Nikki was not in some way mocking a sexual liaison, it usually meant trouble in the end, but there was small point indicating it at this stage. She also circumnavigated the questions about David – yes of course he'd met them at Heathrow, that was all she acknowledged. As for Benjamin – well, yes, she was happy to report that Benjamin had suddenly become talkative over an airline dinner – and a little of Anna's airline wine – had said what a lovely time they'd had, and maybe he'd rather go to Berkeley than Cambridge, assuming he went to university. One reply of hers had contrived to irritate him for some reason, he had snapped at her, then five minutes later apologised for his bad temper, with only the slightest suggestion that she, for her part, shouldn't contrive to rub him up the wrong way, should be less motherly, was how he put it – almost his longest speech of the whole trip – so she had forgiven his ill-temper almost at once. (But then, ever since he had fallen down and shaken, in particular ever since his father had walked out, she'd felt bound to forgive him anything, almost at once.)

At some point during the third call Nikki asked if there was any further news on the epilepsy project.

'Not a lot,' said Anna. 'Jacoman – the wild Canadian – is in Ecuador at the moment. David keeps getting messages via Basel to hold on, there's some problem with Dr Gomez, the local neurologist, so maybe he won't go to Ecuador after all. I don't know. But he's still very keen to do it somewhere else.'

'No more volcanoes, though,' said Nikki. 'Will you want to go, too, hon, if there's no Cotopaxi, or whatever?'

'Of course,' said Anna. 'I'll go anywhere, just about.'

'You mean you and David can't bear to be separated still. How *adorable*, how *sweet*,' said Nikki. 'But don't forget what I told you. About such things being dangerous to marriages.' She made it sound as if she almost wanted it to be dangerous to Anna's marriage. All the more so when she added, ruminatively, 'For one so newly married, Anna, aren't you a bit a dangerously dazzled by the charming Jacoman? *Aren't* you?'

Around this time, Anna, looking for clues to the dissonance she'd felt, re-read the autobiographical account of Nikki's upbringing by her parents in Santa Barbara and her grandmother in Tennessee that was Nikki's first and best-known book. Anna had come across it a year or so before meeting Nikki, shortly after the book came out. It was one reason why she had accepted an invitation to the party in Nikki's honour given by her old friend, Tessa, the chairperson of a feminist literary cooperative; why, too, despite Nikki's disconcerting largeness in the flesh, her very flamboyance – her laugh could be heard from one side of the room to the other – she had begged to be introduced to her. Nikki had been quite famous at that time; in the course of a week in London she'd been on literary chat-shows at least twice. Anna had certainly not looked for friendship; the whole gathering was queuing up to meet the famous author. But Nikki made her own decisions on these things. Having decided she liked Anna, she resisted for a whole fifteen minutes or so all attempts to introduce her to anyone else – this was an informal party she said, she didn't feel obliged to walk on her hindlegs the whole time; if she was enjoying a conversation, why should she stop? When greeted by someone she knew she would shout something like 'Hi, great to see you; talk to you later,' then carry on talking to Anna. Only when they'd exchanged addresses and phone numbers did she consent to move on.

It was the unselfconscious ease with which Nikki achieved this – no one could have been offended by the way she told them to go away – not just what they talked about, let alone her sense of flattery at being singled out by the author of *Grandma Opium*, attracted Anna as much as anything. She herself had been far too conditioned to efface herself; to please; to think of other people first – or at least to look as if she was doing so – to know how to get her own way with any kind of grace. (This did not mean that, often enough, she did not make sure she got it; even while pretending not to.) The only other woman she'd observed as unabashedly going her own way, was David's sister, Anna's sister-in-law Sonia; 'Sonia's bulldozing us again,' David would put it. Nikki was bulldozing everyone now. But it didn't look like bulldozing in the least.

For the rest of the party they'd barely exchanged another word. Once, besieged by a particularly anxious but persistent woman whom Anna heard saying, of a trip to the Stone Circle at Avebury, 'You really have to go there, Nikki. There you *really* get a sense of walking into the Mother's Womb,' Nikki unmistakably winked at Anna, but that was all.

But two days later, Nikki had called her – Anna was not the least expecting it, particularly before eight-thirty in the morning. Something had dropped out of her schedule, Nikki said, she was free till lunchtime, could Anna drive her down to see the Avebury place now – she had to see if it was really like a womb – oh gee what a cheek, she had, at such an hour; what would Anna think of her?

Anna told Nikki that indeed she had a cheek to make such peremptory demands out of the blue on a working day – in any case how did Nikki know she had a car? – but yes, she could take Nikki, she'd be delighted to. It was the middle of January and very cold. By some meteorological quirk, Avebury itself and the country immediately around it were the only places in the vicinity not shrouded in fog. All distances excised, the stones – there was still a rime of frost on the sides the sun had not yet reached – seemed still more extraterrestrial, at the same time still more enclosing than usual.

If Anna had expected noisy enthusiasm from her companion, she did not get it. Nikki said nothing for a little while. Even when they had made a complete circuit, going in and out of the little gates that divided the two parts of the circle, crossing the road in one place, she continued wandering about, touching a stone here, a stone there, with an exploratory finger. 'What a place,' she said, at last, putting an arm about Anna's shoulder. Then added – quite inadequately clad for the climate, she was shivering; Anna had already felt obliged to surrender her scarf – 'Well, Anna, I always heard the womb was kind of homely; not to say warm. I'd say in that sense this wasn't a particularly good example, wouldn't you? Unless you were a polar bear, born with fur on. Is that a pub over there? Do you think it's too early to get a drink?'

At 11.00 a.m. it wasn't too early. Nikki's next appointment was at 1.30 p.m. But they weren't back by 1.30 – they reached her publishers at 3.00 p.m. Nikki wouldn't let herself be driven there any sooner, she said Anna had to get the whisky out of her system first. And besides, they were considerably slowed down by the fog; Nikki would explain the delay, she said, by the fog; not that there was any fog to speak of in London. But then, getting out of the car, she'd apologised, almost awkwardly, for having taken Anna over so completely. People were always telling her she was intolerable, she added; but . . . they had had a nice day, hadn't they; they really had?

'It's been a lovely day,' said Anna, and meant it. Not least, she thought, though she did not say, she'd *liked* being taken over. Few of her other friends showed a willingness to do that; 'You're so wonderfully independent, Anna,' they'd say – this was two years after her husband had walked out; after she'd had to set up life on her own. They seemed to expect – want – her to take them over; often, given such expectations, she did. (David was to accuse her of taking him over in due course.)

On that trip Nikki had been too busy for them to meet again. It hadn't mattered; things had gone straight on from there; they'd kept up, even advanced the friendship, by Nikki's phone calls mostly – twice more they'd met in London; once they'd coincided in New York. Up till the trip to California, however, Anna's first, Nikki had always refused to discuss her past history, at least that part of it which figured in her book. 'It's all there,' she'd say. 'Everything I want to say.'

'And was it really like that, Nikki? How much did you make up?' Anna asked her once.

'Shouldn't I have made anything up? Of course I made it up; how can you tell the truth about those things if you don't? Anyway aren't all grandmothers mythical in a sense? Isn't what you remember from childhood by definition as much myth as reality? Isn't it?'

Anna had heard Nikki making these kind of claims on chat shows. But if the hosts had let Nikki get away with it, she wasn't going to, not having got Nikki this far into the matter.

'You mean yours didn't sing hymns, she wasn't an amazing cook and hooked on laudanum; there were books in her house that weren't the Bible?' she asked, as innocently as she dared. (If she had long ago stopped being in awe of Nikki as a famous writer, she still was, she always would be, a little in awe of Nikki as Nikki. Nikki, she knew, intended her to be.)

'What's with you, Anna? This is my past – what's got you paddling round in it?' said Nikki.

'Doesn't your writing a book about it give me the right?' asked Anna. 'Doesn't it make the whole thing public property, up to a point?'

'What's in the book's public property,' said Nikki. 'What's true or not isn't. That's trying to find out about me. No one's the right to do that.'

Anna, unfamiliar with much literary theory fell headlong into the trap. Her 'And isn't it reasonable I should want to find out about you, in the light of the book?' had Nikki waving a triumphant finger and saying, 'Where've you been, Anna – haven't you heard? the fashion is you deconstruct texts these days; the last thing you do is hunt for authors in them.'

'A bit difficult, not to look for authors in autobiographies, don't you think, Nikki?' said Anna.

But that was it. It didn't stop Nikki pumping Anna about her past, of course. But as far as Nikki's went, Anna had to content herself with what she'd culled from the book; and from a tape her friend Tessa played her once, of an interview with Nikki given before a meeting of her feminist group (in such circumstances, as to journalists, Anna noted, Nikki was quite prepared to talk about her past). There was Santa Barbara on the one hand, home of the lonely, overweight Nikki, whose mother spent her time on beaches, in bars, having plastic surgery, flirting with rich men and film stars and famous professors from UCLA. Nikki didn't talk much about Santa Barbara. On the other hand, she talked a lot about Tennessee.

It was hot in Tennessee. Nikki's grandmother lived in a shabby wooden house with a porch like something out of Andrew Wyeth. Here Nikki had been no less lonely than she had been in California; more so in some respects, there were no other children around; the difference was that she'd been so loved and cossetted the loneliness had been pleasant. Her grandmother was this wonderful cook – her spoonbread was famous – as for her muffins – 'I always came back from Tennessee seven pounds heavier – I was heavy to start with,' claimed autobiographical Nikki; the book at this point had been suffused with remembered smells of food, and also with the comfort of Nikki's grandmother's lap, where, as a small child, Nikki had slept the afternoons away, in her grandmother's rocking chair. And also with the odour that had emanated from the grandmother; not an unpleasant odour, but langorous. Some while back the grandmother, in all innocence, had started taking medicine from a bottle available over the counter those days at the local store, and recommended for that mysterious ailment called 'women's problems'. The soothing medicine contained laudanum unfortunately, but how was she to know? By the time Nikki came on the scene, grandma had been, again quite innocently, addicted. The indubitably opium-induced stupor into which she sank during those sojourns on the porch remained, for Nikki, the image of utmost ease, of being safe, loved, cared for. Only she had not known they were opium induced, not till long after she was too big to be taken on her grandmother's lap, to rock away the sweaty August afternoon.

'So what hope for me?' wrote Nikki; 'On the one hand there was virtue – hell-fire, apocalypse – my grandmother was a kitchen preacher when she put her mind to it, she thumped the Bible with the best of them; on the other this pagan ease, this dangerous heaven out of a bottle. But I didn't know how the laudanum made her suffer. I only knew the peace of her lap, I knew the opium induced visions she mumbled to me sitting there in the same way I knew the thunder of her last judgments, her hellfire. I wasn't afraid of either. I loved them both; as I loved her lap. She loved me with her lap, her visions, her last judgments, her spoonbread. Whereas my mother, if she loved me at all, loved me with diet sheets and tennis rackets, swimming lessons and her psycho-analyst – all aimed at making me thin, making me fit her golden image.'

It was Nikki's grandmother had put her onto the Bible also; though maybe she hadn't reckoned in doing so on Nikki taking above all to the Book of Revelations. But that was later, after Nikki got too big for her grandmother's lap, and had taken to sitting reading in the fork of one of the cottonwood trees above the scuffed red dust of the yard.

Of course she brought books with her from Santa Barbara; but there never seemed to be enough to last her the whole stay. And then all that remained was the great family Bible. It didn't matter, she loved it by then, this huge book with its crude woodcuts of biblical plants and beasts, biblical head-dresses and buildings, and with the names of four generations of her family written in the front. Her parents did not care about the past – the only way Nikki got to learn about her family, who they were, where they came from, was through her grandmother's bible.

Excerpt from tape, property of Tessa's feminist group: (?1977-8. Tessa wasn't sure, exactly. Part of it had been wiped inadvertently; it began in mid sentence.)

'. . . what they looked like, it didn't matter, the very sound of the names was enough – they sounded just like the things in grandma's visions; I would sit up my tree crooning them to myself; jasper and chalcedony, sapphire and sardonyx, topaz and chrysoprasus. Then there were the even more mysterious words like fornication – the word fornication is used a lot in the Book of Revelations. I used to ask my grandmother what that meant and she wouldn't tell me; she'd just say, "You'll know soon enough," (she was quite right I did know sooner enough; I lost my virginity aged fourteen). Then she'd hand out another muffin.

'And then, later, what got me was the grandeur of the phrasing;' (here, on the tape, Nikki drew a deep breath; intoned dramatically), '"I am he that liveth and was dead; and behold I am alive for ever more . . . and have the keys of hell and death."

'Though I liked all the descriptions of heaven – the

place where there was no need of light and candle, and so on, it was the scary bits, the fiery bits, the death and destruction bits, earthquake, the dragon, the seven vials with the seven plagues, that I really liked; I loved the thunder and lightning, the sheer amazing energy of it; I wasn't scared. Why should I be? I didn't think I was evil. Granny in all her thunderings never told me *I* was evil; maybe she should have done, I guess her religion would have told her she should have done; but she didn't. Maybe the laudanum was speaking, maybe it softened her, made her belief in everything, not just evil, fuzzier, altogether less real, like her visions – or rather made it real in a different way – if that was so you could say Laudanum did for my sense of evil and with it my sense of guilt from the beginning. Or maybe it was simply because I was everything to her, none of her other grandchildren came near her, not one of them, ever; their parents weren't glad to be free of them the way mine were of me; besides, sending me to grandma was much cheaper than paying for me to go to summer camp. She cuddled me; she said I was the best girl in the world and I believed her. I was always in trouble at school back in Santa Barbara. But with my grandmother I was good as gold. Which was why I fornicated so guiltlessly I guess, so effortlessly, right from the start; apart from anything else it felt nearer to the Book of Revelations than anything I was offered in my mother's Californian paradise. The feeling it gave me – I'm not talking about clitoral sensation here, no way, though that was wow, terrific, that was the apocalyptic bit, the hallucinatory bit – doesn't everyone hallucinate some during orgasm? – felt nearer to being cuddled by my grandmother than anything else in the world.

'She was dead by then. Since she died, I haven't been back to Tennessee. I also got the hell out of Santa Barbara, soon as I could; I was bright, luckily; aged sixteen I went off to Mills – that's a private girls' school, no state university for me – and it was a good time; it was all happening; all those sit-ins and women's groups – oh God, those rich women, when they get radical, they get most radical of the lot. And I contributed pale horses and all that, only my horseman by now was as female as the Scarlet Whore. I *was* the Scarlet Whore. I loved it. At which point I took another long look at my grandmother's God and decided he might as well be female too. Boy that was a good time – when politics were everything, before disillusion started setting in. When women were really getting together for the first time. The feeling that gave me reminded me of my grandmother, and being with my grandmother. It really did.'

It was in Switzerland that Anna Kern met Carter Jacoman for the first time. As regards Switzerland she was, for instance, struck by the fact that when they arrived, in the pouring rain, umbrellas awaited all passengers at the foot of the plane steps; also by the fact that the immigration officer spent minutes thumbing through her passport because he said one page looked as if it had been cut. Not only had no one else ever noticed, Anna couldn't tell what he meant even when he pointed it out.

From the beginning Carter Jacoman made *his* views on Switzerland plain.

'Whatever you do, Anna, you mustn't forget ever, not for one minute, that this is a Swiss company you're working for, a Swiss company based in Basel, what's more. And the Swiss aren't like anybody else. And the Baselers aren't like any other Swiss; they don't speak the same dialect not least, no one except a Baseler understands another one. It's changing a little. The new Managing Director of Bader-Kleitz comes from St Gallen and he's a Catholic what's more. That wouldn't have been heard of ten years ago. And, you must remember, one reason Basel is different from anywhere else in Switzerland is it's got the three biggest pharmaceutical companies in the country sitting bang in the middle of it, plants and all. That makes a difference. Not least it means Basel is full of non-Baselers, let alone non-Swiss.'

Or again: 'There's this whole neutrality, Anna, this pragmatism of the modern Swiss. They hate extreme

101

disciplines, they're enormously tolerant of other people.'
(Except gypsies, murmured Anna, thinking of the scan-
dal of the gypsy children taken from their parents. She'd
learned over these years that most statements by Carter
needed qualifying in one way or another, whatever their
core of truth.) 'You know the reason they're tolerant?
They think everyone else is a barbarian, except them.
And so they don't expect anything from you, you can't
even insult them. How can a barbarian insult you, he's
inhuman, he's a dog. That's why I can get away with
using "du" here all the time to everyone. And I do.' (But
Anna, later, wondered.)

This was opinion of course. Anna looked up the facts
in publications put out by Her Majesty's Stationery
Office, the *Economist*, etc. A few she set down in her
notebook.

Location, central Europe (i.e. landlocked). Land area
41,293 square kilometres. Population (1985) 6.47 million
(against 56.62m in the UK). Population Density 157 per
square kilometre (in UK 232 per square kilometre.
Presumably, in Switzerland the mountains take up a lot
of space). Income per head, almost double that in UK
(£10,000 odd against £5000 odd, 1985). Exports (1985)
£20,931 mns against UK £78,331 mns – that's approximately £3m per head of population, in Switzerland,
against under £1.5m per head of population in the UK.
(Industrious people the Swiss.) Their trade deficit is more
than made up for by tourism (winter sports, eg) and
financial services (Swiss bank accounts, eg). The main
export is not, as you'd expect, watches and cuckoo clocks
(6%), or even chocolate (food exports 3% of total) but
chemicals (including pharmaceuticals, 21%).

More fact: Switzerland is officially neutral; but spends
a higher proportion of its GNP on defence each year than
any other country, apart from Israel.

Switzerland is divided into twenty-three cantons, of
which Basel is the fourth largest. Sixteen of these, like
Basel, are German speaking, six French speaking, one
Italian. But of the German all speak mutually exclusive
dialects. Foreigners have no rights. They may not even
own houses in Switzerland. Till recently they were not

allowed to own shares in Jacoman's company either, though one quarter of the workforce in Switzerland itself was non-Swiss.

Q: Why in such a chauvinistic country are so many employees foreign?

A: (from one local executive). There aren't enough Swiss.

Q: (one foreign executive). There's this language problem. Which of my colleagues do I address in the second person, informally, as du, and which in the third person, formally as Sie?

A: (another, longer in Basel). Those who leave the doors of their offices open may be addressed as du; those who keep them shut are always Sie. (But see Jacoman's solution to this problem, above.)

(The shut doors in the company headquarters had door bells on them Anna noticed, the one time she actually got in there. The first bell she saw, she assumed meant the door was a lift. She was looking for a lift at the time, she almost pressed it, before noticing that all the other closed doors along the corridor were the same.)

In January 1986 five people sat down in the cellar restaurant of a hotel in the centre of Basel to eat a large meal at Bader-Kleitz' expense; the first of many for some of those present. There were Jacoman himself and his assistant, a tall Dutchman called Piet, with a nice smile and a broken front tooth, who never said one word all evening, at least in the memory of the two Kerns. There was Vittoria de Cordero Mackenzie, a psychologist, originally from Spain, but based in England many years. (A small, very neat woman of forty-five or so, with skin like that of a china doll, she'd spent the whole flight to Basel agitating about whether or not it was ethical to work for a pharmaceutical company, much to the irritation of David Kern, who had recommended her to Jacoman as the project psychologist – 'She could have worked all this out before she got on the plane,' he said to his wife later.) Finally there were the Kerns-husband and wife; the husband appearing even more pale and tired than he felt in his sombre suit – this was a Friday night, the end of a long working week; the wife unusually large and English-looking beside the diminutive Vittoria, her husband thought, though she was not actually in the least large, and preferred to think she didn't look particularly English; but she did. She was wearing a black and white striped jacket, much smarter and more businesslike than she was accustomed to wearing. This had been insisted upon by her husband, who was, she'd noticed, unusually anxious about the impression she would create upon Jacoman – much more anxious than when he had introduced her to his father and sister. It made her more curious to meet Jacoman than ever.

The neurologist's wife was the only one of those present not entirely sure what she was doing there. David Kern and Vittoria Mackenzie had come to Basel to work with Jacoman on plans for the project. The nominal reason for Dr Kern's wife accompanying them was her expressed desire to travel with her husband sometimes, at her own expense; also her suggestion to him that she should do some journalism while she was about it – Dr Kern had noticed Jacoman's immediate interest in this suggestion; what he could not guess was the extent of that interest. Thus not only his wife but David himself had been surprised when Jacoman, in the course of one of his phonecalls, had said 'Why not bring Anna along to Basel? At Bader-Kleitz' expense, of course.'

('I suppose he wants to look you over; make sure you're not going to make a nuisance of yourself,' the neurologist said. 'In which case I'll be very demure,' said his wife. 'Not speak till I'm spoken to.' 'That'll be the day, Anna,' her husband said.)

But what, precisely, had Mrs Kern expected? She knew what her husband had told her; this was not a great deal, describing people was not one of his talents; 'fairish-haired; blue-eyed; same sort of age as me; Canadian.' All that was accurate enough, but not the truth. He was warmer, but not much so when he added, 'His teeth aren't exactly straight.' And added again, 'Oh and he never stops talking.' But if that was all, why did even mentioning this man so animate her husband? Normally, he never talked about projects he was embarking on in quite this way. Normally, he never talked about his work at all. The travelling involved in this project excited him, of course. But it wasn't just that. In the four months that had elapsed between David meeting Jacoman and Anna encountering him, Jacoman had developed, for her, an almost mythical dimension; but she still couldn't see him. When they went down to the hotel lobby for their first meeting, she had a much clearer idea of what the restaurant would look like (padded seats? low lights? paintings of mountains? an elaborate menu? the whole thing more – 'gemutlich' was it? – than elegant? and so on; and she was right about all of it, except the pictures; they were photographs of mountains, not paintings.)

As for Jacoman; *him* she heard before she saw him; the great guffaw filling the discreet lobby space as they turned the corner of the stairs could not be Swiss, could it? Glancing at her husband, she saw that he was smiling; that he looked less tired suddenly. Then, barely a whisper later, she saw Jacoman – or rather she saw his reflection, in the large mirror which covered one wall; her first sight of Jacoman, he was not only flanked by two huge vases of gladioli, he was framed by Baroque gilt.

Where had she heard that, according to mathematical theory at least – it couldn't, by definition, be tested – if you put the worlds on either side of the looking-glass together they would explode? Did Jacoman's mirror image, his reverse universe, skew her view of him from the first? If she had always thought of him as mythical, right side as left side, left eye as right eye, you could say, so he was in that fleeting glimpse. Yet the next instant she was looking at the man himself; right-hand universe Jacoman, head to toe. What had she been expecting then? – someone better-looking maybe? – someone longer-legged, maybe? 'You didn't tell me Jacoman had short legs,' she said to David, afterwards. 'Has he? I hadn't noticed,' said David. 'And you didn't tell me he wore spectacles.' For these were, perhaps, the greatest surprise of all, or rather the last thing she would have expected. Gold-rimmed spectacles, what's more. 'Granny glasses,' she said. 'Or John Lennon glasses. Or Himmler glasses, of course. Take your pick. His eyes are pale as Himmler's – weren't Himmler's eyes meant to be pale? – that's for sure. "What big eyes you've got Grandmama . . . Ve haf vays of making you talk"' she proclaimed, with gestures, stalking the room. 'What's got into you, Anna?' asked her weary husband. 'Come to bed. Behave yourself, sweetheart!' As for the rest; a thinnish man, of medium height, beside Vittoria – it had been for her he was laughing – Jacoman appeared both tall and broad; his face looked twice as long as hers; leaning, nonchalantly, against a chair, he was as if bent over Vittoria, making her giggle.

At the start, Jacoman's effect on David coloured Mrs Kern's view somewhat. Indeed, all the way through, that was what struck her most of all, more than anything about Jacoman himself. But then maybe, his effect on people, the way he fired them with his own ebullience, was the most significant thing about him, more significant than the winter sea colour of his eyes, which she could hardly tell yet in the diffused light of the foyer, let alone in the still more subdued lighting of the cellar restaurant to which they at once repaired; any more than she could realise the actual muddiness of his skin, the fair streaks in his thin, otherwise mousy hair. She saw the normally garrulous Spanish psychologist looking at him, silenced; as a rabbit, a very pretty rabbit, at a lank, lean, nondescript coloured, but altogether dominating, not to say flashy, incandescent from sheer energy, stoat. (On the other hand, as the evening went on, she saw Piet, the assistant, looking sceptical from time to time. Maybe that was the flip side, the one that came later. But why should she be concerned with that, yet? She didn't want to be concerned with that, yet.)

At dinner Jacoman sat himself down beside Anna and proceeded to mesmerise her too, or to try to. She had the sense that still more he was trying to impress her in some way, no less than David was anxious for her to impress him. He talked to her not about medicine, but about literature; names like Malamud, Bellow, Updike, Cheever, floated about her; she had the impression he'd read at least a little of all of these – he established his literary credentials with some quite perceptive yet melancholy comments; but no, he said in answer to her question, he'd never read such Canadian writers as Margaret Atwood, let alone Alice Munro. Proceeding to steer her almost at once to the subject she realised he'd been steering her towards all along; the works of Paul Bowles, of which he'd clearly read a great deal; not to say over and over.

Anna, though well accustomed to being wooed by literature – even David, the scientist, had, soon after they met, tried to talk to her about Proust – could have laughed out loud. David, at least, had not aspired to a cork-lined room; whereas Jacoman. . .

'I got the impression,' she said to David later, 'that he sees himself as the main character in a pharmaceutical version of *The Sheltering Sky*. Of course he's exactly the right type; slightly raffish not quite seedy, well-heeled brashness and sensitivity all mixed-up.'

'That's just the way he wants you to see him, don't fall for it, Anna,' said her husband, laughing. But having been watching his wife all evening, more closely than she'd been aware, he felt proud of her just the same; Jacoman had clearly taken to Anna. David had also liked the way his wife didn't giggle at Jacoman's attentions, the way Vittoria did. He'd liked her striped jacket and wished she wore that sort of thing more often.

Though Jacoman had not totally dominated the evening – David observed, with approval, that he was quite careful not to do so – he made it clear, not just in his fussing with the waiters, with the menu, but generally, the way he manoeuvered the conversation, that this was his show. To the table at large, of course, he talked mainly about epilepsy, though not just as a disease of the body. His use of terms acceptable to medicine like 'social morbidity' alongside more philosophical ones such as 'existential disease', 'spiritual angst', 'ontological crises', and so on had Mrs Kern glancing at Dr Kern expecting to see him as amused, as long-suffering, as he did when she herself used such terms. But he did not. Nor did he look mesmerised by Jacoman the way Vittoria did, the way sceptical Piet, the Dutch assistant did, the way she felt she did. How many times had he met Jacoman? – two? three times now? Certainly not more. But they sparred from either end of the table, above the heads of the rest, metaphorically speaking, like old friends. His wife, used to seeing her husband silent in company, particularly on a Friday, at the end of the week's work, was amazed to see him so animated; and in spite of herself almost jealous. She also noted the gusto with which Jacoman ate, for all he was so busy talking. This was something else of which David had not warned her. Maybe he just hadn't noticed.

Towards the end of the evening – Jacoman was getting above himself now, Dr Kern, beginning to desire his bed more than a little, had fallen silent – an Australian woman came to their table with an armful of red roses. Jacoman bought two, presented one each, with a flourish, to Vittoria McKenzie and Anna Kern.

'The creep,' thought Dr Kern, feeling a surge of the sudden irritation Jacoman could arouse in him at any time: like him as he did.

'The creep,' said Mrs Kern, kindly, in their bedroom later, the rose, more forlorn than romantic all by itself, ensconced in a hotel carafe, on her bedside table. 'You know what really interests him about me, David; why he's asked me to come? It's because I'm a journalist, he wants something from me, he really does.'

'Stop talking about Jacoman, sweetie. I don't know what he's done to you, you haven't stopped since we came upstairs. Come to *bed*,' David begged her for the third time.

He was lying on his back, his eyes wide open, staring at the ceiling. How dark his eyes were – dark as Jacoman's were light. His wife was full of joy suddenly that he didn't wear glasses, except when having problems with a contact lens. 'You have such beautiful eyes, David,' she said, fondly, turning out the light. All the same, lying awake thereafter, too exhilarated to sleep, she found herself thinking not of her husband, but of Jacoman.

Switzerland; Anna Kern's diary. Basel. January 1986.

D and the psychologist, Vittoria, went over to Jacoman's office this morning. I investigated the Art Gallery instead, then spent rest of the day wandering round this cold clean city, wondering what I was doing there. All very Nordic – more than I expected somehow. The huge grey river, neatly corralled by trees and buildings like the Seine in Paris (not the Thames in London) but much wider. Also the Seine doesn't have factory chimneys alongside it, even such innocuous, neat ones; there are no less than three pharmaceutical company plants along the river in Basel, right in midtown; Bader-Kleitz is the one in the middle. It's hard to imagine that this civic and industrial orderliness is about to launch everyone into the seething chaos of the Third World.

Another big dinner in the evening; a Chinese restaurant, of all things in this city – the waiters were Swiss. David says Jacoman's spent a fortune on feeding him lately; now it's my turn. Whole lot more people this time, didn't gather who they all were, despite Jacoman's best efforts.

Jacoman's wife came; very beautiful and dressed in jeans, while the rest of us including me were got up as executive wives – in my case what David thought of as executive wife. She'd topped her jeans, though, with the most wonderful silk and velvet jacket, bands of different fabrics layered together, huge sleeves; all colours – a real Joseph coat that I lusted for the moment she came into the restaurant, before I knew she was even eating with us, let alone that she was Jacoman's wife. Jacoman told me last night she's a painter; looking at her I could quite believe it. She *looks* like a painting; like a Flemish virgin – no, better still, a Fra Angelico annunciation; one of those smooth oval faces; very archetypal in that sense, but without any of the resignation. She'd have told the angel to fuck off. (Or else given him good reasons why she didn't fit the job description.) The only time I saw her talk to Jacoman all evening she looked as if she was telling *him* to fuck off. Jacoman seemed quite upset for a minute, David says. I don't think anyone else noticed. I didn't talk to her myself, though I wanted to; we were at opposite ends of the table.

At the end of the evening, Jacoman came up to me, and said, 'Can I have a word?' Then he said, 'David tells me you've got sociological qualifications?' I blink amazedly, thinking of my fifteen-year-old postgraduate diploma in sociology, my diploma in Social Work which I've never used, what with one thing and another. I don't think struggling with people like Lévi-Strauss and Mary Douglas every now and then quite counts. But before I could explain all this, Jacoman went on, so quickly you might think he didn't want it explained – that my having read Paul Bowles was qualification enough – 'How about you trying your hand at some questionnaires for us on social aspects? Your husband says he doesn't have the time, and we need an anthropologist on the project. If they work out maybe you'd like to run the whole social study for us?' And then he added – and I suspect this was still more to the point, 'And then you'll be able to do your journalism right from the inside.'

I said faintly, 'But I'm not an anthropologist. I'm a sociologist. Or rather I *was* one,' I added, still more uncomfortably. But the next thing was I'd said yes, I'd do it, almost before I knew I was going to. It's called typical Anna, rushing in where angels fear to tread. Particularly given that I've more reasons than he or anyone knows for being interested in such a project; (maybe this will at last give me the excuse I need to tell David about Ben?) I did say doubtfully, 'I've never tried anything like this; I'm not sure I'll quite know

110

what I'm doing.' But that seemed to reassure Jacoman
more than anything, he clapped me on the back and
roared out to whoever was listening – this man,
Jacoman, may be clever, he may have got us all
running; at the same time he's crazy; he's a marvellous
joke – 'That's the great thing about this project. It's
never been done before, so none of us know what we're
doing. Your dear husband included.'

In the art museum here, half way up the great
staircase, there's a huge Jean Tingueley sculpture; if
you can call it sculpture. It's more a collection of
wheels and tubes and pistons and cog wheels, bells and
gongs, all sorts of other old junk. I looked at it vaguely
on my way to find Matisse, but I was hardly in the
main gallery when I heard this huge noise and came
rushing out to see the thing shaking and turning and
banging and chiming and thudding. Amazing and
crazy. But maybe not as crazy as it looks. 'Just a
machine,' David said, when I told him I'd seen it.
'Nothing to do with art. Give me the Holbeins.'
Jacoman on the other hand told me how Swiss it was; I
keep wondering what he meant. To me, in lots of ways,
it reminded me more of him.

Chapter Seven

In the course of one of those Basel dinners, Jacoman, as he often did, mentioned the story of the Pakistani Doctor. This was the story that had amazed David Kern in Jerusalem, that continued to amaze him; the amazement relating not so much to the Pakistani doctor himself, but to the use Carter made of him. He and Anna used to argue about the validity of this, around the time they were working together most closely and finding it hard; the time when they could agree on very little. But from the beginning, from his first hearing the story at the Jerusalem congress, David had teased Jacoman on the subject. Even if Anna couldn't be expected to know better, Jacoman should know better, he said.

'Here you are Carter,' he'd say, 'medically trained, a scientist. And what's the essence of medical research, you don't rely on anecdote; you built up a whole cohort of cases, you take your statistics and arguments from that, you make treatment decisions according to that. And here's you, Carter, basing your whole thesis, on which you base this entire project, on which you are spending God knows much Bader-Kleitz' money, on this one man, this one place; this anecdote.'

'And what an anecdote,' said Carter, laughing, not the least put out.

'But still an anecdote, Carter.'

'But that's what I got you in for, David. To get beyond the anecdote. I mean I had to have a hypothesis. You're the scientist; it's your job – and Anna's – don't let's forget

Anna, her job's just as important in its way – to prove or disprove it. That's what we're all now working our asses off doing.'

Anna was struggling at this point; at such times Jacoman was always suspiciously nice to her. It was part of his technique for handling people, she'd noticed. She said, 'OK, Carter. Don't overdo it.'

David said, 'You know perfectly well, Carter, a hypothesis, at least a hypothesis on which you can base proper research, get research money, has to be based on more than anecdote.'

'Oh well; if you're dealing with a monkey nuts project, medical research council projects, it does. But this is big money stuff, this is international reputation stuff.'

'All the more reason, Carter,' said David, grinning, 'not to base it on anecdote.'

Once, early on, about a month after she first met Jacoman, when he'd stayed a night with them in England to work on plans with David, Anna got Jacoman to tell her the story. It was late; a yawning David had already gone to bed. Anna was not unhappy for once to see the back of him; when he and Jacoman were not talking epilepsy – this she did not mind – they'd swapped Jewish jokes all evening, and this she did; not so much for the jokes themselves, but for the sense of being excluded, because she herself was not Jewish. She was also quite happy to linger alone with Jacoman in the cramped Fulham sitting-room – it looked even more cramped with Jacoman in it. In the bantering yet tender tone they had adopted between themselves from the beginning, one quite different from the exchange of ironies which characterised David's communication with Jacoman, she said, 'You're always referring to the Pakistani doctor, Carter. But you still haven't told me the story. Look, why don't I tape it for the book?' she cunningly urged, holding out the whisky bottle to encourage him still further. Jacoman could not resist any of it; the tape recorder, the whisky, Anna. As soon as he heard the tape going, he took another sip of whisky and started.

'First thing in Hyderabad – it was early May, it was summer, hot, hot, hot, a four hour drive from Karachi – first thing I got taken by the area manager, Mr Patel, to the primary health care centre. It was a large place, not too clean or new, but lots of doctors, lots of charts on the walls, lots of WHO reference stuff hanging round; he wanted me to see what primary care was really like in Pakistan.

'So I talked to the doctors and nurses and there was this and that and everything, immunisation programmes, TB programmes, etc., etc. But I was looking at this thing and I noticed there were no patients. Nobody queuing up.

'So we get back in the car and I say to Mr Patel now let's go and see real primary care, and he laughed his head off. Because it was a test you see, how much I knew, how much I'd swallow. But he could see in this that I knew a little more than your average Basel visitor. (Jacoman sounds pleased enough with himself here, Anna was thinking at this point; she liked it; David when she played the tape to him, on the other hand, made a face.) So he took me to a little village about twenty kilometres outside of Hyderabad; dusty dirt track and sleazy villages. He finally picked one and we pulled up outside the government primary care centre and there was the reality – patients hanging out of the window, two young doctors who didn't give a shit, and we interviewed them about epileptics and they hardly ever saw one. One a year, they said. The rest go to traditional healers; they don't come here. Because they believe it's all to do with evil spirits, things like that. When they do come to us we try to persuade them it's nothing to do with evil spirits, that they have to take drugs. The only trouble is we haven't got any drugs to give them, we have to send them to Hyderabad for that. Anyway they never come back.

'So we left there and walked back up a narrow street to get to the car and I asked Mr Patel if there were private doctors here, and he said yes, of course, the patients prefer them; they only get given aspirin at the primary care centre, so they all go to private doctors. And then, in this street we pass a pharmacy and I go in and see the shelves are covered with anti-convulsants, Lenytol, Phenobarb, you name it. When I ask the pharmacist who's prescribing this – someone had to be, he wouldn't have it otherwise – he points straight across the street. There's the doctor, he says.

'Let's go and see him, I say. But Mr Patel's had enough by now, he wants to get back to Karachi. No, no, he says. Yes, yes, I say. Of course I win.' ('I bet you did, Carter,' can just be heard on the tape at this point. Carter laughs.)

'So we go into this guy's place and there are hundreds of people. To see just one guy. And Mr Patel goes in and says there's this guy from Switzerland wants to see him. And the doctor says yes, OK, but then he keeps us waiting for fifteen minutes just to show who's boss.

'Fifteen men come out of his room, when at last he ushers us in. And inside there are chairs lined up like a lecture theatre, and people peering in at all the windows. And this guy's not a bit what you'd expect, he's a Bengali, he's charismatic, he has brilliant eyes, very big, and wears a brilliantly coloured Filipino shirt. In fact that's what he looked like, a Filipino healer, a dead ringer – you know, Anna, one of those guys who pull chicken blood out of your stomach and so forth. It's called spirit surgery or something like that. You could just see this guy at it, I tell you.

'But in fact he specialises in epilepsy. When I asked him how many he saw he said fifteen new cases a month, now that's a lot.' (David confirmed this.) 'They weren't from just that area either; they came from all over the country. The health centres weren't doing it right, that's why they didn't see any patients, he *was* doing it right, so they came to him.

'The fact is, he said, epilepsy is easy for me to treat in these conditions. I bring in fifteen men at once and I ask them questions. And I'm supposed to know within two minutes what's the matter with them, without even touching them, just looking into their eyes and seeing their souls. And of course, to diagnose epilepsy straight off, you don't need an examination, you don't need blood tests, all you need is a history. So it's wonderful for my reputation. If you know how to take a history of a seizure all you need to do is work it out.

'And so within a year of my starting, people were coming to me from all over Pakistan. It had spread by word of mouth; everyone in Pakistan has a relative somewhere. People go from here to Karachi to have a sheik clear a nosebleed, they come to me from all over Pakistan to cure their epilepsy.

'I asked him how he got people to stay on treatment if they all believed it was to do with evil spirits. And he said, I can't tell them not to believe it's evil spirits, they wouldn't believe me. So what I say is: if you take your pills twice a day, the evil spirits will leave you alone. But if you don't take them, the spirits will be angry, they'll come back and plague you worse than ever. I especially tell them this when they're on phenobarbitone, because if they stop taking that they get terrible withdrawal symptoms.

'I tell you, Anna,' Carter added, 'The guy was brilliant, he had it exactly. I mean why do you think I've got you in here, asking all those questions about what they think caused it? How can you treat a patient if you don't know what he thinks caused his disease, whatever it is? And he understood about it being a spiritual, an ontological problem.' (Anna laughed here, fondly; not because she disagreed with him necessarily, but because she had already after such a short time heard this so often, from Carter in public voice, to Carter in private. He grinned back, aware what she was thinking, but maybe not aware of the mockery. He rarely was.)

'He understood it, he really did. And what did he do about it? He said: "We in Pakistan have a wonderful system; it's called Islam. So I refer them to their local Mahdi, to have things done; that is to get prayers mainly. In Islam you still have a bit of a penance system, so they can absolve themselves of the spiritual pollution or whatever brought the epilepsy on by saying them. And of course the Mahdis like that too, they'll send me patients themselves, knowing I'll reinforce their authority and send them back."'

'What about payment for treatment?' asked Anna, knowing the answer, more or less.

'I asked him how people could afford the drugs in such a poor country. I mean he was prescribing Lenytol for at least half and against their sort of income that's expensive. He said: "People will pay anything. People come to me after giving away their farm and their water buffaloes to some quack, some fakir who's promised to cure them."'

'So that's how you decided this study could be profitable?' asked Anna.

'Oh yes. You know the received wisdom, poor people can't and won't pay for medicines. Well the very poorest mightn't pay, but there's a whole lot just above that line will pay anything, if that guy was right. That's what I realised. That's how we could increase the market, by getting to those people somehow.'

'Suppose this project wasn't going to sell more drugs; not your drug anyway, would you still want to do it?'

'I'd have the hell of a job convincing the company,' said Jacoman, 'but sure I'd want to do it.'

'And if Phenobarb turned out to be just as effective, and not much worse in its effects if you gave it in small enough doses, and David's research all showed that, would you still want to do it?'

'It's not what I'm here for,' said Jacoman, 'but sure, like hell I'd want to do it.'

He paused here. Anna, listening to the tape, imagined him sipping his whisky slowly. She didn't think, though, it was that which loosened his tongue. He was often enough, later, to accuse her of being too garrulous sometimes, not playing things close enough to her chest, of showing her vulnerability and inexperience to the whole world. ('Pretend you're the most experienced sociologist ever,' he'd shout at her. 'Make up a Masters, a doctorate, if you like, these fuckers won't know the difference. In this business, in any business, an inferiority complex is a self-indulgence, self-deprecation gets

117

you nowhere. Sure, people will like you if you admit your ignorance, but they'll screw you every time, my dear, they'll screw you.') Yet he was capable of being still more indiscreet if he wanted, if not in the same way or for the same reasons. Fifty times more indiscreet. As now.

For he said, softly, his thin pale hair tumbling every which way, that here, at this time of night he was not obliged to train back to executive order, 'You know, Anna. If Phenobarb turned out fifty times more effective than Lenytol, if its sales went up – which it won't, it's too cheap, it's not worth anyone's while to sell it – but if it did, and if ours went down I wouldn't care. That's not why I am doing this project, why I want it to work. It's doing the project. It's getting it right. It's getting treatment to all those buggers out there who don't think there is any, who fall down twenty times a week and think that's what it's about. Sales figures for Lenytol? Forget it. I don't care a fuck.'

Anna had been impressed by his rhetoric; even having learned a thing or two since, she did not wholly discount it. Then, she said, demurely, so the tape reported, 'What will you give me, Carter, if I don't forward this tape to your boss?'

As a counterbalance to anecdotes of this kind, David Kern feels it necessary to instruct his wife on the real nature of medical trials. (This is dry stuff; in the interests of accuracy there can be no literary tricks here; in the interests of science the impersonal mode must be used as far as possible, preferably at all times.)

Of the various methods used in medical studies to look at disease and treatment these are the ones relevant to our investigation.

1. Cross-sectional.
– Here the researcher looks only at specific phenomena, a specific disease, or a particular group of patients at one particular point in time.

2. Longitudinal.
– Here diseases, patients, etc, are observed over a period

of time, often in relation to some kind of intervention, treatment, for instance, or lack of it. A control group may also be observed, that is a group as similar to the study group as possible in age, sex, social group, and, if not chosen as healthy controls, disease status.

– The state of the subjects' health or their disease at the beginning of the study is compared with their state over six months, a year, five years, even ten or more years later, depending what is being looked for and on the time limits set.

– The researcher compares the changes that have taken place or have not taken place in the patients and the controls at various points in the course of, and at the end of the study.

3. Epidemiological
– This is the study of a disease in a population – how many cases, what forms of the disease, etc.

4. Prevalence
– Here the job is to find out the proportion of any population suffering from the disease, then, often, to compare the results obtained with the figures from other populations studied in other areas or other parts of the world.

(An epidemiological study is to be done in Ecuador, in a population of 72,000 or so. In a population where very few people are treated for epilepsy, it is also one way of finding patients. The main drawback is that a great many researchers are needed to question 72,000 people. All of them have to be trained and paid.)

So to our particular study: let's take Ecuador; here we have:

1. A basic design:
– stage 1. A cross-sectional epidemiological survey to establish prevalence and to provide patients for:
– stage 2. A longitudinal study of the effects of treatment over a twelve-month period.

2. A hypothesis (rural doctors can treat epilepsy as well as neurologists, phenobarbitone is a better/worse drug than Lenytol, and so forth).

3. A methodology (medical examinations, question-naires, administered at various intervals over a year).

The following have to be decided on:

4. Protocols for the study. (That means what is being studied, precisely. What aspects of the disease to leave out or put in. What patients to include and not to include. What diagnostic criteria should be used to decide they are suffering from some form of epilepsy; and so on.)

5. Questionnaires – number and type. (This is more important in epilepsy than most diseases, since it is often easier to diagnose from what the patient says than from a medical examination.)

Then usually, but not this time, because of Bader-Kleitz:

6. Budgets have to be written; how much will all this work cost.

7. Even more careful grant applications have to be written setting out not only these budgets, but all the medical details and criteria, in order to scrounge the money to do the research out of some medical charity, a university department (unlikely), the Medical Research Council or some drug company, or a mixture of all these. This procedure, which is not only time-consuming but tiresome may not even be successful.

(In the case of the epilepsy study Carter Jacoman's going to have to work out the budgets; the agency he has to convince consists of his peers and seniors at the pharma-ceutical company. Anna can see in this sense why Jacoman's study might have its attractions for David. She'd never realised before how hard he had to fight for money for every project he got into. Oh yes, she'd gone with him in the middle of the night to deliver grant applications to obscure medical charities, before the deadline ran out; but she didn't realise that was how it was all the time; he never told her. Actually money is a major factor in Jacoman's study too. A major factor for Jacoman himself; his headache, more than they and he realise.)

8. At some point (very important) decisions have to be

made as to how all the data is going to be recorded, by whom, where, how it is going to be analysed, by whom, where. And so on.

9. Then, finally, permission has to be sought from the researcher's own hospital or organisation; and the study placed, its design complete by this time, in front of its ethical committee, which may say it is unethical to treat patients in such a way with such a drug. Or may at least, force procedures to be amended in such a way they have to be redesigned completely.

This project of Jacoman's, of course, as an international study, has to face more than one ethical committee. More difficult still, as a tripartite study (financed by a drug company, planned by a scientific institute, carried out on the ground in several different countries, in somewhat different ways in each case, by local doctors and researchers. Exactly how difficult this will be, in Ecuador at least, David doesn't say because he doesn't know yet, though he will learn, everyone will learn.) David and Jacoman have to get every single clause in every protocol, every single question on every single questionnaire, every single one of a list of diagnostic criteria, agreed by an unwieldy group of often non-English-speaking medical men, on the other side of the world. So determined are many of these not to let themselves be browbeaten by Western academic imperialism, let alone multinational commercial imperialism, that they insist on looking at every single word, on taking every single phrase apart, at length, in detail, ten times over. Till Jacoman, David Kern, his wife, various others, are in tears, threatening to go home, living off separate snacks – bowls of Ceviche, for instance – from Room Service at the Cristobel Colon Hotel in Quito, because they have no time to meet and eat properly. And so on.

Anna Kern's diary. February 1986.

I keep thinking about what Carter said – or rather his Pakistani doctor said – about diagnosing epilepsy; how you didn't need to look, how you didn't need to test; all you needed was the history; the story. It sounds more like my work than David's; I'm the one tells the stories usually. Carter wants me to tell his story – that's why I have to listen to him so much. Could you diagnose him too, by such means, I wonder? I daresay David could: it's his job. I daresay he could work out Ben's case, too, from just a history; and come up with some opinion.

If David, at this time, had no attitude or opinion concerning his stepson, Ben's, history of epilepsy, it was not because he thought it inappropriate to pronounce medically on someone so close to him; it was because of Anna's never having told him about Ben's seizures – at times now she could hardly remember why not; she did not want to remember why not. Throughout the three months she spent planning her side of the project, she found herself about to tell him, on several occasions; indeed it began to seem inconceivable she had kept such a thing from him for so long. The reasons she'd had for doing so, even when they touched on Ben's feelings on the matter, did not, at this point, good as they once seemed, seem good enough. But each time it came to it she hesitated; was interrupted by David himself, perhaps, or by Ben himself, by the telephone, or something; the moment passed. Maybe she wanted to be interrupted. It was true that after all this time she was afraid of what he might say, not only at having been kept in the dark, but at having been kept in the dark so long. He could even claim, she thought, she'd married him on false pretences. *Would* he? Did Ben's having epilepsy really so fill her with doubt – guilt even? Yes.

The time she came nearest to revealing the secret was in the months before they went to Ecuador, during a discussion of her questionnaires. Anna had said something about how limiting she felt it was to ask sociological questions in such ways; could you really get at what people felt, had experienced, by asking them questions which only required single word answers; yes, no, and so forth? It wouldn't get at what *she* felt, she said.

122

'Luckily,' said David, 'luckily, Anna, what you feel isn't an issue. Quite the reverse. That's the point.'

'Suppose it was an issue?' she asked then, seeing yet another chance to make her confession, to tell him about Ben. 'I mean suppose I had epilepsy – or suppose Ben did – wouldn't I be able to understand them, the patients, better?'

'It wouldn't matter if you did or not,' said David. 'In fact it would be a disadvantage. You couldn't possibly be as dispassionate as you need to be as a scientist. In my experience involving someone with personal connections in any kind of epilepsy work, let alone research, is a disaster. I'd be telling you not to do this job; not encouraging you to do it, Anna.'

This not only made it even more impossible to tell him. It made her not telling – her having not told him – still worse. No good could come of it, she thought, dismayed. But what to do? At all events, though agonising over the matter often, she did not try to tell him again.

Chapter Eight

Phone conversation between Nikki Kaufton and Anna Kern. February 1986.

Anna breathless and excited. Nikki querulous, not to say what she would call 'picky'. Anna tries not to be deflated, but does not altogether succeed. What particularly seems to annoy Nikki – that's her problem, thought Anna, growing irritated with this – is her breathless accounts of all the work she is doing, her total immersion in the phenomenology of epilepsy, beliefs concerning, psychological effects of; in reading up textbooks on sociological method, in attempts to learn the basics of the Spanish language (the fact she's known no Spanish till now, is another reason she shouldn't be doing this job, she thinks in her worst moments; why didn't she opt for having a baby?); in studying the geography, politics and anthropology of Ecuador and Kenya. All this the result of Jacoman's bombshell, that has turned her into an anthropologist in one fell swoop. (What on earth do those words mean *exactly*, she wonders. 'Fell swoop?' – she's taken the cliché quite for granted before.) If she still wonders why she is doing this; meditates, increasingly, on her inadequacies in this role, not least her lack of Spanish; has the coldest of cold feet as it is brought increasingly to her notice that, very shortly, she must descend on the countries concerned and 'lead' (this is Jacoman's term) a group of professional locals, most, no doubt, much more recently and better qualified than she is, she does not tell Nikki. She does not need to; Nikki points it all out, gleefully. She also asks awkward questions; for instance, 'So you're going to bring light into the life of all these poor sufferers, give them drugs for a year, and so on. Then what? What happens when you all go home?'

Anna does not say that this question has already been asked by her son, Ben, who had been interested in her involvement from the beginning, and had his own good reasons for being sensitive to such things. (Ben always was sensitive to such things, though; he always did ask good questions. He thought first, acted afterwards, unlike his mother.) She gave Nikki the same answer she'd given Ben.

'I asked Jacoman that, and he promised he'd insist the company went on providing the drugs when we moved out.'

'And who's going to get the drugs to them, in these out of the way places?' asked Nikki.

'They do have medical systems of sorts, these places,' said Anna. 'We didn't go to hopelessly backward areas – Jacoman said there'd be no point, you can't function at all without some kind of infrastructure.'

'Oh what big words you're using these days, Anna,' said Nikki. 'And how come every other sentence has Jacoman says in it? What's this Jacoman got that he has this effect on you? I guess I should meet him.'

'He's married,' said Anna. 'He has a beautiful wife called Giselle. There's nothing there for you, Nikki.'

'You mean I'm some old frump; what's with you today, Anna?'

'Oh for Christ's sake. I didn't mean that, Nikki, and you know it.'

'Didn't mean. Didn't mean. And for this I make a call which is costing me a fortune?'

'You can always ring off,' said Anna. 'Perhaps you'd better. At least it would put less on your phone bill, Nikki. Wouldn't it?'

But Nikki hadn't finished; not nearly. Anna could imagine her settling back into her leopard skin duvet cover, beneath the shelf of kachina dolls, one of them faceless, alongside her row of pills and potions. Nikki made most of her phone calls from bed; she'd seen it. Indeed, when she came to think of it, Nikki's phone calls were a form of lovemaking; running the whole sexual gamut, you could say, from seduction through aggression to submission and all the way back. What she had to say at this point, of course, was mainly aggressive; it usually was when she got onto the subject of David and Anna, though the aggression wasn't always so undisguised. What's with her? thought Anna. Why don't *I* ring off? But she didn't ring off – she wasn't paying for this after all, and with Nikki usually it was worth letting the storm die down, just to see what would happen. She kept tapping her fingers on her desk, making faces to herself, all the while Nikki was accusing her of letting David take over her whole life. Of letting medicine take over her whole life. She was a journalist, now, for God's sake, she'd given up sociology years ago, so what was all this about being a anthropologist? Why couldn't she go off and do her own thing and let him get on with his? (Why not indeed; in all this furore, the thought had crossed Anna's own mind a time or two. Nikki's intervention hardened her intentions, though, rather than the reverse; hardened them still more, when Nikki went on; how *dare* she?)

'Believe me, Anna, it'll do your relationship with your husband no good in the end, it really won't. Apart from which, the fact that he's about to start running round the world interfering in the lives of people who've already more than enough to put up with without drawing on themselves the attentions of a medical team from the far side of the globe – maybe you don't realise the enormity of it – the sheer fucking enormity Anna, – doesn't mean you have to join in; for Chrissake. It'd make more sense to go off and have a baby, Anna.'

This was too much. 'Nikki you are insufferable,' Anna said. 'Mind your own bloody business.' She almost put the phone down. When a long pause ensued, she thought for one moment Nikki had put the phone down on her. But then Nikki merely said, coolly, 'OK, hon. If that's the way you want it. It's your life. Run round the world if that's what you want.'

'But I do want to. I *like* running round the world,' Anna said, changing her tone also. 'And I wouldn't be able to run round the world if I didn't do this. Of course it's just an excuse really,' she said, the silence at the other end of the phone making her uneasy again. 'You know as well as I do, I'm not really an anthropologist.' Nikki of course, pounced gleefully on this.

'If you're not an anthropologist, then what are you doing saying you are one?' she asked. 'Don't tell me you're going to spend your time telling the people you work with you're not an anthropologist, really. For fuck's sake, Anna, if you must pretend to be what you're not, you better at least be consistent about it. Don't tell little lies, tell big ones.'

This was, of course, not a long way from what Jacoman had advised her (not for the first time, then, Anna thought he had certain things in common with her friend. Not least she liked them for some of the same reasons; mostly to do with things she missed in her husband, much as she loved him.) But all she said was; 'One minute you tell me I shouldn't be an anthropologist at all, and now you're giving me advice on how to pretend I am one.'

'Since I can't stop you,' Nikki said sourly, 'I'd just as soon not see you behaving like a total schmuck. I don't know what's with you Brits, you turn modesty into a religion. I'll shout my merits, including the ones I only pretend I've got, from the rooftops, any time you like. It's not more dishonest than pretending you can't do what you can do very well. And in my experience, it gets you a darn sight further.'

'It depends where you are,' said Anna.

'No it does not,' said Nikki.

'In my experience as a journalist,' said Anna, firmly, 'you get a lot more out of people by pretending to be an idiot, or at least ignorant enough to be harmless, than if they think you know too much.'

'That's as maybe,' said Nikki. And then suddenly,

quite suddenly, she moved into mode seductive; softened her voice; started to tell Anna about a darling pair of gold shoes she'd seen, and did Anna think they'd go with those pink and black striped pants she'd told her about last week; or did she think they'd make her look a bit too much like a tropical fish? Since, when she came to think about it, tropical fish wasn't a bad description of the way Nikki dressed in general, and since she was, anyway, almost weak with relief – why had it so upset her – that Nikki had changed the subject, Anna could scarcely answer for laughing. Not that it really needed an answer. In two minutes, Nikki was onto Conrad again – she'd been rereading *Lord Jim* – wasn't Jim a marvellous portrait; weren't all the English a bit like that, crazy uptight dreamers, hung up on notions of honour; wasn't David a bit like that? But of course Conrad couldn't describe a woman if he tried. For which reason she hadn't ever persuaded her students to read him. OK, it was their loss, but in the case of what he had Marlowe say about Kurtz's wife, for instance, how could she blame them? Though it had to be said – she couldn't risk the dig, and Anna decided this time to ignore it – the way Anna behaved *vis-à-vis* David, she couldn't blame Conrad for taking such a patronising view, either. The way women diminished themselves, they were their own worst enemies. In China, for instance, wasn't it the mothers, always, called the footbinders in?

'Oh and by the way,' she added, about to ring off. 'Did you ever tell me, Anna, how you met David? I don't think you ever did – why didn't you, Anna?'

'Because you never asked me, Nikki,' said Anna.

'I didn't?' asked Nikki; and then, finally, she did ring off, if not without a vague statement of her intention to come to London shortly that made Anna both delighted and apprehensive. She was left so enraged, though, in all other respects, she rang no less than two editors and said that no, for the moment, she couldn't investigate a self-help group for rapists or eat at, report on, a restaurant for women only in Hackney. She would be in touch. (But she knew that that was it; she'd broken the rules; they wouldn't be in touch with her.) Then she went back to her Spanish grammar.

A digression. Anna Kern's journal. October 1987.

Thinking of Nikki today, I remembered a description of African women I came across after I'd visited Beatrice. 'The mooring to which the vast families tied up, the calm centre of African life, the low undercurrent of reality.' Of course this is a figment of male longing in one way – it's what David wants of me, I can feel it, at some level; the book's by a male writer – but I think it also explained what I felt in those Kenyan huts. Reading it, I am consumed by the same longing. Because we – Western women – aren't like that any more – that role was diminished, prettified, sentimentalised long ago – *kinder, kirche, kuche,* all that. Quite rightly we threw it out. At the same time the very choice of rejecting such a role diminishes us – can't but diminish us, I think. I don't want to be part of that culture. I don't want to be a mooring – I want . . . yet the longing and loss remains at one level. I accept that. I'm beginning to wonder if Nikki does. I'm beginning to think Nikki still wants all of it. That this is the whole problem.

Perhaps one reason why Anna had never told Nikki exactly how she and David met was because the chance on which their meeting rested was so particularly flimsy, that still today, though safely married, she couldn't feel quite sure that any minute it wouldn't blow away or reveal itself as pure illusion. At the same time the fragility pleased her; she hugged it to herself; found herself reluctant to reveal its precious million-to-oneness, even to Nikki.

For only once, ever, had Anna taken her son to the opera. And only once, ever, had David let himself be taken to hear a Mozart opera; it was *Don Giovanni*, both of them sitting high up in the auditorium at Covent Garden. Anna went, took Ben, because of tickets offered at the last minute. (Afterwards Ben said – he was twelve

129

– that maybe he'd wait till grown up before going to another opera.) David went because his then girlfriend insisted that though she would never force him to go again, he really must try Mozart opera at least once. In consequence of which David said he could almost like *Don Giovanni* from now on, not because of the singers or the conductor, let alone the production, not for any reason that might have pleased his girlfriend, on the contrary, but because two rows below him with her son had been Anna for whom he'd fallen – or so he claimed – the very first moment he saw her.

It was Ben's fault, entirely; David's girlfriend, it turned out, taught him music twice a week at his junior school; a day school. (These days, against Anna's will, but on his father's insistence, Ben boarded.)

And that had been it, more or less; not that they had talked much that evening, not to each other; Anna had chatted up the music teacher; David had chatted up Ben. His girlfriend had been surprised, he said – she hadn't thought he liked children – he certainly wasn't good at talking to children; but he had asked Ben where he lived in some detail, what part of London and so on – he'd asked the boy's surname also. Armed with this information, he had proceeded to ring round every phone number in that name in the right area; his sixth call had been answered by Anna, to her great surprise. She had not disliked this silent man – she'd tried to defend Mozart to him quite heatedly, she remembered, and felt herself teased just slightly, but shyly. She'd scarcely taken him in otherwise. This was the first but not the last time that what was going on in David Kern's head eluded her completely.

'What would you have done if I hadn't been in the phonebook?' she asked him, some time later. He hesitated – looked at her – said, reluctantly; 'I'd've had to have asked Cathy, I suppose.' Cathy was his then – but for not much longer – music-teacher girlfriend. 'It wouldn't have been decent would it, though? – to do that, then ditch her.'

'As it was,' said Anna, smiling, giving him no quarter,

'you just ditched her.'

'Would you have rather I ran you in tandem?' he asked, slyly. 'I had to find you,' he added. 'I had to.' (It was David's sister, later, of course, told Anna he was a romantic. Whereas she discovered for herself how obsessional he could be; not to say ruthless.)

'Weren't you alarmed about Ben,' she asked him. 'About my having a son already?'

'Why should I have been?' he replied. 'I wasn't thinking of marrying you at that stage. I just wanted to get you into bed; if not tonight, tomorrow.'

And as for Anna; that was what she'd wanted also. Which is one of the reasons – the first reason – she had not at once told David about Ben. Of course she'd intended to tell him in due course, to get his advice not least, on his view of the likely chances of Ben's epilepsy recurring during his adolescence. But she'd wanted him as a lover much more than she'd wanted him as a doctor. And there was a danger in telling him, it seemed to her; if he had epilepsy all day, at work, would he want it in bed at night, also? In other words, might he change his mind about her, might his desire wane entirely? She couldn't bear to take the risk. If he'd been planning to marry her of course, that was different; she'd have had to tell him. But as he said himself, he hadn't been planning to marry her then, any more than she'd been planning to marry him.

But, then, such a short time later, the haste more characteristic of Anna than of himself, David had asked her to marry him. At this point, she'd decided he must be told. But before she could do so, Ben intervened. And again, maybe she wanted him to intervene; maybe it was a relief still, to have an excuse for silence.

For of course, she'd had to broach the matter with Ben, given his earlier views on the matter. Seeing how much he liked David now, how comfortable he was with him, how little jealousy he'd shown, especially as compared to that shown to her previous lovers, she half thought that he would not object any longer. But it was not so. On the contrary, he begged her harder than ever not to tell

David. He begged and begged her. It wasn't till this point Anna saw how little Ben cared for his father; how he longed for David to play that role. It was no longer embarrassment made him want his about-to-be stepfather kept in the dark. On the one hand, he was much more afraid than he had been, that David's knowing of his epilepsy might drive him away; on the other, he didn't want David as a doctor, anything but; he wanted him as a father.

Chapter Nine

Anna Kern's journal. 1988.

I've been exploring the metamorphoses of the Greek word; physis = nature/ physikos = natural. It makes more immediate sense of the present use of the word 'physics', meaning study of certain aspects of the natural world, than it does of the old term 'physic' meaning medicine, and 'physician' meaning prescriber of said medicines. At least it does until you realise that the physician is someone who knows that most central aspect of nature, the one thing each of us has in common along with a father and a mother; a body. How anthropocentric we are; to most people 'physical' means something pertaining to the body, rather than nature in general. How arrogant of doctors to have stolen 'nature' for themselves so early on – the English word 'physician' goes back to the thirteenth century, according to the Oxford dictionary. It wasn't till the nineteenth century that the word physicist was used for scientists working with the much larger realities of physical laws; till then people like Newton called themselves natural philosophers.

'The anatomical novice . . . styles himself physician, prepares himself by familiar cruelties . . . to extend his arts of torture . . . which he has hitherto tried on cats and dogs.' (Samuel Johnson. Quoted in the *Oxford English Dictionary*.)

'Physicians are like kings – they brook no

contradictions.' (That's from *The Duchess of Malfi* – a play which also has the most touching and ironic use of the word 'physic'. 'Look thou giv'st my little son some physic for his cold' – when he and she (the duchess) are about to be murdered, and she knows it. The littleness of human remedies, against such realities. Yes. (I've just looked up the text, the word's 'syrup', in fact, not 'physic'. But the idea stands.))

The replacing of the word 'physic', the natural substance, by 'pharmaceutical' or 'drug', presumably reflects the latter being synthesized in a laboratory rather than boiled up at home. This didn't mean it tasted any nicer. Of course not. ('As bad as the wrong physic; nasty to take and sure to disagree.' George Eliot in *Middlemarch*. Also quoted in the *OED*).

Anna had not forgotten what Nikki had said about the enormity of what they were doing. Though she did her best to forget most of that conversation, and indeed, succeeded, *that* she could not forget. Partly because, unable to see exactly what Nikki meant, she felt she ought to; that it was obvious enough. Yet the word – the idea – 'enormity' – insinuating itself round the reality of what she was actually doing all these weeks, she could not feel the meaning, no matter how she tried. Maybe she didn't dare to. When she asked David he simply said, 'It's always an enormity. But that doesn't mean you shouldn't get on and do it. It's what people want.'

'Do people know what they want, though?'

'I have to assume they do.'

'But how can you make assumptions about people so far away?' asked Anna.

'You're right,' said David, 'I can't. But people locally can. And all I can do is listen. Anyway, Anna, you're just as involved in this as I am. It's no good asking metaphysical questions. Wait till afterwards. If you must. And then ask Jacoman, not me. He's more up to that kind of thing than I am.'

'I know he is,' said Anna, thinking about metaphysical questions; for there always were, there always would be, metaphysical questions.

A digression.
One metaphysical question – or so Anna thought – she
was prepared to admit it was geographical, also –
concerned a lake. The first time they went to Kenya in
June 1986 they spent three hard but pleasant days
working beside this lake; either in a garden under large
and spreading trees Anna assumed were some kind of
pine at first, having never before seen acacias, or in a
specially allocated bungalow, set in the same garden,
belonging to a lakeside hotel. The nub of this story now,
though, is not why they were there, or what work they
were doing; it was the boat trip they took on the lake,
one evening. They'd walked down a long jetty to meet the
shallow-keeled boat in which the boatman, a huge man,
wearing ragged shorts and an official hotel cap, had
rowed them round the island at the centre of the lake.
Thereafter he'd ferried them as close as possible to the
ruined trees on which stood stiffly, like corpses, whole
flights of fish eagles gazing intently at the water; and
thence right across the lake to the deeper water on the
far side. There were storks, there were huge bobbing
flocks of pelicans, also spoonbills. Once they saw the
great whale shape of hippos almost under the boat. A
huge cloud crept over the sky as they rowed back,
making the very light fall green as water – they'd barely
regained the shore before it started raining.

A lake is a lake is a lake, so Anna thought, not the
least unreasonably. But it seemed that she was mistaken. For when they came back the next year there was
no lake, to speak of; no birds, no pelicans, no fish eagles.
They walked out to the island disconsolately, across
cracked, parched ground that looked as if it had been so
for centuries. Here and there stood the skeletons of trees,
quite fruitless, corpseless. Where had the sea-eagles
gone, Anna wondered? Where had the lake gone – and
why? And would it ever come back?

More metaphysical questions; concerning Ecuador this

time; for it was there that Anna, at last, understood precisely what Nikki had meant; about the enormity of what they were doing. Two hours after arriving in the country for the first time, she also realised, for the first time, that Ecuador *meant* equator. Of course, said David, looking at her blankly. Of course.

They had landed in Quito on Good Friday, in a rainstorm, to be met by a young man in a pick-up truck, into the open back of which he threw their luggage. The rain fell still harder as he was driving them to their hotel. When they started to unpack there was scarcely a garment not wringing wet, they draped them around the room to dry. Then they went out and took a taxi into old Quito; Anna, light-headed from altitude – not that she realised yet that it was altitude made her feel so strange – asked 'Where are the volcanoes,' in her best Spanish. (Except here, in South America, it was called 'Castiliano', not Spanish.) '*Cubierto*,' said the driver waving a hand at the louring sky. That was all he did say. '*Cubierto*,' meaning 'Covered'. At least it was all he said that she understood.

Over the years the project was running, a lot went on in Ecuador. There were riots, filling Quito with helmeted, riot-shielded police, and CS gas canisters. There were strikes, including a doctors' strike ('Good,' said Jacoman when told of this. 'All the more time for them to work on our project.') The president was captured, and held as a hostage against the release of some rebellious airforce officers impounded by their superiors; it was rumoured he'd been tortured. There was an election which this same president lost. There was above all a serious earthquake, its epicentre in the Oriente, that is down in the jungle not so far from San Raphael. When Anna returned to Ecuador for the second time, towers and buildings alike were propped up by huge buttresses made of tree trunks, making colonial baroque appear sadder and seedier than ever; and not liable to stand much longer.

However this was Good Friday – there were no riots or strikes or earthquakes, just processions. The shuttered streets were filled not with the sounds of people talking, but the sounds of people shuffling and chanting to the accompaniment of cracked trumpets and bugles played by men in faded and crumpled uniforms, decorated by tarnished braid. Some carried crosses and images and touched the feet of the Christ outside the church as they passed. Some wore deep penitentes caps over their heads, they looked out through narrow slits. Jet-lagged besides light-headed, Anna felt oppressed by the weight of the sky above the narrow, colonial shabbiness of the streets – even the palm trees in the square they arrived at looked dejected to her eyes, even the occasional whiff of fish and of beans cooked by street vendors, a street or two away, was dreamlike; unreal. The people moved as if muffled by their gowns and hoods. She did not know what lay behind the gowns and hoods, any more than she knew what lay behind the very often flat Indian features of those whose faces were uncovered; who wore trilbies and ponchos, in some cases carried children in shawls on their backs. She could read them as little as she could read the blind eyes of the model heads posed on a hairdresser's balcony above the street. There was not much light or colour. Just the animal smell of people. And the sounds of drums and squeaky trumpets and sometimes even of people crying; and a huge weight of grief which permeated her too, she was not able to escape it, no matter how hard she clutched at the hand of her darling husband; as a Jew he looked quite as appalled, if not more so. It could not just be that grievous death so far away and so long ago, that they, that she, were mourning. It had to be here and now, or here and yesterday, or here and tomorrow. Just ahead of them, as they were walking, a little bright child with gold rings in her ears was carried on a man's shoulders, her face, too, impassive.

They had timed their arrival in Ecuador carefully, five days before the work was due to start. A day later, the Spanish psychologist, Vittoria, arrived. Two days later they and she got on a bus and were driven along what they were assured was a whole avenue of volcanoes – but they could not see them, any more than they could see Cotopaxi when they passed that, also – and down to a place called Banos, four thousand feet lower, the gateway, they were told, to the jungle. It was a spa town with a curious and very ugly twin-towered cathedral constructed of big whitish slabs of something Anna could not identify, each square picked out in black. It also had the gimcrack air of all such watering places, though in the European ones with which she was more familiar you didn't find hibiscus and bananas and pineapples growing. And it rained; once it rained very hard and suddenly as they were walking up a street near the centre of the town. They had almost reached a dirty but empty cafe, into which they hurried and ordered coffee.

There was very little of anything in the cafe; a few battered formica topped tables, pushed against dirty yellow walls, some spindly chairs. Pinned behind the counter, one tattered poster proclaimed Pepsi-Cola, another a gangster film shown in 1983, while in the corner of the room, by the door, crates were piled up, empty mostly, apart from some bottles of Pepsi and Fanta and a few much bigger bottles of pinkish liquid. After peering at these for some while – there was very little else to do or look at apart from the people walking outside; once, she saw a man in a bright orange jacket carrying a teapot carefully through the rain – Anna managed to decipher the label; they were bottles of Tizer – she'd always wondered just what that consisted of.

To judge by his cheekbones, his narrow black eyes, the owner of the cafe was himself part Indian. He wore a baseball cap and a faded blue check shirt. As he emerged from behind the counter with a tray on which stood three saucerless cups, a jug of water, a jar of Nescafé and a teaspoon, the door of the cafe opened, three full-blooded Indians came in. Anna had noticed them the moment before walking up the street, one behind the other, a man, a woman and a child, the woman and the child wearing trilby hats and ponchos, the man's torn leather jacket also topped by a trilby hat. They did not say anything. They did not look at anyone, not even at the cafe owner standing there with his tray. In silence the woman brought out a chipped white enamel bowl and handed it to the child in its green poncho. The man lifted a bottle full of the pink liquid from the top crate and opened it – they could hear the hiss of air as the vacuum lifted right across the room where they were sitting. The man filled up the enamel bowl; at once the child began drinking. He himself drank half of what remained in the bottle, before handing it to the woman; she, having poured a little more of the liquid into the bowl held out mutely by the child, raised it, tipped her head right back and swallowed the remainder in long slow gulps. When she was quite finished – the whole performance had taken no more than three minutes or so – the man took the empty bottle from her and replaced it in one of the crates. The woman meanwhile fumbled under her poncho and advanced towards the cafe owner who had stood watching them, the tray still in his hands, almost the whole time the three were drinking, only to crash it down on their table and flee as the man replaced the bottle. Now safely behind the counter, he took the note the woman offered him, scrutinized it carefully, then shook his head and handed it back. The woman, expressionless as ever, produced another note and this, after the same scrutiny he pushed into his pocket. Still not one word was said, not even nods were exchanged; only as she returned to the man and the child did the woman at last break the silence, murmuring something to her family in a language that was definitely not Castiliano: Quechua presumably, thought Anna.

The door closed behind them. The mestizo owner thumped his hands on the counter and said 'indigenos,' to himself. The psychologist as usual impeccably turned out, in a pink macintosh and a pink macintosh hat, was, they had already discovered, impervious to anthropological nuance; (on the bus to Banos she'd complained bitterly of the garlic seller in the white bowler. 'It stinks the bus,' she had kept on saying, not the least interested when Anna had told her the hat was particular to the garlic-selling tribe). Now she said disapprovingly, 'Did you see how they were trying to cheat him? He sorted them, did he not?' David and Anna said nothing. They just looked at each other in complete yet blank understanding, blank because of what they did not understand; what they could not begin to grasp, any more than they could grasp the shape and nature of the volcanoes the cloud had hidden, or even the true shape and nature of the big stain in the middle of the tray the mestizo had thumped down before them. Anna spooned coffee powder into three chipped cups and poured hot water on top from the jug. If even the cafe owner, the local, was outside it, what hope for them, David signalled, as she handed him his uninviting cup – the water wasn't hot enough, some of the powder still floated on top. Such impossibility, such 'enormity', as Nikki had put it. Yes. Maybe. Yes.

Time, perhaps, since we have arrived in Ecuador, to learn a little more about it. How about this, for instance: courtesy W. J. Turner.

When I was but thirteen or so
I went into a golden land,
Chimborazo, Cotopaxi,
Took me by the hand.

My father died, my brother too,
They passed like fleeting dreams,
I stood where Popocatepetl
In the sunlight gleams.

I dimly heard the Master's voice,
And boys far off at play,
Chimborazo, Cotopaxi,
Had stolen me away.

I walked in a great golden dream
To and fro from school –
Shining Popocatepetl
The dusty streets did rule.

I walked home with a gold dark boy
And never a word I'd say,

140

Chimborazo, Cotopaxi
Had taken my speech away;

I gazed entranced upon his face
Fairer than any flower,
O shining Popocatepetl
It was thy magic hour:

The houses, people, traffic seemed
Thin fading dreams by day,
Chimborazo, Cotopaxi
They had stolen my soul away!

(Sour note by Anna Kern. June 1986, post the first
Ecuador trip: *Obviously he'd never actually been there.*)

Ecuador: Anna Kern's notebook: 1986.

Small country on the North West of the South American
continent, once the northernmost outpost of the Inca
empire, and subsequently of the Spanish empire based in
Lima; it straddles the equator and is divided geographically, like Gaul, into three parts: 1) the Costa, a tropical
coastal region, chief products sugar and bananas (this is,
indeed, a banana republic) its chief city, port and business
centre for the whole country, Guayaquil. 2) a high
mountain area, the Altiplano – wherein lie all the
volcanoes; chief product maize and potatoes; chief city the
capital, Quito, home of the main university, left-wing
intellectuals, ambassadors and so forth; home also of a
general tendency to despise anyone from the Costa,
particularly Guayaquil, whose inhabitants, even the
richest and most successful are all dubbed monkeys. 3)
the eastern jungle below the range of the Andes, the
'Oriente,' seemingly impervious, home only of the most
primitive tribes, in fact the source of 70% of country's
income. Oil, of course. (Wherein lie border disputes,
environmental arguments, denial of the human rights of
indigenous inhabitants; and so on.)
    Ecuador: according to HMSO. Economist year book,
etc. Population, 9.38 million. Area. 283,561 square kil.
Density 33 persons per km. Race: Indian 50%, mestizo
40%, European 8%. Yearly income per person £1,136.
Exports £2,241 million p.a. (67% oil, 9% fish, 7% bananas

(yes!) 7% coffee. 64% of all exports to the USA. Religion
96% Roman Catholic.

Ecuador: Anna Kern's journal. June 1987. Another
digression.

We were hijacked for three days by Lohengrin
Meyersdorf, Jacoman's Latin American colleague,
otherwise known as Grinny, and taken down to Lima.
Which turned out less of a diversion than it seemed,
because now I've seen it, I understand Ecuador much
better. Lima is horrible, to start with. We had a brief
marvellous, blinding glimpse from the plane of the
Sierra Blanca then plunged down into a grey-brown
blanket of cloud in which we stayed for the rest of the
time. Lima is all grey brown, even the sea. At this
time of year, we were told, it always is. It is also under
siege, seemingly. Lohengrin's car is discreetly
armoured, his office has armed guards sitting on the
roof of the gateway who leap into firing positions the
moment his car stops for him to identify himself to the
gatemen, all of them also armed. I don't know about
his house, we don't see it. He takes us to restaurants to
entertain us (also, once, to the Lima Cricket Club, of
which he is a member, where we drank beer and coke
in a bar halfway between a pub and a Midlands sports
centre, complete with engraved mirrors, sports cups,
photographs of cricket teams and ads for Guinness and
Whitbread bitter. I'm sure there's nowhere like this in
Quito.)
    Afterwards he drove us into the centre of Lima; it's
a wide even grandiose Spanish town, it could be pretty,
yet everyone seems to be dressed in black and brown
and khaki, most of them policemen with guns at the
ready, all scowling, glaring at us, at each other. It's not
safe to walk about. The monuments and museums are
full of bones and skulls and tortures; Peru was the
centre of such savage empires, both Inca and Spanish.
We saw the catacombs under the church of San
Francisco, the bones arranged in pretty patterns like

Busby Berkeley dancers, we saw the Museum of the Inquisition, more skulls more skeletons, waxworks of skeletal people being tortured by cadaverous waxwork figures in monks' robes with hoods covering their heads. We saw the Inca Museum – there the skulls have jewels set in their eyes and teeth; there are pottery vases in the shape of criminals having mutilations inflicted on them before their executions.

Afterwards Grinny drove us across a dry river, skeletal brown crates crammed along its bed and up the pointed grey-brown hills beyond – in these, he told us, lives half Lima's population (in which case who can blame them, I thought, but didn't dare say, for supporting the Sendero Luminoso). On this side of the river the streets could have been in Seville except they're drained of colour; had our car broken down there, we'd most likely have been murdered, Meyersdorf said, as we stared out from his armoured Mercedes at barber shops and crumbling churches and lethal looking alleys.

The streets of Quito aren't like this. There is a shanty town of course, but nothing, nothing like Lima's. Also, though there were red slogans on the walls of the old town saying 'Yanquis go home', though there were tanks there, and riot police with helmets and riot shields and canisters of CS gas on every corner, last time we walked round it, although the police with their puttees and guns and round white helmets are just as sinister as the ones in Lima, it still doesn't feel nearly so threatening. But then, as I now understand, Quito was never the centre of anything. Ecuador stood on the outpost of every empire, too far to be more than a pale reflection, too near to be independent, to develop its own identity, let alone an Inquisition, or royal court of its own. (I never saw skulls in Quito, though I daresay they are there.) So they quarrel out an identity, they are edgy, they are uncertain, they question everything, they obfuscate in all directions. All those charts and calendars and diagrams for instance, on the walls of the project house at San Raphael! (Which didn't stop them missing the obvious – may have been the reason they missed it, hence our recent problems.)

David and I flew back today – he left the plane at Guayaquil to catch his connection for Miami, when we said goodbye we were both weeping. I don't know why, it's only for three weeks, but this is such a strange place to be alone in. Also we were both hung over from last night's dinner; the only way to cope with Lima is getting plastered on Pisco Sour. For the rest of the journey I sat with a Canadian girl who's studying law at the university of Quito. She said: 'It's amazing, I'm used to writing straightforward rational analyses of legal matters, if I do that in my papers here, they fail me. Even the first year kids who know nothing are filled up with philosophy and metaphysics. Law in Canada's not one bit like that. There you get failed for obfuscating, not the reverse.' When she also told me that it is considered impolite in Hispanic culture to say no, ever, that no one does say no, you have to realise therefore, that when you think you've agreed something it is not necessarily so, I sigh to myself remembering the interminable meetings, this year and last, discussing issues we thought resolved already. Now I understand it all; too late; too late. No doubt to them we are equally inexplicable. Is there no limit to cultural misunderstanding? Meanwhile the plane swings round, it is clear for once, the clouds aren't creating their usual meteorological obfuscations, we swing between one white cone and another, it is godly and glittering – 'I went into a golden land – Chimborazo, Cotopaxi they have stolen my soul away . . .' except they haven't – except in this moment, oh so nearly . . . oh the innocence in which I quoted those lines once back in 1985 in Northern California – what's happened to it?

I've only been gone three days, but when I arrive back in Quito, there's no sign of a tank, a riot shield, hardly a policeman. I am taken out to dinner by Diego Castra, president of the Ecuadorian Neurological

144

Society, and his wife who is a beautician, (there's a beauty parlour every twenty yards or so in these macho Spanish cities). David, by the way, thinks very highly of Diego Castro. He's a nice, sensible man with a beard which makes him look like Holbein's Henry VIII, only thinner. After dinner, they drive me round the empty streets of the Old Town, all we see are some Indians dancing outside the Cathedral.

'What happened to the tanks? Are the riots over?' I ask him. 'Oh, yes,' he answers, 'Things like that never last for long; Ecuadorians get bored after a few days, they all go home.'

Chapter Ten

The first time Dr Jacoman met the Ecuadorian Dr Fernando Gomez in Geneva, he, too, was favourably impressed Dr Gomez was not only personable, well-dressed, polite, yet not the least obsequious, he was also sophisticated, intelligent, well-informed, he also, in impeccable American English, gave a run-down on the problems of his country's medical service which impressed Carter deeply in terms of its sense and justice. Dr Gomez thought it was absurd, for instance, for a poor country like his to waste medical money on high-tech machinery, scanners and so forth. He apologised for his own private practice – unfortunately the state did not employ doctors; at least not at consultant level. The free hospitals and so forth were staffed on a voluntary basis by doctors like himself who were forced to practise privately for the other half of their time simply to make a living. He considered this unfortunate, hoped for reform. On the other hand he was able to praise the system of rural medical centres across the country, staffed by newly qualified doctors, posted for a year each as a condition of their registration. This system, devised in the seventies, was still being expanded. It meant, he assured Carter, that his country was ideal for an intervention study, if that was what Jacoman was suggesting. He also, from his own experience, knew that epidemiological studies could successfully be carried out in rural areas. Might he, he said, invite Dr Jacoman to visit his country to see for himself, and to set up one of his studies? He himself would offer every available assistance, he would also like to offer himself as principal investigator. It would be an honour to work together with the World Health Organisation and with Bader-Kleitz, and of course with Dr Jacoman himself. Indeed it would.

Put so baldly it all sounds a bit much; maybe Jacoman should have had a few suspicions. But he was not only intrigued by Gomez, he liked him; Gomez' self-conscious, very Spanish charm and formality, not to say the hyperbole in his manner of setting things out was undercut by a nice line in irony – this might of course have been employed for Jacoman's benefit. He told entertaining stories about life in rural practice, and the things the reluctant new doctors got up to. He was also amusing but affecting about the main charity hospital in Quito, describing at length a baby he was tending; it had a progressive disease, its development went the other way to that of most children – backwards. 'Two months ago he could sit up, now he can barely hold up his head any longer,' said Gomez. 'Truly Dr Jacoman, if there's anything I can do for cases like this I will do it. If there is anything I can do to rid my country of cysticercosis, that terrible disease, which is the cause of so much wretchedness in my country and so much epilepsy, incidentally, I will do it.' He seemed, genuinely, to mean it. Cysticercosis is a parasitical disease. A form of tape worm, it does not remain in the stomach, but migrates to the brain; hence its neurological dimensions. ('Very interesting,' David said, his eyes lighting up when he and Jacoman discussed it. 'It's something I've never seen in England.' 'Well you can see it there,' said Jacoman, 'Gomez will be only too happy to show you a few cases.' 'I shall keep him to that,' said David.)

What Anna knew about cysticercosis, apart from the light in David's eyes, apart from the warnings she kept on being given, was that it was a disease carried by pigs; transmitted not only through pork but by water contaminated by them, and by foods washed in that water. Lettuce and strawberries in particular were to be avoided; an American anthropologist got cysticercosis

147

here last year, she was told, eagerly, by everyone, including Dr Castra, when she arrived to do her own field research ('You'd better be careful. She was in a terrible state . . .' And so on.) The liability of anthropologists to contract tropical and other non-western diseases, was not something that appeared in their academic monographs. But it was so. No wonder Anna eyed with suspicion the charming little red pigs rooting round the water tank that supplied San Raphael. 'Cysticercosis on legs,' David called them.

Ecuador, however, as a base for the study seemed probable. Carter Jacoman arranged to take up Fernando Gomez' invitation to visit his country in late September, 1985. He also arranged to be accompanied by Bud Schwarz, the epidemiologist from the National Institute of Health in Washington; the same fat, silent, steak-eating man who had attended the dinner with David in Jerusalem, and who had worked with Gomez on his epidemiological studies for the WHO. It all seemed very straightforward. What was less straightforward was the flurry of telexes that kept arriving, from Gomez himself, from the area medical director, the Colombian, with the unlikely name of Lohengrin Meyersdorf, based in Lima, Peru; about how Gomez was setting up this meeting with neurologists here, and that meeting with neurologists there, would Dr Jacoman be kind enough to prepare this presentation, that presentation, so on and so forth. Jacoman was expecting discussions, consultations with interested parties in the government, the Ecuadorian subsidiary of his company, the local neurological profession. He wasn't expecting a whole conference on epilepsy in the Andes. Still if Gomez wanted it, if the local company was prepared to pay for it, well and good.

It is a long flight to Ecuador from Europe. Twenty hours approximately, longer if you go via Miami, wiping out most of a night's sleep unless you happen to be good at sleeping on planes, which Jacoman wasn't. He met up with the epidemiologist, Bud Schwarz, in Miami – he was no more loquacious now than he had been in Jerusalem a month before. Jacoman discussed the project most of the way. Bud Schwarz, said uh, huh, mostly. Occasionally with one sentence, he demolished Jacoman; not that Jacoman seemed to notice; he just wanted to keep Schwarz happy. In the world of American epidemiology, Schwarz was powerful.

Both were somewhat jaded by the time they arrived, around twelve thirty in the morning, Ecuadorian time. Their plane circled for a while before landing, above a thick layer of clouds through which peered the white conical tops of the much vaunted volcanoes. At last it lurched down through the cloud and emerged, at an angle, into the dangerously narrow looking bowl in the mountains in which sat Quito: skyscrapers and shanty towns, also a grotesquely large statue of the Virgin on a hilltop. Jacoman had not travelled so much he had lost all his curiosity for new places; but nearly. Even as he peered out of the window beside him, he continued to talk about epidemiology to the man from NIH. Bud Schwartz, on the other hand, did not so much as glance out of the window.

Jacoman was still talking as he was getting his bags down from the overhead lockers. It did not occur to him to be surprised therefore, when, the plane door having been opened, all the other passengers in business class were asked to wait, in English and Spanish, and Jacoman and Schwarz were escorted, ceremoniously, to the front. They emerged, blinking, at the top of the plane steps to see a crowd of people waiting for them at the bottom. At the rear was a television crew; in front stood Dr Gomez, in a very well-cut suit and a pair of dark glasses to protect his eyes against non-existent sun, between a man thrusting a microphone at him, and another rather fat man, also wearing an expensive suit. Dr Gomez continued talking as they came down the steps. They were each introduced to the fat man and the television reporter, in Spanish initially, which neither spoke well. The import, however, was too obvious to miss; Carter Jacoman unable to believe what he seemed to be hearing, initially blamed his lack of Spanish, but when, next moment, Gomez switched to English, it really was just as he feared. The fat man – he had enormous gold cufflinks – was introduced as a junior minister of health sent to welcome them on behalf of the government. Dr Bud Schwarz was introduced as the American Minister of Health; Dr Jacoman, as head of the Pharmaceutical division of Bader-Kleitz. These notables, the television man was telling the camera, had come to Ecuador because concerned with the plight of unfortunate epileptics in their country; they were proposing to fund and set up a project to help them, with the aid of Ecuador's most notable neurologist, Dr Fernando Gomez. (Gomez translated all this *sotto voce*. Even Jacoman was so stunned he could not speak. Bud Schwarz just grinned, and after a moment yawned, a yawn he attempted, not very effectively to hide; giving Jacoman the impression he only tried to do so to save the dignity of the Minister of Health he was supposed to be. Bud Schwarz was still fatter than the Ecuadorian minister he noted, but much less natty.)

The television crew disappeared shortly. The junior minister accompanied them to the VIP lounge, and then said his own goodbyes with another generous ration of smiles and handshakes. The passports of Jacoman and Schwarz were taken off to be inspected and stamped; no lengthy waits in immigration queues for them. Instead they sat drinking coffee in front of a low table set with an enormous tray of pastries from which Bud Schwarz took two doughnuts and a Danish pastry and Jacoman nothing, while Gomez not only apologised for all these shenanigans, he mocked the whole thing, ironically self-deprecating in the way Jacoman had always appreciated up till now. He still appreciated it up to a point; at least appreciated it as a performance; this did not stop him being maybe a little more suspicious of Dr Gomez, for all the plausibility of Gomez' arguments about cultural norms, about how in Ecuador you had to do things like this, if you wanted your plans to be taken seriously. He himself, of course – here he indicated, very subtly, his own cosmopolitan background, his much greater sophistication – the mere raising of an eyebrow did it, the wave of a manicured doctor's hand, a minor adjustment of the knot of his tie – he himself found such hyperbole distasteful; but they must understand how in this country such things were necessary; how his and Jacoman's position in their enterprise depended on it. He was sure Dr Jacoman, and of course his good friend Dr Schwarz, with whom he'd had the privilege of working before in Washington, he was sure they were experienced enough to appreciate the way things were. 'When in Rome . . .' he said. And sighed a little. As if he found it all a huge bore; including himself.

Over the next few days, Jacoman's suspicions of Gomez grew. For one thing he discovered that Gomez' practice tallied very little with his high-sounding sentiments over dinner in Geneva. He did not, for instance, unlike many of his colleagues, spend half his time working for nothing in charity hospitals. He had not only a huge private practice, his office was filled with the highest of high tech; EEG's, CAT scans, brain mappers and so forth, exactly the kind of equipment he affected to disdain for his poverty-stricken country.

For another, right from the beginning of the meeting proper, Jacoman was made aware of undercurrents, of secrets; of things going on of which he had no knowledge. As the currents mounted, turned to waves, to great rollers, it became increasingly clear, in subtle ways, that the problem, whatever it was, the secrets whatever they were, had something to do with Doctor Gomez. There were interminable formal meetings in which Jacoman lectured about treatment gaps (that is the number of people who were treated, against the much greater number of people who were not) showed prevalence figures, discussed ideas of social morbidity (meaning epileptics are not happy people); in which Ecuadorian neurologists, Meyersdorf acting as interpreter to Jacoman and Schwarz on their behalf, stood at specially erected blackboards, writing up what they considered essential in such a study, or else presenting work of their own, running busily forward and back from rostrum to board to set out these figures, or that diagram.

And yet not once, in any of these, did anyone discuss the proposed study, or their possible part in it. Every time Jacoman tried to address such matters with them, the subject was changed. Moreover there were things going on round him the whole time about which he also knew nothing. Meetings in separate rooms; people being fetched conspiratorially from his own meetings to join them; conferences in corners – whenever he visited the coffee-shop of his hotel he would, almost always, see two or three of the Ecuadorians, their heads together, whispering, giving occasional glances round them. The Spanish – or Castilian – language he felt was used not just as a language but as a barrier against him also. He could not persuade even Meyersdorf to breach it on his behalf. Only the day before he was due to leave did things at last become clear.

It was not a formal meeting; it was convened at short notice between himself and Meyersdorf, Bud Schwarz, Dr Diego Castra the president of the neurological association and another neurologist, Dr Aguadiente, a nervous dark man with gold-rimmed spectacles much like Jacoman's own, and a thin pock-marked face, who'd made more presentations than any one, all involving endless figures and diagrams, none making any sense to Jacoman. This thin man and fat Schwarz sat side by side today, both chain smoking, otherwise alien; Schwarz never moved a muscle; occasionally grunted; rarely spoke. Dr Aguadiente, on the other hand, was forever putting up a finger to check other speakers, kept saying in English, for Jacoman's benefit – 'Please; please; wait; *un momento*; by example,' – before breaking into rapid Spanish. In this meeting, at last, never mind its original purpose, Jacoman could bear it no longer; he exploded. To hell with cultural norms, not to mention cultural prevarications, he said to Meyersdorf in English – Meyersdorf, translating, clearly toned down much of the language – to hell with it, he'd come to Ecuador to set up a project, so far not an iota of it had been fixed; what the hell was going on? Bud Schwarz, vigorously, for him, grunted. Was heard to say; 'Who cares a pig's ass, let's get to the nitty gritty, Carter.'

The President of the Neurological Society was, as Jacoman had already discovered, a diplomatic and reasonable man. He smiled now, a reasonable smile; checked the eager dark man, who was anxiously putting up his finger, and said, Meyersdorf translating word for slow word, 'I think it is time perhaps that Dr Jacoman understood – I am reluctant to say to him, but it seems it is time now to do so; and of course this is quite confidential between us; the problem is Dr Gomez.'

Of course, thought Jacoman, understanding at last. Local jealousy was often a problem, particularly in this part of the world; and who more likely to attract it than Dr Gomez with his expensive suits, his technology, his huge practice, his foreign travel? How could he have been so stupid?

'If Dr Gomez will run the project then it is not possible, not one of my colleagues will cooperate,' said the Ecuadorian neurologist; his colleague, Aguadiente, the twitchy dark man, whom Jacoman had begun to put down as a high-grade fool, nodded and nodded.

'Then it's simple,' Jacoman said to Meyersdorf when they were alone in his hotel room; 'We just get rid of Gomez.'

'Not so simple,' said Meyersdorf, who'd done his own share of conspiratorial whispering, but had not till now been forthcoming with the results; but then Jacoman always felt he disdained the lot of them; noisy Canadian, jealous Ecuadorians, alike. He himself was not the least provincial. He was an aristocrat, and knew it. Not till now did he deign to use the power his local influence, his language, gave him. 'Not so simple, Carter. You cannot dismiss Gomez like that. He is much too powerful. If you don't use him, he will sabotage the whole event. If you do, someone else will sabotage it. That is what's simple.'

Matters still stood this way by the time Jacoman had to leave. The whole thing hung in the balance; in no way clarified by the comment of one neurologist, who, when asked why he didn't like Gomez, simply said, 'Why not?' On the other hand, he and all his colleagues seemed to like Dr Aguadiente. Though Jacoman had decided he was a fool, this was the man several people told him they would be happy to work with if he was made Principal Investigator.

That did not make Jacoman any happier, either. His disaffection came to a head on the last but one morning, when the Ecuadorian medical director presented him with a bill to take back to Basel; a very large bill covering the costs of the whole meeting. Gomez, it turned out, had persuaded the local company the parent company would pay for it, at the same time as letting Jacoman assume the local company would. When the local man, Dr Navarro, realised this deception, he looked ready to faint. A plump, soft yet hirsute man, more devious than assertive, he had nothing but a certain petulant obstinacy with which to confront Carter. (He had nothing particular by which to distinguish himself from start to finish, except the handbag he always carried, and, Jacoman had already discovered, a desire as intense as the desire of a Chekhov character to remove himself and his family from this country, though in his case to Madrid rather than Moscow.)

The whole of the last two hours before Jacoman left to catch his plane, the four of them, he, Gomez, Navarro and Meyersdorf, spent thrashing the matter out over a lap top computer. The Ecuadorian agreed finally, with great reluctance, that he had only assumed the matter was so, because Dr Gomez had told him. Dr Gomez acknowledged even more reluctantly, with somewhat less of his usual charm and self-deprecation, that no, Jacoman had never told him that Basel would pay for it. The matter had not been discussed between them.

The fact that in the end Bader-Kleitz, Ecuador, had to pay for the meeting did not augur well for good relations between the parent and local companies so long as the project lasted. The surprising thing really, after all this – what in Spanish is covered by the word 'envia' – this 'envia,' was that the Ecuadorian project got off the ground at all.

But then envia, envy is the soul of social relationships

everywhere, one might think, not only in Ecuador; even if in Ecuador the form it took was particularly intense. Not that Jacoman took much note. 'Attention must be paid' – yes; despite such a family edict there were things to which he simply did not pay attention enough. He'd never read Henry James for a start, he told Anna when she enquired. Of course he'd allowed for something like this in Ecuador. He was not that stupid. These were Latins, after all. But inasmuch as he didn't take enough note for his own good of such processes at work in the culture he lived and worked in, it was not surprising he found its management in another beyond his patience, Anna thought. For so it was. The heart of social connection *envia* might be. If so, the restless brain of Jacoman did not want to know about it.

Chapter Eleven

Anna Kern's journal:

The British Medical Association sign on the front of David's car has two entwined serpents. Whenever I go into a museum these days, one with classical remains anyway, I keep seeing statues of Asclepius, the god of healing, with his serpent always. Sometimes at a distance I'm not sure if it's Adam and the serpent I see, or even Eve. You can't get away from the ambivalence of the image. Or the wondrousness of snakes, or the disgust you feel if you come on them at the wrong moment. Who was it sucked a drop of hot serpent venom – or was it just touched half-cooked serpent flesh then sucked a finger – and understood everything the animals said?

All her own life, Anna had tended to fall into things headlong – and often regretted it later. (There were times, for instance, she regretted falling, so precipitantly, into Jacoman's project; she'd assumed she knew better these days than to make decisions too quickly; she thought the business of the baby, not least, showed she'd learned more caution.) Her family, on the other hand, were fence-sitters to a man, not precipitate at all, rather they weighed everything up carefully, much like her son Ben.

When she was twenty-one for instance, straight out of university, Anna had spent three months on a kibbutz in Israel, between the Six Day War and the Yom Kippur war; there, ignoring the attention of assorted Swiss, Dutch and Germans, she had fallen in love with a kibbutznik; who had also, unfortunately, fallen in love with her. It would not have been unfortunate, apart from, in due course, depriving David of a wife and Jacoman of an anthropologist, had it not been for the fact that the kibbutznik, having taken part a few years before in the liberation of the Wailing Wall, was so fired by his Jewishness he insisted on his children being Jewish; thus he insisted Anna converted to the religion he himself did not practise on his secular kibbutz.

Not that Anna minded; Judaism, Israel, seemed to offer her the passionate kind of identity she'd always sought without knowing it, her rational, sensible family having failed to provide her with any such thing – maybe that was one reason why, years later, she felt so affronted when David and Jacoman used their Jewishness, unwittingly or not, to shut her out. She learned Hebrew. She wrestled with the Talmud. When she came back to England to do the postgraduate course in sociology she'd fixed up for herself before she left for the kibbutz, she went off to her local rabbinate, and against all discouragements plunged into the business of conversion.

To satisfy the Beth Din, of course, she was going to have to go the whole hog; cover her head, take ritual baths, eat only Kosher food, separate milk from meat, not so much as get on a bicycle on the Sabbath; and so on. For herself she didn't mind this, she even wanted it, she wanted to be as Jewish as she possibly could be. The problem was her fiancé, in his secular kibbutz. On Saturdays, for instance, he liked to borrow a car sometimes and go off for a day with his friends. So what was she going to do then, about all these religious precepts and instructions? He said it didn't matter. She said if she'd promised to do these things she'd have to. But then, after a while, it began to seem alien to her, also; she suddenly felt herself so dreadfully English, so unremittingly Christian, she didn't know what to do about any of it. Not that she told anyone, not even herself, until the night a boyfriend of her university days, took her out to dinner and got her drunk. When she found herself pregnant with Benjamin a few weeks later, it seemed the obvious let-out; she agreed to marry the ex-boyfriend, and that was that – another example of her leaping where angels fear to tread. (The only problem was her husband never forgave her for so entrapping him; the epilepsy was the last straw, or the excuse, whichever way you looked at it; after Ben's second seizure, when he was eight years old, his father left. For which Ben on the one hand blamed himself, on the other, did not forgive his father; this was one reason he so needed, so wanted, David as a father.)

Meanwhile Anna, having completed her postgraduate year, then done another course to qualify her as a social worker, entered a piece about the kibbutz for a magazine competition. What's more she won it. She followed up that success by publishing one of the few bitchy, not to say disillusioned pieces she ever wrote, about her attempts to convert to Judaism. (This she sent to her former fiancé; from whom, in consequence, as she half-intended, she never heard again.) When she saw the commissions thereafter, gradually, beginning to come in, she gave up all thoughts of social work (though she did not entirely give up her sociological – and increasingly – anthropological interests). It is not true that *naïveté* is always the journalist's worst enemy; on the contrary, when it appeals to the *naïveté* of others, as did hers. She wrote about odd places. She wrote about people in unusual professions. She wrote about eccentrics and aliens and sad people on Scottish Islands, and decaying families in upper New York State. She even wrote about things like knitting machines, with the uncanny precision of someone who did not understand how anything mechanical worked, yet could get its intricacies on paper in such a way that other people might.

Was this why Carter Jacoman seized on her; why, all along he wanted her to write a book about the project, starring him? Who can tell. She couldn't. He never told her he'd read any of her work. But presumably he had, in this case. He certainly never asked her anything about it,

158

or anything else about her life for that matter, or anything about David's, apart from his Jewish roots.

If he'd wanted to know more though, he could always have asked his wife.

Once, when Giselle herself came to London to see her grandmother, leaving Carter in charge of their three children for the weekend, she called up Anna to ask her to have lunch with her; over pasta and a carafe of wine, she told Anna how Jacoman had described herself and David, after their first meeting. 'Small, dark; that's David. Small; fairish, you, Anna,' Giselle said, smiling mildly. (Anna's hair was in fact a light reddish brown; now very short, in those days she had worn it much longer.) 'Pretty also. Oh and very English. One minute indeterminate and unsure; the next lively and opinionated.'

'I asked David what you were like,' said Anna. 'He just said "tall".'

When they had exchanged ironical and sympathetic glances, concerning their husbands' lack of curiosity in such matters, Giselle proceeded to pump Anna about herself.

'Giselle wanted to know my whole life history,' Anna told Jacoman next time they met. 'Sure,' he replied. 'She would. Giselle's into life histories. Especially female life histories. With women she can take bits out of their lives and add them to her own. Since what she's into most of all is expanding her own myth.'

'Can you blame the woman?' said David, informed of this. 'Of course she has to work on her myth in face of someone who makes as much a myth of himself as Carter. Don't be obtuse, Anna.'

When she had finished with Anna's life story, when they had both drunk three glasses of wine at least, Giselle asked Anna about David. Or rather, she leaned across the table, her face as ivory-pale as ever, despite the wine, of which she had drunk rather more than Anna. Her beautiful, spoiled-virgin eyes gazing sadly into Anna's, she had hooked her long dark hair behind her right ear, and hissing rather than asking her questions, demanded to know how they had met? What had attracted them to each other?

This Anna answered much more briefly. Not least it was none of Giselle's business what drew her and David together. She did not always know herself. On the face of it they had little in common. She did not think her flirtation with Judaism of account – David was so determinedly secular; almost religiously so; much more than she was. That his first wife had actually been Jewish, Anna regarded as accident entirely. Not that David told her much about his first marriage; apart from the fact that she'd wanted to have children straight away and he hadn't. (Anna wondered if he'd told her this story as a warning.) As time went on she began to think she knew much more about Jacoman than she knew about her husband; or she would have done had it not been for his much older sister, Sonia, who had gathered her up very early on and told her the whole thing, on the basis that David himself almost certainly wouldn't. Indeed, apart from the fact that his mother died when he was nineteen, and his father had Alzheimers, which she could hardly help knowing in any case, since the father lived with Sonia, all that David was prepared to let out could be more or less summed up in the form of an entry to Who's Who; as follows.

Dr David Philip Kern, MA, DM, MRCP, neurologist, b.1945, son of Dr Leopold G. Kern, neurosurgeon, retired, and of Mrs Naomi Kern (d. 1964) née Cohen. Younger brother (much younger brother) of Sonia Kern, b. 1934. Education, Latymer School, Keble College, Oxford, Royal Free Medical School. Married 1) Diana Goldstein (m.dis.) 2. Anna Owers (née Friston). (And so on.) Interests. Walking. Music (collecting musical manuscripts). Geology. Architecture. (And so on.)

None of this meant anything. None of this told her what Sonia did. How, for instance, David had been such a lonely little boy. Apple of his parents' eyes, she said – yet in some ways, they were more like grandparents than parents. He had suffered, moreover, from their contrary religious convictions. (His father only Jewish on his father's side, and a lapsed Anglican by upbringing; his mother of orthodox background.)

Sonia herself had never married; had never, according to David, shown any interest in doing so. She looked very like David, Anna thought, but what suited him, made her too heavy-featured to be an attractive woman. She was a medical social worker, or had been, until her father fell ill. Now she looked after him, playing the piano whenever she had the time to; her father liked to hear her, luckily, it was one way of calming him. Mostly her life was just feeding, changing, nursing. Anna was awed by Sonia's goodness and devotion; overawed, if anything; irritated sometimes. 'The only trouble with Sonia,' she said to David once, 'is that I can't be wicked with her. I have to pretend all my thoughts are good too.' All the same she liked Sonia; on occasions she went round and sat with her father-in-law to give Sonia the chance to get out.

She used to sit on these occasions looking at the former brain surgeon, this old man, sometimes asleep in his chair, sometimes staring at her blankly, mumbling, even dribbling a little, this once so clever, so dextrous man, wondering where all that knowledge had gone to, wondering about the cerebral intricacies that he had probed with his scalpel all his working life, that kind which, damaged, had caused her son to lie down and shake. She wondered about his – the old man's – own cerebral intricacies, the ones concealed beneath his massive skull, his still bushy white hair – did somewhere, perhaps, in those glutinous lobes the knowledge, the skill, still remain, if you could only make the connections? Or had the disease wiped them out altogether? Would David be like this, ever? If so how she would cope?

On one of the three occasions Anna spent time with Giselle Jacoman, Giselle showed her some of her paintings. Anna did not much like them. All the same she found them extraordinary – and not just because they were so small and so intricate; but because the very nature of the intricacy reminded her of her thoughts about David's father's brain; the knowledge going nowhere; the dead-end paths, the non-connecting connections. For what Giselle painted was gardens. Gardens with flowers and paths and mazes. But the flowers were not quite real flowers, the mazes were never to be fathomed; the paths seemed to be purposeful; but weren't, rather as in Escher drawings, also, turrets and towers and walls were not as they seemed. Indeed in some ways, Giselle's paintings were to the horizontal and to landscape, as Escher's prints and drawings were to the vertical and architectural. They made Anna feel sorry for Giselle in one way. They made her also feel sorry for Carter.

Chapter Twelve

Nikki came to London for a week, two weeks before they were due to leave for Ecuador. Though she had been threatening to come almost since Anna left California, she gave them, in the event, no more than a week's notice.

David said 'Tell her it's inconvenient. Tell her to leave it till later.'

'She can't leave it till later,' said Anna. Nikki had told her at considerable length why not. Something to do with her hovering Indian poet; something to do with her now elderly mother in Santa Barbara; and a book she was writing; and summer courses she was running; and money about to come through. None of this Anna explained to David. She just said, 'I can't tell her it's inconvenient.'

'You mean you don't want to?' said David. But he was too busy at this point to be much put out; his attention was only half on the matter.

'No, I don't think I do want to,' said Anna. Indeed, now it was settled, she looked forward to Nikki's visit, to the chance to re-establish their friendship. Never mind this was not the ideal time for such rapprochement; in David's house, with David around – and with both of them busy organising the trip; with Benjamin around also. And that was another problem, the trip to Ecuador spanned the middle of the school holidays; guiltily – Anna always felt guilty about her son, because of his epilepsy, presumably – she had arranged for Ben to visit a friend for part of the fortnight they were away, and his grandmother for the rest. Though Ben himself seemed not the least put out by these arrangements – on the contrary – in the perverse way of it, it made Anna feel still more split between her son and her husband. And now on top of everything there was Nikki.

It was only by a hair's breadth Nikki missed coinciding with Jacoman's latest trip to London. They all but met on the doorstep; Jacoman's taxi departing for Heathrow ten minutes or so before Anna arrived from Gatwick with Nikki and Nikki's belongings – she might have come for a month, not a week – overflowing the little Citroën 2CV. It was Monday, a day David sometimes worked at home. Anna had to leave him to make Nikki a cup of coffee, while she rushed upstairs to take the sheets off the bed that had been used by Jacoman and was about to be used by Nikki. The room – Ben's room in the loft extension – the disgruntled Ben was camping in her own study next door – still smelt of Jacoman; tobacco; hair-oil was it? Some other rather strong-smelling, almost medicinal unguent. She could not but think, however, that this would soon be overlaid by Nikki's own, much more scented pungency; toilet waters, lotions and what Anna always thought of, particularly since last year, when she'd lain in bed next to her snoring friend, the almost spicy smell of her red hair.

Nikki herself, told she'd only missed Jacoman by minutes, screamed, 'Why didn't you tell me, hon, I'd've come a day sooner?'

'Like I said, Nikki, there's nothing there for you,' said Anna, 'and anyway I doubt if he's your type.' (By which she really meant that, in view of the exquisite Giselle – Nikki, whatever charms she had for men, could not even loosely be described as exquisite – Nikki was most likely not Jacoman's.) 'What about your Indian poet?' she guiltily added.

'What about him?' said Nikki. 'Oh didn't I tell you, *he's* married? What do you expect at my age? If they aren't married they're gay or old-maidish or psychotic; or all three at once. Take your pick.'

Draped across the sofa that evening in the not very

large sitting-room, she too, like Jacoman, looked much too large for it. She pulsated; she glittered; the very furniture pulsated in sympathy as she talked. She quite eclipsed the huge vase of red and white tulips, falling elegantly this way and that on the table in front of her. By comparison, David looked exhausted from a weekend of the indefatigable Jacoman. There were little dark hollows under his eyes; his lips were pinched. Though it was a cold day he only wore a thin shirt; Nikki, on the other hand, kept adding sweaters. After a while, Nikki announcing that at last, since this was noon, California time, she was feeling lively again, he excused himself and went out. Anna did not take much note of it; David, always sensitive in such matters, had already commented she'd want to talk to, to be with her friend sometimes without him around. But when she went to bed, to find David a hump beneath the blankets, seemingly asleep, he rolled over and said, accusingly, 'What time is it?' And then, 'Phew, she wears you out that friend of yours. What's she like when she's not jet-lagged, for heaven's sake?'

'Hug me,' Anna said. She could hear thumps overhead; Nikki going to bed in the attic. She would be sharing the little bathroom up there with Ben. Anna hoped she remembered to wear a bathrobe more often than she did at home. Probably she would; the sexual tease of Ben had not been directed at him. All the same, when Ben came in earlier to find Nikki sitting in his mother's kitchen, saying 'Hi, Ben,' encouragingly, he had, noticeably, blushed, before mumbling something and retreating. Nikki, for her part, had asked straight off if she could come downstairs to take a shower, since there wasn't one upstairs. Afterwards she complained, quite cheerfully, that the water pressure wasn't high enough, but then she never had taken a decent shower in this darling country, what was it about Brits they preferred wallowing in bathtubs, in their own grime?

Anna, who had seen Nikki before now wallowing happily in her own grime, overlaid by a luxuriant froth of scented bubbles, laughed; Nikki looked indignant.

Next morning, when David left for his hospital Nikki was still asleep. He said he reserved his judgment so far on Anna's friend. She was quite amusing. Still she had picked her time to come, hadn't she? After putting up with Jacoman for two days, not least. He groaned – and grinned rather sheepishly, when Anna said, 'But you like him.' 'Yes, I like him. All the same being around him any length of time is like being in a high wind. So's being with your friend for that matter. Maybe we'd better introduce them.'

Of Anna's husband, Nikki said, enthusiastically, 'What a sweet guy. Is he always so *quiet*? And doesn't he just adore you; the way he looks at you.'

Anna hadn't been conscious of David looking at her at all the night before; except sometimes quick glances of amazement at Nikki's more outrageous statements. These glances grew more amazed as time went on. Not that he spent much time with Nikki; he was still working furiously, and Nikki wanted to see this play and hear that concert and of course Anna had to go with her. David said he would have liked to come, under normal circumstances, but just now he had too much work.

In this, clearly, Nikki saw some kind of victory. The triumphalism with which she put her arm around Anna could have been offensive in anyone else. Other things about Nikki were offensive this week – or so David said – but not that. Anna herself found the way Nikki usurped her rather charming; not to say touching; not to say flattering. Not least because, most of the time, David was too busy to notice Nikki usurping her.

Nikki dressed triumphantly also. Anna could no longer see her without being reminded of Nikki's own description of a tropical fish. As for David, he said she looked like a parrot; and wasn't she a bit old for such things? 'Not only sexist but ageist,' said Anna tartly, but sadly. For she was disappointed, though she did not tell herself so, that her husband and her friend had not taken to each other more. She pointed out that Nikki's mode of dress was geared to the strong sun of Northern California, not the chilly grey tones of this London April. She told Nikki herself that she looked like a lilac bred out of the dead land. Nikki's response to this was that Eliot was talking about Massachussets, not England; England wasn't dead at the end of winter like New England. Anyway she was wearing orange (and what an orange, thought Anna) not lilac, oh, hon, what a pedant she was, it was all those years of teaching freshmen who didn't know they'd been born, let alone Thomas Stearns Eliot had been.

Later in the week it came to Anna that Nikki was even more baffled by David than he was by her. And that her growing loudness in his presence was an indication of that bafflement, rather than, as David said, that her jet-lag was wearing off. Her jealousy of him, if so it was, was seemingly exacerbated by the fact he did not, in her terms, let her near him, try as she might. She did things calculated to rile him; she made, for instance, several cross Atlantic phone calls without offering to pay – Anna pointing out that she'd rung him from Nikki's sometimes, and Nikki hadn't asked *her* to pay, didn't mollify him in the slightest. And when she, Anna, suggested to Nikki that in the face of this she might cut the next call down a bit, as tactfully as she dared, she wouldn't mind herself, she said, if she paid the phone bills but she didn't, Nikki said she never could understand Englishmen, and anyway they made lousy lovers, and sulked for the rest of the afternoon, as did Anna over the implied insult to David's sexual skills.

Most of the time, however, they enjoyed themselves, exploring London like the tourist Nikki said she was – she'd never had the chance to be a tourist, she claimed. One day she even demanded to go to the Tower of London – here Anna stood for a long time looking at the Traitor's Gate; she did not think she knew any longer, exactly, what a traitor was. Most people, certainly most of those who went through that gate, were loyal to someone or something; a traitor in their sense, that snake in the grass, was merely someone loyal to something or someone other than their own king or country. Who was Carter Jacoman loyal to for instance? She had already formed the impression that whatever his overall loyalties he was not one hundred per cent loyal to Bader-Kleitz, let alone the pharmaceutical industry. As for her – who was she more loyal to; to her work, or to David, more broadly to her family life? Nikki and David might each think she, Anna, was a traitor, *vis-à-vis* the other. Or David might think her a traitor for being so intrigued by Jacoman. And then she laughed at herself for so inflating her role. But it was their fault in a way that she was tempted to inflate it.

Behind her Nikki said, 'Doesn't it give you the creeps, Anna, thinking of all the people who went through there and never came out?' The way she squeezed Anna's shoulder, Anna, for a brief moment, felt closer to her than she had all week.

Dinner that night, moreover, just Nikki, David and Anna (Ben was off with one of his friends; Anna had the impression he too was avoiding Nikki) was a more comfortable affair than others. Maybe Nikki made her presence less felt than sometimes. At the same time, she seemed to have set out to charm David, almost ignoring Anna. Several times she made him laugh with one of her stories, then picked up the dry humour of his response more quickly than Anna – it was Anna who felt excluded now. She got to her feet and gathered up the dishes. When David and Nikki migrated to the sitting-room, she remained in the kitchen making coffee, a particularly dark blend, brought from California along with a host of other goodies (dried mushrooms, sun-dried tomatoes, raspberry vinegar, and so forth, 'Gourmet food parcels for benighted Brits,' David said when he saw them). She could neither see her red-headed friend, nor her husband, nor hear anything they said, nor wanted to.

Afterwards David went up to work in his room, and Anna and Nikki retired to the sofa with a bottle of vodka; the three of them had finished the wine. Her ill-humour evaporating suddenly Anna felt quite drunk, as drunk as Nikki sounded. Nikki laid her head on Anna's shoulder, and started talking about her grandmother, almost the first time she had ever talked to Anna directly about her grandmother. To Anna's surprise and pleasure, she told her something that was not even in *Grandma Opium*; about a little wart her grandmother had, on the left hand side of her upper lip. 'The Lord set it there with his own hand, the Lord will take it away if he chooses,' her grandmother said, when Nikki, used to her mother's instant recourse for medical help with any blemish, asked, innocently enough, if she was going to have it removed.

'The point was I hoped she wouldn't have it removed; she wouldn't have been my grandmother without it,' said Nikki. 'The only way she changed was getting older. With my mother, on the other hand, I never knew from one day to the next what colour her hair would be; what shape her tits. Isn't that freaky? And all for the sake of men.'

Anna giggled a little to herself; she felt so relaxed – this the first and only time during Nikki's visit, she knew all the old sense of comfort with her friend – that she dared say, forgetting, as usual, how quickly alcohol could swing moods in Nikki: 'Isn't it for the sake of men you had your face lifted, Nikki?'

Nikki abruptly took her head off her shoulder; sat upright; said, dangerously, 'What's the problem? Is there any reason I shouldn't have my face lifted? What a priggish little Englishwoman you can be, Anna. And talking of women doing things for men, I've seen how you are with David, Anna; I've watched you all this week. You nurture him all the time. Sometimes I think you nurture him a bit too much. Are you sure that's not why he wants you to go travelling with him – so that he can keep on getting all his home comforts? And by the way don't forget I warned you about all this business of working together. I hope you don't get to regret it in the end.'

And then she put her head back on Anna's shoulder; did not take it off; even when Anna, annoyed in her turn, shifted herself energetically to make her do so. She still kept it there, provocatively, when David came into the room.

Nikki waved her glass and said, 'I'm drunk. This

woman of yours so maddens me I have to drink.'

'Don't let me stop you then,' said David, 'I'm going to bed.'

Anna struggled to get out, giving herself a mouthful of red hair – but he was gone. Nikki said, 'You English are so uptight. You haven't changed since Henry James. The way you reacted, Anna, you might have thought he suspected us of having an affair.'

At this point Anna did push Nikki vigorously from her.

'Can you blame him, Nikki?' she asked, angrily. 'The way you go on?' But when she got to her feet and looked down to see Nikki smiling lazily up at her, she refused to give Nikki the chance to tell her how adorable she looked when she was angry. Very softly, teasing, she called her friend's bluff. 'Suppose I took you up on it, Nikki? What would you do then?' she asked her.

She knew Nikki well enough to expect a retreat at this point; Nikki always was much less invulnerable than she made out. What she did not expect was the outrage. (Anna told her friend to shut up, in due course; Nikki would waken the neighbours, she told her, not just this whole house.)

Next day nothing was said; they all went to lunch at Sonia's – David and Anna often went to Sonia's on Sunday for lunch. David felt guilty if they didn't. Anna wondered what that had to do with making his long-suffering sister cook one of her heavy English meals (roast lamb today and plum tart made from bottled plums; Sonia did not have a freezer). If there was any matriarch in this family it was the husbandless, childless Sonia. An awful warning Anna thought, much as she liked her. In her view, the life Sonia led hardly bore thinking about. But there it was.

The contrast between her sister-in-law and her friend could not have been more extreme. Sonia, as usual, wore a shapeless black sweater over a yellow aertex shirt and pleated grey skirt, which exaggerated her broad back-side; she had broad shoulders, and surprisingly small neat breasts. Since, unlike her brother, she scorned contact lenses, her spectacles were thick below a fringe of black hair cut brutally short; they were so thick they hid the eyes – just like David's, Anna thought – which were her best feature. As always, the only decoration she permitted herself, apart from a single silver bracelet, was a striking but heavy silver necklace – 'That's a Navaho, squash blossom necklace,' Nikki said almost accusingly, as soon as she saw it. Sonia who kept her eyes fixed on anyone speaking but stared at the ground usually when she spoke herself, glanced at her and to Anna's surprise, murmured, almost approvingly, as if with relief, 'Yes, that's right.' Anna wondered what else she did not know about Sonia. Quite a lot she suspected.

Besides both of them – Anna had jeans on and an old sweater – Nikki was dazzling; Anna had the feeling she'd made a particular effort to be dazzling this morning. She wore her orange jumper, she wore a very short black and white striped skirt and black and white striped stockings, with little black boots. She had fixed her hair up and wore gold earrings like bunches of grapes. Anna thought she looked top-heavy, bizarre, but splendid. David said he thought she looked absurd. What Sonia thought was not clear. Sonia, like her brother, was one of these people who rarely admitted what she was thinking and feeling. Anna's own attempts to elicit feelings from either of them made her feel loudmouthed, indiscreet and stupid at times; in vain.

For today, though, Nikki glowing in that dim room, talking loudly, laughing, Anna felt as subdued, even as discreet as her husband. She also felt as embarrassed as she suspected he did at the way Nikki, sitting next to her demented father-in-law, chattered on to him – she made it seem he wasn't demented, his mumbles might have been coherent replies. But as time went on, she began to think such an approach to him admirable after all, given the constraints most people showed in his presence; she'd heard herself talking in a cheerfully loud voice, as if she was talking to a baby. David meanwhile continued to look disconcerted. Anna was not so sure about Sonia; she

171

noticed her watching Nikki with what might almost have been approval. As for the old man, she suddenly noticed him smiling as he bent his head to the spoon he could barely manage, letting the food dribble from the side of his mouth.

Nikki turned from him at last. She asked David detailed questions about the study with Jacoman, whose name Anna noticed, she pronounced very deliberately, looking at him intently the while. His first replies were suspicious; then, suddenly, he became enthusiastic – he told her – and Sonia – Anna could see he was partly addressing himself to Sonia – how unusual it was to have a previously untreated population of epileptic patients to study; what an opportunity it was. Anna suddenly wished he wouldn't. She guessed exactly the line Nikki'd take.

'Isn't that just another kind of imperialism?' Nikki asked at last, innocently, turning to give the old man another smile as she did so; patting him almost lovingly on the knee. 'Isn't imperialism even with a moral idea behind it, still imperialism?'

'Whatever do you mean by that?' asked David.

'The old kind of imperialism,' said Nikki, 'you went into all these places and grabbed out all their minerals and so forth. Well you can't do that any more. Not without a lot of trade agreements, and these guys are wise now to at least some of the tricks that can be got up to. OK, you're not trying to do that, David. What you're going for is an imperialism of knowledge. OK, what can these poor sods tell me, that I understand my subject that much better. What do they get out of it, I'd like to know.'

'They get treated,' said David, smiling.

'They get treated,' said Nikki. And paused, significantly. But before she could continue, Sonia, to Anna's surprise, leaned across the table, and with a look of fury so intense she resembled her brother exactly, said, 'Gosh yes, David. You just answer that. They get treated these people. But I also wondered if you wouldn't do more harm than good, barging into their lives like that; asking questions. Raising their hopes. What's going to happen to

172

them after you all go home?' She glanced across at her father; as if she knew better than any of them what could be done, what couldn't; the cruelties of intervention, or of non-intervention come to that. Anna wanted to kiss her. As furiously as she wanted at this moment to kick Nikki, why she did not know entirely.

She knew all the possible answers anyway; the ones that David now tried to give, not letting her add anything; when she tried he kicked her under the table, but in a way more conspiratorial than unkind. For weren't they the very same questions she and he had trudged round, night after night, when Jacoman wasn't around to fire them, to make them think their undertakings might, could, transform the world? Ecuador only a week away, they couldn't afford such questions any longer; she and David were united against the rest, now, looking, not looking, at each other; against orange Nikki and black Sonia, even against the old man drooling in his wheelchair, whose knee Nikki patted, whose mouth Sonia wiped so tenderly.

Anna took Nikki to the airport next day to catch a midday plane. They hugged each other on parting; Nikki was almost in tears. All the same, Anna drove back to Fulham with the feeling that Nikki had behaved very badly; or that she herself had done so. Though still nothing had been said about the argument two nights before, she did not think the visit had been a success. She had the impression that since that evening Nikki touched her rather less; even that she made an effort not to do so – but she might have been wrong. Yet the whole balance of their friendship did seem to have changed somewhat; how exactly she could not tell. All David was prepared to say was that he'd found Nikki a bit vulgar. He added, also, that Anna let Nikki bulldoze her too much for his liking; that is when she wasn't touching Anna up. Anna ignored the last bit; she was still trying to make sense of her friend's reactions, it seemed treacherous to discuss it with her husband. Maybe, if Nikki really was so much more vulnerable than she often appeared – she was beginning to think so – could it be

Nikki needed her more than she needed Nikki? – it would be a betrayal to discuss it, ever. She said, 'Nikki bulldozes everyone. She's no worse than Sonia; she just makes more noise about it.' But at her attempts to explain just what she did see in Nikki – 'She gets things so right sometimes, and usually when you least expect it; look at the way she was with your father,' David looked uncomfortable and sceptical together, and she wished she hadn't mentioned this. Lamely, she added, 'I enjoy her. She's fun.' Because Nikki was. 'Meaning I'm not?' said David; but he was smiling, she noticed. He came home earlier this week; Ben, too, now that Nikki was gone, spent more time at home.

After two days, the visit in retrospect more uncomfortable by the minute, Anna could not believe Nikki had enjoyed herself in London; it occurred to her to wonder if Nikki would ring again. But after three days came one of Nikki's more interminable and flirtatious phone calls. Would she get some flowers for Sonia and send her the bill; it had been such a privilege to have a real British family Sunday lunch. (Was she being ironic, wondered Anna, thinking of the drooling old man; of the far from gourmet – as Nikki would call it – food; she feared not – Nikki's – for an American, she thought – quite well developed sense of irony did not, she'd observed all week, encompass or at least did not always encompass, her seeming reverence for English artefacts and institutions.) Oh but Nikki'd had a great time altogether, and she'd been so glad to have the chance to get to know David. Oh and Anna should know, she'd broken with her Indian, she didn't want his name mentioned ever again; in England she'd finally realised at last how impossible he was. Time for a new mindset. Her next trip was going to be celibacy, for sure.

By the way, had Anna liked her orange sweater? She had meant to leave it with her, she was sure it would suit her. How about if she mailed it now?

'Anna,' she said, 'I love you.' Then she hung up, not giving Anna time to say, 'Nikki, I love you.' Though, on the whole, she did; even if she did not know how to explain it to her husband.

(At some point during her friendship with Nikki, she reread *Middlemarch*, came across the description of Dorothea Brooke's relationship with her younger sister Celia; she copied it into her notebook with some relief; it fitted so exactly her relationship with Nikki; she did at times feel very much the younger sister.

'Since they could remember, there had been a mixture of criticism and awe in the attitude of Celia's mind towards her elder sister. The younger had always worn a yoke; but is there any yoked creature without its private opinions?'

In the light of this she asked herself: Why is it everything in my life always has to be validated by literature? And am I in equal danger now of doing what David does and validating other things too much according to science or sociology? Why can't I just trust what I observe, what I feel, myself?)

Chapter Thirteen

Mrs Kern is about to embark on her labours; herewith, for those interested, A BRIEF NOTE ON MEDICAL ANTHROPOLOGY.

What medical anthropology does and is even medical anthropologists aren't agreed on entirely. All would maintain that they are not physical anthropologists, interested in bones and skulls. All would say also that no, they are not the the same as medical sociologists (they are hard-pressed, in places, to define the difference exactly). What most would acknowledge, on the other hand, is that they study ideas of illness, medical systems – and doctors – as aspects of culture just as social anthropologists study religion, kinship systems and so forth as aspects of culture. But whereas some medical anthropologists see themselves as medical handmaids, working alongside doctors, others see themselves as advancing knowledge pure and simple. If doctors want to make use of their conclusions that's up to them, of course, but if so doctors must realise they are themselves as much objects of study as their patients. (Doctors don't always like this: see 'other', below).

In this project Anna Kern is definitely a medical handmaid; a rather lowly handmaid, come to that, way down in a cultural hierarchy, in which doctors are top dogs. (See 'hegemony', below). Her job is to find out what patients in the study designed by her husband, carried out by Ecuadorians and Kenyans, financed by Bader-Kleitz, think cause their illness, their views about treatment, about what effect it has had on their lives and so on. She is to obtain this information not by classical anthropological methods, working in a small community over a long period, but by more sociological means, namely questionnaires – the kind in which those questioned choose one of several suggested answers to each question – such as 'yes', 'probable', 'possible', 'no', 'don't know'. The point of such answers being that they can be counted, that statistics can be made from them; in a medical study done by medical handmaids, statistics are essential.

The pure knowledge anthropologists, in particular, are suspicious of such crude numerical methods. So is Anna Kern up to a point. Partly because she doesn't like statistics. Partly because, as time goes on, she becomes increasingly attracted by the more theoretical aspects of her subject, the kind of which her husband is suspicious, not least because it is the theoreticians who have observed to what extent doctors, even in scientific traditions, are embedded in their cultures, and not as scientifically unbiassed as they'd always hoped. Take, for instance, the kind of unspecific malaise which constitutes seventy per cent of illness presented to doctors anywhere. In Ecuador indigenous doctors – that is healers – witchdoctors – might diagnose it as 'susto' or 'espanto' (fright, literally). They might treat it by rubbing a guinea pig or an egg on a patient's stomach. In the scientific west, on the other hand, French doctors might call it 'spasmophilia' or a liver problem, Germans a mild heart problem or low blood pressure, Britons constipation, ME, stress, or hypochondria – so much for science. In all cases the pills they prescribe are rarely more effective than guinea pigs or eggs; and definitely more expensive.

Theoretical anthropology, of course, develops a language of its own. Kern says this is 1) pretentious 2) meaningless 3) a waste of his wife's time. Mrs Kern has her own suspicions; at the same time she is, increasingly, intrigued; against statistics, she is beginning to think, give me a nice convoluted theory any day.

Here are a few examples of anthropological language. But, be warned. In some cases the definitions quoted are courtesy *Chambers 20th Century Dictionary*. They are not, however, the nice simple even one word definitions you find in medical dictionaries. If they leave you any the wiser, at least in practical terms, it is more than they did Anna Kern often, and probably more than they did many less theoretically orientated, more medically trained

177

medical anthropologists, and certainly more than they did doctors themselves, unless they happened to be called Carter Jacoman. (He used such words all the time, Anna noticed, particularly after he began hobnobbing with medical anthropologists. David Kern did not use these words. When his wife dared to, he'd groan, 'Spare me the jargon.' 'If you spare me yours,' says she, sweetly.)

Be warned also; those who use such terms do so very much on the principles of Humpty Dumpty. 'When *I* use a word . . . it means just what I choose it to mean – neither more nor less.' So don't expect usage to conform to the dictionary definition, even where such a definition exists.

(All interpolations, by the way, are by Anna Kern.)

Explanatory Models or 'EMs' = the explanations for illness held by whoever is concerned with it; those of doctors, for instance, 'scientific' models, tend to be very different from lay models. *(Here's some examples of Explanatory Models to make this quite clear. They are all from one case we encountered, and all of them contradictory – that's usual. The first time we met the patient, she said, 'I have epilepsy because I met a ghost at 6 o'clock one evening and got a fright.' The second time, she said, 'My epilepsy started because of grief at my father's death.' Meanwhile her mother said, 'My daughter got epilepsy because she always was a sickly child.' Meanwhile, on her medical form, her doctor said, 'It runs in the family; it looks like it's an inherited weakness.')*
EMICs = questionnaires designed to elicit Explanatory Models

Participant observation = when anthropologists live in the field as their subjects do, not only observing them but sharing their discomforts, their rituals, and so on, and thereby, they hope, becoming a) less suspect to their subjects and b) more understanding of their subjects' lives. *(The main difference – the important difference – of course, is that the researcher, the anthropologist, like the small child camping in the back garden, can get up and go home any time she likes, to proper medical facilities, hot baths etc; the subject can't.)*
'The Other' = the subject = the person or persons the anthropologist, having observed, then attempts to describe. *(There is currently much debate as to how the describing can*

*be done without inflating the anthropologist on the one
hand, diminishing the 'other', on the other, no one yet has the
answer – except to suggest that novelists, playwrights and so
forth may do it better; it helps of course being allowed to lie
– 'Oh to tell the truth, the plain truth as only a liar can,'
said Katherine Mansfield. I'll have a minor and maybe
esoteric problem in writing the book for Jacoman, in that
one of the 'others' I'll have to describe is my husband; he
doesn't care for this position, who can blame him? Nor do I.)*

Now we get more complicated: (and arrive at *Chambers
Dictionary*)

Ontology: Ontological = 'that part of metaphysics which
treats of the nature and essence of things.' *(Essence of
what? A person, a group, a psyche; of being? This is a
word Carter is fond of. What or who, at heart, is Carter?
might be one ontological question; but not one I can
answer. Maybe it's the nature of ontological questions that
they aren't answerable, or at least not satisfactorily.)*
Hermeneutic = of interpretation *(meaning no words,
actions, symbols, are taken at face value, but interpreted
according to the bias/standpoint/theory of the interpreter
in ways invariably meaningless to the person whose
words/symbols/actions have not only been interpreted but
thereby appropriated by the (medical or cultural) anthropologist, or by the doctor, come to that. David's reading of a
medical history as given by one of the patients on our study
would be quite different from the history as seen by the
patient, let alone by me. He wouldn't call it hermeneutics,
maybe, but what he had to say would be as meaningless in
the patient's terms as what I had to say, without a doubt.)*
Epistemology = theory of knowledge. Episteme = theory
of knowledge current at any one time. *(Classical thought
is one episteme. Post-modernism another. Problem: how
do you define post-modernism? If not according to dictum
that the term is meaningless, so to be used as often as
possible. Carter says project is definitely post modern, all
these different disciplines involved. But I don't think he
knows what post modern means, either. Will my book,
assuming I ever write it, be post-modern?)*
Discourse = different kinds of language and thought
process; *(eg medical discourse is different from anthropological discourse; academic is different from literary;*

179

classical from modern, etc. This word I understand better than most, because of the difference in the ways David and I both look at the world and then describe it. Sometimes I think all the differences and difficulties between us boil down to just this, on all levels, not just him as doctor, me as writer, the old science versus arts culture gap, but him as Jew, me as Gentile, him as man, me as woman, and so on; all the discourses are different, not to mention the reference points. That's what so interesting, of course. But wearing.)

Reify = to think of as material thing *(eg love = Marilyn Monroe??? This, a term used most frequently by thinkers with a Marxist bias, could lead on to the term also used by Marxists, 'commodification' = turning of person, quality, longing into a commodity (eg love as a commodity, see prostitute, labour as a commodity, see labourer; dreams, hopes, relief of fear as commodity, see drugs/medicine; the pharmaceutical industry.)*

Hegemony = leadership; predominant influence *(especially of one state over others. Carter uses this word all the time, but actually in a much wider, perhaps more modern sense; meaning intellectual hegemony, of medicine over anthropology, or western over Latin Americans (specifically Ecuadorians) or pharmaceutical moneymen over mere academics (academics would see it the other way round.) Predominant influence – hegemony – in our project is definitely medicine; as with all weaker states, classes, disciplines, sociologists/anthropologists having none of the clout of doctor, my only hope of undermining it is subversion not confrontation. I've already subverted David, just a little. To the surprise of his colleagues, he's been heard to advocate the merits of traditional medicine.*

That's enough; more than enough: for the moment.

There were two people Anna did *not* encounter during her first trip to Ecuador, though she might have been expected to do so. What happened to Dr Gomez, for instance? What happened to Bud Schwarz? The last we heard of Ecuador, Dr Gomez, in particular, was still a problem; the whole enterprise was threatened. In this case, however, much as the rioters in Quito got bored in the end and went home, so the problem of Dr Gomez evaporated; or rather Dr Gomez himself, after two months of wrangling over who should be Principal Investigator on Carter Jacoman's project, went to Washington and did not come back; it seemed that had always been his intention. Something to do with a girlfriend at the National Institute of Health; something to do with the Ecuadorian divorce laws, or attitudes to divorce, which made it impossible for him to stay put, or at least to maintain his Quito practice if he did stay put; something to do with a job into which the girlfriend eased him.

Jacoman, who had made gloomy calls to David on the subject at least once a week was cockahoop; 'What an omen; if our worst headache can vanish overnight, just like that, it's meant to happen, we're meant to do this thing.' An argument at which David sighed as if at an argument of Anna's, and muttered about Jacoman's fondness for anecdotal evidence. Anna said, when this conversation was reported to her, that it was called reading the entrails; something like that.

So that disposes of Gomez, for the moment. It still leaves Bud Schwarz, of course; with whom David was engaged by this time in an acrimoniously polite correspondence over the epidemiological protocol. David said Bud Schwarz' suggestions were crap. Jacoman told him never mind, shift sentences around, he had to keep Schwarz happy, otherwise he'd rubbish the whole thing in academic journals across the USA. This, in fact, is the sole importance of Bud Schwarz; his making it clear from the start how much approval from the American academic establishment mattered to Jacoman; certainly more than approval from David's academic establishment, which did not, according to David, think much of Bud Schwarz' work, as it happened.

Shortly after Jacoman had handed out this advice, about two or three weeks after Anna had been hauled into the project and so was more privy to such things than she had been, Bud Schwarz dropped dead of a heart attack. Carter Jacoman said what a good guy he was, a hard guy but the greatest, what a waste. What a bugger.

But then he burst out again, irrepressibly, 'Look at that, David, what did I tell you, we were meant to do this, all the cards are falling our way, all the gods are rooting for us.' 'Whose gods, Carter?' murmured David. 'Wasn't there something once called hubris?' 'Yes there was. There is,' said Anna.

Chapter Fourteen

'The chances of the project getting off the ground is now only eighty per cent likely,' said Jacoman, four days into the first Quito meeting of the whole team. Two days later he said, 'Now it's only sixty per cent likely.'

The purpose of this Quito meeting was to introduce the project to the local people – the neurologists, psychologists, anthropologists who were to carry it out on the ground, on the one hand, on the other to finalise all the details of medical protocols, of questionnaires, organisations and so forth. In Jacoman's case, he also had to finalise the budgets, the cost of the project to Bader-Kleitz. All of which seemed straightforward enough; the cultural problem that it wasn't polite or proper to say no, though already encountered by Carter Jacoman, had not been recognised for what it was. David and Anna did not recognise it either – as the anthropologist, Anna ought to have recognised it, maybe. All they realised now, like Jacoman himself, was that nothing was going to be as straightforward as they'd expected. To the point that both of them almost welcomed Jacoman's pessimism. They almost hoped he might be right; that, after all, the project would go no further.

As for the Ecuadorians: to them the ways of Jacoman and his team were quite as baffling, no doubt; not to mention crude, not to mention bad-mannered, at least to those who had not been out of Latin America (most hadn't; they couldn't afford to). There was no reason for them to understand the discontents of their visitors, why should they; this was their country. It was up to Jacoman and Co to adapt to them. On the other hand they almost certainly did want the project to survive; for many of them it meant a job, and/or kudos. In Ecuador, where, as they also told Anna, medical unemployment was running at fifty per cent, Jacoman and the Kerns were rich, by definition. And as for Bader-Kleitz. . .

Anna Kern's journal. April 1986. (Checking this account later, she feels obliged to add footnotes to explain the names she keeps encountering; but then why not have footnotes? This is, after all, an academic project.)

Ecuador. April 4th. Tomorrow we start. Tonight Carter arrived, in Quito, even more manic, jet-lagged, than usual, the effects of altitude, perhaps. We have dinner with him, Piet Van Dyke[1], Vittoria[2], the local company medical director, a petulant looking man whose name I miss[3], his side-kick or whipping boy, whom everyone calls Jacqui[4] – he is small, eager, obsequious, smiles a lot, comes from Guayaquil according to Jacoman (I cannot help thinking every time I look at him that, also according to Jacoman, people from Quito call people in Guayaquil monkeys; his being called Jacqui doesn't help); a man called Aguadiente[5] and some colleague, very fluent, both desperately trying to state position and status. Aguadiente in particular, thin, sallow, pockmarked, keeps taking off his gold-rimmed spectacles – not unlike Jacoman's, apart from that and restlessness they have nothing in common, he so dark, Jacoman so bleached-looking – putting up a finger,

1. Jacoman's Dutch assistant, already encountered

2. Spanish psychologist, ditto

3. Dr Sylvio Navarro

4. Dr Jacopo Sylvestre

5. Dr Virgilio Aguadiente; neurologist, the Principal Investigator of the epilepsy study on the ground

leaning forward and saying '*por ejemplo*' in vain,
Carter steam-rollers him and his colleague both, in
between buttering them up. David meanwhile says
nothing just smiles politely, occasionally raises an
eyebrow at me. I realise how little used I am to seeing
him in his professional context. At home I look at him
and wonder at all the knowledge hidden in his head, at
all that is rolled up in his title, Dr, and feel excluded.
And now here I am, inside is out, us, our marriage, is
the secret locked in his head, in mine, unobtainable in
this place, over my garlic prawns and his Osso Bucco.

The next day, the first working day, is all public meetings and receptions, shaking hands with the minister
(actually sub minister) of health, listening to everyone
telling everyone else, in English and in Spanish, how
wonderful they are, and so forth, drinking thimblefuls of
whisky and eating bowls of shrimp ceviche. Yet what
sticks in Anna's memory afterwards is not ritual, let
alone ministers. It is herself and her husband sneaking
off from the official lunch for an hour in bed, giggling like
schoolchildren. As her keenest image of the week that
follows is not of meetings or of volcanoes – she rarely sees
volcanoes. It is the same one she's left with from Kanterberg two years later; of the green baize table round which
the meetings take place. Green baize tables are what
people sit around to make agreements, in theory; or, in
practice, often enough – this applies to their case also –
disagreements. She seems to remember a ballet once,
called the Green Baize Table; there the agreements the
disputants failed to reach turned into some war or
other – The First World War? – she couldn't remember
exactly – only that the dancers starting out as diplomats,
emperors, generals had turned by the end into skeletons,
corpses.

There are three baize tables, in three separate rooms;
one for the neurologists, one for the psychologists and one
for the anthropologists.

Each day each green baize table starts out neatly;
glasses, carafes of water, empty ashtrays arranged all

along it in order. By each evening the ash trays are full, the carafes empty; the green baize is piled with untidy heaps of paper; the whole room stinks of stale tobacco.

OUR PROTAGONISTS ENGAGE IN A TYPICAL AFTERNOON'S WORK

On the first afternoon of the group discussions, the neurologists in Room 111 discuss further aspects of the study protocol. The morning's deliberations – on which patients qualify for the study – has gone as expected, if too slowly in the eyes of Drs Jacoman and Kern. This afternoon's subject – the problem of seizure classification – is another matter entirely. This is a subject which neurologists all over the world argue about; there is still no generally accepted list, and sometimes conflicting diagnoses; for which reason Jacoman and David's draft protocols have opted for the simplest classification possible –

1. Generalised seizures[6]
2. Partial seizures[7]
3. Other[8]

The Ecuadorians are having no such thing. In vain David, Jacoman and Meyersdorf swear that opting for such simple classifications is not because they have a low opinion of Ecuadorian – Third World – neurologists; nor because they think them incapable of using sophisticated classificatory schemes etc; that it has, rather, everything to do with the size of the study; its being carried out in remote places, in relatively primitive conditions, using specially trained but non-medical surveyors and newly qualified doctors, who

6. Those affecting both hemispheres of the brain, usually, but not always, manifesting as classic, tonic clonic or *grand mal* fits.

7. Those originating in one hemisphere and manifesting themselves variously, according to the location of the defect. Some, for instance, manifest themselves in different kinds of often bizarre automatic actions (one patient of David's used to invent and sing original tunes).

8. Under this were to be included such things as various kinds of partial seizures, manifesting as absences, myclonic jerks or whatever.

would not have been trained to recognise anything but the most basic types of seizure. David's protest that students aren't taught much about epilepsy in English medical schools, either, falls on deaf ears. The whole thing is taken as a slur on Ecuadorian capacity; thereby on Ecuadorian honour.

In the afternoon as the morning, the neurologists come and go. Each newcomer is taken aside by Aguadiente and briefed in a whisper so loud sometimes it makes other discussions impossible; each in turn sabotages any agreement that has been reached. One, a small man with flat Indian features, and, David notices, particularly long ear lobes, off which he cannot take his eyes, only came to this one meeting. He hardly lets Aguadiente finish before screaming out in Spanish first, and then in not very good English – he won't let Meyersdorf translate – that Ecuadorian neurologists are not peasants, they are not barefoot doctors (he calls them 'bare toe' doctors – a weary David has visions of the assembled company all besandalled or with holes in their socks before getting the sense), they are properly trained scientists, just like Dr Kern himself. No Ecuadorian neurologist would accept a study done using short cuts, using simplified procedures that aren't according to international seizure classification standards; and so on.

By six o'clock in the evening they have barely moved one clause from where they started at two thirty in the afternoon; at which point most of the neurologists go home, except for Aguadiente and the president of the Ecuadorian Neurological Society who are scheduled to start the meeting with Jacoman, Meyersdorf and local company people such as Navarro and Sylvestre on that equally vexed subject, budgets.

'And how did Aguadiente behave in all this?' asked Anna, when David recounted this tale of woe. 'Did he have tantrums too?' But no, he said, Aguadiente didn't have tantrums, he was tiresome in a different way; not only with his noisy briefings, but raising niggling little points concerning past discussions, often, not present

187

ones, making objections quite besides the point. 'I'm beginning to think the man's a total fool,' David said morosely. 'The worst thing is, when we go away he's going to be in charge.'

'What does Jacoman think?' she asked. 'What's his reaction to all this?'

'The trouble with Jacoman,' said David, 'is always the problem with Jacoman; he's too impatient. I mean he knows how to handle people in a crude kind of way, he flatters them, strings them along, sometimes he's better than that; clever; subtle; kind even. And then he gets bored, he ups and starts bullying everyone, threatening them almost – how lucky they are to have someone like me, and so on, how easy it would be for Bader-Kleitz to take its money elsewhere and so on – he doesn't quite say that but he hints it; fortunately most of them don't understand much English, and Meyersdorf, I'm almost certain, smooths it down a bit, makes it much flowerier – which is another problem, Meyersdorf explained to me that Spanish *is* more formal, what's acceptable in English is plain insulting to them; by which I think he meant to suggest to me I should try and persuade Carter to keep his mouth shut, though of course he's too Latin, too circumlocutional himself to say it outright. The worst thing is that Carter in bullying vein feeds all the suspicions they have of us as despising them and so on, they get more offended than ever, more argumentative than ever.'

'But *don't* you despise them just a little?' asked Anna.

David threw her a weary look, and disappeared into the bathroom. She heard water running. 'I don't despise them as scientists,' he said when he reappeared, naked, carrying his clothes. 'What drives me nuts is that they can't see it's sometimes more effective scientifically to do things simply. They seem to think that if it's not made one hundred per cent complicated, they're not doing the job properly.'

'Maybe they just do things differently here,' said Anna. 'Why shouldn't they?'

'Because if we don't get things right in our terms, it's

not going to do them any good either,' said David.

'That's what *you* think,' said Anna. 'How patient are *you* with them, David?' she added. How vulnerable he looked, she thought, with his back to her, laying his clothes upon a chair; if the Ecuadorians could see him now – he had a large mole on his right buttock; who else but her knew about that?

David began fumbling around on the desk. 'Not very,' he said, irritably. 'What's all this junk, Anna – where's the medicine bag? I started shouting at them at one point. I think they're beginning to see me as an imperialist bastard like Jacoman. I mean they assume I'm one anyway. If it goes on like this, I'm going to go crazy. I think I'll want to scrub the whole thing. I can't work like this, Anna. I really can't.'

He was almost in tears, suddenly. He'd abandoned the desk, his back was playing up, he complained, searching his suitcase now for aspirin.

Anna had a headache, not backache; her day had been almost as bad. Her team consists of (this is Quito, of course): 1) Dr Aguadiente's mistress; Dolores Yepes, an out of work doctor. (The name Dolores evokes for Anna the idea of someone luscious; Dr Yepes is lean; Dr Yepes is stringy. She cannot be described as luscious.) 2) Dr Carlos Naranjo. Dr Aguadiente's acolyte. Also an out of work Ecuadorian doctor; short, stout, bearded, earnest, would be anthropologist. 3) Dr Teodoro de Valasco. An out of work anthropologist; Dr Yepes' first cousin.

Their job is discussing with her the questions on her questionnaires, her EMICs. For instance: Is your epilepsy caused by a bang on the head? Does it affect your work/your schooling? – and so on: to be answered according one of these alternatives: yes, probably, possibly, no, don't know. But each day, it seemed to her they arrived at exactly the same problem. Why ask questions with coded answers? Yepes, Naranjo, de Valasco asked. All the questions should be open questions. What hope of truth if all people could not make any answer they chose to; if their only option was to answer 'yes' or 'no'?

'They can answer "probably" or "possibly" or "don't

know"', said Anna wearily, the more wearily as days went on and nothing changed; the more wearily because she too didn't think human life and feelings could easily be crammed into 'yes,' 'probably', 'possibly', 'no', 'don't know'; but for statistical purposes they must be. Teodoro told her that in Spanish probable or possible meant more or less the same thing. 'This project will probably come off.' 'This project may possibly come off.' As the days went on, as the latter statement became more accurate than the former, owing to Jacoman's budgetary problems, she puzzled as to how to express such a significant change in nuance in Spanish. Did she care any longer if it could be expressed in Spanish? Possibly not. Probably not.

This is how all the arguments went, roughly speaking. This is Ecuador, it's not like anywhere else in the world, there's no point in comparing anywhere else in the world with Ecuador, even epilepsy is different in Ecuador. You are imperialist tyrants, imposing these things on us; not least your Spanish is lousy.

All is expressed with much politeness; even, as time goes on, with affection. No one seems to dislike Anna; why should they – tiresome as it all is, she concedes they have a point; her Spanish is lousy – and of course they know more about Ecuador than she does – and, of course, given their history they have every reason to be suspicious, even paranoid, and of course she is not as well-qualified as she ought to be; not that they know that; here she is Dotora Kern, no question. On the other hand, they know nothing about epilepsy, and she knows quite a lot – not all for reasons she's prepared to acknowledge (the tireder she gets, the harder it seems pretending this whole thing is just academic; at times she's tempted to acknowledge them; of course she doesn't.) Surely they can pool these areas of expertise? arrive at some conclusion? Obviously not.

Soon it seems as if she has never not known these people. They are like her family; she knows their every gesture, every tone of voice. If they go without saying goodbye to her in the evenings, she almost feels hurt. Hostages too learn to love their captors – the only question here is, which of them is the hostage, which the captor? Curly-haired Teodoro smiles when she agrees with him, flushes with annoyance, speaks petulantly, like a girl, when she does not; his wife whom he insists on Anna meeting looks old enough to be his mother. Dolores, on the other hand, smiles rarely; she has as if two little stops either end of her mouth. Her spectacles are steely, her hair scraped back severely. She wears jeans held up by braces, and a striped sweater. Apart from the large, even sexy earrings she wears some days, she is hardly the image of a luscious Latin beauty – is it her earrings Aguadiente fancies? On the last day of the meeting, Dolores hands Anna a present as elaborately wrapped as she herself is not.

As for Naranjo; outside meetings the small fat man follows her around; begs her, earnestly, to introduce him to English anthropologists. He urges her to send him her academic papers. Inside the meeting he agrees with her in nothing. She learns to dread his leaning forward – his 'Momento, Anna.' His name she now knows means 'orange'.

Between the rooms in which David's neurological group and Anna's sociological group are working, sit Vittoria and her six psychologists. They do not fight. They come out of their room in a group, chattering like sparrows, laughing, embracing each other. All day, on and off, peals of laughter can be heard from behind their closed door. Oh yes their work is well up to schedule. There'll be no problem getting their questionnaires done on time. Vittoria has booked herself a day trip to Cotopaxi.

'Why does she have to look so bloody smug?' said David, of Vittoria.

'Do you think there's any significance in the fact that the only group that isn't fighting is all female?' asked Anna.

'Feminism is all I need right now,' David snapped at her. 'It's just as likely to be because Vittoria's first language is Spanish.'

Anna turned away from him, towards their room, heaped with clothes, books, papers, the remains of hurried room service snacks. On the desk, hotel information folders – laundry services, telephone, room service and so on – fight for space with David's papers from today's meetings. Anna had learned something about her husband in the past week; how in such meetings he could concentrate indefinitely on a plethora of petty detail. But now she saw that the margins of David's notes were covered in graffiti – doodles, and that whereas the notes were lightly written, barely pressed on the paper, the doodles – squares – diamonds – squares within diamonds, diamonds in diamonds, hatchings, scratchings – all angular, straight lines, not a curve anywhere – were black, heavily indented. She doodled herself; but much less heavily, in curves and circles, in figurative things, flowers, people; not abstractions, like David.

On Friday evening Jacoman called for a joint meeting of all groups to report on progress. This meeting, this evening, turned out to be Mrs Kern's nadir. At 3 p.m., Meyersdorf had appeared in Room 113, the anthropologists' room, demanding they produce their full logistics – that is how many manhours their work will take and so on – for the meeting. Weary of being called despotic Anna assigned this task to Drs De Valasco and Naranjo. In the evening, in front of everyone, worst of all in front of Anna's husband – seeing his face darken, Anna cannot help thinking of Nikki's warnings – they got up and insisted 1500 manhours were needed to do the anthropological job properly; the cost of this would, on Anna's estimate, exceed the total budget for the whole study. Anna had gauged rightly the effects on her husband. After three days of fruitless negotiation, Dr Kern now found a legitimate target on which to unleash his frustration, in whispers he accused his wife of sabotaging the entire project – she would not give him the satisfaction of bursting into tears; but she felt like it. Jacoman, on the other hand, was very kind; also diplomatic. First he drew a picture of a very small bottle to fill a very large wine glass; then he urged caution on all and sundry. Then he came to Anna and said she hadn't done so badly – it was all Anna could manage on the one hand not to fling her arms round him. On the other hand she thought, sod him, the patronising git. For so he was.

The Kerns did not retire amicably to bed; only with difficulty could Anna persuade her husband that the figure of 1500 manhours had not been her idea. She sat up half the night and made a new logistical plan -- Yepes, Naranjo, De Valasco, Tom Cobley and all could like it or lump it. ('No more democracy for them,' was how the despot put it.)

It is like being in hospital; or boarding-school; totally cut off from the world. Anna has heard business men complaining how, on their travels, all they see is the inside of their hotels. Now she experiences this phenomenon for herself. It is not that life does not go on elsewhere. It goes on in the hotel not least; tour parties come and go ⌐ on the notices put up for each one, detailing the times of meals, excursions and so forth, only the names of the tour company and the language changes; Americans – Harvey's Home Improvers from St Louis Missouri according to their posted information – are succeeded by Germans, Germans by Swedes, Swedes again by Americans; all of them, it seems, depart for Galapagos after three days in Quito; no doubt they go to look for turtles. Anna wishes that she were German or Swedish or better still a Harvey's Home Improver. She wishes that she could go and look for turtles. When she tells the Dutchman Piet this, he informs her that the name of the hotel, Colon, is the same as Columbus; this is Christopher Columbus hotel – in a meeting, subsequently, driven more than usual to exasperation, she recites, 'In fourteen hundred and ninety two, Columbus sailed the ocean blue,' and sees De Valasco, Dolores, Naranjo staring at her in amazement; 'Just a joke,' she says; thinking that if Christopher Columbus – or Cristobel Colon – she dares enjoy *this* linguistic gap – if he *hadn't* sailed the ocean blue, she and David wouldn't be here probably; nor would the more Spanish of the Ecuadorians be here either; maybe just as well.

193

Outside the hotel the efficient Indian woman in poncho and trilby hat who sells rugs and hats and shawls and other Andean gear to passing tourists, works out the price in dollars on her calculator. Sadder Indians, their eyes on the ground, hold out surreptitious hands for money. At night women walk in pairs along the street; that these wide pavements are the hunting ground for local prostitutes Anna and Vittoria discover for themselves; walking back to their hotel one night they are accosted no less than four times. Vittoria becomes hysterical and has to be calmed down by Anna. She, too, is annoyed – why shouldn't they walk in a street without such problems? – but keeps it to herself in face of Vittoria's loud plaints that it is all to do with chauvinist Latin cultures; that this is why she left Spain in the first place. Having observed for days now the flirtatious manner, the seeming submissiveness by which Vittoria gets her own way with Jacoman, with her husband, Anna is astonished at hearing her voice such sentiments. At the same time she observes the alliance they have formed as the only women among the visitors; an alliance cemented on Vittoria's side by her offering to give Anna her own recipes for this dish or the other. Vittoria, it turns out, is a fanatical Cordon Bleu cook. It was Vittoria handed Anna a handkerchief after her fiasco with the logistics on Friday night. It is Vittoria and Anna, jointly, who comfort Jacoman at lunch in the coffee shop one day, after a particularly difficult budgetary wrangle; he has hardly had more than two hours sleep a night, he says, since he got here. (He has looked very well on it till now, if this is so.) He lays his head on the table and groans loudly. He is performing, of course, but not entirely.

Vittoria knows how to deal with this much better than Anna. She puts an arm about Jacoman's shoulders. She summons up a waiter and orders coffee – Jacoman twists his face round and says, 'And a tomato juice. Two tomato juices.' Then he sits up; he does indeed for once look quite exhausted; his tie is awry, his hair on end, his face even more colourless than usual. Anna puts an arm round him now. He lays his head on it, and says, 'Anna dear, if you knew the half of it. If you *knew*. You can ask your husband about the neurology group but even he doesn't know what's going on with the budgets. The way things are going, there's now only a forty per cent chance the project's going to happen. If the Ecuadorians don't cut down their demands by tomorrow, it won't happen. Look at them. Just look at them,' he waves a hand round the coffee shop. As usual – it is the same in the bar next door – there are heads together here, there, everywhere; Aguadiente and Naranjo, De Valasco and Dolores. 'Plots and counterplots; and all directed against me, Anna, and you Vittoria, and you Anna. Imperialists all.' And he groans again and knocks over a glass of water. The glass doesn't break, but water goes into Jacoman's lap; he leaps to his feet, brushes himself down; Vittoria dabbing efficiently at his crotch with her napkin suddenly becomes aware of what exactly she is dabbing at, withdraws her napkin hastily, blushes. Jacoman looks at Anna and winks, distinctly. Whereupon Anna, also, blushes.

Thereafter, aided by the coffee, the two tomato juices, a ham sandwich and three Marlboros he becomes more cheerful altogether. Colour arrives in his face – inasmuch as it ever does arrive in Jacoman's face. He even starts an argument with Anna about suitable priorities for improvement in the communities they are going to work in. When she says clean water comes before drugs, etc., that there has to be appropriate technology, Jacoman asks, 'You tell me, Anna, just what *is* appropriate technology? You mean you're going to roll up in your Porsche and hand out spades and tell people it's in their best interests to dig wells right now, this minute? Suppose they've got better things to do than start digging wells? Suppose they'd rather have a Porsche – or a combine harvester come to that? Appropriate technology is what *they* want Anna, not what *you* think they ought to want.' And then he orders yet another tomato juice, guffaws so loudly that people at the next tables turn round to look, and says, 'Arguing with you, Anna honey, is just like arguing with your husband. I love it. I just *love* it.'

(Out of their bedroom window, there should be a volcano.
Sometimes there is a volcano – but never for very long;
each time it makes Anna gasp, it is so white, so brilliant,
so even in shape; like a Hokusai woodcut of Mount Fuji.
Each time – for nearly a week – she believes the mountain to be Cotopaxi; like everything else here it's an
illusion. Cotopaxi is to the south; their bedroom, she
discovers, belatedly, faces northwards. The name of the
volcano to the north, the one affords her glimpses of itself
sometimes, at sunset usually, or sunrise, tinged with
gold and pink, she learns at some point, but forgets at
once.)

Anna Kern's journal. April 8th. Quito.

Today I realised that the name 'Aguadiente' means,
literally, 'Watertooth'. When I told Jacoman I thought
he'd choke he laughed so much; it shows the state he's
in, it isn't really so very funny; no funnier than
Watertooth's Christian name: Virgilio, believe it or not,
evoking marine wanderings, tragic queens, the
founding of mythical cities; or it would be funny, it
would evoke such things, outside a culture where
names like Virgilio – Plutarcho – Caesario – are not
uncommon. Apart from this, of course, I don't yet know
anything about him much, beyond the way he drives
David and Jacoman crazy. He's not the least attractive
– in a funny way I find him rather sweet.

One afternoon, Anna arrives in the hall of the hotel and
finds a crowd of tourists all talking at once; in the centre
of them someone is crying. As she draws near, the group
shifts a little, she sees that the fat blonde woman weeping at its centre holds out a white leather bag in which
there is a huge slit – even as she does so a powder
compact falls out of the slit and tumbles to the floor. The
woman weeps louder than ever; 'I saw a knife,' she cries,
'I saw the knife – they cut it.' Anna remembers a warning
she'd read in the South America Guide – how in crowded

places – markets for instance – you'd be jostled by several people, and then, while you were distracted, someone would slit your bag and remove your wallet. She hears people exclaiming now, telling each other the story. The woman keeps on sobbing; 'I saw the knife. I saw the knife.'

Anna for once is taken out of the hotel, away from thoughts of the project. She has a sudden vivid recall of the old town, of its heavy almost animal smell. She sees the beggars, she sees the shoe shiners, the street photographers, the food sellers, the endlessly vicious struggle for existence; like turtles, she thinks; survival of the fittest. Though she's not fit especially, just lucky, she doesn't know the viciousness; or rather she doesn't know the necessity for viciousness. Yet she sees the knife; what was it William James said – that Nikki quoted – 'The path of insecurity beneath the surface of life?' – exactly. Reminded of Ben, as usual by such things, once more she wonders, what am I doing here? What are we doing here? What can we do? Of course we know nothing about this place, these people; they are right to scream at us, to complain how little we know about them.

She has fifteen minutes still before the next meeting. She wanders up the hall to the place where newspapers are strung on a rack of wooden arms for those who want to read them; she extracts the arm which holds a week old copy of *The Times* and reads that on Easter Monday, Chelsea defeated Arsenal, Heart Of Midlothian were beaten by Hamilton Academicals. She is comforted by this; to her amazement she is even more comforted thereafter to read details of how Mrs Thatcher has spent Easter.

In almost all this time, though even her husband stopped working sometimes, Anna never saw Jacoman not working. On the Saturday the whole team, visitors and Ecuadorians alike, were crammed into an ancient bus – it had holes both in the floor and in the roof – and taken up to the Altiplano; still on that day, it seemed to her, Jacoman just kept on working.

In the morning, when they set out, he'd sat in the front of the bus alongside Meyersdorf. But before long he lurched down the aisle to where David and Anna were sitting, turned Anna out of her seat and sat down to discuss something with David, forcing her, reluctantly, to join an equally reluctant, but polite as ever Meyersdorf.

Next time she looked, David was sitting alongside Piet, Jacoman's head was bent to someone else. During the group photographs at the Equator he was still at it (one showed him looking back over his shoulder towards Jacqui Sylvestre behind him, another in close conversation with a disaffected looking Piet, who did know when to stop, unlike his boss; Anna had encountered him in the foyer once or twice, in running shorts). Even when they visited the Indian market, he was to be seen, two Indian dolls in one hand, an Indian basket in the other, conferring with Meyersdorf. Even during the lunch at what Aguadiente assured everyone was a restaurant absolutely 'etnico' – certainly there were musicians with guitars and breathy panpipes – he hardly stopped; when he banged the table and addressed them over the coffee cups, it was to say how wonderful they all were, how hard they were working, what a great project it would be.

Towards the end of the afternoon, the bus turned off the main road back to Quito and started chugging its way up a mountainside on a very rough dirt road. It was a grey cloudy afternoon, no sign of volcanoes, although one was not far off. As they lurched ever higher, the ancient bus unsafer by the minute on such a precipitous, rutted track, the windscreen started spotting with rain; by the time they drove into the village it was, relentlessly, drizzling.

On a Saturday afternoon there was no one much about. Only two or three people, a few pigs and a dog appeared to see the visitors piling out of the bus in a bleak square surrounded by low houses. In the middle, in a scrubby garden, were some unhealthy looking palm trees. At the back, where the bus was parked, stood a white flat-roofed building bigger than all the rest. This was a Health Centre, of precisely the kind they would find in the areas they'd work in, staffed by a newly qualified doctor, of precisely the kind who would treat the patients in their study. This was why they had been brought here.

The place was now empty of patients, of course. The rural doctor, on the other hand, had been extracted from wherever he lived; he looked glad of the diversion; probably he was glad of the diversion. They'd been told how many of the doctors hated these remote rural postings, only accepted them because they wouldn't be registered as doctors without; besides, there wasn't much work going, Teodoro de Valasco told Anna as they hurried up the steps to the clinic, to get out of the rain. Inside it looked like any other surgery anywhere, although the equipment was sparser, more basic; examination couches, weighing machines; stethoscopes, equipment for taking blood pressure, dietary charts, carefully kept records setting out the progress, the immunisation and illness history of all babies born in the village over the past five years, locked cupboards containing basic drug supplies; that wasn't quite the whole of it, but almost. The place was, however, very clean and neat. David said it wasn't bad, all things considered. The careful record-keeping in particular was impressive.

When the inspection was over, they returned to the waiting area to find a patient, an actual epileptic patient – the only epileptic, Anna realised with a slight shock, she had ever met, apart from her son – sitting alongside his wife on two of the grey plastic chairs lined up by the door into the street, talking to Jacoman and Meyersdorf. A short, round, rosy woman in a large poncho with drops of rain still on it, the wife overspread the not very generous chair – the effect, Anna thought, was wonderfully wholesome looking; her husband nodding alongside her, she also did all the talking. They'd both taken to Jacoman, by the look of it; but then he appeared different from usual. His voice was quieter, his gestures much more restrained; he wasn't the least overbearing, let alone hectoring; he wasn't – the only way Anna could put it – 'buttering the woman up'. It made her realise to what extent Jacoman was, usually, a performer, for if he was performing now it was a calculated attempt at non-performance. The kindness and tact with which, even speaking through Meyersdorf, he drew the man's story from the couple impressed her. It made her realise for the first time that Jacoman must have been a good doctor. And made her think, too, what a waste of a good doctor. The woman told him everything; about how bad the seizures had been, how he'd used to fall down in the maize fields – how the drugs – ('What drug?' asked Jacoman – 'Phenobarbitone' said the woman) how they had stopped the seizures; on the other hand they had made her husband sleep all the time, he couldn't do his work properly. (Jacoman looked pleased here; this was just what he wanted to hear. What a shitty drug Pheno-barb was.) So then they had decided he should take fewer pills; they had cut them down to an acceptable level of side effects. It left him with the odd fit at night, but they could live with that, no one saw them except the wife; only if he was to start fitting in the daytime would they consider upping his dose.

Jacoman turned to Anna here and asked if she had any questions. She asked 'What does he – do they – think brought his epilepsy about?' The man gazed at her, smiled, said nothing. The woman shifting her poncho across her shoulders, thought for a moment but no more than a moment. 'I think it is our troubles and suffering as a family,' she said – *'pena y suffrimiento'* her exact phrase, the same phrase Anna had unearthed in her research on Andean concepts and attitudes and used in her questionnaires.

She looked at the couple in awe almost; in those words the project became real for the first time. She would not forget, she thought, that woman's face, her gold tooth; nor the braid on her husband's hat, his hunched back, the way he looked away, where the wife gazed into their eyes not defiantly, but as if she and they were equals.

What excited Jacoman himself about this interview, on the other hand, was the example of what he called self-titration, that is dose adjustment. All the way home he told Anna that it was a perfect example of what he'd always been certain happened, that in regard to drugs people did draw their own conclusions. And why shouldn't they? – doctors couldn't know someone else's quality of life, or what constituted for them their quality of life. Everyone had the right to decide their own.

'What a pity you're not still practising as a doctor,' Anna told him, 'thinking like that. It's very enlightened of you. Most doctors want to play God.'

(Which was ironic, she thought the many times afterwards she did watch Jacoman try to play God.)

It all came to an end at last; how could it not?

Anna Kern's diary. April 14th. Flight to Miami.

Dinners. That's the other thing about Quito, apart from green baize tables; dinners. It's always the same working with Bader-Kleitz; dinners. It's Indian restaurants in London, French restaurants (I'm told) in Nairobi, Chinese restaurants in Basel, Swiss restaurants complete with alpine scenes in Quito.

On the last night in Quito we got – antlers and sombreros – 'Mexican hunting lodge' said David; yes, precisely. Everyone came, all the visiting academics, all the local and visiting Bader-Kleitz people. Aguadiente spent the whole evening describing to David in execrable English what he called his internal torment over leaving his wife for Dolores. Meanwhile I was trying to make conversation to Navarro's Spanish wife; she pronounced the word 'Madrid' as if it was Eldorado. Jacoman, Meyersdorf, the head of the local Bader-Kleitz, all the pharmaceutical mafia were down the far end of the table. Looking at them reminded me of some anthropological theory – Mary Douglas's, I think; something to do with the impersonal social and political control manifest in the pig feasts held by Papuan New Guinea chiefs, otherwise known as Big Men. She says industrialists are Big Men also. Lord Thomson, the newspaper magnate was a Big Man.

Maxwell and Murdoch are Big Men. So indeed is Bader-Kleitz a Big Man – Jacoman perhaps too in that context; I'm sure it's how, waving around his American Express Gold Card, he'd like us all to see him. I'm sure, in his heart of hearts it's what he'd like to be.

This pig feast's a sign that everything is over for the moment; we have a project, God knows how, remembering the furores, remembering how many times we thought we were done for; how many times I thought we couldn't finish the work. I don't think we did finish it exactly; we just cobbled it together, sitting at our green baize tables, huddling over word processors into all hours of every night, kissing each other goodbye at last, and handing round the ritual Ecuadorian presents. 'Beads for the natives,' said Jacoman. (In fact it was me got the beads, there was a necklace inside Dolores' elaborate wrappings; rather a pretty necklace, actually, made out of large Amazonian seeds.) How Jacoman squared the budgets he isn't saying. David suspects he's handed round computers like lollipops, as he would put it, to keep the natives happy, as he would also put it, to us if not to them.

And now we're off to Oxford, Connecticut, USA to give a seminar at Franklin University, no less, on what we have just been doing. Is there no end, Anna Kern, to all this madness? (But one thing: Nikki seems to have got it all quite wrong. After this week David feels closer to me than ever; not further away.)

Chapter Fifteen

Anna Kern's notebook: June 1986. Some thoughts about big business in general; the pharmaceutical industry in particular.

'There's no such thing as Bader-Kleitz, merely a collection of individuals.' (Carter Jacoman.)

'Whatever man's position may be, he is bound to take a view of human life in general that will make his own activity seem important and good.' (Tolstoy. *Resurrection*.)

'Here's the rule for bargains. "Do other men, for they would do you." That's the true business precept.' (Dickens. *Martin Chuzzlewit*.)

'People of the same trade seldom meet together even for ... diversion, but the conversation ends in a conspiracy against the public...' (Adam Smith.)

'Leadership is also about fellowship. You can only be the sort of leader your followers are comfortable with. What works in Scandinavia may well look weak and wet in Mexico.' (Hofstede.) *(N.B. Anna. In other words, what works with us, Carter, doesn't work in Ecuador. Or in Basel, come to that.)*

'Organisations need to supplement the technology of reason with the technology of foolishness. Individuals and organisations need ways of doing things for which they have no good reason. Not always, not usually. But sometimes.' (I can't recall the source of this.) *(N.B. Anna: Carter's way of business, absolutely.)*

'There is no arguing with or explaining to the industrial system any more than there is arguing with the weather. The strongest social controls are not exerted in the personal mode.' (Mary Douglas. Natural Symbols.) *(N.B. Kern. Multinational companies, yes.)*

'[The power of the Big Man] is a purely personal achievement . . . rests only on the consent of his followers . . . Everyone else depends on the Big Man for their livelihood and security . . . He does it all by generosity, hard work, skilful manipulation of the rules of feast-giving . . . The Big Man has the biggest, fiercest demons to work for him.' (Douglas, ibid.) *(N.B. Kern. What are Jacoman's demons; his North American degree? His drug company budget? His computers . . . David and me?)*

(Of Lord Thompson. . .)

'And right from the start, we see him always poring over his balance sheets. Like the game of snakes and ladders, the balance-sheets represent rules which send him to the winning post and his rivals to the starting point . . .' (Douglas, ibid.) *(N.B. Kern: Snakes and ladders is a very good description of life in the pharmaceutical business. I am reminded of Jacoman, too, forever poring over the budgets. However when I made this analogy to Piet Van Dyke, or tried to – he and I became quite friendly over the last few days in Quito, in his own way he is as much of an outsider as I am, and always two steps behind Jacoman in the corridor, like a Prime Minister's husband – he said, cryptically, 'Oh yes, Jacoman's a big man. He thinks he's a big man. And he is building himself an empire alright, you and I are among his subjects, Anna, and for the moment Navarro and Aguadiente. But it may not last. This empire he is building is on sand; and you will see.'*

At some point during that first Ecuador visit – late at night, one of the few evenings Jacoman was not involved in budget negotiations – Jacoman had summed up the attitude of Anna Kern to the business he worked in, as he saw it, at least. It had been another hard day. By this time David, as usual, was desperate to get to his bed; Carter Jacoman, however, was equally insistent that he and the two Kerns needed to get together; he had suggested a drink in either their room or his. 'Your room then, Carter,' David said. Adding *sotto voce* to Anna, 'At least we can escape; if he comes to our room we'll never

204

get rid of him.'

All week Anna had been observing the relationship between Drs Kern and Jacoman, David's attitude towards Carter, shift and change. The honeymoon stage was over, she realised; at the same time, there were occasions when, seeing the level of unspoken understanding between them, she thought; bloody *hell*; they might as well be married, they really might. Yet she wasn't jealous, not really. She liked it. Perhaps because she also observed – and this did give her pleasure, perversely – how David grew more sceptical about Jacoman, for much the same reasons as she herself grew more intrigued. As far as Jacoman was concerned, on the other hand, she'd observed above all his increasing reliance on her husband. What he needed now was reassurance on a point so minor Anna hardly gathered what it was. She retired to Jacoman's bathroom as the discussion began, slipped down her knickers with relief – she had drunk three cups of coffee and a bottle of Guitig water – and sat on the lavatory eyeing Jacoman's brown striped wash bag, his aftershave lotion, his tube of Swiss toothpaste (she picked it up to see where it came from), his two toothbrushes (two toothbrushes? she wondered), scattered hither and thither. There was a wet towel on the floor, another on the mottled Formica surface around the handbasin; Jacoman was not tidy – in the bedroom his clothes and papers lay all about; the more so now, since he'd scrabbled for a document to show David, papers falling to the floor, this way and that. It was amazing, really, he turned up each morning as spruce as he did.

He had a pair of ivory-backed hairbrushes like her father used to have, she noticed. (David's hairbrush was blue plastic, just like her own.) Seeing them gave her a strange feeling of intimacy with Jacoman. It made her image in the mirror as she washed her hands, using the hotel soap he'd left lying in its crumpled package, seem almost as intimately connected with his scattered belongings as two pairs of knickers jumbled together in a laundry bag.

She returned to the bedroom to find both David and

Jacoman laughing. Stretched out on the hotel armchair, her husband still looked tired, but more relaxed; maybe it was the duty free whisky Carter had poured for him. Maybe it was Carter, she thought – she and David did not share a sense of humour the way Carter and David did. Was that why, now, laughing, they did not bother to explain the joke?

Anna demonstrated her own intimacy with her husband by removing the glass from his hand and taking a sip. Carter waved the bottle at her. 'There's another glass somewhere, Anna dear,' he said. 'It's OK,' she said, sitting down on the floor beside her husband's chair, 'I'll share David's. I don't want much. And he shouldn't have much anyway,' she said, eyeing her husband. 'It gives him a headache.' David groaned, took the glass from her, followed it with a healthy swig. 'Well now,' said Carter, 'do I see marital dissension? Oh wow, I thought you two newly weds had never heard of such a thing.' 'Well now you know we have,' said David grinning at him and giving the glass back to his wife. 'Drink up, Anna,' he said, 'it's time we went to bed.'

But they did not go to bed, yet. David stayed where he was and went to sleep. Jacoman, on the other hand, was all energy suddenly, the way Anna'd often noticed in him late at night. God knows where he got it from, after his late start, his sleepless nights. (Her husband was the opposite. Seeing his eyes well shut, she rescued the whisky glass from a limp hand, catching Carter's eye as she did so – they laughed, affectionately, at each other.)

She never could remember afterwards how they got onto the subject. She only knew that, quite suddenly, Jacoman was accusing her of being supercilious; of approaching Bader-Kleitz, in particular, big business in general, discussing it, like an anthropologist approaching an unknown tribe. But then he said, 'No, not like an anthropologist, Anna, I guess that's not it, you're too naïve about it for that; more like Christopher Columbus confronting a new world; did you never read those books of old voyages? That's what you sound like sometimes, I guess you do to me; it's charming, Anna it's cute, but it

206

does you no favours. In the 1980s innocence is pernicious in anyone over twenty, it seems to me.'

This last bit nettled Anna. She scowled at him, but said nothing, because for the rest he was quite right – damn him, how did he know? At times these days she felt exactly like Christopher Columbus or Marco Polo or 'stout Cortes' or whoever – sailors, traders, conquistadors, Jesuits alike; having to try and make some kind of connection, as they did, between past and present, known and unknown; turning priests and shamans into witches, tribal chiefs into kings, indigenous gods into saints or demons. What astonished her also – but then Jacoman was always astonishing her in such ways – she'd put him down as an ignoramus and suddenly he'd reveal himself as anything but – bloody knowall, she thought, sourly; such things annoyed her husband still more – was the quite extensive acquaintance he revealed with such works as Hakluyt's voyages; Marco Polo's travels; even *Purchas' His Pilgrimages*, a much more obscure book, that she had only come across by chance in the course of researching some story. Forbearing to point out that, by the sound of it, Jacoman's reaction to Bader-Kleitz ten years ago had been not dissimilar, she let herself be swept into a happy discussion of literary explorations; complete with references, of course, to the latter day voyages of characters in Paul Bowles; literary discussions with Jacoman always did come round, eventually, to Paul Bowles.

I know what this is like, thought Anna, exhilarated, after half an hour or so – if it was exhilaration fuelled by whisky, so what? – I haven't had anything like this since I was eighteen, since Sussex. How long can I keep it up? How long can he? And then, treacherously, but she could not help it, she thought; why can't I ever talk like this to David? Her husband, all unaware, was by now snoring gently in his armchair; awaking only with a snort as Jacoman, his voice rising, tried to recite, from memory, Marco Polo's description of the Gobi desert at night, of his mistaking the sound of wind shifting the sand dunes for the voices of spirits. 'Much as you, Anna, hear demons in

Bader-Kleitz,' Jacoman said.

And siren voices in you? she wondered. A wave of exhaustion reminding her she was not eighteen any more, that this was not university, that she had another hard day's negotiating ahead, in which she would yet again, like Sisyphus, have to try pushing the same stone uphill, she gave Jacoman a conspiratorial grin – he returned it – and prodded her husband to wake him. 'Really, Carter? Well even if I do find demons where there aren't, it's too late to go into it any more. I need my bed. Oh and by the way,' she added – between intellectual excitement and whisky such intimacy, she thought, was permitted – 'Oh and by the way, why do you have two toothbrushes, Carter? Most people only have one.'

'Mind your own business, Anna,' said Jacoman, grinning, showing all his crooked teeth. Then, unabashed it would seem by her husband's presence – why should he be, it was all quite innocent, of course, she didn't fancy Carter, he didn't show any sign of fancying her other than mentally; why should she feel guilty (but she did, briefly) – he kissed her a whisky tasting, surprisingly fervent good-night.

It was not surprising Mrs Kern did see in Bader-Kleitz such a wholly new world. Though things had changed in her own generation, even one generation back the attitude of her English – oh so English – family to any form of commercial business could be summed up in her grandmother's ultimate dismissal of various unfortunates unwise enough to woo her daughter – 'But he's in *trade*.' Till latterly, no one in Anna's family had ever been in *trade*. Those who earned their living – over successive generations from the nineteenth century onwards, the decline in the family fortunes meant that its younger sons at least had to support themselves and their families – went, if not into the army, the navy or the church, into the law, the civil service, estate management. Anna's grandfather had been a Treasury Solicitor, her father a civil servant. In both these positions they had, then, enjoyed long holidays and relaxed hours. Of work as vocation, work as obsession, work as money-making for other people, they knew nothing; what they called 'daily-breading' for their family was an unfortunate necessity, nothing else, to be forgotten whenever possible and certainly never discussed, either privately or in public.

David's family, on the other hand, doctors for many generations – or, on his mother's side, rabbis – had no such dilettante attitudes to professional toil; far from it. Not only did they know what vocation was, work was what they did to the exclusion of virtually all else – her father was always working, according to Sonia; David had hardly known him. This did not mean, however, they knew any more about 'trade' as such, than Anna's family. But again, just as Anna's two brothers had been forced to prostitute themselves, in family terms – one working for BP, the other an insurance broker, which could also be described as 'trade', of sorts – David himself, unlike his father and grandfather, had been brought hard up against commercial realities; in his case the pharmaceutical companies who financed his research.

All this, perhaps, helps explain the spirit of alarm and adventure in which our anthropologist and her neurologist husband, up to a point, approached the organisation they were to work so closely alongside for five long years. David, despite experience of projects funded by the drug trade, was the more suspicious; as an academic he felt compromised by the alliance. Anna for all her left wing opinions did not feel compromised in the same way. The objections to trade in her family had been social rather than moral.

Indeed, over the years of flying Club Class hither and thither, staying in smart hotels, eating in expensive restaurants, David was to say, smiling at her his fond and weary smile, that she corrupted all too easily. She told him they were earning it, and in any case, excuse her, she was a moral peasant compared to his austere rabbinical standards – not that she noticed *him* fighting to travel Economy Class or eat in greasy spoons. And in any case the brief sojourns in luxury hotels were more than balanced by such hardships as five weeks in the project house in San Raphael, living on a diet of rice, avocadoes and chilli sauce, in constant danger of dysentery, and, much worse, cysticercosis, heavy consumption of Guitig water, as opposed to the pig ridden and intermittent local supply, notwithstanding.

At a conference, a doctor from some school of tropical medicine asked her who was funding their project; informed it was Bader-Kleitz, she had, fastidiously, as if drawn back her tweed skirts, and removed herself from Anna's presence. This annoyed Anna, mainly. David frowned when she told him and said, 'What do you expect, Anna? You are very naïve sometimes.' Jacoman, on the other hand, sighed, shrugged his shoulders, laughed, said, 'That still shows you, my dear Anna, what cloud-cuckoo-land English academics are still living in. The difference between a drug-company and academia is that if you have a good idea in a drug company there's money, big money for it, you can have a big project. Whereas if you're an academic, if you get money it's peanuts, and if all you've got is peanuts, all you end up doing is monkey projects.'

'Carter would say that,' said David, when Anna passed this on. 'On the other hand he's got a point. On the other hand, so's that woman.' And he sighed, in his turn. He and Anna were sitting on a beach at the time, on the island of St Thomas. They were attending a conference, so-called, in fact a promotional exercise set up by Bader-Kleitz' American subsidiary, at an expensive – very expensive – but charmless resort, in which David had only with reluctance agreed to take part, as a last minute substitute for a London colleague. Two hundred American neurologists and their wives had been flown in, Club Class, from places as far away as Hawaii, to be greeted by a company executive, a beefy red-faced man, English in origin, but so Americanised he answered to the name of Chuck, and wore for the occasion a pink t-shirt with 'Lenytol For A Happy Life' blazened across the front, above a pair of tartan bermudas. For two hours every morning the neurologists were lectured to by medical academics such as David on the uses and merits of Lenytol.

The afternoons were given up to free entertainments, sailing, snorkelling, golf, and so forth.

David said if he'd realised what the thing was he'd never have come; made clear his medical independence, his integrity even, was impugned by such goings on. He refused to avail himself of the amusements offered; sat, writing, in their room. Anna, on the other hand, took up snorkelling; she so enjoyed it, that her faint guilt at abandoning her husband to what she could see were appropriate feelings – and which she loved him for, it must be said – evaporated all too soon; as far as she was concerned the unexpected pleasure justified the whole trip. Those half hours or so, flippered and goggled, took her literally, in all senses out of her over familiar elements – her marriage not least; with one flip of her feet she glided like a bird or a fish. Those plump, striped, spotted, finned creatures of the not so deep, darting about, nosing among the tentacles and fronds rooted on the reef below her, reminded her, of course, of Nikki; except that their colours were muted as Nikki's were not, by the refractions of water. Indeed there were times in the upper world, that of the beach resort, where even vases of flowers, even bowls of fruit not only came courtesy of Lenytol and Bader-Kleitz but said so in inch-high letters, that thoughts of Nikki were followed, guiltily, by thoughts that Nikki might be better company here than her embarrassed husband.

On the last evening there was a banquet. The neurologists and their wives, some of them unwisely sunburnt, to Anna's surprise – she thought Americans knew better, she thought it was only the English finished beach holidays with peeling noses – gathered in a large but bleak, half-underground, windowless room. Flowers were arranged to spell out the word Lenytol at the centre of each whiteclothed table; before each place was a menu card also headed by the word 'Lenytol', and by the company logo. On a low stage at the far end of the room, draped in red and gold, every drape, every banner, too, having the company logo and Lenytol blazened across it in foot high letters, sat a small dance band. Throughout dinner they played middle of the road music – Sinatra songs, Neil Diamond songs, once a medley of sanitised Beatle tunes, Anna noticed, once an even blander version of Mick Jagger's 'Have you seen your mother, baby, standing in the shadow?' at least Anna thought that was what it was; she had not quite made up her mind before the band was off into a swinging version of 'Stand by Your Man'. A medley from *Oklahoma* followed; towards the end of this Chuck, in a white tuxedo with a day-glo bow-tie, got up and made the motions of encouraging everyone to join in a chorus of the 'Surrey with the Fringe on Top'. He covered himself neatly by making a joke of it – no one did, seriously, join in, apart from the members of the band behind him grinning away. 'A pharmaceutical Billy Butlins, that's what all this is,' murmured David in Anna's ear. 'If we did sing it might be better, it might at least be fun,' said Anna. 'Speak for yourself,' said David.

By now cigars were being handed round, and liqueurs; the assembled neurological talent and its wives, mostly white Americans, with a smattering of Chinese and Japanese Americans (also one pair of Korean Americans – the wife had gone snorkelling in the same group as Anna; she and a WASP woman from Milwaukee had been sick on the boat on the return trip) discreetly loosened belts, puffed and sipped contentedly as Chuck proceeded, yet again, to tell them how wonderful they all were, what a great meeting this had been, one of the best of its kind he'd ever attended, and this was surely due to all of THEM, you wonderful people. And now, ladies and gentleman, he had the greatest pleasure in presenting in what he hoped would be the highlight of their visit to St Thomas – oh and by the way he hoped they'd had the chance to visit all those great downtown duty free stores – but the entertainer he had to introduce now was by no means duty free, let alone cut price, he was unique in his field; ladies and gentleman, Bader-Kleitz proudly presents for your entertainment, all the way from Manhattan, the one and only . . .

Anna didn't get the name; she was too busy watching

the entertainer – black, not very tall, rather plump and wearing a red tuxedo ('What did I tell you; we've got the redcoats and all,' murmured David) running onto the stage on surprisingly little, light, patent-leathered feet. He pulled the microphone out of its stand, swung round to face the audience, giving only the smallest of acknowledgments in passing towards the now redundant, patently amateur, and suddenly, by comparison, touchingly English-looking Chuck, and bringing it to his lips with a tremendous flourish, as if kissed, as though that was not enough, as if caressed it, and launched, pursued rather than accompanied by the attendant band, into a tune which Anna recognised but could not identify, and words entirely improvised by him; a fulsome, wittily rhymed, at the same time oleaginous tribute to the representatives of the medical profession now perched below him on spindly gold chairs, puffing their cigars, sipping their brandy and liqueurs. Men of healing he called them, wonder workers and so on, people like him he sang, were lesser mortals. And so on.

('How's your self-esteem, now?' Anna teased David. He had his head in his hands. Faintly, she could hear him groaning.)

Having followed this with a more or less straight rendering, sub-Louis Armstrong style, of 'Wonderful World' (he claimed, of course, it was doctors made it a Wonderful World), followed by a song rhymed from words shouted up at him by his now beaming and noisy audience, he improvised, finally, an interminable ditty on the merits of Lenytol. He got any number of rhymes – some of them ingenious – out of the word; ending, it was to be expected, 'I sure *love* you all,' to the glee of most of those present, except, of course, Anna's husband. He now groaned in her ear, 'What am I doing here? What am I *doing* here? This is the final *straw*.'

Anna thought she ought to be ashamed of thinking, as she did, that she wouldn't have missed this horror for all the world. Because she wouldn't have. She had been rereading *Vanity Fair* all week. She finished it as they flew home across the Atlantic, and offered it to David.

But he declined the offer, saying he'd had enough of such things, and, anyway, she knew he didn't like Victorian novels. 'There's always room to change your mind,' she said, tartly. Then she added, more kindly, 'Don't take it so to heart, David. It's just the Americans do things that way. Bader-Kleitz in Basel aren't like that.' Whereupon David gloomily pointed out that a single day of such a jamboree – it lasted four – must have cost at least the same as the year's allotted budgets for the projects in Ecuador and Kenya. As for Bader-Kleitz in Basel; he wasn't so sure they were that different from the Americans, when it came to the hard sell, when it came to the question of profits. They just made less noise about it. 'As even you'll most likely see, Anna, before we come to the end of this,' he said.

Chapter Sixteen

On the return from this Ecuador trip, as if that in itself hadn't been bad enough, Jacoman began seriously to doubt his own marriage. It wasn't for the first time, yet never before had it given him such foreboding, such pain. This was mostly because he felt excluded. His reappearance was made to seem an intrusion into family life. 'What do you expect?' said Giselle when he remonstrated with her – humiliated by the whole thing, he had to get half drunk before he could do so, that is before he could bring himself to state the reason for his unease and ill-temper; he was used to Giselle's propensity for punishing her nearest and dearest, but this – 'If you're away so much we have to make our own life without you.' He accepted that. What he could not accept was the fact that, though his kids seemed pleased enough to see him individually, certainly they flung themselves on him in search of the presents he'd brought home (painted parrots from the Amazon, the Indian dolls, doll's house fruit and cakes and flowers on little painted plates, an embroidered hanging of two lamas and an Indian peasant standing in front of a volcano, a video game for Louis picked up on Miami airport) they did not allow him re-entry to the family group. In particular Giselle did not allow him re-entry to the family group; and, loyal as always, willingly or not, it was from her they took their lead.

Each time Jacoman had come back from a trip lately, his readmittance to the family had been a little more perfunctory, a little more grudging. Yet, till now, Giselle had always moved aside a little, given him a place of some sort, if only a narrow one. Not this time. She even – or so it seemed to him – continued to sleep right in the middle of their matrimonial bed, leaving him to make do as best he could with what remained of the left side which had always been his. It was a week before he got up the courage – despatched his weariness sufficiently – to make love to her. She did not resist, any more than she had resisted when, the day before, exasperated, he had moved the sofa back to its position in their sitting-room in which it had been when he left for Ecuador. She lay there passively until he had finished. He almost wished she had resisted him. As it was he seemed to have as little part in her as in the room he'd rearranged to his satisfaction (inasmuch as such things could, any longer, give him satisfaction, were not simply a matter of rearguard action rather than convenience or comfort, let alone aesthetics).

Everything seemed to resist him; Chantal and Suzette, grave, orderly little girls, fair-haired like Jacoman, dark eyed like their mother, and with a waxen stillness and skin-colour that Giselle said, looking at them dispassionately, like the painter she was, reminded her of Victorian engravings or even Victorian dolls. His twins always had lived, up to a point, in a universe and occupations of their own, but now they behaved as if there was no other universe; at least none that included him. When Jacoman told Giselle that he did not think this was entirely healthy, she shrugged, and said, 'What's wrong with living in a world of your own?' making him realise, as if for the first time, what a long way she lived from the ethos that sustained him; it was not so much that she did not think attention should be paid, more a matter of where she paid it; relentlessly inward, rather than relentlessly outward; like her paintings, of course, and her paintings were getting more and more that way, he realised, despairingly. The series she had embarked on recently, of flowers rather than gardens, all seemingly accurate, botanically, looked at closely were as baffling and as crazed as the edifices and landscapes she had painted before, petals that did not match petals, stamens detached from corolla. These paintings excluded him still more than most things; for once she did not hide them from him, indeed she left them lying about, as if she wanted to emphasize the point she was making; that there was in their deep if disjointed femaleness absolutely no place for a man; a husband; at least for this man, this husband.

She hardly bothered to harangue him any more. She was almost supercilious. Except the once, when exasperated by the garrulousness by which he in his turn attempted to break down the barriers all about him – with rare self-insight, maybe it was jet lag broke *his* defences down, he had this image in his head of the noisy little clown leaping about, making funny noises, faces, to gain her as yet unpaid attention – she said, angrily – he'd been accusing her of total and inappropriate hostility to the sources of her and her children's living – 'What do you expect? If I'd wanted to marry a man who watched baseball on television on Saturday afternoons, I'd've married him; if I'd wanted to marry an executive in a brass-buttoned blazer, I'd have married him. But I didn't. I married you.'

Thereupon she buttoned up her mouth; he could not tell the colour and nature of the buttons; only that her skin though as smooth, as virginal, as ever, looked older somehow. Maybe it was the way she pinched up her mouth. Also there were dark shadows under the eyes whose blackness she flung at him briefly, before veiling them against him.

'Giselle,' he said.

'Carter?' she responded, indifferently.

Outside, all the way down the street, were impervious Swiss; who complained, sent deputations, organised official letters, if so much as a sweet paper was not removed the very moment it appeared on the pavement outside their home. It was still more hideous in the winter, every snowfall had instantly to be cleared from their patch. So far the same neighbours had blocked all Jacoman's attempts to have the tree which shaded their whole

217

garden cut back, though their landlord himself was willing.

Only Carter's son was left; and even his approaches to his father were independent of the rest of his family. He would make demands on Jacoman's time and attention – and his pocket of course – set up temporary alliances with him, but thereafter retreat to his niche among the women, not taking Jacoman with him. He had learned to read recently; now, although only six years old, he devoured print voraciously. On weekends he would come downstairs in his pyjamas, eat cornflakes or whatever, then, clutching a whole pile of books, ranging from *Tintin* to books on castles and aeroplanes, from Roald Dahl to *Finn Family Moomintroll*, he would retreat to the sofa, covered in shabby, faded brocade, that Giselle had found in a French junk shop, the very same one she had moved, symbolically, in Jacoman's absence and that he, equally symbolically, and without a word, moved back.

Jacoman was proud that his son was such an early and avid reader. On the other hand the fact that Louis made it clear he'd be happy to stay where he was all day, in his pyjamas, indeed on occasion did, also aroused all sorts of atavistic feelings he'd never have suspected in himself. Shouldn't the boy be out playing baseball or some such with his friends? Shouldn't he in general be more gregarious . . . shouldn't he . . .?

'Oh, for goodness sake, Carter,' Giselle said. 'The boy spends his whole week in school with a hundred and fifty other kids. If he wants time to himself on weekends, what's wrong with that?'

'But why does he have to stay in his pyjamas?' Carter asked.

'You're very bourgeois all of a sudden, Carter,' Giselle said, smoothly. 'It must be those executive types you're mixing with, these days.'

More than ever Jacoman poured his energy and his frustration into his work. His schemes grew still more grandiose. He was telexing Egypt now and Indonesia; Pakistan and Turkey. He spent hours closeted with Taylor plotting how to present these new projects to the management committee. In two weeks' time Anna, David and the psychologist, Vittoria, were off to Kenya to initiate the study there. Jacoman was not going with them; not because of Giselle, but so as not to tread on the toes of Falconer, the Scots Medical Director (Africa), whom David had met in Jerusalem; there already he'd sensed Falconer's resentment, even dislike of their mutual colleague.

'Falconer's competent enough,' said Taylor. 'He doesn't need you, Carter. Let him get on with it.'

'Competent is all he is,' said Jacoman, 'and English.'

'Scots,' said Taylor.

'Comes to the same thing,' said Jacoman, who for a man with such Talmudic sensitivity to intellectual subtleties was, even after a year in England, surprisingly insensitive to such matters. As Taylor – though he of course did not mention the Talmud – pointed out. 'So a French Canadian comes to the same thing as a Jewish one?' he said, smiling, shrugged, and raised his red eyebrows. This was somewhat below the belt given Giselle's contentious ancestry and both of them knew it. On the other hand it was also fair exchange for Carter's mockery of Taylor's executive phraseology, his rugger club ties. This relationship, at least behind the closed door of Taylor's office, was much more open, much more personal, perhaps because much more conspiratorial, more clubby even than anyone else – Giselle, David – even the secretaries who worked for them and so observed them in closer professional circumstances than their other colleagues – realised. One man – a Welshman – saw more than most; he christened them, privately, Tweedledum and Tweedledee, but kept it to himself because neither his Swiss nor his American colleagues would have recognised the allusion.

Anna would have recognised it, of course; but she hadn't met Taylor yet; she never met the Welshman. And even having met Taylor, would never have suspected the nature of the relationship, the mutual need between the bland Englishman with his mid-Atlantic accent and his Euro-shrug, and the maverick Canadian; each in his way, the puppetmaster of the other. Though whether either recognised playing puppet as well as master was another matter.

Jacoman was on the phone to her husband almost from the moment they arrived home, to their mutual irritation. David said it wasn't necessary. He knew exactly what Jacoman wanted. The rest was up to himself and Falconer, at least at this stage.

But maybe Jacoman wasn't only ringing about Kenya. Maybe Kenya was only the excuse, one he found himself unable to escape from in the end; for he could not yet manage to bring up what he really wanted to bring up, the way he did later, in what David called Anna's marriage guidance period, when, often, after a nominal business discussion with David, he would demand to speak to David's wife; when sometimes, indeed, he rang Anna during the day when David was not at home, hardly making a pretence of talking about anthropology, before embarking on the subject of his marriage.

Yet once, at this time, when Anna answered the phone, and asked him, conventionally, how he was, how his family was, still expecting conventional answers, she got a sudden silence and then this one word, 'Baffling.' And then, after another silence, 'I'll tell you, Anna, one day. I'd be glad of your advice. I guess you know more about women than I do.' But he said no more. Anna felt he could not.

'Carter beaten for words,' said David when Anna reported this. 'I don't believe you.'

Oxford, Connecticut. April 1986.

What distinguished the trip to the University of Franklin – Connecticut's answer to Oxbridge, England, to Harvard and Princeton, USA – was not the talk Anna gave to the dreaded seminar; this was acceptable (just) and very brief, David having kindly used up a whole hour of the ninety minutes allotted the Kerns to describe their Ecuador project. What distinguished it was their first meeting with that other couple, later nicknamed by them

220

the Dreadlocks, or the Twinlocks, the Morticelocks, the
not-Yalelocks; actually Professor Milton Lock and his
wife, Dr Charlene Perkins Lock, leading lights of the
University of Franklin's School of Medical Anthropology.
(Also leading lights of American medical anthropology in
general Jacoman was to claim, later, though other
schools on both the East and the West coast, disputed it.
Franklin's near Talmudic style, exegesis on exegesis,
was not to everybody's taste. 'Yiddish tailoring, English
accent,' someone once described it to Anna. Dr Charlene
Perkins Lock wasn't Jewish; Professor Milton Lock was
for certain.)

Professor Lock chaired the seminar; he was the then
boss of David's long-legged friend, Dr Stanley Heins, an
expert on Islamic medicine and mourning rituals, who
was not only responsible for getting the Kerns here,
setting up the seminar, but also Anna's mentor, author of
the questionnaires, the EMICS, on which she based her
own questionnaires for Jacoman.

Stan Heins introduced Professor Lock to them at the
door of the room where the seminar was to take place.
'I'm glad to meet you both,' said the professor. It was a
very casual introduction. The whole affair appeared
casual at first glance. The low, wooden-walled, windowless room, 20F the number posted on the door, was like
the inside of a nut, thought Anna; into it poured a stream
of people dressed in such clothes – jeans, check shirts,
leather jackets – even some tweed jackets – as made clear
these were anthropologists not doctors. They crammed
themselves round the rectangular table which took up
most of the room space. They laid hands on its surface or
across the backs of chairs, tapped fingers, scratched
necks, laid heads on hands, held pens ostentatiously
ready over notebooks. Some, the later arrivals, lacking
seats, leaned against the walls, heads to one side, legs
crossed. But the eyes of all of them, seated or standing,
were fixed on the far end of the table, where sat Anna,
David, Dr Heins, who was to introduce them to their
audience, and Professor Milton Lock the chairman.
Opposite, Anna noticed, near the door of the room, sat a

white skinned, black-haired woman less informally dressed than her fellows in a brown shirt with a neckbow, more like an office worker than an academic. She wondered afterwards what it was made her pick that woman out – it wasn't her relationship with Milton Lock for sure. Milton hadn't greeted her in any way. So was it the clothes had caught her eye? Or the startling contrast of skin and hair? She'd dubbed her the Snow Queen on the spot; her surprisingly full yet petulant mouth did not wholly, though, fit that image.

The Snow Queen's eyes, too, were fixed upon the Kerns. Indeed it was the eyes gave everyone away; this was for serious, this was for real. Who's afraid of the Big Bad Wolf, thought Anna. (What big eyes you've got grandma – what big teeth.) Or maybe all seminars were like that, had she but known it. Looking at the set face of the Snow Queen, her fountain pen, not ballpoint as with most of her colleagues, poised above a paper, Anna thought better the devil you know, and could have wished herself back among the Ecuadorians, almost. As for David: after one glance at this gathering, he removed his jacket, loosened his tie, but he did not adjust his talk, the eyes demanded the serious stuff, they got it; more than they wanted, to judge from the expressions on some faces, they were medical anthropologists, not doctors; also, maybe, less than they wanted – his assumption of their ignorance of epilepsy appeared to rile them. Impatient though they may have been to hear Anna, the moment he had finished they raised a forest of questioning arms, vying for his attention. Professor Lock pointed his green ballpoint at first one, then another; studiously ignoring, it seemed to Anna, observing the exchange, the arm of the Snow Queen, raised along with the rest. Only when she put it down, did he say at last, smiling interrogatively, 'Charlene?' Whereupon the woman, her pouting lips belied by the deep voice that issued from between them, said 'Dr Kern? Dr Kern? Are you meaning to tell us you can sit in London and know for sure that the patients you are treating, I beg your pardon that your Ecuadorian *colleagues* are treating, are suffering from true epilepsy and not the hysterical form?'

Most of the questions had been of that nature. David sighed and explained yet again how they proposed to validate his diagnoses. Professor Lock rescued him after a while and introduced Anna; but they weren't interested in her – why bother to attack a gnat, she thought, when you could draw the sting of a hornet? Happy to be a gnat in this company, she was more relieved than offended at the desultory questions that came her way. When she sat down, David nodded his approval; Stan Heins patted her on the shoulder. The assault on her husband renewed itself with ever greater fury.

On their release from the wooden room, all was *bonhomie* again, however; everyone was smiling. They had got off lightly, after all, thought Anna, until she saw the woman she'd dubbed Snow Queen hovering, and heard Professor Lock say, his eyebrows raised for some reason, 'This is my wife, Charlene.'

'Glad to meet you, Mrs Kern – Anna,' said Dr Charlene Lock, shaking her by the hand; pinning her slate-green eyes on her. The Locks and the Kerns were lunching together, it seemed to Anna's dismay. Close to, the Snow Queen appeared no more and no less prepossessing than she had from the other side of the room. With that hair and that skin, with those eyes, she'd look better in green than brown, thought Anna dispassionately. Despite the beauty of her hair and skin, Dr Lock looked dowdy; among the jeans and leather jackets she also looked overdressed. Anna, too, in the striped jacket so liked by David felt overdressed. But she at least was not wearing something her own mother might have worn. No she was not. (The way she looked the other woman over, David said afterwards, the way Charlene looked Anna over, they were like two tom cats sizing each other up. 'Wrong gender,' said Anna; not just stating the obvious. The rivalry she had felt was a comic strip version of female rivalry, not at all what she was used to in her relationships with women. But having observed it in others, she'd at once recognised it – to her resentment, even horror – in herself.)

It passed, for the moment. The dreaded seminar over, Anna pushed the unsought rivalry aside too, preferring to take at face value the contradictory hint of female solidarity in the way the wife accompanied her along the street behind Stan Heins and their two husbands. The day was windy yet bright. The red brick Gothic of the university buildings set off in places by thanklessly dark-green bushes, seemed more public school than university, at least by English standards. In such a setting, Charlene Lock's walking in the gutter beside Anna rather than on the pavement equally disarmed and confused her; Charlene was a tall woman, it made her and Anna more or less the same height. She believed in eye contact, moreover; Anna kept turning her eyes away, but looked back each time to find the flint green eyes, heavy brows raised enquiringly above them, fixed, unwavering, upon her. Beware ice splinters, thought Anna, lowering her lids discreetly. Charlene's black hair did not seem to be affected by the wind, she noted; she kept on having to pick strands of her own out of her eyes and mouth. Once, tenderly yet impersonally, as if she hardly noticed what she was doing, Charlene Lock did it for her.

The response of the increasingly disconcerted Anna to Charlene's questions was by now in what she, asked by a maddened David to explain it, had once defined as her Proustian mode. ('Answer the question I'm asking,' he'd say, 'not one three questions forwards or back.'

'But I can't answer that question till I've explained the other things,' she'd protest, patiently.

'Yes you can,' he'd say. 'Of course you can.')

'Why are you so defensive, Anna?' asked Charlene Lock, after a little. 'No, let me guess. You had a hard time in Ecuador. But you don't need to project that on to me, dear.' At this point she smiled, very kindly. (What big eyes you've got grandmama.) Then she herself changed the subject; quizzing Anna at length about all the neurologists on the project, who they were, where they came from; when Anna, fumbling, tried yet again to explain the set-up, Charlene, yet again, accused her of being defensive. Anna, red in the face, and ever more

224

wind-blown, was rescued by Charlene's husband – hearing their by now raised voices, he turned back to join them – she seemed to have done a good job, he told her, bending his head down towards her, kindly; of course she must go back to Ecuador in due course, to check on how the field work was going. Anna nodded at David. 'Make sure Carter hears that,' she said to him. Her colour subsided a little.

She was flanked now by both wife and husband. Milton Lock towered above her. Soft-voiced, his shock of prematurely grey hair topped a benevolently round, even youngish face, sporting gold-rimmed spectacles and a big moustache. At the same time his legs were long; he wore boots and a leather jacket; he was in his way almost dashing – she could have imagined him on a horse, in a cowboy hat, even. Roy Rogers, she thought; Prince Charming. If she preferred him to his wife, Charlene, maybe she was meant to prefer him; for all the steeliness of her approach, against his smiling benignity – he was light to her dark, also, soft to her hard, bland to her vinegar, his very features were amorphous-looking, alongside her sharp ones – there was a hint of collusion in the way husband and wife glanced at each other. Talk of being defensive; aggression was the best defence, according to Charlene's tactics. Had Anna picked this up sooner, so much the better. She was reminded of the fierce Dolores; much more disconcertingly – Charlene Perkins Lock was so thin, almost skinny – of her friend Nikki; for all that the flamboyance, the style, the colour of a Nikki had been as if leached right out of this one. Like Nikki, Charlene looked older, close to, than at a distance. She pinched her full lips into a grudging smile that corralled her Snow Queen glitter.

Over lunch in a refectory like a school hall; black oak, gothic vaulting (no high table in this egalitarian country – Anna ate cauliflower cheese; David green peas and a Welsh rarebit; the Locks both settled for a chef's salad) Mrs Lock gave up her siege of Anna, transferred her attention to David; her husband made one or two desultory and vain attempts to curb her. 'Well, David,' she'd say, for instance, 'I was very interested in the way you said it was possible to distinguish hysterical seizures from genuine ones – are you saying . . .?' and so on. Though David smiled at her, with unfailing politeness; though he gave her, neutrally, the same answers as earlier, Anna could almost see the sparks flying off the knife he used to saw at his Welsh rarebit.

Milton, meanwhile, said little. He smiled, nodded or shook his head, as appropriate, from time to time offered Anna salt, ketchup or whatever, thoughtfully forked up his salad – the fastidious manner of his eating disguising the speed of it. He finished eating long before the other two. From time to time he broke off to murmur something to one of the hoard of what Anna could only describe as acolytes, who descended on them throughout the meal. She observed the deference in the manner with which they approached Milton. Those who first bearded Charlene were, if less deferential, warier, even at times belligerent, like people confronted by a receptionist when they wanted the boss – Charlene, of course, was dressed like a receptionist. One portly man with a beard, his yellow and black shirt hanging outside his jeans, muttered something about the professor, to make clear it was Milton he wanted, not his wife; when Charlene dismissed him he looked resentful for a moment, then adjusted the set of his mouth as if it wasn't politic, with her, to look resentful; he departed smiling not at Charlene, though, but Anna.

Over ice cream and coffee people still kept coming. Now, imperiously, at a nod from Milton, Anna noticed, Charlene waved all of them away.

'Bloody power games,' exploded David afterwards, when hands had been shaken, polite goodbyes said, and the Kerns were on their way back to Stan's apartment. (Stan was a bachelor; he'd told them he'd never had time to get married; seeing the way books and journals absorbed his rooms, Anna could quite believe it.) 'She could have stopped all of it from the beginning.' 'Could she?' queried Anna. 'Of course she could bloody well have stopped it. No one has to be interrupted all through lunch when they've got guests. It was a set up, that's what it was, to show just how important they were. God what a frightful woman. She knows fuck all about medicine, what's more,' he added with a satisfaction that so riled Anna she felt for the first time a flicker of sympathy towards Dr Charlene Lock.

'David's problem,' she said to Stan, 'is he doesn't like American women. Full stop.'

Stan chided David. 'Hey, go easy, Dave. She's not so bad. It's not easy for a woman here in Franklin, particularly a woman anthropologist in a medical department . . .' Such a defence surprised both Anna and David; Mrs Lock had been offhand with Stan also, when he arrived to meet them. She hadn't offered him coffee. Yet he didn't even stop there, going on to insist how much harder it was for a woman competing so directly against her husband, in particular where the husband had a medical qualification of some kind and she did not; and where the woman concerned was somewhat older than her husband, had been senior to him at some stage; as he now informed them was Charlene's case; adding, finally, 'She'd see everyone as about to screw her, and can you blame her?'

'I'm not about to screw her,' said Anna. 'How could I?'

'Watch it, Anna. You got your job on the strength of me,' said David.

'Maybe she thinks people see *her* as getting jobs only on the strength of her husband,' said Anna.

'She's good, Anna, she's a bright lady,' said Stan. 'But in this place you might be right.'

'Is that why she's so angry?' Anna asked. For in retrospect, an underlying rage, not to say fury, was what most remained with her of Charlene Lock. At which she felt another flicker of sympathy, even identified with the woman for a minute; partly, maybe, because of her husband's extreme dislike. She was too surprised by this to explain further, though both men were looking at her, blankly, as if unable to understand what she meant.

When David asked, 'Are they always such a double act?' she nodded; she understood exactly what *he* meant.

'Creepy,' she said. Stan who had a habit of glancing quizzically, then silently holding out a hand, now did so, while David came up for the first time with his joke about the Twinlocks. Anna laughing raucously in sheer relief, contributed 'Dreadlocks'. Stan looked awkward – they were his bosses, after all, David pointed out – or perhaps this kind of humour was simply too English for him. David and Anna, however, pursued the joke for the rest of the way; Anna, at least, felt the better for it.

They were home within two days; Anna relieved as usual that in her absence Ben had been all right. Within three days, she had talked by phone both to her sister-in-law, Sonia, and her friend, Nikki. The second conversation, of course, was much the longer; Nikki, having got over her initial annoyance at Anna's raising the subject (her propensity to give intimate details always had been balanced by a tendency to bridle when Anna mentioned them afterwards; how dare you gossip about me, Anna, was how she put it; how can it be gossip to your face, Nikki, Anna would protest) went on about the pleasures of celibacy – afterwards she asked about Sonia. Sonia, in an altogether briefer, not to say laconic exchange, asked about Anna's friend, Nikki. Serve them right if I exchange their numbers so that they can ask each other, thought Anna, almost piqued. She could not imagine what they would have to say to each other, however.

Behind Sonia's voice, meanwhile, she could hear the old man burbling, almost moaning.

'It's nothing,' said Sonia. 'The district nurse is here to do his dressings. He always makes a fuss.' Anna's father-in-law had ulcers on his legs, on top of Alzheimers. How appallingly life treated the old, Anna was thinking. She'd read that the very genes that made reproduction possible were precisely those that in causing cells to wither and die, ensured human obsolescence. In other words having children was the real fly in the ointment; no, not fly in the ointment, what was a fly but dirty little feet, flies were nothing. Snake in the ointment would be better. The serpent's tooth in the jar full of a substance that might even be made from its own venom, that might otherwise help you live your life for ever.

It reminded her of an African story, in which stones, men and animals had to choose between immortality and having children – only stones opted for immortality, not reproduction. Till some pharmaceutical whizz-kid came up with a mixture that could stave off the ageing process – what a fortune would be made by someone – they – men and animals – were stuck with the consequences of choosing to live for ever only in the flesh of their children. But if you had no children? Would she and David have children? she wondered. She was getting on for forty; there were dangers already, her cells were dying by the million, and so were David's, also. Soon, soon, they'd have to come to a decision.

Chapter Seventeen

Three weeks after returning from Quito, David, Anna and Vittoria, the psychologist, flew to Nairobi, to repeat the whole business for the Kenya project.

Kenya, according to Anna, who not only knew no poems about it, but apart from vague memories of the Mau Mau, had no preconceptions, no particular interest in going there; Africa had always seemed to her less interesting than Asia or the Americas. Yet, after all, their time in Kenya – they went three weeks after their return from Ecuador – was delightful; the work, compared to that in Ecuador was like chamber music against a symphony orchestra; or, better still, against Grand Opera. There were no government ministers, no opening ceremonies, no speeches. The one official lecture David was invited to give, at the university in Nairobi, he and Anna turned up to find a lone and embarrassed professor in an empty hall; all the medical students had gone down to Mombasa, for what purpose they were not told. There were no jealousies, no pride, no histrionics. That there was to be no epidemiological survey might have had something to do with it. That there was no Carter, ditto. That there were no neurologists, other than David, ditto again – the only Kenyan neurologist worked in Nairobi, in private practice. What the project had was a small Kenyan sociologist, a tall Kenyan psychiatrist, a Ugandan medical assistant, a Chinese psychologist, a Scots medical director. At that time there was also a lake, as we have seen. And four days of hard but agreeable work in cabins converted from bedrooms to offices for the duration, or else sitting beside the lake under acacia trees, during which proposals were advanced, amendments made, amicably, according to what was needed rather than according to the egos of the protagonists; no need of a ringmaster, let alone a conductor (or two or three would-be conductors).

At the end of four days they had the full medical protocol, 2 medical questionnaires, 2 psychological ones, 2 psychological function tests, 4 sociological questionnaires and a full logistical analysis of two years' work; no problem.

Kenya according to the neurologist: 'These people are serious,' said David, approvingly.

('Sometimes,' said the Scotsman, Falconer, looking disaffected. 'If you stayed longer, you'd see Africa isn't always so simple.'

'Maybe it's just Carter not being here,' said Anna, who had, perversely, been disappointed when told he was not coming to Kenya. 'It's less exciting without Carter,' she added, 'you must admit.'

'Who wants more excitement when they're trying to work?' said her husband.

'Me, sometimes,' she answered; but only to herself.)

Carter not there to bully them, Kenyans and Falconer alike determined to keep their weekend work free; David, Anna and the psychologist, Vittoria Mackenzie, were sent down to a game reserve the night after they arrived, a Friday evening. It was the start of the love affair Anna hadn't expected; like the love affair in a marriage arranged for practical reasons, without obvious enthusiasm; (Ecuador, you could say, was disillusion following a love match.)

Anna Kern's journal. May 1986.

'Africa is to the horizontal what the Himalayas are to the vertical . . .' Discuss. Even Vittoria who says forty-eight hours is as long as she can stand being outside a town, even she's impressed, for her; she likes the lions. Since her safari outfit consists of a bright yellow shirt, and her shiny pink mac, it's a wonder we see any lions. But we do. Last night we also saw a cheetah. Also baboons, elephants, zebra, hippopotami – any number of Thompson's gazelles – no snakes – no one ever mentions snakes in game parks. Maybe there aren't any. (There *are* snakes in Africa, of course – I think of the bi-coloured python rock snake, but when I mention this to David and Vittoria they both look blank; neither, evidently, were brought up on the *Just So Stories*; lucky them, dearly beloved. Vittoria didn't even know at first I was talking about snakes. As soon as she did realise she gave a little shriek and threatened to rush back to Nairobi forthwith. No one had ever told her there were snakes here, she said. We had to work hard to convince her there weren't any we knew of.)

This morning we went by jeep to a Masai village. The hut we were invited into had an earth floor, a fire circle with a hole in the roof for the smoke, stacked pots, wooden stools, low bed frames covered in animal hides, no place to stand upright. Vittoria came out looking dismal; and saying, 'It is for animals, it is not for people to live like that.'

No use my pointing out that the Masais are clever people, that they are educated many of them, they just prefer to maintain their old traditions; Vittoria kept repeating, 'It is for animals, not for people.' Next morning she says 'I cannot sleep for thinking of those miserable people.'

(This last was Kenya, according to Vittoria, from then on, no matter what else she saw and did.)

Kenya according to Carter, on many occasions: 'Kenyans are an ex-British colony, they know a red pillar-box when they see one; that's why you like them, Ann, you and they understand each other.' In one conversation, he went on, 'African culture isn't macho like Latin American cultures; people don't need to defend their honour all the time.'

'You mean it's a more female culture,' said Anna.

Carter laughed. 'You would see it like that, Anna. You

and Giselle should really get together,' he added wrily, without animosity, Anna not being his wife.

'Bennet thinks honour has to be defended,' said Anna recalling her friend, the sociologist. 'He thinks Kenyan honour has to be defended. He wants to prove Kenyans as professional as Europeans and Americans. He goes mad every time Meaki hijacks the project truck to visit one of his mistresses.' Meaki was the tall psychiatrist, a distinguished enough man, English trained, with not only a complicated love life, but something mysterious in his past which stopped him making his fortune treating private patients in Nairobi like most doctors of his training and background. David respected him, however. Dr Meaki had an epilepsy clinic of longstanding, knew his job. 'Meaki believes in what he does,' David said. '*And* he gets paid peanuts. Why do you think he can't afford transport of his own?' But then the neurologist had never found himself, like Anna, waiting three hours with Bennet and a team of young health visitors for Meaki to return the truck. Bennet's embarrassment had been almost the worst of it, as with every such problem (the offices being locked when they should be open, two of his team not turning up one day, the Ugandan's hijacking of some funds, and so on). But as Carter Jacoman pointed out, Bennet's embarrassment notwithstanding, the problems in Kenya, compared to the problems in Ecuador, were relatively unimportant, practical ones, not ontological problems.

'The problems in Ecuador, on the other hand, are definitely ontological,' Carter said throwing back his head, laughing.

'What do you mean, ontological?' asked David, giving Anna an irritated glance. Carter ignored him. 'As for that Bennet,' he went on, 'he's the one of the few Africans I know with European hang-ups. That's why he's so good, poor guy. Why do you think I suggested him for this project?'

'His problems are also ontological then,' said Anna, grinning at David; who raised an eyebrow; threw up his hands.

Kenya, according to HMSO, the Economist, etc. Land area 224,961 square miles, less than Ecuador a bit less than the UK, quite a lot more than Switzerland. Like Ecuador the country straddles the equator. Population (1985) 20.33 million, 39th in the world, but still well below half that of the UK; more than double that of Ecuador, getting on for triple that of Switzerland and growing all the time – at 4% p.a. it has one of the highest growth rates in the world; 51% of the population is under 15 years old.

(A particularly African problem, this one; no one has yet solved the conundrum that on this continent the worth of men and women is measured in sexual potency. It is a creed more powerful than religion; the birthrate in Kenya is almost double that of Ecuador where contraception is forbidden by the Catholic church. Nor is it likely to be countered – it is not countered, if the birthrate is anything to go by – by the large posters Anna Kern sees pinned up in some clinics and hospitals, on one half of which a melancholy looking woman is surrounded by ragged children, on the other a woman smiles at two smart, school-uniformed children.

AIDS may counter it, of course. The government, hence also the press, is coy about AIDS at the time of the Kerns' visits, to the extent of barely acknowledging the problem let alone releasing the figures. The only sign of any attempt to confront it are some poor little hand-printed posters they see stuck up on walls in Nairobi, advising husbands to be 'true to their dear wife', wives to be 'true to their beloved husband'.)

Average national income $270 p.a., less than half that of Ecuador. *(But then Kenya has no oil.)* 27% of produce agricultural, 75% of its workforce in agriculture – including forestry workers – timber is a growing export. A high proportion of the agricultural workers, and the poorest, are subsistence farmers producing food mainly for themselves. *(It follows that, as in Ecuador, a high proportion of the patients in this project are agricultural or forestry workers, or the children of agricultural or forestry workers.)*

Race: African 98%, Asian 1/4 of 1%, of Africans, tribal breakdown is Kikuyu 21%, Luhya 14%, Luo 13%, Kamba 11%, Kalenjin 11%. Swahili *(Jambo, bwaná, safari, etc.)* and English are the official languages, plus all the tribal languages, some of them Bantu-related, some, remotely, more Semitic. Religion: 70% Christian, 6% Muslim, 20% Animist *(tribal religions, ancestor worship and so forth).*

Literacy 47%. *(Against 80% in Ecuador.)*

Climate, hot and humid on the coast, temperate in the central highlands – Nairobi is at 5,500 ft above sea level; Likuru, in the centre of the rift valley, 6,000 feet odd.

(The equator is a few miles further north, slap through the middle of the study area. It is higher there and cooler. The day Anna and the team of health workers went up, the temperature was twenty degrees or thereabouts, the Kenyans put on jackets, complained of the cold. Unlike Ecuador, where it rains all the time, there is not much rain except in the rainy season, April, May and June. It is warm and pleasant most times, not too hot, not too cold. On Anna's second visit, purple jacarandas were flowering along the roads into Likuru. To the North East of the town and up into the hills ('blue remembered hills' she thought, with one of those inexplicable aches of nostalgia evoked sometimes, far from home, by the most unfamiliar landscapes) coffee plantations were flowering. Directly to the north lay big estates, once white colonist country, some still in the hands of big land-owners, all still good, profitable farming land. Here after independence, Kikuyus came from the high country, their tribal land, and settled, shedding tribal traditions in the process. Many had prospered, some to the extent of owning tractors and other mechanical aids. Industry in Likuru, for obvious reasons, was mostly agricultural processing and parts for farm machinery.)

Kenya: epileptic eye view.
'What is the reason for someone having epilepsy? It can be caused by a lizard in the head. It might be caused by breaking a taboo, or the patient's mother breaking a taboo. My community thinks it can be caused by

witchcraft, I too think it might be. I think these people are dangerous to the community, and I would not like my son or daughter to marry one of them. I am a pastor, I know I should not think these things, but I was brought up in the reserve, it is hard to shake off such beliefs; I cannot.' (Local Pastor; leader informant, no 12.)

'Since I had epilepsy I am useless in my family, to my children. I rely on relatives to keep us.' (Patient 153)

'I feel tired all the time. I cannot work.' (Patient 106)

'She is lazy she cannot go to school.' (Patient 17)

'We do not get on with the neighbours, because sometimes the patient fights their children.' (Patient 83)

'I am a teacher, aged 23. I am married with four children. Please do not send your health workers to visit me at school, people will know what is wrong with me and society at large has beliefs on epilepsy that would be embarrassing to me and my family. They think it is a curse from ancestors. They believe it can be transmitted by touch. You are looked down on as a handicapped person.' (Patient 178)

'My name is Peter. I am eighteen years old, I wear smart clothes, I try to look good, for the girls. But often I feel very depressed, sometimes I want to die, because I do not think any girl will be interested in someone suffering from kifafas.' (Patient 57)

'Our daughter has this disease; we have to watch her all the time. She could have a fit – kifafa – any time, fall in the fire or in the river. We cannot let her cook or go swimming.' (Patient 116)

(There were others with epilepsy who claimed to lead normal lives, function normally; there is no reason to doubt them; look at the teacher, but even they gave the same answers to some questions as the more afflicted. Viz:

Q. What do you think this epilepsy treatment will do for you, apart from preventing seizures?

A. I'll get married, go to school, go swimming, get my brain back, stop having headaches/stomach aches/ depression . . . my husband will come back. I'll have a happy life. . .

Q. How much would you be prepared to pay for this treatment?

A. What is costs. Life is more precious than money.)

Anna's journal. May 1986.

We've seen three hospitals so far; the one in Likuru, Meaki's, where the patients will come for the project, is a show hospital; clean, even pleasant, except for Meaki's psychiatric unit at the back, where men in blue overalls, women in green dresses like sacks, mill round a bare compound. They do ECT here without anaesthetic; not from lack of compassion – these are Meaki's patients – just lack of resources. There was an ex-police inspector, a huge man, his English perfect. When I commented on this, he said, in a baleful monotone, his eyes, hot and bloodshot, staring as straight into mine as Charlene Lock's cold ones, 'Of course I know English. I learned it from you, our masters.'

Other hospitals are worse. Falconer drove us up to the one at Moro, two hundred patients were waiting in the open to see one young doctor. The wards were filthy huts, stinking of urine, with broken windows, peeling paint, concrete floors, neon lights so grimy they gave no light, virtually. Nothing much else except beds, strangely lumpy-looking we thought – till we saw the three patients in each of them, head to tail and tail to head. In one corner of the compound was a hut full of oxygen tanks, where the same doctor operates on appendices; hernias, and so forth. He came out to talk to us – he said this was only his second posting. He also said, looking around him, shrugging, pre-empting what he must have thought we were thinking, that the hospital did have its uses. Last month, he'd successfully treated a man with tubercular meningitis. On the other hand when we talked of treating epileptics, he just laughed. He said that once the seizures stopped, epileptics wouldn't keep taking pills; when the seizures returned, they'd claim the tablets were no good. They all kept running off to traditional

237

healers anyway and getting rubbish, so what was the point?

'Look,' he said pointing at a man lying near us, eyes glazed, a zombie. 'He's epileptic. What can you do for him?'

He'd have gone on talking, if we'd let him, sitting on the burnt grass of the compound. But there were all those patients still waiting, so we took ourselves off. Falconer said, 'If you think this hospital is appalling you should see the ones elsewhere in Africa.' I wonder if he thinks this project worth doing. He is generally cynical, though cosy.

Kenya: a case history.

Before going down to the lake, to the Rift Valley, they had spent a morning in Nairobi. Anna went with Vittoria, the psychologist, and her fellow sociologist, Bennet – a slight man, very serious, nervous, eager to please her, in a suit that would have looked flashy on a European but not on him – to the big public psychiatric hospital to talk to the Chinese psychologist. It had been raining earlier. The red mud steamed in the shafts of hot sun; among tall fir trees, single-storey ward blocks were fronted by barbed wire cages in which blue-overalled patients roamed like wolves. The psychologist took them to watch a clinic in the children's ward, run by an Indian psychiatrist. It held nothing but empty beds, on these the visitors sat – there was only one chair, for the doctor, who did not sit down. Pinned up on the walls were cartoon pigs and kittens, chubby children, filmstars, cut from colour magazines and papers; none of the children, filmstars, none of the animals even, were black. The Indian psychiatrist told Anna offhandedly – he was clearly not interested in his visitors, why should he be interested in them – that he couldn't do his job without traditional healers, they took the neurotics, the psychosomatics, they had time to talk to them, he hadn't. What he could treat was organic illness. Yes, he was authoritarian, he told people what to do; that was what they wanted. By implication he mocked the liberal attitudes he assumed in Anna; at the same time his ironical smile suggested that in some respects he shared them.

The children came in then, one after another; stumbling, staring, twitching; some all too heavily drugged, it was clear. None were epileptic; until, after an hour or so, there shuffled in slowly, led by a nurse and an elderly man, a thin little girl called Grace, her head covered in a yellow kerchief. She was twelve years old, the Indian psychiatrist said, but she looked much younger. She kept her eyes cast downward; both her arms were bandaged.

Grace waited; the man – her father, the doctor said – waited, while in an undertone the doctor went on to relate to his visitors Grace's story. How she had been a good girl, meek, did what she was told, as required of young females in that culture, got high grades at school, at home helped look after her younger brothers and sisters. Three months or so ago, however, her mother and grandmother decided it was time for her circumcision, till recently an automatic rite of passage for both sexes. But times are changing. Her schoolfriends told Grace it hurt, it wasn't necessary. The girl went home and instructed her mother and grandmother well then, she didn't want it. They said she must, otherwise she would shame them; she wouldn't be a proper woman. (Anna could not help remembering here Nikki's frequent assertions concerning mothers and footbinders.)

For a few weeks, impasse; the girl's school marks went downhill. Then the grandmother came home and said she'd fixed the operation. The girl cried but said nothing. That night she'd had a *grand mal* seizure. Hysterical, could be, said the doctor; he was checking that out. The next night she had another. On the third night – the mother and grandmother were still insistent the circumcision must go ahead – she had taken a kitchen knife and mutilated herself, cutting her arms deeply; this was what the bandages covered. She had gone on screaming all night long, been brought to the hospital next day, put on Phenobarb for the epilepsy and Largactil for the mania.

The psychiatrist ordered the Largactil to be stopped, and the Phenobarb also. He asked the gaunt old man, the father, what he'd been thinking of to allow this situation. The father said the mother and grandmother did what they thought, they didn't care what he thought – what made the doctor think *he* could stop them? The doctor ordered the mother and the grandmother to come to his clinic next week, nonetheless. Through his white coated assistant, he then spoke to the girl herself, telling her in Kikuyu not to worry, nothing would be done to her without her consent. When he'd finished speaking she was led out by the nurse and the father. Not once had she raised her head, they'd caught only glimpses of her doped eyes, swivelling every which way.

'What are you thinking?' asked the psychiatrist, turning to his visitors. Encountering silence, he challenged Anna directly. 'You are the anthropologist, you tell me.' He not only challenged, at the same time he mocked her, yet almost perfunctorily, as if he could hardly be bothered. Why pick on me? she wondered, glancing at Vittoria, at Bennet. Because she'd been introduced as an anthropologist? Because she was a woman? Because she was the youngest person present? Her skin the palest? But when she opened her mouth to answer, he put up his hand, picked the words right out of her mouth, 'As an anthropologist, Dr Kern, you're going to say, quite rightly, so long as you realise that all such things are also over-simplifications, that she's a victim of changing cultures. She was brought up to be submissive, to do what she is told by her elders; yet today she has an option, choices, the norms are not so certain, there's room for fear and doubt. Fear fights against her conditioning to do what she's told, she cannot take it out on anyone, she takes it out on her own body. This is what happens to the weakest. They fall between the cracks in the culture, particularly one changing so quickly. And then they end up, here in my clinic.'

'And the epilepsy?' asked Anna, throwing another glance at Bennet, the sociologist who had been sitting on the bed beside her all this time, saying nothing, not even with his face, not even now, his smile both eager and guarded.

'Oh yes, the epilepsy,' the psychiatrist shrugged. 'We have to see about that. There is a history in the family. It might be it is organic. If it is maybe we can do something.' He sounded still more impatient; he was gathering up his files.

'Can you help this girl?' asked Vittoria, anxiously. From her expression, Anna could see the story adding itself to that of the Masai hut, in Vittoria's Kenya demonology; people living in huts too low for them to stand up in, and, besides, mutilating their daughters.

'I can try,' said the psychiatrist. 'At least I can try not to make things worse. Can I not, Dr Kern?' he asked, glancing at her. He was dark-skinned; his face narrow, yet heavy; his expression sardonic yet benign. His eyes were set beneath prominent lids in a way that reminded her of David's. He wore a dark suit with a tie under his white coat and brown shoes, highly-polished, their toes rather pointed. He looked at Anna as if to say even looks were too much bother, he was so busy.

She did not ask what she wanted to ask, thinking of the patients she'd seen, of the barbed wire compounds; how he found his job tolerable in such conditions. Was *their* job tolerable even? Or at least was it worthwhile? She thought of the cafe in Banos, the deadpan faces of the Indian family. She shrugged. He shrugged. He said, as if he read her, 'Sometimes things work out better than you think. People are more and less delicate than they seem. Societies crushes some, some survive no matter. To that end I must play God, though I am not. Though I do not believe in God even. I do just what I can.'

'You have to be a priest, as well as a doctor,' she asked him, 'in such a job?'

'Not a priest. No. Never. Priests believe in God. I told you I am an atheist,' he mocked her, and when she went on, 'What makes you think all priests believe in God?' held up his hand, would not let her explain further.

Falconer drove them down to the lake that afternoon in his company Volvo. The new fast road above the Rift Valley was lined almost all the way with traders. They sold live rabbits in cages – this upset Falconer's young daughters, so he said. They sold – there were racks lined with things that looked like metal platters or even shields, flashing in the sunshine – it took Anna a while to see what they were – hubcaps. They sold the spread pelts of sheep and goats; lengths of cloth; straw handbags.

Not once did she see cars stop though, except at the vantage point, at the first wide view over the Rift Valley. There were traders there, also. Below, in the far distance, was a lake tinged pink all over. 'That lake . . .?' asked Anna. 'Flamingoes,' replied Falconer in his clipped Scottish accent. He sat often, she noticed, with his mouth a little open. He was driving with his mouth open. He looked, she thought, like a teddy bear; a sandy man; chubby. 'Oh flamingoes; *pink*,' she said, after puzzling for a moment. 'Flamingoes,' at first, seemed no answer to her question. 'Are they there always?' 'They come and go,' said Falconer. 'Some years there are none or far fewer. No one's quite sure why. Something to do with what they feed on, the level of drought and so on. But it's not directly obvious; it's not clearly related to wet years or dry ones. It's a mystery like most things.'

Anna looked at the pink and distant lake, at the red walls of the Rift Valley and thought of Grace; of whose story she'd never know the ending. Their work – David's work most of the time, she realised, with an acute sense of pain – seemed more than ever like throwing a pebble into a huge, heedless, ocean tossing so wildly the pebble hardly raised a ripple. Just so flamingoes, mysteriously, like the winds, like the weather, like meanings, like possibilities, like war, peace, ecstasy, tragedy, like Africa now, in her consciousness, came and went.

Let us state correctly – rigorously as David would say – the chief differences between the two studies in Ecuador and Kenya and the way they were carried out.

Both were intervention studies – terms already explained. In both countries patients were to be randomly assigned to one of the two drugs and treated for a year. Their progress was to be examined, medically, psychologically, socially. But:

1. Medical Resources.

a) Kenya. All the patients were treated at one centre, the hospital at Likuru, by the principal investigator, Meaki, or his junior.

b) Ecuador. The project team was based at San Raphael, in the north of Ecuador, near the Colombian border, but the patients were to be seen and treated at local medical centres, scattered widely over two provinces, by local doctors, all new graduates, doing a compulsory year on behalf of the government, before being granted registration. At the same time the work was to be supervised by the Principal Investigator (Aguadiente), based with the other neurologists, psychologists, sociologists etc. at a house especially rented for the duration in San Raphael, the study centre.

(NB. The fact that all these rural doctors were employed by the Ministry of Health, responsible to regional government bureaucrats, was one reason for the need to involve government institutions and to butter up health ministers. In Kenya, with two doctors only, there was no such problem.)

2. Administration.

a) Kenya. The recruitment of workers, the day to day overseeing of the project, the disbursement of monies, the making of timetables, the checking to see all patients were duly seen at the right time, by the right people, was organised by the sociologist, Bennet Mbara.

b) Ecuador. Above functions were performed by Aguadiente, backed up by Jacqui from Guayaquil, the pharmaceutical man, seconded to San Raphael for the duration. The sociologist here was a functionary recruited by Aguadiente and responsible only for sociological aspects of the project. There was no one with overall responsibility to see that all investigations, visits etc., were up to date; this was to cause problems, later, leading to the promotion of Jacqui, the demotion of Aguadiente in all administrative matters.

3. Data computerisation.

a) Kenya. Was to be done in Forrester's offices by his functionaries. Not much thought was given to this early on.

b) Ecuador. Data was entered from the start of the

243

project by a team working round the clock on the roof of the project building.

4. Recruitment of patients. (This represented the most significant difference between the projects).

a) Kenya. Patients were recruited to the project by the Key Informant method. A team of workers would go into a village somewhere, stick up posters about the project, then ask anyone around for the name of the village headman, pastor, or other leading community members; any one of these located (the Key Informant) would be asked for the names of epileptics in his/her community; who would in their turn be surveyed by trained team members to find out if their problem was indeed epilepsy. If it was they were told of the project, asked to come to Likuru.

(It might seem lackadaisical at first sight, this method, slow to turn up patients. It certainly seemed so to Anna the one time she observed it, during her second trip to Kenya, in 1987. As she, Bennet, and the health workers he and Meaki had trained – about eight in all – sat on the grassy patch at the centre of the village, the team leader accosted a woman who happened to be passing; she in her turn pointed out a man in the usual woollen hat (sludge-green in his case, frayed at the edges) and wearing a blanket over his shoulders. This man was a village elder; he claimed to know a family in which there was an epileptic.

Bennet issued further instructions then took Anna to lunch in the local restaurant, located as such restaurants usually were at the rear of an unsalubrious butcher's shop, all bones and bloodstains. Bennet, always correctly dressed in a suit and tie, was very protective of Anna on these trips; not only did he carefully wipe the plastic chair, the plastic table, warn her not to lean on the peeling and dirty blue wall beside her, he wouldn't let her use the lavatory at the back, let alone touch any of the food on offer. 'Our stomachs are used to it,' he said, eyeing the plateful of goat stew and a maize porridge called ugali, set down in front of him. 'But yours is not.' He allowed her a cup of tea, however; to eat she had two bananas left over from her breakfast which she'd brought along. Meanwhile two of the health workers went in search of the suggested epileptic. Having failed to find him they stuck up posters about treatment for 'kifafas' all round the centre, and that, so far as this village was concerned, was that. On went Anna and Bennet and the rest to the next place. In due course, she was told later, news got about; two patients came in; when treatment had halted their seizures twenty odd patients from that village and the surrounding area, presented themselves to the study: lackadaisical or not, the method worked.)

b) Ecuador. Here the method of recruitment (and the source in Ecuador of many problems, given Aguadiente's ambitions) was a large scale epidemiological survey. It involved ninety specially trained surveyors, questioning, door to door, the entire population of two provinces of Northern Ecuador, approximately 72,000 people, across an area of 1500 square kilometres. (Many of the bright orange labels attached to the doors of every one of the 15,195 dwellings successfully surveyed were still visible when Anna got there.) The cases thus identified were assessed first by local doctors, then by neurologists. Those fulfilling certain criteria – having epilepsy of course the most essential, also not being in treatment, not being pregnant, and so on – were assigned to the intervention study and treatment.

(This method of recruitment meant all patients were identified from the start of the intervention study, as was not so in Kenya. Like the use of the rural doctors, it meant also the need for government support. Though this part of the study was a hangover, you could say, from the days of Bud Schwarz and Gomez and the WHO, and the one of least interest to Bader-Kleitz – counting patients did not obviously or speedily lead to selling drugs – it was the part of most interest to David, with his epidemiological ambitions, as also to Dr Aguadiente with his. Jacoman, too, of course, relished its medical interest; being Jacoman he relished equally the very ambition, the very size of the thing. This was why, maybe, he showed so much more interest in running things in

Ecuador than in Kenya. More seriously, in terms of the project, it was yet another example of how this pharmaceutical executive still remained, at heart, less drug company man than doctor.)

Chapter Eighteen

Anna took to visiting her sister-in-law, Sonia, much more that summer, partly, but not entirely because Nikki, maybe, had made her look at Sonia more closely. As for Sonia herself, she seemed less cautious with Anna. She sometimes, almost, looked her in the face. She gave Anna a key to her front door. 'In case of emergency,' she said.

One afternoon when Anna went round, about a month and a half after their return from Kenya, David's father was asleep in a corner, Sonia playing the piano. Hearing the music – a Bach prelude – as she came up the path to the front door, Anna had rung the bell as warning but let herself straight in. Sonia nodded at her but did not stop playing. Anna hardly knew if Sonia was glad to see her. But then she never knew; she still could not even be sure if Sonia liked her. It did not seem to matter very much. She was happy to throw herself down on Sonia's sofa and listen to her rendition of Bach – not a particularly good rendition, usually, no more than competent in fact, not always even that – precisely because Sonia made no issue of her being welcome.

Nor did Sonia seem to care about revealing her limitations as a pianist. She never so much as mentioned her skill or lack of it, let alone apologised. If she missed a note or two, she either went back and replayed them or else ploughed on, without comment; thereby making it quite clear she was playing for, attending to herself, no less than the music, with its mathematical yet human precisions attended to, retained itself.

The old man asleep in his chair, meanwhile, twitched sometimes, whimpered, like a sleeping dog. He too remained locked within his head; in his case he had no option. Anna wondered about his dreams, if they were any clearer than his waking impressions, or if Alzheimers stole your dreams also. Turning from him, regarding Sonia's dark profile intent upon the music, she thought of the Indian psychiatrist; there was no obvious reason why this room, apart from being shaded, as the ward had been shaded, should remind her of him; or that the old man or Sonia should; but still they did.

As for the room – despite its being part of Sonia's father's house, full of his furniture, his belongings, with his Kazak rugs scattered across the parquet, it had always seemed to Anna entirely Sonia's. Long, low-ceilinged, it contained nothing even half new; books, pictures, wooden surfaces, covers, curtains, rugs, were faded, subdued by age, in places definitely shabby. There was a tall turreted clock, ticking so loudly even the Bach could not quite drown it. There were bowls of flowers but few ornaments. Sonia called the friendly crowding of objects that Anna went in for 'clutter'; sometimes, seeing the calm spaces of Sonia's shelves and mantlepiece, Anna thought she might be right. One wall was books; half medical – Anna assumed they'd belonged to old Dr Kern, the father. The other half held poetry at the top, and a few hardback novels, big books on architecture at the bottom; all these were Sonia's. There were books on the most stylised architectural forms; buildings in India, Victorian houses and churches, art deco. For all the austerity of this room Sonia was not interested in plain buildings, in classical forms. She belonged to the Victorian Society, the Edwardian Society, the Thirties Society. On Saturdays, when she could get away, she went on trips, organised by these institutions; she undertook walks round Victorian or Edwardian suburbs, from Kilburn to North Oxford. After David's first marriage broke up, before he ever met Anna, Sonia used to invite him to go with her sometimes; sometimes he did go with her. But not any longer. Looking at the society programmes still lining the mantlepiece, Anna wondered if Sonia minded.

Sonia came to the end of the prelude she was working on, and went into the kitchen at the back of the room. She returned five minutes or so later with a tray of tea things and a plate of home-made biscuits. Sonia always did produce tea, whether or not it was teatime. She never asked if it was wanted. (The only complaint Anna had ever heard David make to his sister, he'd said, 'Sonia, why can't you make coffee sometimes; you know I prefer it.' But Sonia never did. And David always drank the tea provided – and almost always ate the biscuits.)

The scented steam rising from the cup of Earl Grey tea before her, still too hot to drink, Anna told Sonia about the Indian psychiatrist; about the little girl, Grace. Sonia cradled her own tea and made no comment.

As much to break the silence as anything, Anna said – irritated at hearing in herself, too, the kind of schoolgirl language Sonia's own use of it often evoked in her (Damn Sonia – not least because she'd grown to wonder if in Sonia it was a deliberate form of self-parody; whereas in herself it was not ironic at all, but an unwilling reversion to type, into which her sister-in-law pushed her – at times she even suspected that Sonia did it on purpose.) 'I suppose psychiatry isn't so bad actually, is it? I mean psychiatrists can get somewhere with some people, can't they? It's not incurable, degenerative diseases as with neurology.'

Sonia took a biscuit and nibbled on it reflectively.

'Gosh yes. That's why a psychiatrist's the only kind of doctor I'd want to be, if I was a doctor. Psychiatry has some uses. And it's not all done by pills. I should hope not.'

'Did you ever want to be a doctor?' Anna dared ask her.

'Oh yes,' said Sonia. 'Of course. That's how I started.'

Anna looked at her, her mouth open. Sonia, as usual, did not look back at her, but sipped her tea, gazing into the distance. 'To be precise,' she went on, 'I read medicine at Cambridge, for my Part One. But that was the end of it. In my third year, for Part Two, I read fine arts and

249

architecture. And afterwards I didn't go to medical school to do the pre-clinical; I didn't even apply. No. I went off and did my social work training.'

'David never told me you'd read medicine,' said Anna.

'Oh *David*,' said Sonia, pronouncing his name as in Hebrew, the accent on the last syllable, the way his mother, he said, always spoke his name. Anna had never heard Sonia do so, though, not till now. She had never seen or heard her reflect on her and David's Jewish origins in any way at all. Perhaps Sonia meant to disconcert her – for Anna was disconcerted – certainly she looked across at Anna briefly, as if to gauge the effect. Then she smiled, softening the heaviness of her features for a moment, and raised her hand in an almost elegant gesture, her bracelet catching as she did so the silver necklace lying as usual between her small, angular breasts, on her faded black t-shirt. She pronounced her brother's name again, the English way. 'David never remembers anything past yesterday,' she said. 'Besides he was young, much younger than I was. It was all over long before he left school. I doubt if he would remember. And if so I doubt if he's interested.'

'I don't imagine he thought it was any of my business,' protested Anna – why did she feel a need here to defend her husband? she wondered. As for the kindly detachment with which Sonia answered, 'No. I don't suppose he did.' It had her asking, almost crossly, 'Well then, what happened? Why didn't you go on with medicine?'

'Having been brought up surrounded by doctors, I found I didn't want to work surrounded by them as well, I suppose. No, probably not.'

'But you were a medical social worker,' ventured Anna.

'Only because it takes time to wean yourself completely,' said Sonia, not choosing to explain what exactly she meant by this. 'Anyway it wasn't for long. Not more than five years. Then Mummy got ill, someone had to nurse her. So that was that. And afterwards there was Daddy to look after.' She paused and added, 'My father never wanted me to be a doctor anyway. He wanted

David to be a doctor, but that was different, David was his son not his daughter.'

'And you didn't fight?' asked Anna.

'I did two years of medicine, didn't I?' said Sonia. 'That was a fight to start with. That was enough. And besides, I think the only reason I ever wanted to be a doctor was because Daddy didn't want me to be one. In some ways I'd rather have been a nurse. You get to know patients much better. But he wouldn't have liked that either. He wouldn't have wanted any daughter of his to be patronised by doctors.'

Anna thought for a moment, and risked it. 'Is that why you don't mind having had to nurse your parents, Sonia?'

'Don't I mind?' asked Sonia, with an ironical smile, that prevented Anna – it was obviously meant to prevent her – from pursuing the point. 'Well, at least on this ward, I can play the old piano. I wouldn't be able to in the Charing Cross hospital; or Guys; or St Thomas's. Gosh no.' She glanced at her father; he showed signs of waking up, suddenly; and more than signs of waking.

'Quick, Anna,' she said, 'help me.' This was something Anna always dreaded; it happened at Sonia's sometimes – she should be used to it by now; but she still wasn't. Sonia could manage alone, she usually had to, but with Anna's help it was easier.

Anna fetched the commode from a corner, while Sonia prepared the old man. They were in time, fortunately – they weren't always – a faint smell of disinfectant lurked within the room; walking him from armchair to commode, unbuckling his belt, easing his trousers off the withered and useless shanks, extracting his limp white organ. As the yellow stream poured from it – these days it was the old man's only vigorous-seeming function – Anna couldn't help thinking, with amazement always, that this otherwise now useless organ had engendered her husband; and Sonia too for that matter; who was, at this moment, despite the strong reek rising from between her father's legs, managing these matters as calmly, confidently, as if such intimacy between father and daughter was only to be expected. David never managed

251

these things so well with his father. Anna had observed his embarrassment; she had picked up his faint, half-ashamed disgust, also. She did not blame him – she couldn't have imagined performing such rituals for her own father, while he was dying. Sonia's matter-of factness surprised her much more. But for Sonia's sake she concealed her feelings, steadying the old man while Sonia zipped him up. Sonia, not Anna, of course, emptied the commode after.

Then Sonia made another pot of Earl Grey tea; and now, her father awake, listening, not listening, as usual, as he nibbled on a Marie biscuit, sipped from the cup that Sonia offered, it was she asked Anna questions. Since the lunch with Nikki, she had taken to showing interest in the thing – what was happening about the project; was it all up and running?

Anna groaned. 'I thought it would be. But it isn't. They keep sending letters wanting to change my part of it. And I keep writing to say they'd misunderstood entirely the information we needed to get. And besides I thought we'd agreed all this in Quito.'

'And had you, Anna?' asked Sonia.

'Not according to the Ecuadorians,' said Anna. 'Not only that, there seem to be different people running my bit of the project, not the ones I dealt with at all. Carter is trying to find out what's going on, what's happened to the people I worked with; but he hasn't so far. And mean-time, he says, even if I think it's all cuckoo could I please make some amendments, so they won't think I'm over-riding them completely. Which is rich, actually, coming from him. I've written three letters so far, sent three revised questionnaires, with changes in. I have to keep running after the psychologist, Vittoria, to make sure the Spanish is right, and now she's getting fed up, she says, smugly, all the psychology was agreed in Quito, so why wasn't the anthropology? And on top of that, I'm having to work out the codings for the answers to the questions, for statistical purposes, that's something else we should have done in Quito, and never had time to, and I keep sending versions of these out, and they keep ignoring them, because they are only interested in rewriting the questions. Which doesn't mean to say that in due course they won't start querying the codings too, and I'll have to start on those all over. In fact I almost certainly will have to. Actually, Sonia, it's driving me crazy.'

'What does David say?' asked Sonia.

'He's still having hassles of his own, over entry criteria and so on, so he's not the least sympathetic. He says I took the job on and I just have to get on with it, same as him. Which is true. But at least he has assistants, and knows just what he's doing. After Kenya, I began to think I knew a bit about it. But now I'm not so sure I have a clue. And when I ring Jacoman to ask for help, he just says, if I reach him, I often don't, "You're doing fine, Anna, if you want help on the details, just ask your husband.'''

All this came out in a rush. Perhaps it was at that point Anna realised how much the matter was getting her down. Not least because between Jacoman and the Ecuadorians, she never could be sure of the ground on which she was standing. Hearing the plaintive tone in her voice, she was not surprised when Sonia asked drily, sounding just like her brother, 'Do you wish you hadn't taken it all on then?'

'Yes,' cried Anna. And then, thinking of Kenya; and even of Cotapaxi (but no, it wasn't Cotopaxi, the other volcano), pink-tinged, at dawn, 'No, Sonia, no, not really. No, of course not. And I knew it wouldn't be easy. But I didn't expect so much politics, so much sheer human obstreperousness. I'm not very good at playing politics; it all seems so unnecessary – the Kenyans aren't like that. And that's the other problem, the whole point is that we can compare the two places; and the more the Ecuadorians change things, the harder it makes it.'

'Who does like being used as a number to compare with or set against another number? *I* wouldn't like it,' Sonia said. 'It was one of the quarrels I had with medicine, as a matter of fact. All that scientific impersonalisation. I prefer the personal, I prefer particulars myself, I really do,' she said, getting up at that moment and going to

253

stroke her father's head; he was beginning to whimper. When he sighed and quietened, she sat on the sofa by his wheelchair, holding his hand. 'Where's Sonia?' said the old man, turning his head from side to side. 'Where's Sonia?' It was almost all he ever said these days. Except, occasionally, 'Who is Sonia?' And even more occasionally, 'Where's David?'

'Sonia's here, Daddy' she replied, continuing to stroke him. 'Sonia's here.' 'Where's Sonia, where's Sonia?' he kept on insisting. Sonia did not seem to mind his denials. She smiled even. She shook her head at him, and then shook her head at Anna.

'You needn't defend science to me, Anna. I know the general is how things advance; evidence against anecdote and all that. But don't you give it to me, too. Spare me.'

Anna to her own surprise had been about to give it to her, taking for once the side of her husband (to him, of course, she took Sonia's). She laughed instead. 'William Blake said something about science, like art, having to stick to particulars. But the Ecuadorians aren't on your side. They love science. What they object to is having their work compared with that of Africans. It's that simple.'

'Do the Kenyans mind being compared with Ecuadorians?' asked Sonia.

'Not as far as I can see,' said Anna. 'But the Kenyans are different.'

'Perhaps they're just more used to being nice to Westerners,' said Sonia.

'Jacoman always says it's because Kenyans recognise a red postbox when they see one. All the same they're not the least subservient. It's not a bit like that. Not a bit.'

'Some would believe you,' said Sonia, her scepticism aimed at Anna's left ear, approximately.

'Now you're maligning them, Sonia, aren't you?'

'Maybe I am,' said Sonia, knitting her thick eyebrows. She not only was a plain woman; at this moment she looked almost ugly. 'But how should I know anything? I'm just a stay-at-home daughter and pianist. I know nothing about these things, nothing. Truth to tell, Anna dear, I jolly well don't want to. It reminds me of a world out there I'm not part of. That I hardly want to be part of, any longer. That I don't know how to be part of.'

She smiled as she finished speaking, though at her father, not Anna. Flat, unemotional as her voice had been, Anna had never before heard Sonia talk so personally. Her desires, her motivations, deep, mysterious, were seemingly right outside Anna's own, unlike David's, she thought, for all that he kept insisting he was different from his wife. (For instance, though he did not expect to be happy, he made it clear he wanted to be; whereas with Sonia it was not a question of being happy or not. Anna did not know if Sonia was happy – the point was that happiness did not seem to be an issue.)

Sonia was unlike her brother in another way also. Rare as it was she did not seem to resent having such a confidence drawn from her. Indeed she behaved as if Anna had not drawn it from her; Sonia had simply stated her position, quite neutrally, for reasons of her own. If she had, thereby, let Anna nearer her than before, what of that? Her almost fond, if hasty, not to say awkward peck on Anna's cheek as they said goodbye was that of a tentative sister.

'Have you heard from your friend, what was her name – Nikki?' she asked, as Anna bent over her father-in-law to kiss him goodbye, also. (She made a point of doing this, for all she disliked the grating of his moustache against her cheek. She did not know if it pleased him; he raised his face to her sometimes, sometimes jerked it away; but she did not do it to please him. She did it to please David and his sister.)

'Not lately,' Anna said, turning to the door; glancing as she did so with relief, almost with recognition, at the right-hand end of the mantlepiece where stood the room's one significant ornament, a terracotta pot. Nikki had recognised this as Indian – Hopi to be precise. Today, its very solidity, its decisive curvilinear patterns, black and dark terracotta, against a lighter terracotta base, seemed as unfathomable, as intractable, yet at the same time as unambiguously of itself, as Sonia.

You'd have thought that Nikki had heard them talking; next day she rang Anna. She too asked how Anna's project was going. She too responded as Sonia had, and David, but much more brutally, as usual. Anna had taken it all on willingly. She just had to get on with it. People were obstreperous, if she'd ever worked in organisations she'd know it. Part of your job always, was not just doing the job but managing human relations, sorting out jealousies. And talking of jealousies, what did David think about Anna's seeming infatuation with Jacoman?

Anna, first taken aback by this, then furious, said nothing for a minute. Deciding finally to ignore what Nikki had said, she replied simply, 'Thank you, Nikki, Thank you very *much* for that little seminar in human behaviour. And just what's your experience?'

But of course Nikki had an answer, as usual. 'Those places I teach in, what makes you think they're any different? Academic institutions, they're all cut-throat, a hotbed; everyone out to trash everyone. Wasn't it you that told me Franklin was the pits? Well, there you are. What's so different about the Ecuadorians? The education of Anna, you could call it. Hang on in there, you ain't seen nothing yet. And at the end of it all you'll be a much better writer – I promise.'

Anna had nothing to say to this; except, irritably, 'How you go on, Nikki.' Only to be disarmed by a great peal of laughter from her friend. 'I always was a loudmouth, don't tell me you took till now to notice? How's your sister-in-law, Sonia?' she asked as she rang off. 'Give her my love or something, won't you?'

Chapter Nineteen

Jacoman went back to Ecuador in September 1986; he went, he thought, to check the preliminary pilot studies, to sort out any final details; but mainly just to give the scheme the go ahead.

It did not turn out like that. Jacoman told Anna about it quite cheerfully on his return. Home in Basel, Giselle was being more reasonable than sometimes, and at work he'd been given a department of ten – slaves he called them – including a new secretary; she wasn't beautiful, unlike the last. 'So what,' he said, 'I don't have time to sleep with her. So what?'

But in Ecuador – 'Would you believe it, Anna,' he told her. 'Would you believe it, they were still arguing, just the same things as in April. You and David would have thought you'd never been away, if you'd come, just as well you didn't, no matter how much I like the company of you and your dear husband, I'd have hated to have had to deal with *you* in those circumstances. As for David he'd have withdrawn his whole backing; as I wanted to, Anna, dear, as I wanted to. Because there was Navarro with his handbag and Watertooth with his flipcharts running around everywhere,' (after Anna translated Aguadiente's name, Jacoman always referred to him as that; once, in Anna's hearing he called him Watertooth to his face – Aguadiente just looked bemused; did not appear to realise Jacoman was referring to him). 'And would they get to the nitty-gritty? No, they would not.

'And I have to tell you, Anna, your sociology lot was

257

the worst. Watertooth had suffered a whole lot more internal torment since you left, in the course of which his mistress, Dolores, got the push; and with her went Teodoro, because he was a cousin of Dolores and the way things were any cousin of Dolores was Watertooth's enemy for life. He told Piet he never wanted her name mentioned. Talk about cognitive dissonance, Anna, hearing about Watertooth's emotional problems when I'm trying to get agreement on six questionnaires and a whole medical protocol, that makes for cognitive dissonance in me, I tell you. Particularly when he and Naranjo are trying to sabotage you at the same time. There's the two new anthropologists, also, of course, they have to have their dime's worth. And I get all this stuff from all of them, even the ones who never met you, about how much they liked you really, but how autocratic you were, and how of course you hadn't spoken enough Spanish, and how shallow the questions were and so forth. And then Watertooth comes back with the medical questionnaire and he's changed that right the way through as well. And when I protest another guy gets up and starts shouting – that's the guy wants the epidemiological statistics done in Ecuador so he can rake in the fee – didn't David tell you about that extra little hassle, Anna? – and what he shouts – in English, in an American accent – is "Who are you foreigners to come and do medicine, tell us where to put computers, in our country? You are an imperialist. The national language of Ecuador is Spanish. I'm going to talk Spanish." So he proceeds to; but Meyersdorf doesn't translate and everyone else looks uninterested, I guess he didn't say anything that important. As for me, a Jewish Canadian, working for a Swiss company, I'm tickled pink as usual to be called an imperialist. I get up and say so. And then I say, OK, in their eyes I'm an imperialist, and imperialists are big bosses aren't they; well I have to play big boss now, this project is bigger than all of us; if anyone wants nothing more to do with it, let him walk out now this minute, I won't hold it against him. And of course no one does walk out, even the statistician, they can't afford to.

And no, Anna, don't look at me like that, OK I'm playing economic bully, but it's not my fault their country is worth shit, that they need me *and* you and David, Anna, to help them pull themselves up by their medical and economic bootstraps; this is their big chance; it's my big chance, your big chance, Anna. Don't let's any of us blow it.'

'And did you say all that to them?' enquired Anna sweetly.

'Not in so many words,' returned Jacoman, with a look that was not shamed exactly, there was a defiant smile, lurking, but a look that wanted her to like him; at this moment she didn't know if she liked him or not.

'What I did do was tell them why I was in this project really; what it meant to me. I told them about the woman in Pakistan; I think I told you about her, Anna? Didn't I? About the woman who tripped and fell in the well, had epilepsy after? About her devoted husband?'

Anna nodded. But Jacoman launched into the story once more, regardless. 'The two were living in his mother's house, you remember, he and his mother took his wife off to a clinic in Karachi, which started to treat her with a charming cocktail of valproate, carbemazepine, phenobarbitone. Incredible. Incredible. And of course in the end she was doped out of her head, she couldn't add beans, she was sent to the store to buy sugar, she would lose her way. Or if she got there she'd forget what she'd come to buy, or they'd short-change her and so on. She'd lost all her short-term memory that was the point, and though she could cook a bit now, she didn't have fits any longer and fall on the fire, she was totally useless because she couldn't remember how to do it. And she was completely miserable, but her mother-in-law and her husband were happy because she wasn't shaming them any longer, she wasn't having fits.

'And if you want to know, I told them, just as I told you, Anna dear, that that's why I was doing this project, why we were all doing this project to prevent that kind of thing happening. To prevent people having to choose between having seizures all the time or, if they can afford

it, being doped out of their heads. Till they can't add
beans. Or cook a pot of rice or corn cobs. And don't think
it doesn't happen in Ecuador, because it does, you've seen
it, if you blow this, Watertooth, the lot of you, it's not just
you fucking up your own chance of a lifetime, you're
fucking up all those poor buggers' chances also.

'I started shouting at this point. I said I'd had enough
of reaching agreement one day and finding no one agreed
with what had been arrived at the next. Either they took
the questionnaires as agreed, back in April, over the
summer, here in Quito, this month, September, either
they took them, or that was the end of it, the money was
being withdrawn. No project.

'So of course they caved in; they had to. And we all
parted good friends, or seemed to. Not least when they
asked how many jeeps they'd be allowed and expected me
to argue, I pulled the rug out from under them by saying,
"That's up to you." They're all smiles over that, wouldn't
you know it. And the next thing I hear, back in Basel,
Navarro's sent Jacqui Sylvestre up to San Raphael to
rent this house for the project team to live in, and
Watertooth's out buying double beds for all the bedrooms, you can imagine what he thinks he'll get up to,
what he doesn't know, poor bugger, is he won't have the
energy left for fucking once this thing gets going. But
never mind all that, it's nothing. The point is, Anna,
we're up and running; almost.'

That was Jacoman's version of events. Piet's was somewhat different. For Piet not only knew what it was like to
come under fire from Jacoman, he too came from a small
country. He could understand Ecuadorian feelings better
than Jacoman, also, unusually for a Dutchman – he
never would explain why, even a Dutchman, he said, had
a right to his secrets – he spoke good Spanish.

Jacoman derided Piet's mild Dutch scepticism, somewhat; he called it lack of drive. At the same time he found
it useful. David found it useful – as Jacoman's marriage
deteriorated, he used Piet as surrogate increasingly in
discussions with David. Piet liked details for a start,

which Jacoman never did. Someone had to nail down the details. It suited David, moreover, not to have to assign one of his own over-worked research assistants to the job.

Everyone liked Piet; he threatened no one. Because of this he was, of course, despised by some people. Hicks, known as Hicks the axeman, Taylor's successor, was to call Piet 'a piece of grit in my shoe'; the company hierarchy in Ecuador also despised him. Yet this, too, had its uses. The underestimate of Piet's abilities meant he got given information, almost in passing, he never would have been given if rated more highly. It also meant that the medical team in Ecuador trusted him as they would not have done had he been seen to be hand-in-glove with Navarro, like Jacoman.

In Piet's view, the main problem during that last trip to Ecuador before the project started was Jacoman himself; everyone hated him except for Jacqui Sylvestre, for whom Jacoman had produced a leather jacket from a duty free shop somewhere. Jacqui Sylvestre would shit his pants if Jacoman asked him to, Piet said. (Piet, when goaded, could and did put things coarsely, but at the same time so carefully, so pedantically, in his flat Dutch voice, you thought you must be mishearing; until he smiled. Piet had one broken tooth; it made his smile as wicked as a child's, and as disarming. In his last year in Basel it drove Jacoman insane; but then in his last days in Basel almost everything and everyone drove Jacoman insane.)

At the same time, Piet said, there was a lot of infighting; infighting in the local company, for one thing. (Jacqui Sylvestre hated Navarro, called him a snake, while Navarro despised and overworked Sylvestre.) Infighting between the company and the neurologists, for another.

Aguadiente, in particular, tried to subvert Piet to his side, and that of the other neurologists. He called Piet his friend, more than his friend, his companero, fellow-sufferer at the hands of Jacoman, and so forth. He tried to get him drunk; in vain; drink was not Piet's problem, and never had been – he did say that this experience drove him nearer it than anything had previously.

A month after the trip with Jacoman, Piet returned to Ecuador; this time he went straight to San Raphael to observe the process of setting up the project. On the night before he left, ten days later, there was a party, its nominal purpose to say farewell to him – Jacqui, who, of course, had to pick up the bill was not invited. All the local rural doctors, the ones to take part in the study, were invited. So were some of the more presentable of the surveyors involved in the epidemiological project. Naranjo played his guitar and cuddled his fat girlfriend, called Carmen, a rural doctor with a ribbon in her hair. Everyone who had girlfriends cuddled them. The girl-friends without boyfriends tried to cuddle Piet; up to a point he could see they were teasing him, nevertheless as the evening went on and everyone grew drunker, he had to explain ever more loudly and insistently that he was a happily married man with two small children – he even got out his wallet at one point and handed round photographs of his wife and children. Everyone crowded round then; the photographs were passed from hand to hand, getting covered in thumbprints. Soon the entire gathering had viewed Piet's Dutch wife and children, soon everyone was exclaiming 'guapas' (that is how pretty the girls were) also how fair their hair was. (Piet was losing his hair so fast, its blondness was much less obvious.)

Piet's family arrived in Aguadiente's hands eventually. Very drunk by now, he stared at them at length. 'How beautiful is your wife,' he told Piet in his most orotund Spanish. 'You are so fortunate, Piet, to have a beautiful blonde wife. A happy family life is of all things the most blessed' – he wiped away tears here; Piet was not embarrassed the way David would have been, or cynical, like Jacoman. Certainly he did not feel the least sorry for him, the way Anna might have done, despite herself – she never did manage to dislike Aguadiente even at his most tiresome. He just stared at Aguadiente, dispassionately, stolidly you might say. He did not remind him – assuming he thought of it – that his present domestic problems were most likely his own doing; had at least partly, in Aguadiente's own account, come in a package called Dolores.

'More blessed still it is to have a son,' Aguadiente continued. 'What a fine boy your son is, Piet. But at least I too have a son, in that way I am blessed also. My son, Tristano, he is the light, he is the greatest joy of my life.' Here, he extracted his wallet in his turn; having scattered this way and that (Piet, reminded of Jacoman, almost laughed out loud) a variety of – used tickets was it? – folded pieces of paper seemingly covered in figures, a credit card, his driving licence, two well-thumbed letters, folded up very small, even tattered, he succeeded in fetching out a photograph of a boy of nine or so; a miniature version of himself, he looked to Piet, apart from the lack of spectacles and pock marks. The boy's hair was slicked down. He was dressed in a suit and bow tie as if for some formal occasion. '*Mi hijo*; my son,' said Aguadiente, proudly. And breaking into tears again he told Piet how little he saw of his son these days; though he did quite often look after his daughters, his wife kept his son away, simply, he believed, to spite him.

Before long, still a little tearful, he was telling Piet how sexually frustrated he was; also, he hadn't had a woman in four months, not since Dolores. He was almost thinking of going back to his wife, for that reason.

Piet thought, but did not say, that in this case Aguadiente too would be restored to the most blessed of things a happy family life. To the light of his life, his son, besides. So why didn't he? But instead, Aguadiente, grown suddenly much more cheerful, to the extent of teasing Piet for his Castilian accent – wherever Piet had learned his Spanish it had not been Latin America – went off and pursued boyfriendless girls, one after another. If they'd been happy to suggest cuddling Piet, none were so eager to cuddle the lonely but by now tottering Aguadiente. He ended up waltzing alone, precariously, to the strains of Edith Piaf on cassette, to which he sang along loudly, missing the tune altogether, but drowning Naranjo's guitar as he did so.

Anna, for whom a similar party was held upon her own departure, eight months later – Aguadiente got drunk at that party also; he sang a doleful song, its refrain 'Anna Maria, Anna *Maria*' over and over, looking at her sadly – could imagine the scene. She could imagine that big, low, shabby room with its wooden floors and wooden benches, its wide fireplace, more often than not empty since any fire in it smouldered rather than burnt.

Above it even then would have been pinned, all the way along the wall, Aguadiente's interminable rotas, his elaborate charts and indecipherable diagrams, in different coloured pencils. She could see and smell the thickness of the air – to a man, to a woman the Ecuadorians smoked – she could see the counter that divided this part of the room from the narrow dining area at the back with its big wooden table, at which she herself had sat so many evenings, amid too rapid Spanish, eating, without enthusiasm rice, avocado and chilli. Aguadiente's cassette recorder sat on that counter always; if it was not belting out Latin American music, it was always playing Edith Piaf. She only had to taste chilli on her tongue, to hear La Vie en Rose – she only had to imagine them all sitting round the table, to see the door to the filthy kitchen open, to see the equally filthy, fat, but very amiable cook, Blanquita, emerge from it wearing her poncho, flashing her gold teeth as she intoned, on this evening presumably as on all others, *'Buenas noches, a todos'*; followed, most evenings, by her small fat son, also wrapped in his poncho, intoning in exactly the same singsong, *'Buenas noches, a todos'*.

The party grew livelier after Blanquita's departure. Edith Piaf replaced by Latin rock and salsa, the centre of the room filled with jiving figures, Piet sat by what there was of a fire, talking to the sociologist, Lastenia, who had just arrived in the project; 'That's a sensible woman, Anna,' he told her solemnly. 'She wasn't dancing with anyone.' About them swayed and bent the lonely figure of Aguadiente, crying no longer, grinning, jerking his head to the music. But when Piet came to say goodbye, he started weeping again; he threw his arms round Piet, he said Piet was his only friend. Piet inquired, mildly, 'Why do you have such a chip on your shoulder, Virgilio?' At which Aguadiente cried the harder; how did Piet know he had a chip on his shoulder? he asked him. This really proved that Piet was his only friend.

(Piet said he wished he, too, was drunk, at this point; but to get drunk he would have had to like the taste of the alcohol in question – all that was on offer was coke and aniseed, a fearsome mixture.)

'Don't be fooled, Anna, by Piet's Dutch accent, by that quiet, seeming understatement,' said David, after Piet, having told the Kerns all this, departed. 'Piet exaggerates a great deal; he's not a one hundred per cent reliable witness.'

'Does it matter?' asked Anna. 'Don't you think what people think went on is at least as significant in some ways as what actually did go on? *And* more interesting sometimes.'

'But not more truthful,' said David.

'Oh yes more truthful sometimes; at least more useful. Don't you know that from taking medical histories, David?' she asked him.

'Not exactly,' replied David. He did not look at her as he spoke. 'I'm working,' he added. 'Could we continue this discussion some other time?'

What was quite certain was that there was a project house now, in Ecuador; there were surveyors, there were neurologists, there were rural doctors, psychologists, a sociologist. In Kenya, meanwhile, Bennet was interviewing and training healthworkers and interviewers, and drawing up timetables. In Pakistan and Turkey they were writing questionnaires, planning surveys (not that either David or Anna knew much about those; Jacoman would turn up now and then and demand validations or statistical tables; he would produce plans to send them both to Karachi or Ankara. But nothing ever came of it. The Kerns had virtually nothing to do with these projects till they met the protaganists at Kanterberg.)

'Funny old business we're in, Anna,' said Jacoman, around Christmas. 'Dye manufacturers. Chemical synthesisers. Brewers. Turned dream-makers, pill-makers, an unholy alliance. You mean you didn't know about the brewers? Sure it was a strange story, and you'd better not tell the Pakistanis. The thing was that in 1945, they wanted to mass manufacture penicillin but didn't have the facilities; the existing companies couldn't do it, they were growing the stuff on saucers. Then someone had this bright idea, 'What about the brewers? They've got the means for large-scale fermentation.' So in came Distillers and Fisons and God knows who else. Like I said, don't tell the Pakistanis. And now there's us, hand-in-glove also, and look what we're doing, you, Anna, David, me, Watertooth, Meaki, the lot of them, all over. We've got this scheme going at last, we're dream-makers like anyone else, setting snakes to climb ladders.' (Anna, trying to visualise this phenomenon, did not have the heart to tell Jacoman that the snakes were what the players fell down; *they* didn't climb the ladders, the players did. And who knows who would be climbing in the end, who falling.) 'In other words we're up and running.'

BOOK 2
Up and Running

Chapter One

Anna Kern's diary. March 1991

Chronology; it's a problem. I mean things happen, days pass, weeks pass, years pass, more things happen; but it isn't simple. And I think, increasingly, and perversely, it's not a simple matter, say, of date order; that date order and chronology are by no means always the same thing.

Because so many things happen, so many things bearing on each other, affecting each other, but which affects what, what leads to this and what to that, that's the problem. These deep thoughts are prompted, now that the project's over, by my attempts to sort out on paper what happened exactly, and when. Quite simple things, actually, like when Jacoman arrived at the company, when Taylor gave him a list with epilepsy at the bottom, when he met Gomez, when he rang David and so forth. It's not that you can't get those things right; but it's only one part of the picture. And though each one of these events may be links in one big chain, it doesn't stop there, the affair is not so linear and not nearly so simple. Each one is also a link in a whole series of chains leading every which way; macrocosmic chains, microcosmic likewise. There are different chronologies co-existing, also; Kenyan ones, Ecuadorian ones; commercial chronologies, political ones, private chronologies (our marriage, Jacoman's, David's father dying); so on and so forth. In the course of everything the eighties have shaded into the nineties; boom into recession; the brute entrepreneur into the new man; the 'magic of the marketplace' (was that Reagan or Thatcher – I don't remember, does it matter?) into the hardheaded responsibilities of what our pharmaceutical mentors call the Social Market. Then of course there's the demise of Communism. Can I leave that out? It has all, except perhaps the last, a bearing on the activities of Dr Hicks the axeman, for instance; what brought him in, the sad end of our affairs, wasn't just Jacoman overreaching himself was it? It was part of it, obviously. Yet the chronology – the chain of cause and effect – inasmuch as chronology is, at least implicitly, a chain of cause and effect – was fed not only by the wider world but also the narrower one; by the state of the Jacoman's marriage not least; by the advent of Nikki; by Carter's passionate desire to get down to California in due course, which wasn't simply the result of the earthquake in San Francisco, though that figured (as it did in my waning friendship with Nikki; because she rang Sonia then, not me, to say she wasn't one of the people crushed to death on the freeway).

Of course, if not easy, it's easier, to describe the beginning of the story rather than the middle or the end of it. Particularly from my standpoint. People – by people I suppose I mean Jacoman, mainly – can and do describe to me the stages that led to the beginning. I just take it down; I wasn't involved. But later, once I was, and particularly once the thing was up and running, they expect me to know, to be a party to what happened. But I wasn't. I wasn't there for the most part, and nothing much seemed to be happening my end; or rather I didn't see much of it. In particular I didn't see anything of Jacoman's flirtations with the Locks, expensive as they were, I only saw the result of them. Over those two years the project was running, before the Kanterberg meeting, the only times I plugged into it were during Jacoman's visits to us, on the one hand, during the trips to Kenya and Ecuador on the other; but those times were mere snapshots and what's more, in the case of Kenya and Ecuador, distorted by my presence (and the arrival and departure of others). Subjectivism, the fact you see some bits and not others, distorts chronology in a real sense; because no matter how dispassionate you try to be, how hard you try to distance yourself from your own centre, feel the existence and the labour of others, events you observe have weight like no others; this happened to me; and this did not. Thinking my way round it even helps me understand better David's objections to working with people with an emotional connection to epilepsy – to see how anything which stops you dissociating yourself may distort your judgment. (In my case, of course, Ben's history of epilepsy most likely skewed my perceptions still further.) And of course, I have to expect my informants' pictures, too, to be unbalanced; for most, the story of the project wasn't the politics in Basel, it was the work they were doing on the ground, of which I saw much more than David or Jacoman, but not nearly enough.

In late April 1987, the year the project was up and running, as Jacoman put it, Anna made a second trip to Kenya with her husband and Vittoria, to check on how the work was going; in June, with her husband and Jacoman, she made a second trip to Ecuador for the same purpose; this was just as well, considering what Aguadiente had or rather hadn't been up to. The Kenyan project, on the other hand, was going more or less to plan. In each case Anna stayed on in the country after the others had gone, to do what was grandly called field work; less grandly, she went round visiting patients. In Kenya, meantime, she stayed in a large and gloomy hotel in Likuru; in Ecuador she lived in the project house at San Raphael, along with Lastenia, Aguadiente, Jacqui Sylvestre, and an ever changing assortment of the psychologists and neurologists who took it in turns to gather project data.

Apart from a social science conference just outside Barcelona, that was it, that was the project for her, for that whole year; if you did not count the friendship with

271

Jacoman, that is, her many conversations with him (of the fact that around January '87, he mentioned meeting the Locks, quite by chance, at a conference in the Maldives, she thought nothing; except perhaps; good luck to him). In betweenwhiles, apart from the sheer intellectual excitement of the – for her – new theoretical material she was reading, her life went on as ever. It seemed no time at all since David had first met Dr Jacoman in September '85. She and David had been married more than two years now, but even that seemed no time.

Indeed, often, it seemed to her that the only real gauge of its passing was, not the things they'd done, the places they'd been to; it was Anna's son, David's stepson; Benjamin; the changes in whom she watched with the more disquiet because of the slight added risk at puberty, of which the GP had warned her, of his seizures recurring. Would she have noticed, worried less, she wondered, if she wasn't surrounded by epilepsy these days, also? Being so involved with the disease was in those respects a mixed blessing; as David could, would have told her, had he but known.

(She almost did tell him about Ben at least once; it was after finding a scientific paper which claimed that for epileptics and their families the worst thing of all was not the seizures themselves, but the fear of having them. Recognising her own experience, precisely, she had given David the gist of it, then added; 'But of course that must be right. I know it is.' When he replied: 'But how can you know, Anna? You can't afford to assume any such thing, not until you've got the figures to prove it,' she'd wanted to scream out, 'What have figures got to do with it?' And then to tell him the whole story. But as usual did not; what better proof would he have that in such matters involvement distorted your judgment? And, besides, as time went on, the lie, or rather the concealment, ranked so much larger in her head, the effects of disclosure seemed all the more uncertain. Not only Anna's guilt grew, concerning the matter, also her fear – her husband did not forgive easily, judging by the tone in which, very rarely, he mentioned his first wife.)

As for Benjamin; how he had grown even that first year. By the end of the second he was as tall as David. His voice which in 1985 had still swung between registers, to his great embarrassment, by 1986, had broken entirely. By 1987, he was two inches taller than David. Anna viewed these changes in her previously slight, smooth-skinned son with trepidation and amazement. This was a man she'd bred; or a man potentially; but, for the moment, his unfamiliar deep voice, his widening shoulders, his height, his added hairiness (one day she noticed, with the same sense of shock as a gardener might observe an onion coming up where he'd previously planted delphiniums, hairs on his chest); all this made him seem not less vulnerable but more so. Partly because of the GP's warning of course. But not entirely.

Ben's disaffections with the changes in him, if any, turned mainly, to Anna's distress towards his relations with his stepfather, her husband; to David's reluctance, after all Ben's hopes, to be a substitute father for him – or to any child, Anna could not help beginning to think sometimes, ruefully. Was it in 1987 – or not till 1988? that David stopped mentioning the matter, if not altogether, less and less?

The fact that till the summer of 1987, after Ben had left boarding-school to do his 'A' levels at school in London, these dissensions only took place in the school holidays, did not make things any easier; far from it. The day he came home the arguments would start up as if they'd never been discontinued. Anna began to wish she hadn't listened to Ben's pleas to go to day school. If it was like this just in the holidays, how would it be when he lived at home all the time?

Not that his confrontation with David wasn't inevitable, she supposed. Ben saw less and less of his own father, and had liked David from the start. Though he did not quite say so, she suspected he liked him better in many ways than he did his real father. Once, just after David and Anna married – he was joking but not entirely – he told David he was thinking of calling him Dad. Maybe it was the look on David's face stopped him

273

repeating the joke if it was one; let alone carrying out his threat. But why was it such a threat to David? Anna wondered. Was it something to do with his own father's illness, the attenuation of that relationship, if it was an attenuation; she did not know how it had been before his father became ill – she asked Sonia once or twice, but Sonia always sidestepped her questions. She would have liked him to play father to Ben; not least because she too preferred him to Ben's real father; not least because of Ben's epilepsy – increasingly she wished she could tell David about that. In the end, circumstances being what they were, she had to settle for his treating Ben more like a younger brother, the much younger brother he'd never had; as he treated Jacoman, she realised, like the near-in-age brother he'd never had.

Ben had seemed to accept this in the beginning. But as time went on, he seemed less and less willing to. Why else did he keep goading David, forcing Anna to nego-tiate between her son and her husband? At times it felt more like negotiating between two sons. 'Stop treating me like Ben,' David would tell her angrily, when he noticed. Anna wanted to respond, nearly did respond, though it was only a half-way fair judgment, 'Then stop behaving like Ben.' But nor could she tell Ben to stop challenging his stepfather in these ways, because she was not sure Ben realised he did so. It could be his hanging around David at inconvenient moments, asking interminable questions about medicine, for instance, was because he was genuinely thinking of medicine as a career, that he genuinely wanted David's advice on the matter. (But if so, why did he tell funny – he thought they were funny – stories against doctors at every meal-time, just about? Which David listened to in silence.)

Yet David could handle such goading more easily than he could handle the rest; in the summer holidays of 1986, Ben, his GCSEs due the following year, started invading his stepfather's room, leaving his schoolwork all over David's desk, using the telephone in David's room when he was in there; and so on. David, tight-lipped, never said anything to Benjamin. He projected his rage on to Anna;

a fact Ben observed after a while and, in his turn, exploited.

'David,' said Anna urgently, after one explosion, which she knew for certain Ben had overheard, 'you're playing Ben's game, don't let him. Tell him, if you got complaints; don't tell me.'

'It's your job to control him,' said David. 'He's your son, not mine.'

'He's your stepson, David.'

'You don't behave as if he is, you're very proprietorial. He's your son that's the end of it.'

'You mean you think we shut you out?' David never liked such direct statements. 'Just look at yourself, Anna,' was all he responded, for now. But next time David came in to find Ben's books all over his desk, Ben on the telephone to one of his schoolfriends, he marched down to Anna in the kitchen and they had a shouting match, almost the first ever. Or rather Anna had a shouting match – David's fury erupted in vicious whispers. 'What would you say if it was your own child?' she asked him. 'Who says I want my own child?' he hissed at her, to her dismay. To add to such injury she was waylaid upstairs by her son asking anxiously, 'You had a row, Mum?' He did not ask what he feared, what she knew he was fearing; if this might precipitate breakup, as with his father. Still less could either of them mention their fear that what had followed that first breakup, a seizure, might as easily follow a second. Still too upset, too angry, to know how to reassure him, she said; 'It would help if you didn't leave your stuff all over David's room. If you didn't just march in there and use his telephone.'

Ben looked both surprised and injured. 'David doesn't mind. He'd say so if he minded,' he protested. In spite of the surprise, Anna suspected him of being disingenuous; like many children of divorced parents, Ben knew more about adults than most. 'Why don't you ask him if he minds then?' she challenged him. Ben looked shifty. 'If I had a decent desk in my room,' he muttered. 'If I'm going to do my "A" Levels from home, I'm going to have to have a decent desk . . .' In her agitated state, she took the bait, let herself be sucked before she knew it into an argument about the desk in his room, which he'd chosen, which David had generously paid for. When what Ben really wanted was not a desk but a father, what he was really trying to do was provoke David into shouting not at her, but at him. A losing battle, she knew it and maybe he did, as they bickered about furniture and what was the appropriate gear for school; while all the time, she could not forget it, David's own father sank further into oblivion, only a few streets off.

Ben was terrified of David's father, Sonia had once told Anna; how did she know? Anna wondered. Ben had never said so to her or Sonia. But Ben liked Sonia, he always had; and Sonia seemed to like Ben. When she could get away, she'd arrange to meet him sometimes, and feed him ice-cream and coffee, or even take him to the cinema, or to hear music; she'd started doing so soon after Anna and David got married, in case his nose, she said, was out of joint (or was it hers, Anna wondered?). But still Ben didn't go near her house if he could help it; he'd only once ever, been to Sonia's Sunday lunches. Left to herself Anna would have made him come. But Sonia herself insisted that she didn't.

'Maybe he thinks that one day David might end up like Daddy,' she said. Anna looked at her in terror and amazement. And wondered, not for the first time if Ben had told Sonia about his epilepsy; the way Sonia looked sometimes, she thought he might.

During Anna's stay up on the Altiplano, they never left San Raphael later than 6 a.m. The draggle of people on foot that they passed then, most mornings, just outside the town, remained for Anna her abiding image of that country.

At that hour, at 12,000 feet, the mist was down almost always; it was almost always raining. The people, in twos or threes, but silent, barely bothering to glance at the truck as it passed, were agricultural workers on their way to the haciendas. They carried spades, hoes, mattocks, other agricultural implements over their shoulders; they were wrapped in ponchos to keep out the wet and cold, wore hats, woollen or more often trilby hats, pulled down over heads bent against the weather, as their shoulders were stooped against the implements they carried. Their doggedness could have been of any age, any place; man against unfriendly elements, man against unremitting poverty, as in a picture by Breughel, perhaps, or in the small carving Anna remembered from a church at Wirksworth in Derbyshire, of a twelfth-century miner with a mattock on his back, bent, seemingly, as these men and women were bent, not by the weight of their tools, merely, but by the weight of the whole world.

At the same time it was not just any time, any place; it was here, now, this misty, drizzling June morning. It was an endurance, what's more, of not just any element, just any grief, but of the particular elements, the particular burdens past and present of this high place. The Incas had been there, for instance, then the Spanish conquistas and the Inquisition, then the governors in Lima; later there were the governors in Quito, the hacienda owners, even the business syndicates from Guayaquil – all of them augmenting in some way or other the centuries old, inescapable '*pena y suffrimiento*' of people who expected no different; who expected indeed nothing, certainly not from teams of doctors and sociologists; people whose *pena*, whose trials and triumphs alike, were sent by God, a Catholic God, what's more, with Andean annotations, a very niggardly God, heavy-handed with the *pena* and *suffrimiento*, not so generous with the cash, the kudos, the triumphs.

If '*pena y suffrimiento*' was thought the most likely cause of epilepsy in this place (in anthropology-speak the most frequent 'Explanatory Model') you couldn't blame them, thought Anna, seeing the sad procession every morning. As for her friend and colleague Lastenia, not only was she a member of Aguadiente's Marxist-Leninist group, she sat up in bed at night, next to Anna, perusing an enormous life of Lenin. She believed in political remedies for injustice; she talked, all the time, pointing out examples of poverty and oppression as the truck lurched down and up the mountains, about the miserable exploitation of peasants in her country by the land-owners on the one hand, the businessmen on the other; the wretchedness of all these lives. She did not believe it was God that sent the misery; she believed it was Anna and her kind, imperialist exploiters all of them.

Lastenia, a stocky woman, with a flat, clearly Indian face, much less impassive than she looked, and much less introvert, was one of those who had never been able to afford a trip to the United States, let alone Europe. Nor had she ever, she said, been exposed to any languages other than Spanish and Quechua; that was the trouble with Latin America – you were so far away from other languages and cultures. At the same time you were brought up on Europe; on European seasons, winter and summer in European classics – the Brothers Grimm, for instance. At this point Anna and her colleague dis-covered a mutual liking for such elemental frivolities as fairy tales: Anna did not have enough Spanish, alas, to find out how Grimm fitted in alongside Lastenia's admit-ted Marxism. Watching children running around in the warm evenings of the Chota Valley, she could not help wondering, also, poverty or no poverty, what Lastenia would make of the outskirts of Liverpool, say, in winter, or of Chicago come to that; it was all relative, wasn't it? But her hintings at such notions fell on deaf ears – to Lastenia, knowing nothing else, nothing could be worse than the situation of these children, of all poor Ecuador children. Yet they did not, either of them, let such things affect their growing friendship. They washed their hair and themselves alongside each other in fast-running rivers, watched by curious village children. They helped dry each other's hair, lent each other soap and tooth-paste, fed each other peppermints at weary moments. As far as their language gap allowed, they laughed together more and more; as time went on they even dared tease one another – Lastenia mocked Anna's very English accent in Spanish; Anna, tentatively, pretending to col-lapse under its weight, mocked the huge biography of Lenin.

Increasingly, too, Lastenia defended Anna against her sometimes suspicious colleagues. In her turn Anna praised Lastenia's work, encouraged her; successfully – Aguadiente complained to Piet Van Dyke once, that after Anna's visit Lastenia had become quite insubordinate – to assert her own position against Aguadiente's tendency to interfere with her work at every turn. They embraced on parting. '*Adiós, amiga*,' they said, and meant it. Both, years later, still thought of each other fondly.

Once during that time Lastenia involved Anna in quite an extreme form of that activity known in the trade as Participant Observation. Or so it seemed to Anna, shivering in her knickers, up near El Angel, one chilly June evening. Such an extreme form, she felt queasy about it, in some ways. Partly because Jacoman, having been told before he left for Basel what Lastenia was suggesting, said it wasn't ethical. Though Anna couldn't be sure he wasn't motivated in this instance by mere propriety, a drug company executive's view of propriety, at that, she worried about it, she never dared tell him afterwards she had done it, that she had done it willingly, moreover. It was, you could say, one of the odder uses for drug company money, if not the most immoral; she did not know if Lastenia saw the joke. But it was one.

What Lastenia suggested, in short, was that given the interest Anna had expressed in the functioning of local healers, the best way to find out how they treated people would be for herself, Anna, and their driver, Antonio, to visit various grades of curanderos – healers – declare an illness and ask for treatment. She and the driver each picked a 'local' disease to suffer from; Lastenia herself settled for espanto (the local name for susto – the 'fright' disease); Antonio claimed he'd had a spell put on him by a jealous girlfriend. English Anna, of course, would be unlikely to claim she was suffering from such indigenous diseases. It was decided therefore that she would be the one to seek treatment for epilepsy. Participant Observation, this, with a vengeance – the more so, Anna thought, sadly, than Lastenia could have realised; oh, the irony of it.

279

Epilepsy was serious enough, of course, to warrant visiting the highest grade of healer – the witch – the *Brujo* (the word 'witch,' it should be said, in this context, lacks the European connotations of *Walpurgisnacht*, of pointed hats and broomsticks. Sorcerer might be nearer; but even that's not quite right.) Lastenia went to see the healer and booked the appointment in advance; just like the dentist, thought Anna. She'd been told to tell Anna to bring eau de cologne with her and also – as soon as she heard this, Anna became apprehensive, in a foreign – very foreign – land, it felt too intimate altogether – a sample of her own urine. Just the same, she found an aspirin bottle and meekly provided what was asked for.

Setting out, as usual, at 6 a.m., they did not go straight to El Angel; the appointment wasn't till 4.30 in the evening. They spent the earlier part of the day down in the Chota Valley; arriving finally, as usual, at the only passable restaurant, for a late lunch. (Jacqui Sylvestre was always wondering why, almost daily, their team, like the other medical and psychological teams, traversed the valley end to end, using so much more petrol than they needed to; after two days Anna could have told him. He should have known, lunch was sacrosanct in this country, particularly when paid for by someone else – here Jacoman paid, finally – and particularly where work started as early as theirs did, and ended as late.)

After lunch they drove back up to the cold heights. The sun was out, not a generous nor friendly sun up here at this time of day, the tracks they lurched along, passing men leading horses, once, and further on a herd of black and white cattle, Friesians thought Anna, homesick once again, were muddy from recent rain. The soil in the fields alongside was dark, heavy-looking, the green of the trees and the grass livid in the low light. Anna was apprehensive; still more apprehensive when she saw the *Brujo*'s house; it was as she expected substantial, far more so than the houses of the lesser healers she'd talked to in the villages, who took payment in kind, often, and lived much like their neighbours.

This man did not live like his neighbours. He lived in a

big low house, painted white on the outside, a Ford pick-up truck parked opposite. The main door to the house was like a stable's, hinged at the top. When they knocked, he opened this top part immediately, wearing, despite being indoors, a hat with a feather in it, and, over a checked shirt, a heavy green poncho braided round the edges. He was an aristocrat among *brujos*, part of a long dynasty, Lastenia said, if Anna understood her rightly. He looked aristocratic. He was tall and thin, his nose long, his eyes deep, his skin wrinkled, the two-day-old stubble on it white; he had the dignity of an Indian chief, without such pronounced cheekbones; indeed he looked more Spanish, less Indian, than Lastenia.

Lastenia introduced Anna to him as her English sister-in-law – this they had agreed earlier to explain the inadequacy of Anna's Spanish. He shook hands with them and with Antonio, the driver, over the upper part of the door before opening the lower part and leading them into the house. The entrance room had whitewashed walls and a rough wooden floor, was bare apart from chairs, a small table, and, on the wall opposite the door, a mirror, in which Anna caught sight of her own white face and wished that she had not. There was another stable door, its top part open, leading into the main part of the house. They saw a room twice the size of this one, almost as sparsely-furnished, though there were easy chairs and a sofa, a plaster statue of the Virgin carrying the infant Christ, and a big print of the Sacred Heart. An old woman pottered in and out, carrying a steaming saucepan. After he had seated his visitors, the *Brujo* closed that half door, they were left with the cold, yellowy-green light of the sky and the trees through the door that opened onto the street. Inadequate as the light was, the one bulb dangling from the ceiling was not lit. No light had been lit in the inner room, either.

The *Brujo* went out then. There was the sound of the pick-up truck starting. He did not come back for a long time. Anna could not understand the explanation Lastenia gave her; she thought the man had seen she was a fraud, and had departed accordingly. Her head worse than ever, she felt more and more apprehensive, more and more queasy. She hoped he wouldn't come back, almost as much as she hoped he would, her curiosity not quite superseded, though nearly, by her desire to get back to the project house, to lay her head flat on her pillow, thus avoiding what lay in store when the *Brujo* returned; if he returned; she was beginning to doubt it.

It was not hard for her now to feign being a sick woman, she was sick in a way; sick at heart, homesick. Aguadiente, the night before, had diagnosed her symptoms as missing David (indeed he'd been so kind to her, she'd felt quite guilty for the way her heart also, taking its cue from David and Jacoman, mocked him). She still felt nauseous, her head was still throbbing. Even Lastenia looked at her anxiously, she hardly had to feign the concern with which she explained Anna's case to the *Brujo*, when the truck brought him back at last, a good half hour later. Anna herself hardly had to feign sickness. 'Heal me,' said Anna's heart to the *Brujo*. She feared him; at the same time she believed in him absolutely. She did not want to tell him lies for research purposes. He looked at her so very kindly, so very deeply, he said her disease was terrible. And so it was, she felt in this moment, the world, the mountains, weighing her and her companions down, more terrible, maybe, than the guilt of their deception – of all her deceptions. 'Heal me,' her heart cried out. She was no different from anyone, she wanted and needed what the whole world wanted and needed – what was it again – the path of insecurity beneath the surface of life? – yes, that was it, that was the universal sickness, the one she too suffered from. In the end she was not lying entirely when she named this sickness epilepsy, even if it was her son's epilepsy, rather than her own. 'Heal me.' If she could have demonstrated malaise at this moment, proved her good faith, by falling at his feet herself in a *grand mal* fit, she would have.

All the same, as things turned out, she was glad participant observation went so far and no further. The *Brujo* took her temperature first; left the thermometer in

282

her mouth for five minutes or so, he said that was necessary. But when he took it out he shook his head; her temperature was suspiciously low, he told them (and no wonder thought Anna, shivering, she was beginning to feel that not the least of her current ailments was likely to be hypothermia). Was she a *Señora* or a *Señorita*, the *Brujo* was asking; in other words was she still a virgin? If she was a virgin he would extract hormones from her with a syringe, he had done that very successfully for a *señorita* from El Angel, he had taken out half a litre of hormones from the *Señorita* from El Angel. Lastenia looked at Anna now, appraisingly, with a half smile, teasing you might say if the smooth impassivity of cheeks and her mouth, allowed such things; but they did not. No, she said at last; her sister-in-law was a *Señora*, a married woman. 'Thank you, my friend, Lastenia,' said Anna, in English, *sotto voce*.

What she got was difficult enough, anyway and chilly, too, before that open door top; to preserve her modesty Antonio was sent away – as soon as he'd gone, she was told to strip to her underwear. Then the *Brujo* made her stand in the middle of the open room in her vest and knickers – hypothermia appeared more likely than ever – while he took a large bunch of green herbs, like a besom, and with this part brushed, part whipped her all over, lightly, for about five minutes; I felt like a well-swept floor, complained Anna later. The herb had smelt of mint, and had an effect like nettles – the *Brujo* explained that he'd fetched it from Columbia, it didn't grow anywhere else. It brought her skin up in little lumps, making him exclaim with satisfaction; the epilepsy germs, he said, were coming out. It was cold. It was uncomfortable. It was ridiculous really, as well as unscientific; she must be the only person, she thought, who ever underwent – who would ever undergo – a curación in the Ecuador Highlands, for a disease she'd never had, clad from neck to crotch in underwear from Marks and Spencer.

He was not ridiculous, on the other hand. She did not think he was a crook either. She trusted him so much indeed, she longed as much as ever to ask for healing of her real ailments. He had kept his hat on throughout, but removed his poncho. As he rubbed her all over afterwards, with her own eau de cologne, his hands on her bare flesh were warm and firm and gentle. Though rough, knotted at the knuckles, they were quite clean she noticed, apart from his finger nails. So was the skin beneath his white stubble and the brown skin in the v of his open-necked shirt, which for some reason looked much older than the rest of him. There were lines about his eyes, but he didn't smile; he didn't need to. As for his fee – if Lastenia told her the right figure it was by no means exorbitant (despite being paid for, in ignorance, by Jacoman). His work included not just the whipping with the herb like mint and nettles, the massage with her own cologne, the advice to live quietly which followed, she got also a huge bottle containing some pink liquid, so newly distilled that it was still hot (the room from which he fetched it, seen again through the half door, was full of people now, slumped on the sofa and the chairs, before the flicker of a black and white television).

One thing the healer forgot though; so did she forget it. That night, turning out the bag she'd bought in Kenya, and still used to carry her possessions every day, she found the pill bottle. She was about to open it, looking for aspirin, when she felt its dubious slopping, only then remembered the urine sample he'd asked her to bring. With some relief, almost a sense of having been saved in some sense – the man was a bit too powerful for comfort – she ditched it.

As to that poignant – or not so poignant – figure, depending on the way you look at it, of ANNA ALONE – Jacoman was fond of pointing out, as if he needed this image of Anna somehow to justify his interest in her, how often she was, in the course of this project, alone; not only was she an English imperialist among oppressed Ecuadorians, she was a white among blacks in Africa, a woman/non-medic among men/doctors; in Switzerland, in Ecuador, in London, she was a journalist among sociologists, a non-scientist among scientists, and so on. This was not of itself interesting, at least her perception of uniqueness was not interesting or her response to it; she herself came to distrust, deeply, as much she enjoyed, this extension to her myth of herself. What was much more interesting and much more significant, looking back on it afterwards, when she could begin to extract herself from memories of the sensual, emotional, social morass which engulfed her much of the time, permeating her journal entries – not to mention the sheer pity she felt for some of the patients and their families, the times she wanted to shout out, 'Yes, I *know*' – was the way the different groups responded to her. It came to her, increasingly, that these responses in themselves were her keys to knowledge and understanding not only of the groups themselves but of how she could best, most usefully, describe them.

In this respect at least, therefore, she ceased, professionally, to be so wary of her feelings as evidence, as what David might call 'data'. The pleasure, loneliness, homesickness, and so forth, she noted at the time, were often a useful – sometimes her main – clue as to what was going on in the group itself. Part of her pleasure in Africa, for instance, was precisely the way the group were not suspicious of her, indeed the way they almost sported her, the white woman, as a kind of mascot, never mind she also thought she should distrust this flip side of racism; for so it was. Contrariwise, in Ecuador, what lay at the heart of the alienation, the longing for home, was not only the language difference but also the suspicions of the previously colonised towards each other, as well as towards her.

The attitudes of the two Kerns, husband and wife, shifted markedly over the years of the project; sometimes one way – sometimes the other. In most respects Anna grew less defensive, more sure of her position; as far as her feelings about Ben were concerned she grew more defensive, on the other hand. As for David – who only knew the half of it – after sitting in on one of his wife's interviews with Jacoman, he remarked, 'Why do you keep bringing yourself into it?'

'How do you mean?' asked Anna.

'Well you keep saying – well to give an example, when Carter was telling you about the relation of his bit of the company to the rest of it, you kept telling him about some meeting you had with some Welsh colleague of his who told you this that and the other, and what you felt was his reaction to whatever it was. And then another time you were trying to compare his and Giselle's first meeting with yours and mine. What's that got to do with it?'

'Everything,' said Anna, who herself distrusted this approach more than she used to. The problem was she didn't know, she'd never been taught, how to work, creatively, even humanly, except by using her own feelings and experience as part of a blueprint for understanding other people's feelings and experience; as a journalist, more than one editor had told her, over the years, that it was precisely her ability to communicate herself as well as her subject matter that distinguished the features she wrote for them; now, to her surprise, some of the anthropological theory she was reading confirmed her feeling that it wouldn't make sense to deny herself entirely. If science in many respects demanded a different approach from anything she'd done before, it didn't have to be that different; she was still herself. As Einstein had been himself. As David was himself. Still, she was careful; in the case of the epilepsy project where she still thought – half-thought – she could usefully have interjected her own experience, she didn't do so; or she at least tried her best, not always successfully, not to do so. Debarred, of course, from pointing out this heroic self-denial to her husband, she asked him instead, almost humbly, 'How else am I suppose to test out different sources – set one against another – Carter and that Welshman, Owen, were telling me opposite stories; I didn't want Carter to think I was contradicting him outright, the only way to do it was make a funny story about my interview with Owen. So I did. Oh and the other thing. Carter and Giselle are so different from us; I mean Carter has this story about meeting Giselle and all that, but I need to get behind it.' 'Why,' interrupted David here, 'what's it got to do with you?' But Anna ignored him. 'If I want Carter to be open with me,' she said, 'then I have to be open with him.'

'The equivalent in medicine,' said David, 'would be me starting to take a history of a man with a bad leg, by telling him about my bad leg. The point about taking histories being that you listen to the patient only. You don't bring yourself in ever. Yourself is a distraction, that's the point. Yourself is not science.'

'Mightn't the patient,' said Anna, 'at least some patients, be reassured by the fact you'd had a bad leg, so might know what they were feeling? Mightn't they want humanity, as well as science?' (This she realised was special pleading; how tempted she'd been sometimes, sitting in some hut, up some mountain, to shout out: 'I know. I know.')

David was smiling; unaware that Anna's argument was special pleading, he felt on sure ground here. 'Most patients,' he said, 'most patients want to be cured. They don't want to swap symptoms, not with their doctor anyway.'

'And where you can't cure them?' asked Anna; if here, she felt more sure of herself, David felt less so. He shrugged. It was a stupid argument, anyway, and they both knew it. This did not stop it getting more and more heated. Not just because Anna, in trying to become more analytical, if not over-analytical, was increasingly conscious of her limitations in that respect; as much if not more because David – his protests all the more heated and unhappy – was trying, while his father sank slowly out of life, to fight his way through a morass of the kind of feelings he'd tried to avoid contemplating before, but could do so no longer.

Heaven help Anna, if she tried to use her own feelings to understand his, he kept trying to make clear to her; he did not know entirely why he did so object to it. He just knew that he did.

'You're not the same as me, Anna, don't pretend you know what I'm feeling, don't tell me what my feelings are. They're different,' he said.

'I know what it feels like when a parent's dying,' she said.

'Yes but my father's not yours. I am not you,' he said, feeling angrier the closer to him the subject got. Why should he be forced to think about it? He knew what his feelings were. He thought he knew what his feelings were.

'You're behaving just like the Ecuadorians, David. The Ecuadorians aren't like anyone else in the world, they don't feel the same things, they don't believe the same things, how can we possibly understand it? Oh come off it, David. We're all human, aren't we?'

Her husband had the grace to laugh; he admitted it. Well, he admitted it in passing. At times Anna despaired of him, he was so tired, always, no less than he said he claimed to despair of her. They influenced each other, they got nearer to each other all the time. At the same time it seemed, often, they got further and further away. Marriage was like the sea, she thought, it surrounded you, you were so close to it, you knew it so well – at the same time, like the sea, its depths were more unknown, more mysterious, than the surface of the moon many thousands of miles away. The Ecuadorians might be the moon, for instance; yet at times, like any other wife, she truly felt she knew more about them than she knew about her husband; or than he knew about her.

Chapter Two

They spent three days in Quito at the beginning of the second trip to Ecuador, went up to San Raphael for two days – thereafter they were to go back to Quito, and from thence, in David and Anna's case, to Lima for three days. David would then go home, leaving Anna to return to San Raphael to do her fieldwork.

Going through the records in San Raphael, however, they had discovered that Aguadiente had been so busy chasing up the results of the epidemiological survey, that he hadn't had the health visitor records checked to make sure whether the health visitors were visiting the patients as they were supposed to, providing their drugs, ensuring that they took them. 'How the hell can you do a medical trial if half the patients aren't taking their medication?' asked Jacoman.

Anna almost found herself afraid of the anger this discovery had provoked in him – for a whole day, nearly, it had been so black, so all embracing, it had sucked in all his energy, his manic glitter, as inexorably as a black hole in space sucked in matter about it. God help you if you let yourself be sucked in also; she and David both judged it best to retreat.

'Carter's under a lot of pressure, I think,' David said. 'I don't think it's just Aguadiente; I think they're giving him a hard time in Basel.'

They were due to stay for a second night at the only decent hotel in the area, two thirds of the way up between San Raphael and Quito, run by a pair of Swiss gays – however had they fetched up here? Anna wondered – and staffed by local Ottavalo Indians. It was always cold in that place, in Anna's memory, the skies almost always grey. The hotel bedrooms were in bungalows, each made up of two rooms with a common verandah. Carter occupied the room next to David and Anna. The altitude had affected her quite badly, she couldn't eat or sleep. Besides they'd spent till midnight in anguished discussions on how to limit the damage to the project of what they had discovered. Jacoman wasn't so angry by this time, if not resigned.

At one o'clock in the morning, after tossing about for an hour or so, she got dressed again and went out onto the balcony. It was a starlit night for once, so bright she contemplated a walk. The volcano that was supposed to be visible from this point had been shrouded since they arrived; it was more than likely to be shrouded again by morning.

But as she was hesitating on the step Carter's door opened; he did not see her at first – turning, she cannoned straight into him, or almost.

'Hey, Anna,' he said. 'What are you doing out here? Did you know you left your tape recorder on my table?'

He hesitated for a moment; then he said, 'Well then, how are ya doin'? Can't you sleep?'

She told him what she'd been thinking of doing. At once he insisted on coming with her. And, just as she'd hoped, they had hardly walked any distance when there the volcano was, a mystical cone glimmering in the starlight; even as they were watching, the moon came up and then, icily, it started blazing, wisps of cloud making a nimbus around it.

'Chimborazo, Cotopaxi,' she thought, 'have stolen my heart away.' (Except this volcano wasn't Cotopaxi, although seeing it from their hotel room in Quito at sunset, a year ago, she had thought it was.)

Carter, too, just looked at the volcano and said nothing. He must have concluded, as she had, that there really was nothing to say. But after a minute he put his arm round Anna. He kept his arm round her, when, after another minute or so of standing watching, they walked down the path a little further. Which did not stop Jacoman the next minute talking about the project in even more pessimistic terms than earlier. 'If the blood tests are going to come up negative because the fuckers aren't checking the guys are taking their drugs,' he said, 'it's going to skew all the data. Jesus, we'll all have been working our asses off for nothing, especially you, Anna, yours is the bit of the study that would have to be axed first.'

Things were not quite as bad as he made out, though nearly. They'd discussed it and discussed it. Jacoman and the usually bland Medical Director for this part of Latin America, Meyersdorf, had gone so far as to shout at each other about it in the car on the drive back down from San Raphael. They'd had to be calmed down by David. Anna felt sorry for Carter in a way; if he didn't put it out of his head, he'd never sleep. Besides, she'd heard all she wanted from David, and had nothing further to offer Jacoman (apart from wanting her side of the project preserved – she'd made this quite clear when the Colombian who, from the beginning, had mistrusted this sociological 'nonsense' about what patients felt and what they believed, had suggested reducing it, in view of this crisis, to almost nothing. Fortunately, at the time, Jacoman had backed her up, to the extent of shouting some of her arguments at the Colombian in a mixture of English and pidgin Spanish as the car teetered along steep precipices, down into and up out of huge valleys, in places skirting the stony remains of earlier rockfalls half-blocking the road. Anna prayed new rockfalls didn't coincide with their passing.)

Back at the bungalow, without discussing it, they went into Jacoman's room. Jacoman though, removed his arm from Anna's shoulder, they moved apart, almost guiltily, just inside the door. Anna did not look at Jacoman as she went to the table to retrieve her recorder. To cover the awkwardness she felt, she asked Carter to tell her again the story he referred to almost as often as the story of the Pakistani doctor; in this case the story of the Pakistani woman who couldn't add a can of beans. For good measure, her recorder to hand, she taped him. When she transcribed the tape later, it brought first the magical volcano to mind, thereafter the fireplace to which they had retreated as Carter was talking, huddling over the dying fire to warm themselves after the cold of the night outside. When Carter revived it with more logs from the basketful provided by the management, the flames had flickered on the white arched walls of the room with its decorated floor tiles and Spanish furnishings, with its huge poster of the volcano they'd just been gazing at. In her mind Anna saw that room, also; was reminded once again of the sense of understanding, not to say collusion, between her and Jacoman. The moment of awkwardness over, she had never in her life felt so relaxed and companionable with a man with whom she hadn't previously had a sexual relation. Perhaps that was something else made possible by her marriage with David. How amazing, she thought, to be able to sit quite innocently at 2 a.m. in another man's bedroom. How simple. Even now she assumed it was simple.

She assumed it not least because of the nature of their friendship. Because far from being two one to one friendships: her and Jacoman, David and Jacoman, it was, much more, a three way friendship, herself, Jacoman and David. At times, still, Anna felt the two men excluded her by their Jewish jokes and so forth; at times, her growing friendship with Jacoman might have seemed to David to exclude him (maybe that was one reason he played the Jewish game with Jacoman). But more often, at this stage, Anna was for Jacoman what David was not and vice-versa, Jacoman was for her what David was not and vice-versa, the existence of the third person implicit even when only two were present. Indeed on this trip, even more than last year, the presence of Anna had proved not only much more felt but much more necessary than she had expected; she was not just tagging along; as her contributions to this tape made clear. In earlier tapes she'd been spiky, somewhat hesitant. In some of her later interviews with Jacoman, on the other hand, made just before he left Basel, fifteen or so months later, she'd done far too much of the talking; maybe because Jacoman himself was much more subdued at this point, almost valedictory in the way he talked of what had happened, and she was trying to generate in this much wintrier Jacoman, vainly, some of his earlier fire and enthusiasm.

But here it was not like that; maybe the whisky Jacoman had poured for them both helped. Here enthusiasm was still enthusiasm, even in spite of the problems they had been discussing; and if there was not the exhilaration of other times, there was in its place a real tenderness in the way they addressed each other; more than she had realised at the time – it startled her, listening later. Partly because, in contrast to the confident, almost boastful tone in which Carter told his story, it made him sound almost vulnerable. Better not play this tape to Nikki she thought, with an extraordinary sense of loss. Better not to play it to David.

Anna forgetting to turn off the machine, the tape did not end with the end of the story, but went on to repeat the desultory and not so desultory conversation that followed. Jacoman, for instance, had talked to her about Giselle for the first time; it wasn't marriage guidance exactly, not yet; but more than Anna realised at the time it initiated her role as counsellor – it might have been the reason he encouraged Giselle later on that year to look her up a time or two, she now realised, hearing him all over again; maybe he'd hoped she could talk to Giselle about their marriage as she had talked to him. (A vain hope; Giselle spent the whole time asking questions about Anna's.) Afterwards he'd changed tack; told her how useful she was to the project, brought up this beguiling romanticism, as she saw it, about Anna alone.

Afterwards – this, the tape didn't record; by now she had stopped the machine – they'd lingered by the fire saying nothing very much; and maybe the whisky did it – David hadn't drunk it – maybe the volcano – he hadn't seen it – maybe it was the warmth of the fire David couldn't feel; in all events there were only two people in

293

the room suddenly; Anna and Jacoman; if this was a familiar enough occurrence in the relationship between David and Jacoman, it wasn't yet so for them. As she gazed down at the fire at the dying embers, Jacoman said, 'I love the way you listen, Anna.' And he bent his head, and kissed her good-night. Not the way a lover would have kissed her, it is true; but not the way of a colleague either; more, give or take the taste of whisky, more like a husband. Even if she still couldn't see him as a husband, let alone a lover, it made her feel guilty, slightly, though not in an unpleasant way. It made her blush. She liked it.

A digression. Visit to another local healer.
Anna Kern's field diary. Kenya: April 1987.

My cavernous, dimly-lit room, 9 p.m. (I tried to ring David; no luck. Now the telephonist's gone home; very pretty, very pregnant, hair in a frizzy plait, she sits knitting a baby jacket, couldn't be more sympathetic, more helpful, but achieves nothing.) We keep hearing about local healers – witchdoctors – from the doctors themselves – how people go to them, are fooled by them; from the pastors, village chiefs and so forth who are answering our questionnaires; from the patients too, sometimes. But the healers are very suspicious of outsiders. Today I got the nearest I'll probably ever get to one of them. A strange story; the patient we were supposed to be visiting was the healer's own patient; a fourteen-year-old girl, brain-damaged; the parents had sent her to live with the healer, but he'd not been able to do anything for her; he'd referred her to our project. So now here we were, bearing our questionnaires and so forth. The end of a long day – three villages – four patients. To get here we'd climbed a long dirt track behind the village to which we came ten days ago looking for patients. There was another village – much smaller; much less substantial; no road, no village store, just the usual flimsy huts, closed up with big padlocks. We tried to find a patient there, to no avail.

So then we went to the far side of the village, to the healer's house. It was very obviously the healer's house – three times the size of any other, and with an upper storey, made not of wood, apart from the roof, but stone. Seeing it I could believe, really, I don't think I'd done so before, how successful the healers are, how influential. In local terms at least this man, this healer, was rich, I could see it; everyone was meant to see it.

The healer, of course, was absent; just my luck. Or they *said* he was absent; it could be he just didn't want to see us. We were shown in through a dark passageway – kitchen and cupboards on one side, both relatively empty apart from some boxes, which I saw because every door was open – into a big room taking up the ground floor of the house. There was one window, with glass in it. There was a big wooden staircase rising to the rooms upstairs. There was a wooden floor, a wooden ceiling, wooden walls, a big stone fireplace, surrounded by a swathe of wallpaper, pretending to be red brick. The rest of that wooden wall and the one next to it was all shelves, of the same forbidding wood, all empty, except for one, on which sat a knife and a large green cabbage. A wooden table took up much of the room, under the window sat a big sofa, covered in torn red plastic. The weight of all that dark, cheap-stained wood was overwhelming. As for the cabbage – why a cabbage? The mystery obsessed me, I have to say; as the only non-Kikuyu speaker in the room, I had no incentive to focus on what was being said; no one seemed willing to speak English any longer.

The patient was a thin girl of thirteen or so. A hopeless case, you could see at a glance; but graceful in a strange, almost animal way. She cowered under the staircase like a wounded deer, her eyes flickering about her. Sometimes she hid her face in her hands and peered out at us between her fingers; she was terrified, I think. But I couldn't be sure entirely, she was so completely other. I would have liked to reassure her, we were the only women in the beginning; but there was no way, no language. I did reach out a hand once; she shrank away.

I was led to the end of the room facing the door and made to sit on the torn red sofa, beside our three health workers. The team leader, Elisha, a young man almost as serious as my friend Peter, but better-looking (Bennet has great faith in him) set his clip board and his questionnaire on the wooden table, and sat down with two young men, the healer's assistants; they'd been delegated to answer our questions in the absence of the healer.

They weren't obvious medical assistants these two, in their woollen hats and torn jumpers, at least not in any sense a Westerner would recognise. Elisha said afterwards – he was almost as bemused as me – that they, too, might have been the healer's patients. Even with my lack of Kikuyu, I could see the problems; not least the way they answered Elisha and each other back. Sniggering, nudging each other, picking up the words from each other's mouths, looking round – uselessly as far as I was concerned – for applause from the rest of us, they were more Marx Brothers, more Laurel and Hardy, than Guys Hospital or Barts or Thomas'. Not, of course, that I could vouch for the quality of the backchat. But the gestures, the giggles were telling enough; so was Elisha's increasing confusion as he continued to wrestle with his clip board, his questionnaire, his little lead pencil. Sorry for him as I felt, committed to the business as I was, or ought to have been, I still could not help feeling some treacherous amusement, not to say sympathy with this subversion of all our efforts. There *was* something ridiculous about our sitting in this wooden room in the middle of Africa, asking a lot of questions – silly questions maybe – devised in London. After a bit I gave up trying to see the answers Elisha set down – he was writing in English, shaking his head – and contemplated the lonely cabbage so deeply it took me a while to notice that the room was gradually filling up with new people; female mostly; some of them elderly.

One, especially, in a brown and black bandana – the healer's wife? – was deferred to by everyone, even, in passing, by the two obstreperous young men. Though they didn't stop clowning, if anything they tried still harder, they kept a plain eye on her, I noticed; to gauge the effect of their behaviour, presumably, maybe to modify it, if necessary.

The old woman had brought in a big brown enamelled teapot and a big enamelled plate of Marie biscuits. She set them on the table then sat down opposite Elisha and the two young men and began to speak. She, too, I assumed, was also answering the questions; all Kikuyu is alike, to a non-speaker. I was tired, practically falling asleep, so I didn't notice how different her tone was, or even the fact it was monologue, not dialogue, she spoke in; that Elisha, his pen still poised, had ceased to ask questions. But suddenly I saw that everyone but me had their heads down, piously; even the two young men had their heads down, piously, except they kept peering out sideways at me, giggling, unpiously. At that point I realised – I was a long way the last to – that sociological enquiry had turned into religious meeting; the old woman was actually praying over all of us; saying grace before teatime, possibly? – a very long grace though; the only person still taking no notice was the epilepsy girl beneath the stairs. Thank God Ben wasn't like that, I kept on thinking, watching her continue rocking herself, bending herself sideways with that awkward, deer-like grace, making little, barely audible, grunts and moanings.

Afterwards we partook of the tea and biscuits in thick white china mugs, on thick white china plates. Elisha continued to ask his silly questions and get what appeared to be silly answers. He had never had an interview like it, he told me afterwards with a rueful smile. He did not think the answers should be taken seriously, any more than I did. I told him it wasn't his fault – how could it be?

Chapter Three

Anna met the Locks, the Dreadlocks, three times in all. The second time she met them was in October, just outside Barcelona, at the social science conference. It was Jacoman who suggested she attend it; not telling her, though, that as far as he was concerned, her meeting the Locks was the main object of her visit. He did not tell the Locks it was the main object either. Yet the Locks, at least, knew Anna would be there; while she had no expectation whatever of seeing the Locks. Jacoman had not yet got round to telling her he'd involved them in the project; all she knew was that he and they had come across each other at some conference somewhere, and that he had invited them to Basel to explain to a meeting of Bader-Kleitz executives the importance for the successful use of the products they were engaged in selling, of enlisting the skills of medical anthropologists.

In fact it wasn't Jacoman had told her about this. It was Falconer who had been present at the Lock's briefing of Jacoman's colleagues. He'd told Anna all about it in Kenya, six months before. A load of nonsense he called it; a load of suspect nonsense. Having come to visit Anna during her stay in Likuru, he eyed her gloomily over stale cucumber sandwiches at what was still called the English club (it was appropriately shabby, and run by a left-over Memsahib, all limp cotton and fierce spectacles, who shouted at the black servants in their stained white jackets and turbans, about their demeanour, bringing the tea, about the absence or presence of teaspoons, about whether or not the water was hot, about everything to do with it, except the most important issue, the staleness of the cucumber sandwiches). Then he told her – or rather hinted – that she should on no account trust Jacoman. But amid Falconer's rant about the Locks, about the hour they had spent on the platform drawing little diagrams of this model and that model to explain the different influences on patient perceptions of illness of this factor and that factor, while the assembled executives looked blank at best, yawned and fidgeted at worst, she did not take the message in as she should have done.

Falconer added, with bitter satisfaction, 'Jacoman did himself no good in the company by all that tarradiddle. He did himself no good at all.' But it seemed his only satisfaction. His hatred of Jacoman at this stage was overwhelming. Three days before, Bennet, the sociologist, normally a man punctual to the minute, had been two hours late in meeting Anna for dinner, his excuse for this the time it had taken him to smooth down Falconer straight off the plane from Basel, from what he saw as humiliation by Jacoman and Taylor. (Falconer liked Taylor even less than he liked Jacoman; 'At least Carter believes in what he's doing,' he'd said at a calmer moment.)

'Ian,' said Bennet – only he pronounced it very lengthily 'Eee-arn'. 'Ian is not very happy. Not happy at all.' But he did not explain further. And all Falconer himself said, three days later, was that Jacoman was being more high-handed than ever, and that he, Falconer, a man by no means as placid as his teddy bear looks suggested – he had a ravening, red-headed, Scots temper – was beginning to feel he'd had enough; that he was proposing to leave the company as soon as he could find another job.

It was the first time Anna had been alone with Falconer, a man more comfortable with men than women. He had previously addressed himself to David, even when she was present, even when discussing her part of the project. But David was not there this time. To put her companion more at ease, Anna found herself starting almost every statement with: 'David thinks', or, alternatively, 'David says'.

Now she said, 'David thinks this obsession with Franklin is because Jacoman is hung up on his family prestige; you know half his family are professors of social medicine; he wants to make his mark in the same field.'

'Well he won't make it in the eyes of Franklin or any other university while he's working for a drug company,' said Falconer, sourly, who'd had some experience of this himself, having been turned down, flatly, not to say brutally, as an M.D. student by one university department precisely because of his pharmaceutical appointment; though a more honest, ethical man, almost pigheadedly so, David said, it would be hard to imagine. It was one of the reasons Falconer came up so hard against the also honest yet much more sophistical and slippery Jacoman.

'He doesn't think that,' said Anna.

'Well he'll find out,' said Falconer.

There was a long silence. They both shifted a little in their wicker chairs. The only sound was the fan over their heads, superfluous at this time of year, and the sprinkler going on the lawn, which ought to have been superfluous but wasn't, the rains so far having failed. To break it, Anna said, her voice too high now in the face of Falconer's unabated discomfort in her company, 'David says it's uncanny the way if any two people on this project get together, they instantly start talking about Jacoman.'

'I've no desire whatever to talk about Jacoman,' said Falconer, stiffly. Taking another cucumber sandwich, he proceeded to grill her instead about how she thought the project was going in the field and the competence of Bennet's team, and the problems of Dr Meaki going off with the truck; this was, after all, the purpose of the meeting. But naturally, in due course, they reverted to Jacoman.

Anna and the Locks also talked about Jacoman in the seaside town outside Barcelona, with more excuse, perhaps; so far as she knew, Jacoman was the only thing they had in common, apart from her friend, the Lock's colleague, Stan Heins, and there was no reason to discuss *him*.

The three met first, quite by chance, in the lift of the austere and gloomy hotel in which the conference was taking place (social scientists, their work less well-funded than that of doctors, did not meet in hotels like the Sheraton or Hilton). Anna failed initially to recognise the Locks. The light was dim; she had not, after all, been expecting to see them. But they recognised her. They smiled, she half smiled back in embarrassment, only realising as her smile faded whom she was smiling at.

Charlene Lock said – the lift was lurching to a halt, Anna hoped she and Professor Lock would get out on this floor; but they did not – 'It's Anna Kern, isn't it? Carter Jacoman told us you'd be here.'

Even the reference to Carter did not alert Anna. It wasn't till later she remembered Falconer's warnings about Jacoman. Not that the Locks made a nuisance of themselves; on the contrary, they went out of their way to be friendly – some of the time – it was she who not only felt churlish, but out of her depth. She had never, she realised, felt out of her depth with Jacoman.

The next time she saw them, they did not see her. It was nine o'clock in the morning, the conference delegates were gathering in the front hall of the hotel, spilling out onto the steps, onto the road on the other side of which a grey, irrelevant, out-of-season sea reached into the distance, towards the unseen North African coast. This was not a conference like those David attended, with keynote addresses on the one hand, separate symposia on the other, in which the participants had come mainly to listen. This was social science in medicine, not medicine. The delegates had been offered in advance a choice of workshops (Anna had chosen one on community participation in medical policy and practice) in which all were expected to take an active part. But for now they were awaiting buses which would transport them to some central hall for a preliminary address on the aims and purposes of the conference. Until the last morning it was the only occasion when the participants would be gathered in one place; all the better, thought Anna, coming downstairs, for avoiding the Locks. And at that very moment she saw them.

Even there, standing in the middle of the hall, surrounded by people, they looked indissolubly united. It was warm still, despite the clouded sky, the grey sea, the empty beach; many of the women wore cotton frocks, if not jeans and t-shirts. Milton, a light jacket slung casually over one shoulder wore a yellow Franklin t-shirt; his bare arms were unexpectedly brawny as well as tanned. Charlene's sleeveless dress dropped at the hem; she had tied back her black hair with a scarf, more or less the same yellow as Milton's t-shirt. It did not quite look as if she had chosen it on purpose; but almost. Her skin looked even whiter, alongside Milton's, her arms unexpectedly skinny. Professor Lock was deep in conversation; until called to the buses, his head remained bent to one person or another – was he really so much taller than anyone he talked to; or did he just give the illusion of being so? – he did not move from that spot. Charlene, on the other hand, made little forays to right and left. Sometimes she would take one of the people she'd accosted back to Milton, as a hunter might take his mate back some titbit from a foraging trip.

Anna lost sight of the Locks when the buses came. But in the hall there they were, a few rows behind and to the side of her – she didn't see them, unfortunately, until it was too late for her to move. They were not sitting side by side. As Anna's eyes found her, Charlene leaned behind the woman in the next seat along to confer with Milton; he leaned his head towards her; then they parted, both heads nodding. Charlene noticed Anna looking at her on regaining her place. She smiled and waved in a regal manner. Reluctantly, Anna waved back.

The first sessions in the workshop began at three in the afternoon. Anna went off to hers with trepidation, hoping that neither Lock had picked the same group.

Piet was due to arrive today; she suspected Jacoman of despatching him to keep an eye on her. Not that it mattered. She'd be glad of his company when he came, she thought, as she sat waiting for the meeting to get going. She seemed to be the only person in the room who did not know at least one other person. Even the two East Europeans knew each other, though they were not, she discovered, compatriots. For a moment she would almost have been glad to see the Locks walk in.

But neither of them appeared at the workshop on community participation, not that day, at least. There were eleven people in the workshop, including herself. There should have been twelve but the chairman failed to turn up. He was on his way from Australia, someone said; it was the only accessible, quantifiable statement made all afternoon, by a group consisting of one short, fat social psychologist from somewhere in Sussex, a dour Hungarian (male), a dour Pole (female) – there was a daunting array of shoulder straps under her transparent white blouse; two young Frenchwomen who whispered together all the time; two male mavericks from Manchester and Birmingham respectively, wearing beards, sandals, in one case a large hat, in both cases sour opinions, on the pharmaceutical industry in particular, which they aired whenever given the chance to do so; a plump Canadian health administrator in a patchwork cotton dress; a cynical Indian civil servant, formally dressed unlike the rest in a dark brown suit; an elderly American who'd spent his whole life in a Mexican village as far as Anna could make out, who said little, but smiled benignly, puffing at a pipe bound in silver; a Cape coloured South African doctor. In charge of a clinic in a rural area of the Cape, this doctor appeared to be the one person with any real idea about what community participation could mean on the ground; among other things, in his experience, it meant unwelcome attention from the South African security forces; but there you were.

Finally there was Anna; who kept her mouth shut mainly, grateful to be allowed to; remaining grateful after two hours round yet another green baize table, in which nothing was agreed whatever, not even what was meant by the words 'community' and 'participation' – the Frenchwomen, in particular, appeared bewildered by the lack of definitions; the suave Indian mocked them. 'How do you define death then?' he asked them towards the end of the session, shouting down the length of the green baize table. 'Could you say perhaps, it's the point at which a patient can take no more medical intervention?'

Anna met Piet later. They ate dinner together at a fish restaurant on the front. It was full of people she recognised from the conference but did not know, though they all appeared to know each other. Piet insisted on walking her back to the hotel afterwards; sometimes he remembered to match the stride of his long legs to her short ones; sometimes he did not – she had to run to catch up; he would turn then and watch, laughing at her without any more hint of malice than there had been in the analysis he'd given her over dinner of Jacoman's marriage, or his references to Aguadiente, come to that. What a nice man, she was thinking; what a good one – for so he was, though trying now to persuade her to skip the session next day and walk round Barcelona with him. But she would not; virtuously she said she must do what she came for; only to have her virtue rewarded by walking into the room next morning to find not one but both Locks sitting at the table opposite her. Twinlocks; she thought; Dreadlocks – to armour herself against them.

They had all the advantages. Not least they were sitting with their backs to the window, to today's bright sunlight, whereas she was sitting facing it. They could see her face, see her eyes screwed up awkwardly against the light. She could not see theirs; again it was not their fault, but she blamed them for it – she wondered if they made everyone feel as paranoic.

Though Milton had been chairing a WHO meeting the day before – he would, thought Anna sourly; where his wife had spent the day was not clear – they were both free this morning. Milton was now chairman of this group, the one certainty it had arrived at the previous evening, the incoming flight of the scheduled chairman, having turned out erroneous – he was definitely not coming.

Milton did not raise his voice, ever; he did not speed it,

the impression all along was drawling, lackadaisical. But it was not lackadaisical; he dealt with the problem of definitions in ten minutes. When he himself – Anna was impressed against her will, he really did have the capacity to snatch thoughts out of the air and make sense of them all at once – had summarised the brief discussion he'd allowed on the subject – 'Hey folks,' he'd started, 'Hey folks, surely we're not going to let ourselves get hung up on this one,' – Charlene, in a brown dress today, smock-like, with a yoke and an embroidered collar, wrote the definitions arrived at on the blackboard at the end of the room. It was not Milton himself who had arrived at them, of course; the group did. Milton was like a juggler throwing one after another into the air, and keeping them flying, at a dizzying rate; or like a conductor pointing his baton first at the violins, then the horns. If it was logic he wanted, he pointed to the French girls; if dissension, to the beards; if he wanted cynicism, the Indian; if collectivism the Eastern Europeans, and so on. The baton had not yet fallen on Anna; he had looked at her enquiringly once or twice – held her eye – both Locks had held her eye, as far as she could see, their faces still shadowed; but he'd taken pity on her or something, he'd passed on.

The Frenchwomen were not quite satisfied afterwards; one continued to wave a hand in the air for Milton's attention. Studiously he ignored it. As he ignored the rebellion of the beards. Once the hatted beard said, 'Hey man, there's some people round here can't think further than getting their next research grant from the academic boards.' Milton, who had been outlining a scheme for researching different kinds of community participation, starting at home, in an ethnically mixed section of Oxford, Connecticut, asked, smoothly, 'Wasn't it Unicef funded your last project, Roy?' (The man's name was actually Ray; having established that the vowel shift riled him, Milton took every opportunity to address him as Roy.)

In the coffee break, Charlene advanced on Anna. 'You haven't had a lot to say, Anna.'

Anna determined, coolly, to play modest. 'This isn't my field,' she answered. 'There isn't a lot I can say. I've come to learn, basically.'

'The innocent eye, Anna,' said Charlene, adjusting the strap of her shoulder bag, 'the innocent eye has its uses.'

Anna wondered if her eye really was that innocent. Charlene's eyes certainly weren't. Forced to gaze into them again, she sought there the anger she had felt last time – but the one certainty she arrived at was that in her suspicious way Dr Charlene Lock was quite genuinely trying to be friendly. Why? She wasn't very good at it; any move she made towards Anna had to be countered by a move away – Anna had no impression it had anything to do with her; that Charlene Lock had any real desire to be friends with her particularly; rather, Charlene gave the impression of not being very good at making friends with anyone. Anna was again reminded of Nikki; in contrary ways as well as positive ones; the Snow Queen, though beautiful, did not have the advantage of Nikki's ebullience, let alone her charm – let alone, and this was the key point, her sex appeal. Moreover, while Nikki's calculations did not appear to be calculated, Charlene's did. But both of them were ridiculously defensive. (It was observing Charlene Lock made Anna realise, almost for the first time, just how very defensive Nikki was.)

Even at a distance Milton seemed better at wooing Anna than his wife. He, too, waved a hand at Anna, smiling at her across his coffee cup, though he did not bother to come over to speak to her thereafter. He looked taller than ever in this room, she noticed; he wore an open-necked cream-coloured shirt and a light cream-coloured jacket; he looked elegant, unlike his wife.

Charlene's next question, however, made things quite clear. What she wanted from Anna at this point, undoubtedly, was Jacoman, above all.

'What's *with* this guy?' she asked Anna. 'What's *with* him? He seems to know what he's talking about one minute, the next he's all over the place. Is he really the nephew of–' here she named Jacoman's famous, psychoanalyst uncle.

Anna laughed. 'You're confirming the hypothesis that any two or three people gathered together who know Jacoman, are bound to end up talking about him. Yes, I think he is.'

Charlene looked at her coldly. Confirming other people's hypotheses was obviously not something she cared for.

'I don't want to gossip, Anna. I just want to know if he can be relied on. He doesn't . . .'

'You could say he's not standard pharmaceutical executive,' said Anna. But if she felt that about this at least there could be no possible argument, she was wrong. Charlene bridled – that is she made a curious sideways movement with her head, frowning as she did so. Holding Anna's eyes, a slight flush staining her white skin, she enquired, in a loud whisper, 'How would you define then, Anna, a standard pharmaceutical executive?'

Anyone would think I was maligning him, thought Anna. How can I talk to, how can I understand anyone who thought I was maligning Carter by saying that? Laughing, in embarrassment, mainly, she said, at last, 'Someone not like Carter Jacoman. Well, not very like.' And then she thought, Charlene's expression unchanging, so we do have something in common; we do understand each other on one thing; she too has fallen under Jacoman's spell, just like I did in the beginning. Is it because he's so different from Milton? You wouldn't, on the face of it, call Milton Lock manic, would you? Even if he is much less lackadaisical than he looks.

What was Jacoman offering the Locks exactly, she wondered? And in which case what threat were they to her and David, if any? Maybe the only real threat was in Charlene's rage – she was still unable to fathom why Charlene, retreating from her overtures of friendship, was directing it at her, this minute.

But Charlene, mind-reading it seemed, stopped glaring at her all at once; she removed her eyes from Anna, after a minute smiled, almost conspiratorially, as if she too knew that they did after all have something in

307

common, and the something's name was Carter Jacoman; as if she too would like to sit in a corner with Anna and gossip with Anna about him, but had over the years become too wary for such things. Suddenly, smiling her irrevocably wolfish, irrevocably icy smile, no matter what – Anna for a moment felt quite sorry for her – she was trying to be charming again; shifting the conversation from Jacoman to Jacoman's project; how marvellous it was; and so forth. She talked about it as Anna's project – if you want any help with the analysis, dear . . . The irony being that there was nothing Anna would have liked better than Charlene's help with the analysis she'd be faced with in due course, that she was already dreading. Charlene would be ideal, if only she trusted her; if only she knew just what her communication had been with Jacoman. Here there stirred in her for the first time a faint suspicion, the briefest memory of Falconer's warnings. Was Jacoman to be trusted? Was Charlene, come to that?

Even so, she opened her mouth to suggest that yes, Charlene might be able to help; too late. Maybe Milton thought there was danger in his wife and Anna getting together; maybe it suited his wife to have him think that. Anyway there was Milton now, saying to them, to the entire room – why did Anna suddenly have this sense of a chance missed – because she did have that sense; 'Time to get back to work, folks. Time to get back to work.'

In the next session, Charlene and Milton between them, contrived not to let Anna alone. They told the group about the epilepsy project; at the mention of Bader-Kleitz, the heads of the bearded mavericks swivelled towards her, both gave her surprised, but not hostile looks – their dislike of Milton exceeded even their dislike of the pharmaceutical industry, evidently – as Anna was asked to describe her role in the project, the degree of community participation involved, and so on. It did not seem malicious attention. All the same Anna played hookey that afternoon with Piet, sat on the gritty beach almost till dusk, watching him exercise his long limbs.

To this end, at one point, he acquired a volley-ball from somewhere and a gang of local kids whom he instructed in the art of passing it between them, in what sounded like demotic Spanish. The next morning she exercised her right to attend a different workshop, on maternity services in primary health care, guessing, rightly, that this was one place she might not expect to find either Lock.

The afternoon of this third day was given over to conference excursions. All who wanted were to be taken in buses either to tour Barcelona or to see the Black Virgin at the Monastery of Monserrat in the foothills of the Pyrenees. Anna and Piet opted for the Black Virgin. So, unfortunately, did the Locks. Almost the first thing Charlene asked Anna when, having borne purposefully down on them outside the bus, she'd managed to separate her from Piet, was what was bugging Jacoman's Dutch colleague, what was his problem, why was he so *hostile*, for God's sake?

Charlene Lock was wearing the kind of strapless cotton sundress with matching jacket that Anna thought only Englishwomen of a certain type, her own mother, for instance, were ever to be seen in. Though it was cloudy, sunglasses hid her Snow Queen eyes. She wore sensible canvas shoes and carried over one shoulder a raffia handbag, over the other a camera. She looked like a serious tourist, as did her husband, who was also carrying a large camera.

'Anyone would think you were trying to avoid us, Anna,' said Charlene, almost coyly, when she had finished with the subject of Piet. 'We were sorry not to see you at the workshop this morning. What was the problem? Were you having difficulties with it?'

'Not especially,' said Anna, too irritated to feel intimidated. 'It just didn't seem to me to be getting anywhere much. But then I'm not sure you could expect that number of people from so many different backgrounds to get anywhere with anything so nebulous. Could you? The workshop on maternity services was much more specific and down to earth.'

Charlene took off her dark glasses. Shifting the strap of her raffia bag, she raised her eyebrows and poured the icy green stream of her gaze straight into Anna's.

'I guess you're just not used to academia, Anna.' (It was only afterwards Anna grasped the implications of this; and raged.) 'Where do *you* think we should be getting to, as you put it?'

Anna shrugged. 'Your guess,' she said, 'is as good as mine.'

Charlene raised her eyebrows again. 'I guess it is,' she said, adding a moment later, 'Carter Jacoman suggested you and I should get together on this trip, sometime. You're not making it very easy for us to get together, Anna, are you?'

Bloody hell, thought Anna.

'*Did* Carter suggest us working together?' she asked after a long pause, Charlene looking at her enquiringly as if expecting an answer. 'He never told me.'

'Why are *you* so hostile now, Anna? Has Dr Van Dyke been subverting you?' asked Charlene, sympathetically, patting her arm.

On the rush to get on the bus, they were separated, fortunately. Anna managed to regain the increasingly dear – by comparison – Dr Piet Van Dyke. The Locks were trapped three seats back among a noisy group of English academics, at their centre an exceedingly camp, well thought of, professor of sociology from London. Anna did not know if it was the bus itself made the Locks look so uncomfortable, or the group of English sociologists, or the Catalonian patriotism fed them from the front of the bus by the Catalan guide – he was not to know, poor young man, that this was not likely to be the most receptive, let alone the most reverent of audiences for lengthy statements in garbled English about the extraordinary, martyred greatness of Catalan people/art/music and so forth (the plaintive tone of this reminded Anna of Ecuador somewhat; the guide said 'by example', all the time, just like Aguadiente). Milton Lock's legs were too long to fit the narrow space between Catalan seats; names like Picasso, Casals, Gaudi, ringing all round him, he thrust them out into the aisle. Charlene Lock made loud remarks about passive smoking – one of the sociologists had lit a Catalan (or Spanish) cigarette. The gay professor, amid the guffaws of his companions, moved from mocking the statements of the guide – to which Charlene Lock at least, her camera at the ready, appeared to want to listen – to an inspired, if obscene, mock-anthropological dissertation on the precise significance of the little black Virgins – replicas of the ones they were going to see inserted into glass bottles stamped with the Catalan flag, and on sale everywhere they went – as against the ships inserted into little bottles for sale in England.

Meanwhile the bus was climbing awkwardly, slowly, among sinister grey hills, more like architecture than landscape – like pinnacled French castles, for instance, obelisks and gargoyles; Anna did not the least like them; partly because they made such a fit setting for the Snow Queen, Charlene Lock; they might have been climbing into her mountains, to the heart of her castle. Not that Charlene Lock actually looked any more at home here than Anna felt. She seemed to have given up trying to hear the guide above the guffaws of the sociologists; the professor's dissertation was reaching its climax. She gazed out of the window as blankly as Anna, occasionally raising her camera. Once, catching Anna's eye, she smiled brightly at her, seemingly without calculation.

Anna played hookey altogether for the rest of the conference. She missed the last session of either workshop, she missed the closing speeches to the whole conference. She took the train into Barcelona instead, with Piet; at the very least it was a way of avoiding the Locks, to whom she did not speak once after the trip to see the Black Virgin. When, at the airport, she thought she saw them, she flung herself on Piet, crying, 'For God's sake save me, Piet, there's the Locks.'

'Are you afraid they will think I am your lover, Anna?' asked Piet in his flattest voice, but with one of his delightfully evil smiles. A safe enough question; there

311

was not even a hint of such a thing, the question itself proved it; which did not mean to say she and Piet didn't like each other, very much.

To Anna's relief, the two figures in the distance turned out not to be the Locks. Piet celebrated by sliding like a schoolboy, thin hair flying from his balding head, across the huge and empty, highly polished floor – it immediately ceased to be empty, he almost cannoned into a professor of anthropology in earnest discussion with the more sober of the two mavericks from the workshop; the one with the biggest beard, the most outrageous sandals but no hat. Contrary to appearances, Anna had discovered, he was a distinguished, not to say influential, health economist. Anna nodded at this man, and hastily led Piet grinning more than ever, even blushing, to the bookstall where he encouraged her to buy a copy, in Spanish, of *Don Quixote*.

What an innocent Piet was, she was thinking, for all his matter-of-factness and sound commonsense. Such innocence, such sheer niceness made him vulnerable, more vulnerable than Jacoman, who wasn't nice really, not in the sense Piet was nice. A Jacoman could fall far and fast, could, like Samson, pull the ruins of the temple down on him. But a Piet could be swept away in torrents not of his making, simply because he was both too nice, too innocent, in some ways, to look for trouble, to understand that there might be torrents of a certain kind, let alone read their nature. Indeed he was, you could say, a much less likely pharmaceutical executive than Jacoman, though Jacoman mightn't like to think so. The sight of that *Don Quixote*, sitting on her shelves years later, still unread, always made Anna remember the then gleeful, the then quite youthful Piet, sliding across the floor of the airport in Barcelona.

It was on the way home she began seriously to wonder if, in the light of her inexperience, and in the light of his increasing respect for anthropology, Carter Jacoman actually was considering replacing her on the project with Charlene Lock. Next time Jacoman rang for one of his marriage guidance sessions, it did not surprise her to hear him ask if she had met the Locks at Barcelona; and when she said she had, how she had got on with Charlene.

'Why? Was I supposed to get on with her?' Anna asked.

But all Jacoman responded – he sounded quite unabashed – was; 'Isn't she *great*? Isn't she just great, Anna? I hoped you picked her brains, she's so bright that girl, there's nothing she doesn't know about analysing the figures in a study like yours, on that side she's much more clued up than Milton; he uses her for all his work. She could really help you break your stuff down. She could really put you in touch, Anna. What's more if she and Milton take you, take us, seriously, everyone will, we can't afford not to have Franklin on our side. Oh and by the way, isn't Charlene just so beautiful to look at, Anna? *Isn't* she?'

Fortunately, as usual, he did not wait for an answer.

There was a park in Barcelona, Anna and Piet had visited; like a small scale – very small scale – Disneyland for adults, you could say, designed by Gaudi, having all the mystery and oddity that such places ought to have and usually don't. Small as it was, and though it had its due entrances and exits, you could not for the life of you tell even so much as where it began and where it ended. The joy was that you really did not need to know, it did not matter, except in the most limited, practical sense, where it began and where it ended. After three days of academic subtexts, rationality, pretended dispassion, Anna had smiled, laughed with relief at the Parc Guel. Its mystery was not like that of the faceless kachina doll, disturbing; nor, unlike the equally bizarre Tingueley sculpture in Basel, was it noise and frenzied activity, hard edges and straight lines; it was blue and white mosaic glitter, curvilinear shapes, towers or walls, seats or tables; and all of it quite silent, at the same time as genuinely humorous even joyful as the Tingueley was not. But then this was Catalonia not Switzerland. In Switzerland she had not seen a single black virgin, let alone one forced into a bottle.

313

Chapter Four

One thing that came out of Anna and Carter's late night talk in Ecuador, was an invitation to Basel, for Anna without David. Jacoman said she couldn't write this book, she couldn't begin to, if she didn't understand how Bader-Kleitz worked; how the pharmaceutical industry in general worked, for that matter; he would brief her himself, then fix her up with some interviews, and so forth. Anna said she wasn't aware she had even agreed to write such a book, yet; because she hadn't. (Not least she had never, till now, written any thing much longer than 5,000 words – her pieces usually were a good deal less.) To this protest Jacoman did not appear to be listening. Driving down to Quito the following day, his good humour seemingly quite restored, despite the fact that they were on their way to confront Aguadiente with his failure, he alternated between discussing research matters with David, and firing pharmaceutical jargon at his wife. Some words she asked him to explain; some definitions he gave her; others she came up with for herself, later.

Altogether it is high time for a pharmaceutical digression.

Anna Kern's notebook; 1987-8.

Corporation = (courtesy, Ambrose Bierce) an ingenious device for obtaining individual profit, without individual responsibility. (*N.B. Anna: I'm being naughty*).
R & D = Research and Development of new drugs. For the drug trade, this is the expensive part of their business; the development of a new drug can cost up to £10bn;

314

indeed a company may spend £5bn on some compound which never reaches the market. Such figures are used by pharmaceutical companies to justify high prices and to show what good boys they are spending all that money on spec for the good of the world.

Ethical drug = can be unethical drug = one dangerous enough to be available by prescription only, not OTC.

OTC = Over The Counter. Eg headache powders, cold cures, vitamin pills, etc. Also big business.

Me-too = a reformulation of an old drug; another version of aspirin, say, as opposed to something entirely new – an effective migraine specific drug, say. Bader-Kleitz' current lack of genuinely new drugs, as opposed to me-toos, partly explains eagerness to expand the market for older drugs like Lenytol, even though such drugs are no longer in patent and can be copied by any company.

Detail man = drug salesman.

ADR = Adverse Drug Reactions (death: for instance).

Retrospective/reactive = acting/devising policy after some event or crisis (for instance on ADR).

Proactive = anticipating problems – eg an ADR – in advance, and having strategies worked out to deal with them. Companies, in particular Bader-Kleitz are getting smarter at this these days. It isn't *just* better PR; but it helps.

Biodata = biographical material/CV.

Mindset (a word Jacoman is *very* fond of) = more or less what it sounds like. Mindset as chess set. Change ivory/ebony for plastic or vice-versa. Being able to change your mindset thus, eg from seventies soft-edged to eighties hard-edged, consumerist to monetarist, is highly regarded.

Social market = selling something with regard to social sensitivities, that is as if you've got the customer's needs/situation in mind at least as much if not more than your profit; an especially important strategy, public relations-wise, if you're selling anything as sensitive as drugs. Bader-Kleitz, at senior management level, at least, was one of the first pharmaceutical companies to get this point. (Be warned however; pace Baudelaire ... 'for the merchant even honesty is a financial speculation'.)

Product = drugs in this case; but virtually anything otherwise – from your body if you're a model, or a prostitute, come to that, to a medical service, to a church, to an opera performance . . . to this book you're reading.

Customer = consumer of any product including any of above; is superseding useful words like passenger, audience, pupil, client, even patient, in commercial-speak. Even reader; alas.

Interface = point at which any one person/institution/ section interconnects with another; eg customer meets seller, marketman meets medical director, executive meets board, book meets reader, etc., etc. *(N.B. Anna. Point at which public life – professional life – meets private life come to that. Exactly where this interface is put is a significant issue: how far public life intrudes into private lives, private lives into public, could almost be said to define the differences in general between different cultures, ethnic, professional, commercial, the cultures of gender, as between David and me, not least. David excludes his private self – his private life – much more rigidly from his public/professional life than I would think either possible or desirable. At least he thinks he excludes it. Whereas I, and the Ecuadorians, for instance (Aguadiente with his emotional torment, and, much more significantly perhaps, his using, giving jobs to, his own group, his own tribe in effect) acknowledge our private selves in the work much more than my husband would think appropriate, as a scientist, as a doctor, as an Englishman; as a male, even. Actually, I think it's a delusion we're all so very different. No one can be detached from themselves entirely, not even a scientist in a lab. It's just that some cultures, professions, genders mind less than others having their private agendas on show. What could be more publicly correct, businesslike, detached in a Western sense, than the way the Swiss go about things? But in the final analysis who could be more tribal than the Swiss? Who could be more tribal than doctors, come to that, in England, at least?)*

Despite his marital and professional problems, Jacoman did not forget his invitation to Anna. Although much postponed, her visit to Basel to investigate the company took place at last the following summer, shortly before he left the company, but after Giselle and his children had departed for Canada. A visit at such a time inevitably had implications for their friendship. What she set down, however, was simply what she learned of Bader-Kleitz itself, hoping to understand better thereby the problems relating to the company that beset the project; in particular the problems that related to Jacoman.

Anna Kern's notebook. July 1989.

Bader-Kleitz according to its employees:
'I tell you, to be a doctor working in this pharmaceutical company, any pharmaceutical company, if you want to be promoted to be medical director, for instance, you have to compromise. *I've* compromised some of my principles. (Disaffected English, ex-Medical Director, met by chance at a medical dinner.)

'The medical department has autonomy as long as they're making money.' (Marketing Man.)

'The thing about Bader-Kleitz is that when a project is accepted there are some clear guidelines, the bottom line is that you're accountable, but after that you work it out yourselves.' (Ditto.)

'We are very freely organised. We have personal decision, things are more spontaneous than in Kleitz in the old days. Negatively you could say, if someone didn't like you, you had problems.' (Communications manager, Swiss, ex Kleitz, gives impression he himself would prefer much less spontaneity.)

'Decisions here are never a one man show, it always goes through allies which you pull in – it would otherwise be very vulnerable.' (International Relations Manager. Smooth. Academic. Clever. Rumoured to have Big Brothers on Management Committee, unlike Carter. One of Piet's few fortunates who do all the nice things. See below.)

'In any company you have conventional and unconventional jobs. In a company like Bader-Kleitz you will employ bookkeepers and suchlike and people you actually need to do the business. The unconventionals I would say are in a very elastic position. When sales go up, they employ far more of them. But in Basel we have a six or seven strong basic group who do all the nice things and get the credit – it's very remarkable it's always the same people doing the nice things . . .' (Piet Van Dyke.)

(Comment – do I detect a sour note here? cf. F. Bacon. 'Young men are fitter to invent than to judge, fitter for execution than for counsel, and fitter for new projects

317

than for settled business.' True of Jacoman?? But not true of Piet? He does, he's always done, all the donkey work . . .)

'There was this English colleague of mine. He had to go to the States for some conference along with two of his bosses, both Swiss. He was relatively junior, he sat in the back of the plane while his bosses sat in the front. But half-way through the flight, one of them came to the back and said, to this guy's surprise, "Well, Philip" (I mean it was his name, Philip, but none of his bosses had ever called him that before, even when they got on the plane, he'd been Doctor Watts, as usual, while this guy was Herr Kreutzer, and his colleague still up in First Class knocking back champagne, was Herr Dr Fankheim.) "Well, Philip, things must change for a little while, now that we will be in the United States. You will call myself Heinsli, Herr Dr Fankheim's name is Franz. And when we talk in German we will address each other as *Du*, not *Sie*. Of course when we go back to Basel, we will return to Swiss ways. But in the USA, we have to do as the Romans do, isn't that right?"' (American Journalist, working in Bader-Kleitz Information department – an iconoclast. On his desk he had a paper stars and stripes, and a little plaster model of Ronald Reagan.)

'You've got to remember that in Bader-Kleitz there's no one guy making all the decisions. It's all committees, all various people, everyone's guessing what the guy above him's going to think. So he can make the right judgment. If he doesn't he's not going to get promoted. But his boss is never going to tell him what judgment to make, no one tells anybody what to do in this company. But Heaven help you if you don't do what's wanted.' Carter Jacoman.

'Do you get sacked in the end, if you keep getting it wrong?' Anna had asked in answer to this. Jacoman laughed, mirthlessly.

'No one in a Swiss company ever gets sacked, Anna. They just get moved sideways, into a corner. Given some meaningless title, that's all. It's only in American companies you're out on your ear, like yesterday, if you don't reach your targets, if your face doesn't fit.'

*

Bader-Kleitz: the sociological/administrative view. In all organisations, Jacoman reminded Anna, there are tensions between certain forces – why should Bader-Kleitz be any different? – it wasn't. Indeed the tensions Anna Kern herself particularly noted in the course of her brief visit between the aims and views of the ideas men, the policy/image-makers, the would-be innovators, and so forth, and what were seen as the cruder commercial ends of the marketmen, both clarified and expanded the understanding she'd acquired from observing, listening to Jacoman, over the preceding years.

She discovered, for instance, that most people outside the marketing department despised the marketing-men; it wasn't just Jacoman despised them. 'They don't know how to use data. They're not trained,' she was told. Or, 'Medical men end up in gaol if they make a mistake – marketing men don't.' Or, 'Of course marketing men don't understand these long-term projects, they only think in terms of more sales, instant results. You get resistance all along the line from them. They think all our social projects should be left to charities and churches.'

That Jacoman didn't consult with marketing men was something else Anna heard, over and over. Aided and abetted by Taylor, he'd spent large amounts of money not only without any reference to short-term market advantage, but without so much as a nod towards the marketing department. This was not the way of others in the organisation, even those who said such rude things about the marketing men. It was certainly not the way of Hicks, Taylor's successor.

On her second evening in Basel, Anna was invited for a drink by a Chinese woman from the Third World department who had worked hard to interest her in the wonderful things Bader-Kleitz was doing for lepers in Taiwan and Thailand. In a room overlooking the by now glittering river, a glass of Cinzano in one hand, Anna smiled innocently at this woman – about to play tennis she'd changed into a white tennis dress, revealing the straight slim legs of a twelve year old – at her English fiancé, a financial whizz kid in a tropical suit, with a disconcertingly soft, fair skin, at two other young women also from the policy department (neither of them Swiss). And she had asked, innocently, why no one had thought of letting her interview someone from the marketing department. Whereupon they all laughed very loudly – how could she possibly *want* to talk to marketing men? they asked, when they stopped to draw breath. Marketing men were so *crude*, and also so *stupid*. They *always* picked up your ideas two years later, claimed them as their own and garbled them *disgustingly*. Still more innocently – perhaps too innocently – Anna said, 'I don't understand this. Most of the flak – the bad publicity – the company gets arises from its marketing methods. Yet inside the company you despise marketing men. So why don't you employ better people – ones you don't despise – then maybe their methods would be better, you wouldn't get the flak?' This question being followed by a stony silence, and then, coldly – from the financial whizz kid – by, 'What do you mean, exactly?' Anna made a tactical retreat. But she still thought it was a fair question; thought it even more so, when the one marketing man she did finally manage to meet, a Frenchman, took her out to lunch and made faintly anti-Semitic insinuations about her husband between fussing with the waiter over how he wanted his steak cooked and the precise balance of ingredients in his salad dressing.

Bader-Kleitz: the figures. (According to company fact sheets, pharmaceutical journals, etc., lavished on Anna in the course of her visit.)

Multinational company with a turnover in 1988 of around 18 billion Swiss Francs, almost double what it was in 1979; of which 29.3% – the largest share – was earned by the pharmaceutical division; 45% was earned in Europe, 29% in the USA. Labour force around the world 90,000 approx of which 21,000 were in Switzerland, a third of these non-Swiss.

As regards pharmaceuticals: in 1985 it had 3.5% of total world sales, in 1986, a bit less, 3.1%, in 1988 3.8%.

Its continual desire to expand its share was the basis of Carter Jacoman's claims for his project; Lenytol is one of the company's major sellers.

Bader-Kleitz continued. Anna Kern's diary. 1988.

People's offices are interesting; the extent to which some impose their personality on them and some don't. Carter's office is a mess, papers stacked on every surface, and falling onto the floor, his secretary making vain attempts to tidy them up. Piet's office, on the other hand, is jokey. He has a large picture of Arap Moi on one wall, General Zia on another, and Jacoman on a third. Their department is in a very small building; rooms like boxes, low ceilings; not the least prestigious-looking, except the room just vacated by Taylor – that has a huge desk placed at an angle – plants large enough for the Tropical House at Kew. The headquarters I was escorted to later by Piet, sits alongside the Rhone and alongside the manufacturing plant with its metal chimneys and pipes, and is quite a different matter. Austere, high-ceilinged. Shiny floors. Leather sofas. But again, when you go through from the lobbies to the various departments, the atmosphere – and the decor – changes completely. The information department, for instance, is gloomy and shabby, shambolic, filing cabinets tucked into corners everywhere. The policy department, the company think tank, has new carpets and primary colours. While the department that deals with Third World issues, and has been around much longer, is more like the lobby, austere, carpetless, etc. – but with the odd ethnic rug from Africa or Latin America, ditto objects – raffia baskets – African heads – etc., displayed on walls and shelves.

The head of this department, Reiner, a university professor in his spare time, is the ultimate in PR men – a bit like Robert Redford, without the sex appeal. He was, Piet implied, one of Carter's arch rivals. They'd coincided somewhere in Africa, and not got on. Carter told me Reiner didn't matter; the Third World

321

Department is peanuts, employs less than ten people. But Piet insisted I had to see him, that Reiner was an unconventional, one of those he said got to do the interesting things. He had at least two big brothers on the main executive committee, and given the way this company works, was worth keeping on the right side of. Carter's refusal to consult, let alone make an alliance with him, on the ground that if he did Reiner would steal his ideas, was one of the two prime examples (the other was his refusal to throw sops to the marketing men) of Carter building his empire upon sand. Now that Taylor has gone and Carter is going, the marketing department and Reiner, both, are sniffing round the ongoing epilepsy projects. That is, if they continue, once the main project is over. Piet thinks – Jacoman dismisses such an idea – that they may not. Given the reputation of Hicks, the man who's succeeding Taylor in a month or two, he thinks he may close down – I beg your pardon, close *out*, Jacoman's projects altogether.

A slippery character, Reiner, whatever the case. I saw him give a perfect example of commercial tight-rope walking in moral terms. On a low table, there was a beautiful silver and ivory bowl, in the form of a head. Piet picked it up and made a joke about ivory being a bit politically contentious at this time for a department like Reiner's. But Reiner just smiled, took it away from him to put back on the table, saying smoothly he'd had it at least ten years, long before anyone made a fuss about elephants. End of subject.

On an earlier visit to Basel – Anna had accompanied her husband this time – a few weeks before Christmas the previous year, the relations between Giselle and Jacoman appeared amicable enough, if cool. David said he hardly noticed them exchanging a word, but Anna pointed out that there wasn't much chance for them to do so, given that he and Carter spent most of the weekend in Carter's office. She also said how helpful Carter claimed to have found the talks with Anna about his marriage. 'I should hope so,' said David, smiling, 'you spend enough time on it.' On the Saturday evening, Giselle cooked them all dinner – a very good dinner, defiantly French, *poule au pot*, with a saffron rice stuffing and a *tarte aux pommes*; Carter ate enthusiastically, congratulated his wife loudly, and waxed quite jovial; Giselle, when she was not attending to the food, looked, mostly, at her plate. Alone with Anna during the day, she contrived to be both distant and, as before, inquisitive, probing about the Kerns' marriage; she did not relax until on Sunday afternoon, at last, Anna persuaded her to show some paintings. Though the tight, logical, illogic of these, their defiant, yet perverted femaleness – flowers like clamped vulvas and so forth – made her nervous, at the same time their sheer power and skill genuinely impressed her. Giselle, hugging one of her twins as Anna leafed through the folder, was clearly pleased by her admiration. She even kissed the twin – Chantal was it? – or Suzette? the two were, really, ridiculously alike. Anna had noticed before that Giselle, though seemingly devoted to her children, did not show them much overt physical affection, at least not in front of Anna. After this she was not only less distant with Anna; she embraced her children more in Anna's presence.

Sometime during that winter of 1987-88 – had Giselle, Anna worried, observed the rapport between her husband and the two of them that weekend and felt excluded – had it made things still more difficult? – the marriage of Carter and Giselle Jacoman went from bad to worse. Inasmuch as Carter was sensitive to these things – and he was away a lot, though maybe a bit less so than the year before – he felt the problem lay less with him than it had done; that much more now, it lay with Giselle. Even he could see she was depressed. She could not be bothered to argue with him any longer. All arrangements he made, involving her and the children, she accepted in silence; she herself made no arrangements, of any sort, not for the family, at least. If he had not said, this weekend we will drive out to X, or take the children to Y, they would have done nothing, gone nowhere. Whereas

323

on his instructions she would make a picnic, put the children into snow-suits or whatever, and only sometimes, herself, cry off at the last moment, saying she had a headache or some such. Maybe she did have a headache, these days she almost never looked well. But Carter, mostly, forbore to ask her what was wrong; the few times he did she refused any answer beyond a shake of the head; at best she muttered, 'What do you care?' beneath her breath.

At this time, she not only stopped talking about setting up an exhibition of her paintings, as she had done ever since they arrived in Basel, she did not appear to be working at all, apart from one painting weekend she arranged and the one night a week she went to a drawing class, getting in a baby-sitter if Carter was away. Those were almost the only nights she did go out. Even so, these days she rarely waited to eat with Carter; instead she shared the kids' tea – or claimed to – she'd grown so thin he wondered if she did eat – leaving food in the oven for him; not her home-cooked French food, either, pizzas more often than not – though up till this time, she'd always cooked, no matter what. Sometimes she went so far as to get the food out of the oven for him and lay the table. More often she did not. While he ate, at the big table overlooking the garden, she would either remain upstairs with Louis or the twins, or else sit on the brocade-covered sofa at the far end of the room, alongside her array of carefully-tended plants, watching one of the video cartoons that, Swiss television being incomprehensible to all of them, they'd got in for the children. Or rather Carter had got them in; to begin with Giselle said her kids watched video cartoons over her dead body. But now they watched them all the time. *She* watched them all the time. Carter tried to tease her about it. She hid behind her hair, her eyelids, her imported magazines, *Elle* and *Paris Match*, her much-thumbed copy of *Madame Bovary*, in French of course. She would not be teased. She could not be teased. Baffled, Carter retreated.

She claimed she hated Basel; she claimed all the expatriate wives hated Basel, and in that she might have been right. She claimed the children hated Basel. She claimed she had no friends in Basel, the children had no friends. Little Canadian flags drawn by the children appeared all over the place. The children said daily, twice daily, three times daily, 'When we go back to Canada ...' or 'In Canada, we ...' or, 'Dad, when *are* we going back to Canada?'

Not that Giselle herself ever talked about Canada, at least not to him; she'd always claimed she hated Canada anyway, she could hardly start being sentimental about it now, that wasn't her style. So that when, driven to exasperation by maple leaves everywhere, Carter shouted, 'You're all as bad as Navarro, wanting to get to Madrid; no, we are not going back to Canada; not next week not *ever*, if I can help it,' she could and did look innocently blank.

Two weekends that winter she went away, to her painting course, and once, to visit her grandmother in London, leaving Carter to look after the children; on account of the painting course he had to move a trip to Ankara back four days, to Taylor's polite fury. ('I would submit, Carter, it is not the behaviour of an executive to let his wife's arrangements get in the way of his business commitments ...' 'Poor Jennifer,' said Giselle, of Taylor's wife, when Jacoman reported this. Not that Jennifer Taylor failed to do exactly what she wanted, all the time, as Carter was well aware. Giselle, in any case, loathed her even more than she loathed Taylor – Jennifer Taylor's idea of what she'd call leisure wear was a designer track suit and high-heeled boots; 'Ugh,' said Giselle, with an exaggeratedly French shudder.)

Two other weekends out of those when he was scheduled to be at home, Giselle indicated she did not want him there. 'How about you going someplace else?' was the implication. It wasn't quite as crude, as direct as that; what she said could have been interpreted quite differently, if Carter wanted. But Carter didn't want, or didn't know how to, he didn't pay enough attention you could say. He read the message crudely, added it to his list of resentments related to his wife, and made his arrangements. In each case he went to London, to stay with David and Anna.

On the first such visit, Jacoman coerced Piet into coming with him, brought endless figures and files on files, spent most of the two days locked into the Kerns' sitting-room with David and Piet, papers all over the floor. By the end of the weekend the room reeked of tobacco smoke; Piet kept coming out into the hall, to cough, ostentatiously. Twice he insisted in taking himself off to run round Bishop's Park.

'It's nice to see one of you not totally obsessional,' said Anna, smiling at him as he came in, sweating. None of this work involved her. Getting on for a year after her second trips to Ecuador and Kenya, still some time before the data from the projects was due to arrive and put her back to work, she felt a long way outside of it; a long way from Carter, also; he had stopped ringing her to talk about his marriage; to talk about anything, come to that. These days what took up her time, ironically enough, was research for a series of articles about crisis points in marriage. (She considered, at once rejected, the idea of using Carter's marriage as an example of the stress in an executive's marriage. As she also rejected discussing the effects of Ben's epilepsy on her first marriage; even anonymously, it wouldn't do.) Though suspicious of the superficial line the editor concerned expected her to take – had working academically caused her to be more dissatisfied with such an approach, she wondered? – she was enjoying her journalism again; beginning to be apprehensive – of course she did not admit it – at the prospect of having to break off again, to work on the analysis of the project.

The second weekend Carter came to London, in late February, early March, he just said he needed to get away; that was all. He gave them two days warning only, too late for Anna to delay the arrival of Nikki, who had also announced her imminent arrival in London somewhat belatedly, but in her case the week before. She was due to arrive on Sunday, around lunchtime. Carter arrived at nine o'clock on Friday night; overlapping with Nikki by one night; one of them, Anna was not sure which, would have to sleep on the sitting-room sofa. It was a meeting she looked forward to in a mixture of curiosity and irritation, not least because of the triumph with which Nikki would greet the coincidence she had been angling for ever since she'd first heard of Carter. She wondered, too, about the effects of such a meeting on her relationships with Nikki and Jacoman, both. Nikki, also, had seemed a long way away from her recently. As for Jacoman, but for the tape she'd made of their late night talk in Ecuador, she might have assumed that she had dreamed it.

Carter scarcely tried to pretend work as an excuse for coming on this occasion. He talked project to David for about an hour; at one point he drew Anna aside and mentioned, to her disquiet, something about having met the Locks again, about his hopes she could liaise with them. But that was all. David's edgy attempts to get more from him about the Locks were fruitless. Giselle he didn't mention.

'I don't think that marriage is going to last,' David said, in bed that night.

'They can't talk to each other, those two,' said Anna. 'Piet says he keeps telling Carter he should do something about it, but Carter takes no notice; *he* claims it's Giselle can't talk, not him.'

'What are you doing, gossiping with Piet about Carter? Carter's Piet's boss,' said David, wryly.

'Don't be so hierarchical, sweetheart,' returned Anna.

'Ever my anarchical wife,' David teased her. 'You're worse than Carter, Anna.'

In the morning, early – Nikki was due at eleven – they walked Carter around Bishop's Park. He insisted on their linking arms as they walked, talking about the three Musketeers, crying 'here we are again' and so forth, guffawing a lot. But it didn't make him look any better, happier. Even the keen March wind could not put colour, Anna noticed, in his sallow cheeks. Half-way round the Park, near the football stadium, he began talking about his future in terms that shook them both, given what a long way the project had to go. For the first time he made it clear he was thinking of leaving Bader-Kleitz, sooner rather than later, if he didn't get Taylor's job which was coming up any minute. He was increasingly sure he wouldn't get it.

The moment she heard him use words like 'leave', like 'departure', Anna, for all her surprise, believed he was serious, that he would leave Basel; she believed him absolutely. At the same time, her sense of impending loss made it clear how much the pleasure of this work, for her, depended not on working with David so much, as on working with Jacoman. It meant almost more to her, even, than her commitment to the project, because of Ben. What would it be like after all this time having no Jacoman to talk to? she wondered, forgetting that she had hardly talked to Jacoman at all during these past few months.

'I don't want to be identified with the pharmaceutical industry for the rest of my life,' Jacoman was saying now, so loudly it caused, or seemed to cause, a sparrow to fly out of a bush.

'What's brought this on, Carter?' David asked.

'The bottom line, David,' said Carter, 'that's what's brought it on. The bottom line is I've just got to get you to buy more and more drugs; more and more Lenytol; that's the beginning and end of it.'

'Now he discovers it,' said David, drily.

'Don't get me wrong, you guys. Don't get me wrong. I've still got nothing against drug companies intrinsically, I've got nothing against Bader-Kleitz, intrinsically, it's a great company. No, Anna I'm not trying to be subversive. All I'm trying to do is get across the idea that if you bother to look more closely at what the consumer wants and base your market policy on that, your market will grow more slowly but be much more solidly based.'

'And won't the company acknowledge it?' asked Anna.

'Up to a point,' said Carter gloomily, drawing out another fag and then tossing the empty packet into a wire bin full of crisp packets and takeaway containers, 'up to a point. But at the same time they want miracles. They want their loaves and fishes.'

'And do you give them any?' asked David, glancing at Anna.

'The odd loaf, the odd fish,' said Carter, still more gloomily. 'But it's never enough. Especially when any of them gets wind of Watertooth, and what he's up to. I tell you that man gets crazier every day, what he does to himself and his career, I don't mind, what he does to mine is the problem.'

'Surely he can't damage you *that* much?' asked Anna.

'Only inasmuch as he demands all the energy I haven't got,' said Jacoman. He added, with a wry smile, that he was reminded of the old Chinese superstition that a corpse had to be buried in the foundations of every building. 'Guess who the corpse is in our project,' he said, 'I give you one guess. If Watertooth comes out of all this intact, then I'm a Dutchman.'

Here Anna looked at David, and David looked at Anna; each of them wondering – and wondering whether the other'd had the same thought – if the corpse, assuming there was, there had to be a corpse, wasn't easily as likely to be the corpse of Carter Jacoman.

As soon as they got back to the house, Anna went to fetch Nikki from the airport. ('Why can't she come in a taxi?' asked David, rhetorically; he had asked the same question last time.) All the way back in the car, when she was not speculating on the meeting with Jacoman ('You mean I'm really getting to meet this guy at last, Anna, that you've been keeping to yourself all these years?' – Anna forebore to point out that, given geography, work, the price of air fares, a meeting between Nikki and Jacoman was hardly something she could either prevent or arrange; what was Nikki doing coming in termtime anyway, what about the classes she was supposed to teach?) Nikki declared how tired she was, how she hadn't slept a wink, she was going to have to crash out right away, the moment they got in.

But of course she did not crash out; the moment she

walked in the door, her jet-lag appeared to vanish. She did not even take her luggage upstairs, she only contemplated for a moment changing out of the turquoise cat suit in which she had travelled, declaring, immediately, she was too tired to think of any such thing; besides she'd be going to take her nap, any minute. (Anna thought it was as much that the cat suit suited her very well; she wore little turquoise suede boots to match; round her neck was a big gold chain.) She used the downstairs lavatory to brush out her red hair and apply more lipstick, before the meeting with Carter. And in due course it was David who, tired of falling over her assorted bags in the hall, took them upstairs for her, as it was David who brought Carter's bag back down; Carter, having agreed, gallantly, to sleep on the sitting-room sofa, was too busy talking to her to fetch it down himself.

More than ever that day – it seemed an inordinately long day to him – David Kern became aware that he really did not like Anna's friend Nikki. Though not a man who said much about his feelings, he was reasonably conscious of them, and, inasmuch as he thought them important – often he did not – reasonably honest about them, to himself at least. He knew he felt jealous of Nikki's friendship with his wife (not because of the way Nikki made up to Anna, though; he recognised that as mere tease much sooner than Anna; all that did was make him dislike her more than ever). What he did not let himself admit was that he now felt jealous of her instant rapport with Jacoman; but then he'd never let himself admit he'd sometimes felt jealous of Anna *vis-à-vis* Jacoman, and vice-versa. He attributed the worst of his disaffection, therefore, to the fact that he'd been left to carry the luggage, upstairs and down. He certainly did not speculate, like Anna, on the possibility that in the event of the Jacoman marriage breaking up – it certainly looked likely to – Jacoman might get together with Nikki.

What had most struck Anna about the meeting, however, was that it showed how very subdued Jacoman had been by his standards, until Nikki walked into the room; and how little she and David had succeeded in cheering him up. Whereas he let Nikki cheer him up; or seemed to – if his being much noisier, suddenly, his jollity much less forced, indicated his being more cheerful. She minded more about that, curiously enough, than about the pair's long-term prospects, assuming there were any. The moment she led the freshly lipsticked and hair-brushed Nikki into their kitchen, Jacoman, looking much too large all at once in the space where the table was, got up, stubbing out his cigarette as he did so, and held out his hand; at the mere sight of the red hair, the turquoise cat suit, he'd actually laughed; as if a Nikki was the very last thing that he expected. And immediately, for Anna, there was this contrary, at the same time complementary juxtaposition; gold and silver you could say; or maybe, more appropriately, platinum and bronze. A mass of red hair against Jacoman's bleached-out wisps – high colour against lack of it – deep brown eyes against icily pale ones – negative against positive you could say, except that neither image was more forceful than the other; neither superseded the other.

It was only for an instant. The world turned; the images settled; became Anna and David's kitchen on a bleak Sunday morning in early spring, of which the only sign yet was one solitary yellow crocus in the garden outside – amid the drab remains of winter it looked as exotic as Nikki did, as Jacoman and Nikki did greeting each other, surrounded by Sunday clutter; newspapers all over the table; half drunk cups of coffee; a sink full of breakfast dishes; and so on.

'Pleased to meet you, Carter, Anna told me so much about you,' Nikki was saying. She was holding Jacoman's hand somewhat longer than seemed appropriate, at least by David's standards, and even by Anna's.

'Well I'm glad to meet you too, Nikki,' said Carter in the bemused tone of someone who'd heard nothing about the woman he was meeting, hadn't expected what he got, but having looked at and taken her in, knew exactly what to do with her; she might have been the sort of woman he'd sparred with all his life – it was Giselle now who seemed unlikely. Even at this point Jacoman and Nikki were sparring, or so it seemed to Anna, thinking about it afterwards. As for the hand business; it had all happened so quickly she might have imagined it. Jacoman did not try to take his hand away. If anything he clasped Nikki's tighter. Whereupon Nikki withdrew hers like something wholly within her gift she no longer chose to grant him, and again Jacoman laughed, again for no apparent reason. The next moment they had both somehow fitted themselves at opposite sides of the kitchen table; David was making a fresh pot of coffee, Anna clearing a space among the newspapers. Jacoman took out his packet of Marlboros, now, extracted one – glancing up at Nikki, seeing the expression on her face, he offered her the packet; grimacing, she shook her head. Jacoman at last took the hint. 'Do you mind if I smoke?' he asked her.

'Sure,' said Nikki, sweetly, mocking him in a way that was more tender than triumphant. Jacoman, to Anna's astonishment, put his packet away, and proceeded to mock Nikki in his turn about such an attitude to tobacco, so cheerfully, that you'd think banter was as effective as nicotine for soothing his battered soul.

('Doesn't it make you feel weary, listening to those two flirting with each other all the time?' David asked in bed that night. 'No,' returned Anna, 'just miserably English. Anyway,' she added, 'it wasn't what I'd call flirtation.')

And Anna was right. It was not flirtation – Nikki flirted with her, yes, she could see that now; presumably it was quite safe to flirt with her. But the tone between Nikki and Jacoman contained more comradeliness than sex. This did not mean to say there was no sex. Anna was reminded of women in the kibbutz she'd nearly married into; who worked with men all the time but could not afford to stir them up; or at least could not be seen to be doing so. (Next day, it was true, Nikki did tell Anna how sexy she'd found Carter; and Carter said something to David about Nikki being quite a woman; gee, a real *woman* – Giselle wasn't? David wondered. At the same

time he'd behaved like a man too worn out for actual sex.)
Most of the time they just mocked each other. Jacoman
mocked Nikki for what he called her right-on opinions;
for her pc – politically correct attitudes (this was the first
time either Anna or David heard the term pc – where'd
they both been? Nikki and Carter asked, in concert for
once, before turning their attention back to each other.)
He told her she spoke in psycho-babble, he mocked
California and Californians in general – meantime Nikki
had made much of their both being West Coast – 'Oh Gee,
Carter, you come from *Vancouver* – I don't believe it,
that's really *something*.' (Whereupon she'd winked at
Anna, to Anna's relief.)

What Nikki mocked Carter about mostly was his being
a pharmaceutical executive; Anna could not believe he
would take it so well, but he did; his eyes blazed in almost
the old way; the glitter on him, on his talk, though
ghostlike, shone through. She mocked him about bla-
zered executives (Anna thought of Carter's blue blazer
and giggled). She mocked him about pharmaceutical
ethics, pharmaceutical scandals – she seemed to know a
lot about pharmaceutical company scandals – had she
been reading it all up? thought Anna; bloody hell; and
bloody hell; given the times Nikki had lectured her about
the need for her, Anna, to become more of a commercial
realist. Whereas here she was mocking Carter for being a
commercial realist; for compromising his medical principles; and so on. Bloody *hell*, thought Anna. (The point
was, what was she, or Jacoman, or David for that matter,
to believe? Who exactly was Nikki sending up by this
stuff? All of them possibly? Herself possibly? Nikki kept
on turning to wink at Anna. Carter threw both Anna and
David shamed glances from time to time.)

Once Nikki told Jacoman, who had just leaned across
the table to take another slice of bread, that his table
manners were gross. Anna thought Nikki must have
gone too far, this time; for a moment even Carter looked
taken aback; the next he seemed to have absorbed this,
too, as part of their heavy not – what could you call it but
'*not*' – flirtation.

After dinner that night, after they'd all moved from the table, Anna became, for the first time, aware, strongly aware, of Carter as not actually American, like Nikki, the way he so often, tacitly, made himself out to be, but as Canadian. Maybe it was just seeing him alongside Nikki that did it; or maybe it was not.

The two had calmed down now, somewhat; sat at either end of Anna's sofa talking quietly, sometimes to each other, sometimes to David and Anna. And suddenly, also the first time Anna had ever heard him do so, Jacoman was telling all three of them about the two years he'd spent after qualifying as a doctor, working up in the northern wilderness of Canada, by a lake, amid forests, with the Eskimo people. It was not so much what he actually *said* which struck her – though some of his stories about his patients did remind her of her perception up on the Antiplano that he must have been a good doctor. It was the way he said it; the kind of emotion he showed; as if in the end this had been the best time of his life; as if it had been the place in which, even as a stranger, a white man, a Jew, amid Eskimos, he had felt most at home. 'In his skin' was the way he put it, looking at Nikki, suddenly. 'In my skin.' He spoke with such nostalgia – Anna had never heard him nostalgic for such things – was it Nikki aroused such feelings in him? she wondered, with a pang which was sadness for all of them for their changing friendships. He spoke the way Nikki spoke of rocking on her laudanum-soaked granny's lap – as if this, this northern place, by far the greater part of Canada, far beyond the pullulating towns crammed to the south, the prairies to the centre, these wastes of snow, of forest, inhabited by bears, by wolves, reaching up to a white Arctic wilderness, as Nikki's home country on the other hand, reached down to the arid heat, the deserts of Texas, and California, New Mexico and Arizona; as if this was his cradle, his heartland.

Carter didn't belong in the overheated spaces of the south, whatever he said, thought Anna; he did not finally belong in India or the Sahara. These weren't the source of his wanderlust, at least. His eyes were Baltic, his parch-

334

ment skin like a troll's skin, his hair pale also. He was a northerner; his disappointment just now, she could feel suddenly how disappointed he was, how disillusioned – by his work these days? – by his marriage? – was wintry, as of someone who'd struggled his way across snowy ridges to the Klondike and failed to find gold; the story he came out of was not by Paul Bowles after all; maybe more like something by Jack London.

Next day, Carter left early. To her relief, Anna'd had no impression there had been any nocturnal creepings between the beds in sitting-room and attic. Nikki didn't even get up to see Jacoman off. Her goodbye to him last night had been a platonic kiss on both cheeks. When he demanded her phone number and address, she'd asked, innocently, 'Oh gee, after all that, you're thinking of coming to California?'

'It's just so I know where to start digging you out after the next great earthquake,' said Carter. 'I guess there's one due pretty soon.'

'Didn't you ever have earthquakes in Vancouver?'

'They don't make people like you in Vancouver,' said Carter, 'that's why I left.'

'And why you never came to California?' asked Nikki. 'Well I tell you what, Carter, when you do come, except there's an earthquake, I'll take you to Chez Panisse for one thing.'

'And to a men's consciousness raising workshop for another?' broke in Carter, laughing. Whereupon she rounded on him, furious – Anna had the impression that for once it was no game, Nikki really was furious – 'OK, Carter,' she said, 'if that's what you want. If you're so hooked on the stereotype, you don't want to see the real thing – you Canadians are as bad as the Brits when it comes to that – I'll find you a men's workshop; like it or not.'

'Is that a promise?' asked Carter, looking at her more admiringly than ever.

'It's a promise, Buster,' said Nikki.

Her tone was so unrelenting, Anna found herself

interjecting here, to her own surprise as much as theirs – she could not imagine what came over her – 'As long as you don't forget he's a married man then, Nikki,' she said.

Both of them looked at her; she had the impression neither of them were pleased at such an intervention.

'How could I forget that Carter's a married man?' returned Nikki, and kissed him, for the third time, on the cheek.

For the rest of the week Nikki hardly mentioned Carter. What she did do several times was go over and see Sonia. It turned out that she had called Sonia from California a time or two. But Sonia had never said. If Anna was annoyed, not to say put out, it was because of that, of the secrecy, mainly, or so she told herself. For she was annoyed. And all the more so, the one time she saw Nikki and Sonia together, because in each other's company both Nikki and Sonia were so very different; Nikki less noisy; Sonia more animated. Sometimes Sonia even laughed out loud. Anna had never managed to make Sonia laugh out loud; nor had David, in Anna's presence. Even if she was better than Anna at picking up David's oblique humour, Sonia rarely did more than smile, wrily, at his jokes.

Yet in all other respects it was a good week, better than on Nikki's last visit. Nikki did not try to ingratiate herself with David this time, let alone compete with him for Anna; she kept saying what a sweet guy he was, but why did he have to work so hard? She appeared in all other respects to have given him up; as David appeared to have given her up, going out early most mornings and appearing late most evenings.

'It doesn't matter, enjoy your friend. I've got more than enough to occupy myself with just now,' he told Anna, when she apologised for being so tied up with Nikki. In many ways their friendship was more like it had been before David appeared on the scene; as if, what with Carter, what with her secret friendship with Sonia, Nikki had stamped out ground for herself, and so, surer of Anna, wanted, needed, much less of her. They teased each other as before, discussed clothes, food, inconsequential things, as well as books, as well as God, science, Walter Benjamin, religion, as well as Nikki's love life. At the same time Anna was apprehensive; there was something autumnal about this; she had a sense of things changing, shifting, of a process of loss, of a relation that from now on never would be regained; a relation represented as much as anything by Nikki's renunciation of her former castigations of Anna, the former sharpness of her tongue, by which, lemon followed by honey, she had always wooed her dear friend. Partly it was because Anna herself had changed, more than she realised till seeing Nikki again; teasing her, castigating her, must be much less fun now than it had been. But partly it was because Nikki seemed much less concerned to woo her. Maybe she had surrendered her friend at last to marriage. Or maybe, as in an ongoing marriage, she no longer felt any need to woo her.

As for annoying David; Nikki only made one transatlantic phonecall. Even then she offered to pay. Later that same day, she even accused Anna of not being nice enough to David. (She had heard Anna snap at him at breakfast.)

Two days before leaving, Nikki produced a present for Anna; the faceless kachina doll from the shelf above her bed in Mill Valley. 'You always liked it, Anna,' she said, 'and I never did much. To tell you the truth it gives me the creeps, it really does. But since you seem to like it, it doesn't seem to worry you, I'd like you to have it. And no, hon, I never did find out why it hasn't got a face, what the significance of it is. One day I will, Anna, then I'll tell you.'

Till now Anna had never told Nikki about Benjamin's epilepsy; it was not she'd never thought to, but when they first met, there'd been too many other things to talk about. And besides the thing was too close to her still, too raw; Nikki was too far away, geographically speaking, to be involved in, to be part of that; to put it bluntly, it was none of her business, thought Anna – it was not often, anyway, Nikki let her get sufficient words in edgeways to explain any such thing. And as time passed, just as with David, she thought that whether it was her business or not, Nikki might be offended by not having been told something so intrinsic to Anna's life. This became, also as with David, another reason for not telling her.

But Nikki was quieter on this trip. And Anna did not care too much if she was offended. In any case it wasn't Ben really she wanted to talk to Nikki about; it was more the silence; her not having said anything to David. This weighed on her at least as much these days, if not more than her fears for Ben himself, and there was no one else she wanted to talk to about it. Certainly it surprised Nikki that she had not told him; but she did not make much of it, after all; any more than she made anything, or anything much, of Anna never having told her, either; she implied that everyone had their secrets, including her; why shouldn't Anna? And she took Anna's point completely about David not wanting to have epilepsy in his marriage bed as well as clinic; as she also took Ben's point about wanting David as a father, not as a doctor.

But if this surprised Anna, even reassured her some-what – maybe she had been making too much of this guilt, after all – she did hope so; on the other hand Nikki didn't know David and she did – what surprised her still more was the point at which Nikki, furiously, took David's part, not hers. The point of academic detachment; how Anna's judgment might be less good, when it came to the patients she was working with, not better, because of Ben, her experience of Ben's epilepsy; that David's expectations of bias in such a case was right.

If there was anything Anna had not expected to hear from Nikki, it was this. Perhaps Nikki was just missing her point, she thought; to make sure Nikki was not missing it, she told her a story; about one of the patients she had seen in Ecuador, a thirteen-year-old boy; to which Nikki listened in silence, as if it would never have occurred to her to interrupt, as if all she wanted to do was listen to Anna. Whereupon it occurred to Anna, not quite for the first time, but nearly, that if noisy Jacoman was, contrary to appearances, a good doctor, so might her noisy friend be, contrary to appearances, a good teacher.

'I've forgotten the boy's name,' she said, 'but he lived half-way up between the Chota Valley and the Altiplano, in a house only just off the road. He was the most beautiful boy you ever saw; but very thin; he was wearing nothing but red swimming trunks and a pair of gumboots, so you could see how thin he was. He was also very miserable, sitting outside the house, on a wall, kicking it, his head down. Lastenia talked to him, and he smiled a little. He said his mother was inside the house, but he wouldn't come in. And we sat for hours with the mother, and she told us how many seizures he had – the pills didn't seem to be helping much. And how he'd been sent home from school, because the teacher said it wasn't any good educating boys like him. And I looked at her and thought how lucky I was with Ben. Then Lastenia asked when his last seizure had been; and the mother said, "When he was out riding." I don't think I told you, Nikki, anyone who can afford it in the slightest rides there. And this family did; they had three or four horses. And then it turned out the boy'd had fits several times when he was out riding, and I thought how enlightened of them it was to let him do such things, I'd never have dared to. And then I heard they let him go out riding alone, in fact no one went with him ever. And that every time he had a seizure out riding, he'd have to lie there unconscious for a bit, and then pick himself up and come home on his own. And I couldn't bear it. I mean he might have been killed any time; it was a wonder he hadn't been. And I thought, how could they? But when Lastenia asked why they let him go riding alone, the mother shrugged and said there was too much to do on the *huerta*, no one could afford the time to watch him all the time, let alone go riding with him. He had to take his chances; it was all the will of God. And I wanted to shout out, "Blow the will of God." But of course I didn't.'

'And are you saying she didn't care a damn about him?' Nikki asked. 'Oh no. I think she cared,' said Anna. 'It was just that sort of fatalism. And just letting him go out and lie where he fell. And the way he looked so miserable – he was still out there kicking the wall when we left, still looking desperate.'

Oddly enough, though, having told this story to Nikki, to suggest how much better she, Anna, understood the situation of such a woman, such a family, because of Ben, how indeed she had the right to judge the way they handled the problem, because of Ben, the very telling of the story, the way the words came out, showed different; she was aware of it, even before her friend had time to point it out.

And after a while, after she'd listened to her own voice and Nikki's on the subject, at length, it was like one of their old arguments, going here, there, everywhere, this way and that, there came into Anna's head from somewhere, a long way ago, a long way back, Jacoman's story about the insect spray and the dead chickens; and the people saying – what was it? – 'Chickens is cheaper?' In this case, you could say, the boy was more expendable than the growing of food; the work on the *huerta*. And if she Anna couldn't, wouldn't see it that way, why should she, her situation was quite different, that was no reason why they shouldn't. Was it? Putting that moral conundrum to Nikki, she was quite happy to sit back for a while and let Nikki work it out. Which Nikki did, at length, to her satisfaction and with a detachment David himself would have applauded, Anna thought angrily, hating them both somewhat, and Jacoman, too, for taking such a line, for being right about it; if they *were* right. For if so what to do with feeling? With pity? What to do?

Two months or so later, on the telephone, Anna asked Nikki, curiously, 'Did Jacoman ever get in touch with you, by the way, Nikki?'

'Of course not,' said Nikki, almost indignantly. 'Didn't you keep saying he was a married man?'

Anna did not tell her that the signs were Carter wasn't a married man any longer. She did not think it was her place to; never mind if her motives for such purity were suspect in some ways. Chiefly she thought, snuggling up to David that night as many others in the brief lull before the meeting at Kanterberg, what a relief it was to be out of all of that sexual hope and manoeuvering, that fear of loneliness, that never satisfied itch of longing that belonged to the single predatory life. Marriage was a loss in some ways – briefly she'd felt that talking to Carter sometimes; marriage on the whole did not involve such late night, mental and emotional intoxication, was certainly both puzzling and troublesome; watching Carter and Nikki, she had missed for a moment or two, passionately, that excitement, that simplicity, that unfolding mystery of a new relationship between man and woman; between woman and woman come to that. At the same time, it made her feel, more than for a long while, contented with her lot. Marriage was its own kind of mystery; much less immediately exciting and much less satisfactorily simple. Yet still, despite an ache of longing, for the old precious friendship with Nikki not least, that this marriage had disrupted; despite missing Carter, now, seemingly, gone far beyond her reach; despite, too, the failure of the efforts she was presently making to arouse the lust of her overworked, sleepy husband, Anna was glad at this moment to be where she was and not still emotionally questing, like Nikki; or like Jacoman by the look of it. This was her granny's lap if you like, this her northern haven, this her place where there was no longer any need for light or candle; that was how contented it made her feel. At its best, anyway. Sometimes. She hoped so. But dared, still, be sure of nothing.

'Go to sleep, Anna,' David was muttering. 'Go to sleep. I'm much too tired.' Almost contentedly, she did what he asked her.

At first back in Basel, after that weekend, things went a little better for Carter with Giselle. As if invigorated by Nikki, he asserted himself rather more. He insisted, for instance, that in the evenings, if Giselle would not actually eat with him, she came and sat at the table while he did so. To his surprise, she obeyed, almost meekly, as if she'd been waiting for him to assert himself in some way, as if that was what she wanted. She even began to cook him proper meals, most days, in the old way. But he could not consciously keep up such arrogantly masculine behaviour, not with his wife – the Ecuadorians might have been surprised to hear him say so – nor did he have enough self-insight to compare or equate the way he treated them with the way he felt he ought to treat his wife. Yet such behaviour towards her did go against everything he believed in; it wasn't, in his book, paying enough attention. (And, besides, the maple leaves still kept on appearing.)

Giselle, paler and thinner, ill-looking sometimes, was more beautiful these days than ever. Looking at her sadly, Carter appreciated her beauty, remembered as if in a dream how crazy it had once driven him. If it did not still mean much to him, it was partly because he meant so very little to her; for all their seemingly improved relations, he knew that this was so, even though she treated him, these days, with a kind of weary if resentful affection that made him ache with longing, on the one hand, on the other had him dying to bang her head against the wall. It was at such moments he would remember, with relief, if fleetingly, Anna's large friend, Nikki; how she had mocked and teased him; how he had mocked and teased her; how much they'd both enjoyed it. Giselle had never in her life teased him, any more than she had ever, in her life, accepted being teased. Teasing, even the crude variety of teasing, needed blades, needles of some kind. For all her fragile looks, her pallor, for all the delicate instruments of her art, Giselle had no time for emotional blades or needles. Her own preferred weapon, emotionally, psychologically speaking, he thought bitterly, was a bludgeon. Just as a bludgeon was the only weapon she could recognise, used upon herself. Why else was he always forced to use one?

He took to teaching his son to play baseball, most weekends; that certainly annoyed her – the more so when Louis himself became quite keen on the business; he brought friends home once or twice to play along with them; sometimes they all went to the nearest park to practise. This represented a triumph of some kind for Jacoman. On the strength of it he felt able to suggest that Anna and David Kern came to spend the night at their house before the project meeting at Kanterberg at the end of May; it was all arranged; Giselle was to play hostess whether or not she wanted. But then, six days before the meeting, Jacoman rang David to say he'd had to change the plans, would they mind staying at the hotel in Basel after all? – he'd looked at the schedules and the time the plane came in, the time they had to go out in the morning, it wasn't practicable for them to stay in his house.

As this conversation coincided with a stiff complaint from David as to why he and Anna had learned first from Stanley Heins, not Jacoman, that the Locks, the Twin-locks, the Dreadlocks were also attending the meeting – to sort out some projects of their own, that Bader-Kleitz were financing – also 'to rap with them all' as Jacoman put it – neither David nor Anna felt inclined to reflect much afterwards on the reason for Jacoman's change of plan. Their schedules remained exactly as when they'd made the plans; they'd already discussed them at length – what *was* Jacoman about?

But this was something that Jacoman was not saying; the very fact he did not do so made them in due course guess the substance, if not yet the precise, the awful nature of the ultimatum. One week before Kanterberg, Giselle had announced that in September, latest, she was going back to Canada; if Jacoman wanted to keep contact with his children he'd have to leave Basel himself. She couldn't stand Switzerland any longer. Oh and by the way, she wasn't having her children monolingual in English, that meant she wouldn't live anywhere in Canada, except a French speaking area; which meant it had to be Montreal or Quebec. She'd got a friend there already hunting for an apartment for them. She'd been on to her father to pay the first quarter's rent. Even in Montreal, even in Quebec, he'd said he would do so. Of course. He'd objected to his daughter marrying a Jew, even more than he'd objected to Giselle's mother's

343

Frenchness, Jacoman knew that.

'If you live in Canada without me,' he said, coldly, 'how are you going to keep yourself? I'll support the children. But I'm not going to support *you* in those circumstances.'

'I won't want you to support me; I won't need you to support me; not in Quebec,' Giselle said. 'I'll be able to sell my paintings in Montreal or Quebec; I'll be able to teach art in Quebec. And in any case, if you come back to Canada too, I will live with you, surely?'

'In Montreal?' returned Jacoman. 'In Quebec? My French is lousy, for one thing.'

'You can learn,' Giselle said. 'I had to learn to speak English.' There were tears in her eyes now. But he would not let her sway him.

'Don't give me that, Giselle dear,' he said, thinking of her paintings; paths which led nowhere, hedges without ends or beginnings, petals detached from sepals. 'There just ain't no end to your crazy illusions.'

'There's no end to *your* crazy illusions, Carter,' said Giselle, petulantly. 'What does it matter, anyway? We're going back, with or without you. *I'm* going back. So make up your mind, Carter. Now it's up to you.'

'A bludgeon, as usual, fuck you, Giselle,' said Jacoman, amiably. 'Why, with you, does it always have to be a bludgeon?'

But she looked blank, as usual, as if she did not know what he was talking about. Most likely she really did not know what he was talking about – so, what hope had they? Not a lot, he suspected.

Chapter Five

Ecuador. 1987.

Patient 079 was a little girl, Elisa. They found her alone, dressed in a dirty pink dress and a dirty red baseball cap, in a very poor, dirty house, its floor piled high with rags. Lastenia had told Anna the girl's story as they were lurching along dirt roads toward her, on a morning wet enough to set successive rainbows across the hills; once, almost, a double rainbow. Elisa's father did not believe this child was his. Not only did he beat his wife for her supposed infidelity, he punished the innocent result of it. 'He beats me all the time,' the girl told Lastenia, today, at the end of a long silence. She was eight or so, her face filthy, her nose running, her upper lip encrusted. Though she said little, and that in a whisper, not looking at her, she seemed to like Lastenia; but then all the patients liked Lastenia, the same way Anna liked her. They smiled when they saw her. They told her about their symptoms – they even swapped gossip with her; teased her, as she teased them; conversations with Lastenia were somehow careless, more like conversations between neighbours, between equals, like those between herself and Lastenia, than consultations between social worker and client, in Anna's observation. At the beginning of the visit, often, Lastenia had something to give the patients, if only the answer to a question, or a promise to talk to the doctors. At the end of the visit, they handed her big bags full of vegetables. Elisa had no big bags of vegetables to give away, she barely had a smile. But when Lastenia asked

her what she did when her father beat her, she looked
Lastenia in the face, momentarily, the one and only time;
she even looked, though sideways, at Anna. She said,
without smiling, this was a serious matter; this was a
means of survival: 'I bite him back. That's all I can do.'
Lastenia nodded. She gave the child a peppermint first,
then handed one to Anna.

'Are you having fewer fits now, since the medication?'
Anna asked, through Lastenia – this child could not
understand her Spanish; she could only understand some
of the child's. 'Maybe,' said Elisa, but she would not say
how many fewer. And what hope was there for her,
anyway, in this high, cold, muddy place, the tops of the
livid green hills misted over, the rainbows on them only
rainbows and fading almost as you saw them, scrawny
chickens wandering about pecking at the sodden, dung-
spattered earth? Epilepsy was but one of the child's
problems; except, there was this at least, the child said
her mother loved her; loved her enough to disobey the
father and fetch her drugs.

Love and hate, beatings and tenderness; none of it
seemed to Anna to have much to do with arguments in
smoky hotel rooms, let alone with Jacoman sitting in
expensive restaurants, thousands of miles away, a hundred years ago it now seemed, debating what he called
social morbidity; plain misery in other words, epileptic or
otherwise – what they were now looking at; what most
people turned their backs on. For what help could you
give in the long run? Throughout the world there were
billions more people living the way these people did (and
worse), than those living the way the Kerns did, or
Jacoman did, or even Lastenia. Just as there always had
been people crushed for one reason or another in the
wheels of the social machine, there always would be, no
matter what you did to change governments and systems. In the best, most profitable societies, husbands
beat wives, some marriages were hell-holes. All you
could do really was remind the happy men that such
things existed, persuade them to hand over a little
money, or a little time, as hostages to their own good

fortune. But even this, like all the rest, was mere drops in a vast ocean.

Luckily not all people felt as she did, thought Anna. Look at Lastenia, sitting up in bed reading the biography of Lenin. Look at Sonia, come to that, tending her father. Look at Jacoman, paying attention with all his energy, his fury – but for that energy, that fury, they wouldn't be here, this child would have no hope whatever. She still didn't have much hope. (And what of Jacoman when such energy left him – if he still knew to pay attention, what if he ceased to know exactly where to pay it? As time went on Anna feared increasingly that he was ceasing to know where to pay it; which was his tragedy, of course, no one else's.)

There was another woman she came across in Ecuador, a day or so later, another very poor woman, (patient 112 – Señora Amada Simballa) whose husband loved her. She lived in a hut with a dirt floor so uneven it had hillocks and ridges and valleys among which ran a tribe of guinea pigs, under the feet of both hosts and visitors. These guinea pigs – cuyos – bred for eating, looked just like the long-haired beasts which Anna as a child had kept as pets, on which she had lavished love, yet which had, just the same, carelessly, viciously, bitten her. Maybe, after all, you might as well eat them. And besides, if this woman's husband reared his guinea pigs for food rather than affection, he had married his wife, and her epilepsy, for love, precisely. They'd had four children together. But all the time, all those years he had worked to support them, as paid agricultural labourer on a local hacienda, or on their own *huerta*, he had gone on worrying about his wife alone at home with her children. He would not let her cook or carry things. Even while they were talking, he fussed around her; she sat with a bemused smile, nodding and saying nothing. He wore his trilby hat inside the house, he was unshaven. Her hair was braided, she was wrapped in a torn red poncho. Both husband and wife were small – they came up to Anna's shoulder more or less, their eyes were dark, their skin brown, just beginning to wrinkle. Inappropriate as it

347

might seem, the word 'pretty' came to Anna; in the literal sense she found them a 'pretty' sight. Maybe it was because they were so patently devoted to one another, because they were both smiling, urging bags of aubergines and green peppers on Lastenia. And they sat in this rough, wooden, really quite big house, with its mountainous floor, another big windowless room through a door behind them, cooking pots and bags full of clothes and possessions hung on hooks from the wall, with a fireplace in the far corner emitting wisps of smoke and the odd spark, with the little ratlike animals running from other, dark corners and veering away, no more and no less nervous than the people. The man looking at his wife gladly, said she hadn't had a fit in eight days, he worried about her less now. His wife smiled, nodded, continued to say nothing.

Anna was more hopeful for this pair than for some of the others. But what of later, when the project was over? She would never know; not that it mattered. What mattered to them was that the pills kept on coming and that the seizures did not. Lenytol for a happy life – yes: it went without saying. But how could you gauge a happy life, over the months and years of cold and hard labour? A cockerel that kept crowing and crowing outside had no answers; it neither contradicted nor confirmed a single word, merely drowned at times the tale the man told of his wife, in response to Anna's questions, to her seeking, earnestly, as she was paid to do, 'Explanatory Models'. His wife had her first fit, he said, aged sixteen or so, after she'd been foolish enough to go out at a bad time – six o'clock in the evening – to a bad place – a ravine – and met a white figure that she was sure was the ghost of her recently dead father.

This meant that in return for her papers and questions, in return for the little white pills that had stopped the wife falling down nearly so often, Anna, Lastenia and smiling Antonio, the driver, went away not only with eggplants and red peppers in a plastic bag, but with a ghost story noted down carefully by Anna in her black-backed notebook. She tried to translate 'fair exchange is no robbery' into Spanish for Lastenia's benefit; but if Lastenia understood the words, she did not understand their sense, or rather why Anna was saying them; after a while nor did Anna.

That same night when she mentioned the guinea pigs, Aguadiente told Anna how people killed the guinea pigs they bred for eating; by smothering them first, and then, not always troubling to make sure they were wholly dead, dropping them into boiling water – this made it easier to skin them.

She was sure he did not tell her such a thing to upset her. He never meant to upset anyone she was concluding. It was just his usual bad luck; he couldn't get it right, ever. How could he possibly know what guinea pigs meant to a middle-class English woman? No, of course not. He told Anna quite kindly, dispassionately, a piece of interesting information that he thought she'd like to hear. It was not his fault, it was his tragedy, rather, that when she heard about the fate of Aguadiente's only son, she thought of the guinea pigs dropped, alive possibly, into boiling water.

In the months before Kanterberg, neither Kern had much to do with the project. Jacoman, too, more than they knew was losing interest; it was Piet made most of the arrangements for the Kanterberg meeting. Yet it went on for the people who mattered, for whom it was most supposed to matter, though, these days, that was easier than ever to forget. Some of the patients' lives were transformed for the better; some, their hopes first raised, then bitterly dashed, for the worse. Not that Anna knew which, for the most part; individuals were hard to track down through the record books that had begun to arrive in London; the patients in them were mostly referred to by numbers, not by names. In Kenya, Beatrice was patient 076, for instance. But locating her – and Anna wanted to know her fate – was hard. She tried and failed to track Beatrice a year after meeting her; gave up for the time being. She couldn't find the little girl, Elisa, either.

One patient, a boy of eighteen, she did know about. Bennet sent Anna a clipping from a Nairobi paper which described how he drowned himself around this time. That was the danger of such projects the article said: he had seemed to do so well, this boy; his seizures were controlled completely. But contrary to all his hopes, and in spite of all the health workers who visited him could do to reassure him, he still couldn't make friends; girls wouldn't have him, he was still terrified of having a fit any minute; in the end he'd drowned himself in the river from which his family fetched their water. The article – on the health page of the paper – made the point that with these sorts of diseases the years of fear and derision went deep, and that to cure those was harder than curing seizures; it could not be done with pills, only.

A week or two later the news came, via Piet, of Aguadiente's son, Tristano, the light of his life. He had been knocked off his bike in Quito, and died of brain damage two days later. It had happened three months ago already, before any of them knew, and all this time Aguadiente had continued driving David and Jacoman no more nor less crazy than he had from the start.

Once Anna asked David, 'Why is it tragedies so often happen to the people it's hardest to feel for? Someone we knew lived next to a survivor from Belsen once; they weren't a bit heroic; they were petty and snobbish and horrid. And there's Aguadiente – he still drives you mad, yet how can you laugh at him, any longer? Poor man; it's awful.'

'What a tidy view of life you have, Anna,' said her husband. 'In my job you learn pretty soon that people with tragic histories aren't usually the least like Oedipus; let alone Hamlet.'

'Stop laughing at me, David. I don't have to deal with Aguadiente. You do. You know exactly what I mean.'

'Things like this happen all the time,' said David. 'I see them. People survive. You have to keep working. Life has to go on.'

Life has to go on, thought Anna, even when your elixir of life, your guarantee of life has gone for nothing – just as you, just as anyone, always feared it might. She thought a lot about Aguadiente. Even after her stay at San Raphael, after coming up against him there, being driven crazy by his vagaries, his insistence on this, one day, and that tomorrow, his paranoia, if so it was; after understanding, at last, why David and Jacoman so complained about this man, for reasons beyond the obvious problems of cultural difference, she continued rather to like him; she remembered how once, when her headaches continued, he dropped everything to look for headache pills. He didn't send a junior for them; he went himself.

She had also watched him, there, up at San Raphael, if not with his son, with his little daughter. She and Lastenia returned one cold evening around five o'clock to find Aguadiente sitting at the big table, the girl – she must have been six or so – on his knee; the cassette player, as usual, blasting out Edith Piaf.

Aguadiente didn't see them at first, nor did the child. She was leaning over the table drawing on the back of one of his old charts with a blue crayon, her tongue tucked to one corner of her lip, her concentration absolute. She wore a blue t-shirt, matching blue hair-ribbons tied back her long dark hair. Her father, meanwhile, absently stroking her hair with one hand, held her steady with the other. He wasn't attending to her otherwise, he was having a furious discussion with a fellow neurologist, the one helping him carry out what he called his inventory of patients (that is the list Jacoman had forced him to make after discovering that no one was checking on whether or not anyone was chasing up the patients, let alone seeing they had their drugs).

The whole thing looked odd, somehow. Aguadiente shook his head so furiously, his eyebrows shooting up and down, his shoulders shrugging beyond any necessity. It took Anna a moment to realise that this was because he did not have the free use of the hands he normally used to emphasize everything he said; because he was having to peer at his fellow round the body of his oblivious little daughter. She must have seen him in such guise before, must have felt and heard him and learned to take no notice. She was scratching in clouds now on her picture, it looked from upside down. But as Anna watched, Aguadiente so far lost himself in the argument that the hand tenderly caressing the little girl's hair suddenly forgot to caress, shot up in a furious gesture, in doing so caught on a lock of hair, pulled it – only momentarily, not a hard pull exactly, but hard enough to make the little girl's head jerk up, to make her to cry out, indignantly.

At which Aguadiente, suddenly, noticed Anna standing there watching him. At once he stopped playing neurologist, started playing father. 'Anyone would have thought I'd caught him abusing her,' said Anna, reporting this incident to her husband when she got home. 'He went right over the top.' For Aguadiente had kissed his daughter on the cheek, on the head; he'd lifted up her little hand, the one that held the pencil, her left, Anna noted, and kissed that. He insisted on discussing her picture with her, on showing it off to Anna; a process the child watched quite coolly at first; then buried her face against her father's chest, from which she turned to peer out almost flirtatiously at Anna, the stranger. Indeed all the time her father was playing with her, showing her off, dancing her up and down, acting father, Anna had the impression the child was colluding with her, with the other spectators, to humour him. She could have sworn she saw forbearance in the way the child glanced at her father. He was putting her down now; he was straightening her hair ribbon; pulling up her white socks; making sure the blue crayoned picture, on the back of which one of his complicated coloured timetables was plainly visible, did not get crumpled.

That scene came back to Anna clearly, when Piet was telling her of the fate of the boy, his Tristano. She hadn't seen Aguadiente with this boy any more than Piet had; she had, on the other hand, like him, been shown a picture. Not the neat boy in a bow tie in her case, the photo she saw was of a boy in jeans, laughing, his black hair on end, standing astride what might have been the very cycle that killed him.

Such bolts from the blue; such unseen pits in a dark

street could wait, like seizures for epileptics, for anyone at any time. And how could you bear it? How could anyone bear it, no matter what David said? If any such thing were to happen to Ben ... But of course she spent her life fearing such things for Ben. Every time he went swimming; every time he rode his bike – she was no different from any parent with an epileptic child, even if some of her decisions, courses of action, might be different from theirs – look at the mother of the boy half-way up from the *Val de Chota*, who was so busy she let him go off riding by himself ... (this still shocked Anna; she couldn't help it). Aguadiente's son hadn't been epileptic, the odds against him had not been so great; just the same the pit had opened up and taken him. If it opened up for Ben, Anna thought, she'd lie down and die. Life could go on without her, thank you. She admired Aguadiente for not lying down and dying; even, in the circumstances, for making a nuisance of himself with David. It was the whole problem with having children – there was always this danger, of the ultimate adverse reaction, the real snake in the ointment. From the moment of conception, no matter what, you never had another moment's peace. Was this one reason David was so reluctant to take up that elixir, to drink it, seeing what he saw each day of his working life?

She'd jotted down a passage by Chekhov once in her notebook; she hunted it out.

> ... the real tragedies of life are enacted somewhere behind the scenes. Everything is calm and peaceful, and the only protest comes from statistics ... clearly this kind of system is what people need ... the happy man feels contented only because the unhappy ones bear their burden without saying a word; if it weren't for their silence happiness would be quite impossible. It's a kind of mass hypnosis. Someone ought to stand with a hammer at the door of every happy, contented man, continually banging on it to remind him that there are unhappy people around and that however happy he may be at the time, sooner or later life will show him its claws and disaster will overtake him ... and there will be no one to see or hear him.

Chapter Six

Anna Kern's diary. August 1988.

Bennet came through London last week; I asked him – I forgot at Kanterberg – if he knew what happened to Beatrice; but he didn't. He didn't seem interested, particularly; this was just one patient among many. But then he's a man, of course, men in general seem less interested than women in what happens to people. Whereas I prefer working on stories where I can pick up a human thread – and follow it through to some kind of conclusion. (What she'd first written here was *'confusion'* – she'd scratched it out, with an exclamation mark, before putting in the right word). The people I write for – mainly women I'm told – must want this too – or they wouldn't read me. Even David says I'm good at 'that kind of thing' meaning something he'd never choose to read left to himself. Actually it always surprises me how someone as kind as David, so much better at sorting out other human beings than I am, shows little real curiosity about what happens to them outside his clinic. It's things that really interest him; no, I'm wrong, not things so much as processes, the origins of processes and the results of processes; though I suppose that has at least as much to do with his being a scientist as being a man. He doesn't read what I write, mostly, unless I ask him to. As up till now I've only read his papers when he's asked, usually because he thinks the English needs

354

improving; which it doesn't; he writes well. Now, of course, I'm reading what he writes as a model for what I'm trying, God help me, to write myself.

Anna liked Bennet, the Kenyan sociologist. Sometimes when she thought of Piet, the Dutchman, she thought of him. Maybe it was because, as with Piet, she liked him so much. He was much more ruthless than Piet; she saw that in his reaction to his colleagues; it wasn't his wish that Meaki, for instance, should be given the clapped-out project truck, in due course – that was Falconer's doing – Bennet opposed it. Even so she liked him the way she liked Piet, quite simply and easily, without the equivocation, the high colour, the sheer exhaustion in her liking for Carter Jacoman. One image she had of him, particularly, stayed in her mind; it came from the beginning of her second visit when she was being driven round from village to village to talk to patients.

This particular village was a forest one, that is one temporarily set up for foresters and their families; after six years or so, when that section of forest had been worked out the people would be moved on to another place, another village would be built for them.

Not that this looked like a temporary village; it looked like any other village Anna visited; wooden huts, dirt streets, *shambas* reaching away beyond it, all at this time of year dotted with bent figures, planting. The only difference was that it was, like the other forest villages, a long way from anywhere, up the far end of a red dirt track used by forestry vehicles, and heavily rutted; the sort of track, Bennet told Anna, on which, ten days before, when the rains were still falling, had not, so unseasonably, stopped, the project truck had got bogged down at least twice.

Bennet had come along that day – much of the time he left Anna to his juniors; he had too much to catch up on back at the hospital or even in Nairobi. Although later in her visit he relaxed a little, maintained his tie but wore it beneath a leather jacket, he was clad for this first trip as if for a day at his desk in Nairobi. A handkerchief peeped out of his breast pocket. His suit was dark grey, his shirt white, his shoes gleaming with polish. Only the tie hinted at rebellion. Although striped discreetly enough, in grey and white, it was much wider than more conventional ties, those worn by David, for instance; practically a kipper.

At the end of the road, in front of the village, was a wide grassy space. Here the truck was parked; here they all got out. Bennet's chief assistant, Elisha, went in search of village elders and patients, while the rest of them waited, standing in the sun. In the distance a woman was coming towards them leading a donkey, carrying two large plastic petrol cans on either side of its back; the cans did not contain petrol, Bennet said; they contained water from the village well. The donkey did not seem a particularly slow donkey, as donkeys go, it wasn't recalcitrant; maybe the distance across the grass was further than it looked. For its coming seemed interminable, Anna felt her whole life slowed down to the donkey's pace, all the more so by contrast with the speed with which children had suddenly gathered around them, bare-legged, bare-footed children, in some cases bare-assed. Their clothes were ragged, faded to one colour with long use; their legs were dusty; their faces encrusted; around the mouths, under the snotty noses of many, flies were crawling; this did not appear to worry them in the least, they barely bothered to brush them away, they were too busy pestering the visitors, particularly Anna, the one white face; they were holding out their hands for sweets, crying out hullo, goodbye, how are you, laughing at her, and so on. Once or twice, on the other hand, Bennet, speaking crossly in what Anna assumed was Kikuyu brushed them away like flies. There was no malice in it; there was not even pathos, these children though thin, though dirty, looked well fed and healthy. Some carried on their backs babies almost as big as they were.

After her last trip, after these two days in Kenya, none of it surprised Anna. What surprised her was Bennet's reaction. He stood there in his suit, in his kipper tie, smiling fixedly at her. She could have sworn at one minute he was actually shaking a little. He was not unkind; not even when he was shouting in Kikuyu, brushing the children away from Anna. But suddenly he turned on his heel, marched off into the narrow streets of the village, bordered by their roughly cut, bleached wooden stockades, behind which could be heard the grunt of pigs sometimes, the cluck of hens, once the thin whine of a cheap radio; but scarcely a live human voice. He did not stop even when Elisha appeared and told them he'd found no patients, all but the old and the young were out working on the *shambas*. She had this image of him thereafter, scurrying up these streets, past the hen noise, the pig noise, the curious faces, the scents of people and animals, the gaggle of children at his back, like a man haunted.

At lunchtime, as they sat drinking tea in one of the usual squalid cafes, he told her what haunted him, in an accent so strong, as usual, she missed some of the words, if not the essence.

'You see, Anna, that was just the sort of village I was brought up in. Once I was just as dirty as those children. Once my mother had to fetch water like that from the well; only we were so poor we didn't have a donkey even, we carried those cans of water on our backs. I live in a nice house now, we don't have to carry water, my wife keeps our children clean. Also they wear shoes to school, they don't have to chase after strangers in the street – I buy them sweets, all the sweets they want. But every time I see children like that, villages like that, I think of my childhood. I think how it would be to live that way again. And then I am afraid. I remember how the dirt felt on my face, I remember the flies under my nose, I remember the weight of the water-cans on my back. And I am afraid. I don't want that for my children. I fear it for myself.'

Bennet, very formal usually, very correct, did at times offer such confidences to Anna. He did so throughout the time they worked together. Once, he told her about his marriage – why? she always wondered – to establish his sociological credentials? – in exchange for observing her and David's marriage? Never mind.

Later, as a journalist, she used the story of Bennet's marriage; for an article for the so-called 'in-depth' series on the strategies by which different couples coped with marital stress. (Her own marriage was under stress at the time; where *it* was going was one of many questions at the time to which she did not know the answer. Never mind.)

Bennet's wife is much younger than Bennet; what's more, much to their parents' chagrin, she comes from a different tribe – she's *Luo* and he's *Kikuyu*. A generation back in Kenya you only ever married within your tribe, that was still true in Bennet's home village. But he was an educated man, he lives in the city now and things are changing.

Alas, he and his Loise weren't happy for long. She was very young, he worked long hours. Staying at home with their children she began to grow bored, and bored she grew troublesome. She nagged him all the time, she neglected his house, she cast eyes at other men. In due course Bennet was so fed up with this he even thought of divorcing her.

But Bennet's a clever man – he thought, no, I am a sociologist, I should understand these things, I should understand about women, not surrounded by their tribe any more, but living in a small family, in a city. As a sociologist I've read the surveys about bored middle-class wives living on tranquillisers. What my wife needs is an occupation, an interest.

Unlike Bennet, Loise hadn't been to college, he hadn't given her the chance to finish school before sweeping her off. Now he decided to pay for her training in any profession she wanted. He went to her and asked her what she wanted. And she said to learn to type and do shorthand, and be a good secretary as well as a wife. So Bennet sent her to secretarial college, and then, she wasn't so sure about this but he insisted, to business school. And she did so well, she did better than shorthand

and typing, she now has a little business of her own, selling, even exporting jewellery made by women of her tribe; she employs more secretaries than Bennet.

The last thing Bennet wants these days is to divorce his wife; and all because, he says proudly, as a sociologist he'd thought the problem through. At least that's his version, of course I haven't heard his wife's!

N.B. Anna: I'm not used to writing like this about people I know. In fact there's only one editor demands I write like this about anyone. Does it always sound *that* patronising? Never again.

Anna told Sonia about Bennet's marriage once, in the course of a conversation about her marriage, hers and David's; these conversations occurred every now and then as she and Sonia got to know each other better, always to Anna's surprise and usually against her better judgment. Just then, in particular, she did not want to talk to anyone about her marriage; in particular, she did not want to talk about it to David's sister. Lately, David had not once mentioned their having a baby together – he pretended not to hear any hints Anna might make. She preferred not to reflect on what that could mean or not mean about his feelings towards her.

Getting to know Sonia better, she had, unfortunately, unearthed this wretched ability in her to hit nails on the head, without seeming to have any obvious intention to do so, and certainly without any sign of malice or even curiosity; it was more as if members of that family, on the surface seemingly distant from each other, detached in Sonia's case, were on another level so organically bound up Sonia could take both her uncanny insight and her rights to such insights for granted, whether Anna liked it or not. Anna entirely assumed by now, for instance, that Sonia knew about Ben's epilepsy; whether Ben had told her or not.

Today she mentioned, quite casually, just for something to say – Sonia, wearing an uncharacteristically garish red sweater that did not suit either her or her

Navaho necklace, seemed restless and uneasy, forever casting her eyes to the ceiling for any sounds from her father asleep upstairs – how disappointed David was that Jacoman was not staying to see the Bader-Kleitz project through. And at once Sonia had removed her eyes from the ceiling, and said that David did tend to disappoint easily, he always had; he'd set his heart on something, then be upset when it turned out differently from the way he'd imagined. She glanced at Anna pointedly here. And Anna heard herself saying, to her entire surprise, her voice high with shock and even sorrow – she might have been so brainwashed by Sonia she, too, took her involvement for granted – 'Sometimes I think he's disappointed in *me*.'

'Gosh yes,' said Sonia. 'Gosh yes. But he was bound to be disappointed.'

Anna looked at her, appalled not least by Sonia's cold certainty; she did not want to believe what she was hearing.

'Disappointed in me?' she asked. 'In *me*?'

'Not in you particularly, Anna,' said Sonia, with what Anna took as an air of disapproval – Sonia had this capacity to make her feel paranoid sometimes; even David noticed, he had mentioned it once or twice, indicating as he did so that the prickliness it engendered visibly upset his sister. (But this Anna had not noticed. She was of the opinion that Sonia, though fond enough of her sister-in-law, did not care in the least what Anna thought of her; much more it was David cared what Anna thought of his family, at all times – how he had turned on her, when once, quite kindly, she had mocked Sonia's oddly dated slang.) 'By marriage,' Sonia went on. 'He was bound to be disappointed by marriage. He was the first time, too.'

'But why, *why*?' cried Anna, helplessly. '*I'm* not disappointed. I mean we fight, we're different. But it seems a good marriage, mostly.' It was a comfort to her to realise as she said this, that she did actually believe it was so. How clever Sonia was at pulling out of you what you actually thought, but till that moment had not

360

known you thought. Was she some kind of witch? In that moment Anna loved and hated Sonia equally; pretty much the way she sometimes felt about Sonia's brother.

'David's a romantic. Surely you realised?' said Sonia.

'Jacoman always used to say David was a romantic,' Anna said. 'But then Jacoman can't talk. He's even more romantic.'

'Is he? How super,' said Sonia, a dry note in her voice that always appeared when they talked of Jacoman, whom she had never met. Anyone would think she thought Carter was cuckolding her brother, was my lover, decided Anna.

Sonia was sitting on her piano stool; she swivelled it round now, faced the other way. Her back looked as if she was still listening for sounds from upstairs, presumably, where her father, and David's, now slept away much of his addled days. (This was but three months or so before he died.) Anna did not break the silence therefore, did not say to Sonia what she had said to Jacoman; that yes of course, David was romantic about things like wedding anniversaries, Valentine's Day, the kind of things she herself forgot – on that score she herself wasn't romantic in the least; as he also preferred tragic plays and operas to comic ones – that is *Othello*, for instance – and *Otello* – to *Twelfth Night* or *Così Fan Tutte*; she, preferring irony, was the opposite. But romantic in a broader sense? Of that she was not so sure. What did Jacoman mean, precisely? What did Sonia?

Sonia had swung round to face her again; she still did not look Anna in the face, she rarely looked Anna in the face, though Anna staring straight at her, sometimes dared her to. She dared Sonia to now, as her sister-in-law said, 'David always had a romantic view of marriage; based I suppose on our mother's romantic view of it, which survived all her differences with our father. I suppose that's why he was so desperately disillusioned when his first marriage went wrong. I suppose that's why he waited so long before hitting on you. But he doesn't seem to have learned anything, waiting. This time round too, he assumes it's like some kind of pill, some kind of magic potion; once taken it cures you forever, provided you've taken the right one; first time round, he just thought he hadn't taken the right one.'

'Don't people always think that at some level?' said Anna, thinking with a sigh of her own first marriage. 'Before they're forced to learn better?'

'Of course, but it jolly well takes time to learn better,' said Sonia.

'What in particular,' asked Anna, 'did David expect marriage to cure him of?'

'Oh the usual things; loneliness, depression, boredom; his nastiest nature. Assuming he'd got the right person this time, that is.'

'I'd say,' said Anna, remembering the times she'd found herself shouting at her distressed husband – in his family people didn't shout – as if he were her son Ben, or going on, relentlessly, about this or that, disliking it herself but unable to stop – 'I'd say that even if you have hit the right person, marriage tends to bring out your nastiest nature.'

'Of course,' said Sonia, twiddling her silver bracelet. Anna had seen it before often enough; but for the first time she noticed – why had she not done so before – because her attention had been drawn more by Sonia's necklace? – that it was a snake bracelet; that its clasp was snake's tail, devoured by snake's jaw, snake's head.

Let me be David's right person, she was thinking, please let me, even if there's no such thing as perfection, even if romantic love the way he saw it is an illusion. Meanwhile she looked at Sonia – who still kept on twiddling her bracelet, did not look at her, except for an almost shy, almost amused glance, as if she knew what Anna was attempting. To punish her – by now she almost assumed Sonia could read her very thoughts – Anna asked herself, over and over, what does Sonia know about these things? How can she know anything? She's a spinster. (Deliberately, insultingly, she used that word.) I don't even know for sure if she's been fucked, ever.

Sonia's hand abandoned the bracelet; she pushed her glasses to the end of her nose and peered at the music sitting open on the open piano. Any minute, thought Anna, she will start playing. I don't usually mind Sonia's playing; but just now I cannot bear the thought of all those wrong notes.

Sonia looked her in the face at last. With her glasses still at the end of her nose, she gazed at Anna blindly, like a female Tiresias, knowing everything, revealing nothing. It was when she turned back to the piano – raised her hands – that Anna, to stop her playing, as to stop her talking, hastened into the story of Bennet's marriage. Immediately it was over she wished she hadn't.

'What a super story. But what a pity David's a doctor and not a sociologist,' said Sonia. 'Do I assume the point of this saga is that David doesn't ask you what you want, Anna?'

Anna blushed. 'I'm the sociologist in this family, it's up to me to ask,' she said, and then, Sonia more sardonic than ever – again she looked at Anna squarely, it was Anna who looked away, added, lamely, 'At least I pretend I'm a sociologist,' not having the face before her sister-in-law to take up the brazen stance urged on her by Jacoman and Nikki. (Though these days, come to think of it, she wouldn't put such things past Sonia.)

'And do you ask David what he wants?' enquired Sonia.

'Yes,' said Anna. 'But he never answers. I'm not awfully sure he knows what he wants,' she added, thinking of the business about the baby.

'Do you know what you want?' enquired Sonia again.

'Do you, Sonia?' But Sonia did not answer. Is she a witch? Anna was wondering, again; without any obvious intent, without even asking any obvious questions, Sonia had extracted from her – not painlessly exactly, but almost insouciantly – the precise condition of her marriage; extracted it in such a way she had made it appear she knew the whole story already, not from asking or being told, merely from observing; as usual, in the process, revealing very little of herself. Feeling an irritation towards Sonia, again not at all unlike that which she sometimes felt for Sonia's brother, Anna got up and prepared to go home before Sonia could ask if she and David were planning to have children; today she wouldn't have put such mind-reading past her.

'By the way,' she added, to make sure Sonia was diverted until she made her escape, 'by the way, I never noticed your bracelet was a snake before, Sonia. It's marvellous.'

'Isn't it,' agreed Sonia. And when Anna asked if she could look at it more closely, she not only took it off and held it out to her, she said, 'Keep it if you like. I've got two, as a matter of fact. I never wear them both at once.' Anna hesitated. Sonia had never given her anything before, except at normal times such as Christmas and birthdays. She wanted to accept, of course – *should* she? Yet as she stood there, the bracelet between her fingers, examining it carefully – the eyes in the snake's head were crimson she noticed, they looked like tiny rubies or, more likely, garnets – Sonia said, almost pleadingly, 'Please take it, Anna. I'd like you to.' They smiled at each other and embraced, lightly. And then Anna, happy on the one hand, a little ashamed of her irritability, her suspicion, on the other, went home, the snake bracelet on her wrist, its mouth engorged, its eyes glowing. 'What did Sonia give you that for?' asked a surprised David.

The earthquake in Ecuador occurred in March; Anna Kern's second visit to Ecuador, accompanied in the beginning by her husband, Carter Jacoman and Piet Van Dyke, to check on the progress of the project, took place in late May and June. The epicentre of the earthquake had been down in the jungle, in the Oriente, a long way from San Gabriel, let alone Quito. Yet it had been felt everywhere, it had had its effects, everywhere, quite profound ones. It had broken the oil pipeline to the coast, for instance, thereby cutting off seventy per cent of Ecuador's export income. More immediately obvious, however, by the time Anna arrived, were its effects on what had not been to start with stable and healthy buildings; wherever she went, from Quito northwards, she saw battered and shabby churches, Spanish baroque mostly, stucco crumbling, paint peeling from façades and bell-towers, propped up with huge baulks of raw timber. There were no signs of repairs being begun or even intended. Anna doubted – she might have been maligning the country, but she still doubted – whether five years later repairs would have been set in train; she suspected churches would still be crumbling away, along with the baulks of timber. And that in due course, the country would get the better of them altogether; they would crumble to nothing as their congregations would crumble to nothing, and what's more be expected to do so.

What the earthquake had done to the people was no less profound if much less visible. Lastenia, mostly, told Anna about this; how much more jumpy patients had grown, how, at the same time, they had gone in on themselves; it had become far more difficult to get answers to their questions. How the women cried more; how they got sick, claimed to be suffering from *espanto* or *mal aire*, or to have been bewitched by their neighbours. Anna wondered if the unrest which had led to riots in Quito, filling the streets of the old town with tanks, with police carrying riot shields and canisters of CS gas, with graffiti – 'Yanquis go home' – had been in part triggered by the earthquake.

In his kinder moments Jacoman claimed that Aguadiente's behaviour, too, the near collapse of the project because of his failure to check on the health workers, had been exacerbated by the jumpiness the earthquake engendered. It had pleased him to make a parallel between what they had to do during that visit to shore the whole thing up, and the shoring up of all those churches with great baulks of timber; the effect was no less ramshackle in Anna's opinion. And she should know. It was she not David, let alone Jacoman, or even Piet, who spent the two weeks during which the process of Aguadiente's *inventario* took place sitting up at San Raphael, observing Aguadiente and his junior visit every patient to see who had received a supply of medication, who was taking it, and who was not. The fact that, despite the non-functioning of many health visitors, barely a quarter of the patients were in danger of dropping out of the study, was remarkable, really, though it had reflected little to the credit of Aguadiente himself, who should have seen that health worker activities were not only timetabled but checked on.

Indeed Aguadiente, you could say, was fully responsible for the failure; what's more, he knew it. After they had gone through the papers up at San Raphael, and the awful truth about the health workers had been revealed, when they had all left the Altiplano, when Jacoman had convened the meeting in his hotel room in Quito, to discuss their findings, Aguadiente had, literally, hung his head. Anna had never known what that expression 'hang your head' meant before; but now she did.

You could also say, of course, that the survival of the project thereafter, against such odds, had nothing to do with Jacoman roasting Aguadiente. It had, much more, to do with the patients themselves, with their dogged persistence. When the health visitors failed to turn up, some of them had been forced to walk an hour down a mountain and two hours back to get their anticonvulsants; the fact that three quarters of them had gone to trouble of that kind, was the main reason the study could be shored up, had not collapsed entirely. Subsequently Jacoman was to claim that one of its important findings was the extent to which the majority of patients suffering from epilepsy in these out of the way places not only wanted treatment, but persisted with it in the most difficult circumstances. This contradicted previous theories that it was pointless to treat such people because they would not persist with taking drugs. His view was only half endorsed by David; it was an incidental finding; he said, not short of anecdotal; Jacoman was as usual making the best of things, whistling in the dark. It had been touch and go, nip and tuck, for the project; shored up it had been, no less than the churches. Like them it had continued, against the odds, to stand up.

The shoring-up image was one Jacoman seemed to like, however; he produced it years later at Anna's dinner table, when he and Nikki were over in London, briefly; watching him throw back his head with some of the old ebullience, guffawing, Anna had the impression he was still, after what – four? five? – years, since their first meeting in her kitchen – showing off to Nikki. How amazing that he needed to, or that she encouraged him; far from looking the other way, miming exaggerated boredom, the way Anna and David had observed Giselle doing when Jacoman started up, she kept her eyes glued to her husband, her expression no more and no less mocking, no more and no less admiring than it had been the very first day they met. Nothing seemed to have changed except the way she dressed; tonight the only remnants of the tropical fish look – had it been, all along, some biological device to entrap a mate? Was that, no less than her mother's, Nikki's ultimate aim in life? – were her enormous and gaudy earrings; here at least, to her relief, Anna found traces of self-mockery: they took the form of tropical fish. Perhaps Nikki's present outfit, too, was an example of biological adaptation. Anna had heard Jacoman mock the power-dressing of female executives in his trade; their macho suits, their padded shoulders; and here was Nikki herself in a macho black suit with padded shoulders. If the effect, topped by Nikki's still red (redder?) hair was indeed powerful, not to say over-powering, this did not mean she looked the least like a pharmaceutical executive, let alone a pharma-ceutical wife.

Nor did it stop her teasing what she called her phar-maceutical husband, nor Jacoman from deriding in his turn, her 'amazing' feminist opinions, with precisely the same note of comradely flirtation as on the day they had first met. 'Carter's a real executive, he has himself a blazer, with brass buttons,' said Nikki. Given her own get-up, this, too, might have been ironical, David noted; adding that, alas, most probably, it wasn't ironical.

Anna, in the meantime, found herself wondering, do David and I seem exactly the same with each other as when we met? Casting her eyes to the ceiling, towards the fourth member of their family sleeping overhead, she decided it was unlikely; but that Jacoman and Nikki were much too bound up in each other to notice if they were or not.

What had actually gone on that second week in Ecuador, Anna as usual remembered better than David; she was also more interested than her husband in hearing Jacoman's side of it. At the time both she and David had suspected that Jacoman was under pressures, facing agendas that he only hinted at, never acknowledged directly. Subsequent events had proved this to be the case. But her husband did not seem interested in hearing Jacoman's version. He sighed, ostentatiously for him, fiddled with his fork, at one point offered brandy in a vain attempt to stem the flow; long before the end he'd slumped in his chair and fallen asleep. He'd had two clinics that day, he said later; he didn't dislike Carter, he was still fond of Carter, but after listening to his patients banging on all day, having to listen to Carter banging on was the last straw.

'What a misanthrope my husband is,' said Anna, fondly.

Jacoman ignored David's disaffection. He took them through the whole thing from the beginning.

'Wasn't it that trip, David,' he asked him, 'you got to tend a stiff with an American Express gold card, at Heathrow, before you'd even left England?' (It was: Anna and David had both forgotten this, both preferred to forget, especially David, who'd tried vainly to give the man, a Spaniard, the kiss of life, behind hastily erected screens in the departure lounge of Terminal Two. Anna observed him now, doing his best to shut out what Jacoman said. It was not surprising, he'd had the worst of it, apart from the poor man himself, that is; he had come back to her, she remembered, white to the gills and complaining he had the taste of the Spaniard's vomit in his mouth. 'Who would be a doctor?' he said, even as she thought it. It could be that Jacoman's reminding him of this incident, was, more than weariness, more than misanthropy, his reason for not wanting to hear the rest.)

Jacoman, however, was relentless. 'You kept going on about that card, David, like you'd really thought a gold card ought to protect a guy from fatal heart attacks. You remember, Anna?' he appealed to her. Ruefully, she nodded.

'And wasn't it that trip too,' Jacoman went on, 'they took us all up to Tulcan, to that weird cemetery in Tulcan, a dead culture, Inca heads cut from yew trees, and the ashes of the dead stacked up in rows of white boxes; what's it you call those things, Anna, a columbarium is it? – like a dove house, only no doves in the holes, just caskets full of ash and bones. Amazing. Latin America is all about death, I tell you. Deathly. Maybe they took us to that place as a warning.

'And then there was that stuff with ministers. Will you guys please tell Nikki it really happened, that I'm not making it all up; don't you remember, when we got back to Quito, the morning before we had the showdown with Aguadiente, going to see that guy in the Ministry of Health, don't you remember those offices; the outside ones kind of shabby, the seats torn plastic, the nearer you got to the middle, the more cushy they got, the minister's office itself all gold and real leather and in the middle of it one man reading a newspaper and three others watching football on television, none of them turning an eye when we came in, not taking a blind bit of notice? When the minister came in they didn't take a blind bit of notice; that was the day an Ecuadorian team got to the quarter finals of some Latin American cup; even the minister, the man from Guayaquil with gold teeth, even his sidekick, the guy you always got to see along with the minister because if you didn't laugh at the minister's jokes, he would – even they wanted to talk about football, their eyes kept sneaking across to the little screen set on the huge leather-topped desk; and every now and then everything stopped because there'd be one of those great bellows you only hear in Latin America. Goo-al; Goo-al.' (Jacoman's imitation of Ecuadorian football commentators was passable but very loud. It even woke David. Nikki put her hands over her ears, and said, 'Now then,

Carter, cool it.') 'And in between whiles we kept patting each other on the back, how utterly wonderful *they* were, how utterly wonderful *we* were, how wonderful the project was, how wonderful the ministry was, the Society of Ecuadorian Neurologists was, and so on. David here, of course, thought all that buttering up ministers stuff was crap, pointless. He thought all the publicity stuff was crap, pointless; but it wasn't. Hey, do you remember the sexy redhead who interviewed us for one paper, who Aguadiente tried to get off with. It was amazing, or maybe not amazing, what bad luck that poor sap had in the sexual line; this one wasn't having any either, she kept on shutting him up and asking David the questions.

'By the time we finished there can't have been anyone in Ecuador didn't know what we were doing, from the ministry downwards; epilepsy never had such a high profile anywhere, it was all because of us.' ('What modesty, Carter; don't you mean *me*?' interpolated Nikki.) 'As for the ministry; I couldn't have done it without buttering up the ministry, David, whatever you thought. There we were using all those doctors employed by the ministry of health, they could have put thumbs down any time they chose to; that's why we had to eat dinner with them, talk football with them. Yeah I know we didn't do it like that in Kenya, but we didn't *have* to do it like that in Kenya; we weren't surveying 72,000 people, we weren't using local doctors; compared to Ecuador the Kenyan project was a monkey-nuts project, a can of beans.' (Anna looked at David here – he returned her look; presumably they were both thinking, that was to Kenya's advantage. For wasn't it in Kenya, not Ecuador, the project long completed, that work on epilepsy was still ticking over, years later?)

'And the irony of all this, there we were spreading it round the country that we were the best thing since the Statue of Liberty, that we topped the Trump Tower even, and all the time *I* knew, we were teetering on the edge of it; this time next week there mightn't *be* a project, what with Aguadiente screwing it all up. That that was the real death. Or nearly. Which, though I guess I knew from the beginning that any project in Ecuador was bound to get into problems, I'd never expected. Not like that. Not through a cock-up like that. It would have been the death of it; if you, Anna, hadn't been so quick on the uptake, got Piet to check out the health visitor data.

(This was actually not fair on Piet; who'd been the first to suggest checking it all out, even though he had only suggested it to Anna, leaving her to report the idea to her husband, who had, in his turn, reported it to Jacoman. But then it always was Piet's misfortune, that, very rarely, did he get his due.)

'And that's leaving aside all the shit I was getting from Bader-Kleitz, which was lethal enough, but which I never told you about, never even hinted at before the show-down with Aguadiente. That's leaving aside Bader-Kleitz, Ecuador, digging its heels in, not wanting to give us any more logistical support whatever . . .'

('Which was all your fault, Carter, and you know it,' murmured David at this point. 'You went over their heads all the time, you sent them curt telexes saying do this, do that. Even after the business with Aguadiente, you stole Jacqui Sylvestre from them without asking, I was told, just said you'd seconded him to take over the administration, and that was that. No wonder they dug their heels in.'

'Yeah; and if I hadn't? If I'd hung about while they made up their minds? We wouldn't even have *had* a project,' said Carter.)

'So what with one thing and another it couldn't have been a worse time for the whole thing to fall to bits. And yet still in the middle of all this mess, Aguadiente kept on asking for more money; told us they couldn't do one thing more without this, without that. Yeah, what I told Aguadiente that day I hauled him over the coals, was the truth, more or less. Back in Basel it really was, all the time, chop, chop, chop, I was having to move funds from this project to that one to hide the costs; thank God Taylor let my budgets alone, God help us all if I hadn't been able to manipulate them the way I wanted, all along.'

He paused here; took in the expression on Anna's face,

or seemed to. He added, more quietly; at the same time much more belligerently; at the same time as if appealing to her in some way, 'It was all perfectly legitimate by the way, Anna. Don't look like that. It's only American accounting, Hicks' kind, wants it set out precisely, ass to head – if he'd been in charge, I'd've been screwed at that point. Jesus. Wouldn't I have just been? *Jesus*. I mean there was the thing already one hundred per cent above budget, what Aguadiente and company was asking was going to take it another one hundred per cent over; I couldn't hide that, it'd be a disaster; curtains, for all of us. Which I'd been warning. And still the demands kept coming, more cars, more people, more computers. Those trucks, I tell you; those fucking trucks. Sylvestre kept sending me photos of the happy team at work, a line of the bastards outside the restaurant in *Val de Chota*, where they all went for their lunches, yeah, I knew all about the lunches, that was the least of the bills I kept getting. And there those guys would be with full bellies, standing alongside the line of bloody trucks. When I showed one of the photos to Giselle, she said, very sweetly, "I thought you were a medical director, Carter, not a used car salesman." As a matter of fact, for once, she had a point.

'Sure I knew how it was in the field there when it rained, I knew they needed everything they could get, practically speaking. But they also had to know they couldn't have it. I mean someone mentioned a helicopter at one point, no, I am not kidding. We were rich Americans, rich Swiss, they could take us for everything we'd got; everything; the sky was the limit.

'That's why it got to be the way it was with me, why it had to look back in Basel as well as in Quito like what I was chiefly interested in was getting that bloody drug trial right. That was what I was in the business for, to do drug trials, I might swing the rest for a bit, but in Basel, for most of them – I don't count Taylor, he was always on my side – that wasn't worth *zilch*. What I had to show was that the drug worked there, with those people, and what's more it worked better than Phenobarb, at least it didn't leave the guys so doped. Which as you quite rightly pointed out at the time, Anna – naïve as you were in your husband's terms, in my terms, you could still see the wood for the trees sometimes when we couldn't, not being medical – everyone knew anyway, so what was the point of spending all that money finding out? The epidemiology was worth much more, *and* your sociology, Anna dear. I saw your face when I was talking drugman, but I had to talk drugman, that was all that counted by then, back in Basel. And the key thing was I had to do a drug trial, be seen to do a drug trial and what's more, do it properly, and there was Dr Eternal Torment, Watertooth, Aguadiente, who I paid to do it, fucking it all up because he was too busy down in Quito writing up the survey so he could shine at some local conference, and start being Mr Neuro-epidemiology, Ecuador, and in the end, the sky's the limit, Mr Neuro-epidemiology, Latin America, da da da. The result being that fifty per cent or more of our patients might not be taking their drugs. And how can you do a drug trial with fifty per cent of the patients not taking their medicine?

'And if that got back to Basel, the chances were they'd close the thing down, just like that, without even knowing what was happening to the costs. What was it to them, they'd just write it all off, they could afford to; what they couldn't afford, at least I couldn't afford it any longer, was any more of that endless haemorrhage of money on trucks and cups of coffee and fancy dinners to show the Ecuadorians what big guys we all were; da, da, da.

'It's not that there hasn't always to be some flannel, even the Swiss know that; you have to make a presence in these places, you have to be seen to be spending money, the trick is you've just not got to spend too much of it. But since I was spending too much, or rather they were, it meant that all the time I had to cover my back; and the way things were getting, this wasn't just my problem any longer; this was Aguadiente's, yours, everyone's problem. Which is what I was trying to explain. Who cared in Basel if they closed the project down? But Aguadiente would have cared; Lastenia would have cared; the Society of Ecuadorian Neurologists would have cared; all those rural doctors working their asses off for us would have cared. You would have cared, Anna, you and David.' (David woke up at this point, said, 'Speak for yourself, Carter,' and went back to sleep again. Carter ignored him. Nikki looked conspiratorially at Anna, winked at her; but then returned to gazing at Carter; who had, Anna, noticed, since they last saw him, had his teeth fixed, insofar as Carter's teeth were possible to fix. It was not much of an improvement; Carter with straight teeth almost looked sinister.)

'That meant we all had to live within our means. Like I told Aguadiente, "Virgilio, why do you think we're having this meeting in my hotel room, why do you think we haven't got a conference room this time? Why do you think I have to keep talking like some tight-assed house-wife in Saskatchewan, any minute I'll be urging us to cook our own dinners; bake our own bread." Did you think I liked going on that way? but that was what I'd had to listen to the seven years past; apart from drug R and D, there's no notion in Basel of spending money to get it, over the long term. Spending's the first law of economics in my opinion, I'm a gut Keynesian, but tell that to a marketing man, marketing men are all Hayek or Milton Friedman.

'But then everyone has their dirty words I have to say. And if mine aren't the same as marketing men? – well my family's dirty words were never the rabbi's either; in my family you could say fuck any time you wanted, what you weren't allowed to say was "God"; not ever.'

('As you're always saying, Carter,' murmured Nikki; 'Over and over.' And again she winked, conspiratorially, at Anna. Observing a certain stiffness, this time, in the contortion of Nikki's eye and cheek, Anna wondered if she'd had another face lift; Nikki was quite a bit older than Carter after all. Certainly she'd laid out on her bedside table as many little bottles of creams and lotions, of oil of evening primrose, of products like Ginseng and Guarana, as ever she used to. Anna had seen them when she took an electric blanket into their room before dinner.)

'So now what I had to get across to Aguadiente was this; "Work with what you've got; or else ..." Still more I had to get it across that without the drug trial going right, the thing wasn't worth anything. That was the first thing. And I had to put it to him, all guns blazing, he didn't know what hit him, Nikki, I tell you that guy couldn't keep still usually, he was always waving his finger at me, leaping to his feet and saying, "*Momento*, Carter". "By *example*, Carter," getting his own words in not so much edgeways, but by the front door, by bludgeon, but now he just sat there, hunched, not saying anything, not even smoking, he was so stunned.' (Hanging his head, Anna interpolated, quietly.) 'Because of what I told him. And then I had to tell him he was going to have to answer to Jacqui Sylvestre, the monkey from Guayaquil, for everything except medicine. And third, what I had to tell him was that it didn't matter what he was supposed to be doing the next two weeks, if he was supposed to be putting cream on the President's haemorrhoids, forget it, he was going to spend that time checking up every patient on that project, what their drug status was, and so on. And he just sat there, he took it on the chin, even the haemorrhoids, neurologists treating heads not backsides; he didn't have any choice. And I tell you by the end, don't you remember, Anna, I had that shit eating out of my hand. And I felt as much of a shit myself. Don't look at me like that, Nikki, it wasn't my finest hour, I know it. But it had to be done.'

Jacoman looked so pleased with himself, however, even six years later, it might have been his proudest hour. The expression on his face reminded Anna of the dislike she had been so surprised to feel, especially given the way she'd felt, only thirty-six hours before, looking at the volcano with him; how indignant she'd felt – how disillusioned, even – at being made, now, to dislike him so. (Just as David, she supposed, looking back, had been disillusioned by being made to dislike *her*, sometimes.)

Sitting over dinner so many years later – five or six was it? – it felt more like a hundred – Anna remembered the ambivalence of her feelings; or rather, did not so much remember, recreated them. For some reason they had not, as usual, taken their coffee into the sitting-room. They were still round the table in the crowded kitchen. All but two of the candles were near burning themselves out. Their haunted flickerings hollowed faces, deepened eye sockets. The soft light which had, in the innocent beginnings of their reunion meal taken years from all of them (Nikki, in particular, had looked ten years younger – she and Jacoman had fenced with each other joyfully, like adolescents – an uncomfortable sight, in a way, as well as touching) now aged them; turned heads, faces, to skulls; corpselike – Anna contemplated turning on the overhead light. Across the table lay the detritus of the meal; crumbs, napkins, orange peel, dirty coffee cups, the caked grounds at the bottom of the *cafetière*. It felt like a meal that had not only lasted a long time but had gone on well past its proper hour, past its season if you like. The more so, because for the past few days, in Anna's garden, early summer had been more like the end of it, vicious winds and rain ripping off the blossoms of her dark blue ceanothus, knocking flat her late tulips, her early delphiniums. It served them right, really, she thought, sadly – she really had drunk too much, hadn't she – they had also blossomed before their time. Even behind Jacoman's voice she could hear the sound of the wind and rain; augmenting a melancholy that Jacoman himself, growing ever more manic, ever more excited, tried to dispel, vainly.

He had always showed himself able to be vulgar; yes, she thought. But if the vulgarity in him, the lack of inhibition, had in those dangerous days appealed to a vulgar streak in her, entirely lacking in David, just now it made her feel sorry for him. The scene with Aguadiente, she realised, despite the triumph, the appearance of victory, in which he had recounted it, had not been a triumph, really; it had been damage limitation, the beginning of an end, not a climax. It revealed, not just then, now, the way Jacoman told it, what precisely had gone wrong; what had been bound to go wrong, Jacoman being Jacoman. It demonstrated, more clearly than ever, his hubris.

'That poor guy,' said Nikki, meaning, it was almost certain, Aguadiente. But she could have meant Jacoman; even though she followed it up, by adding, thoughtfully; 'I wouldn't have liked to be in his shoes.' She got up from the table, squeezed round the back of it – she really was much too big for Anna's kitchen – and leaned her head against Jacoman's. The fish earring nearest Anna, the only one she could see from that angle, flared up suddenly in the guttering light, assumed a grotesque importance. Just as in all their views of the project, hers, Anna's, no less than anyone's, this aspect, that aspect, assumed more importance than the others. None of them, least of all Jacoman, had been paying enough impartial attention, and in Jacoman, even more than Aguadiente, that had been fatal; not fatal for the project in the end, they did the project, they finished it, even without Jacoman; but for Jacoman.

And he minded. You could see he minded from the way he'd talked of it tonight. The way he now, with an apologetic look at Nikki – the small nod she gave, Anna thought, might have been endorsement – took out his cigarettes.

What was it he had said once – about the need for a corpse in the foundations? If so whose corpse was it, Aguadiente's (as he'd suggested)? – his own? – or both of them?

Jacoman, incidentally, had not been the only person who had over-reached himself, at that time, who had failed to listen to advice about economy and so forth. Not only did Anna have Jacqui Sylvestre pleading with her almost as soon as she got up to San Raphael, telling her that Aguadiente, despite his humiliation, had bounced right back, was going on as usual, even though he, Jacqui, was now supposed to be in charge: barely a week later, in a break from making his *inventorio* Aguadiente had also demanded a meeting with her, to discuss what he called sociological resources. These, it turned out, what he was asking her for, involved virtually a full census, to validate the selection of twenty per cent of patients to receive the further, locally written questionnaire he and Naranjo had devised, plus extra sociological time in which to apply it; a film crew to film the indigenous healers Lastenia had located; another truck for the use of Carlos Naranjo (Anna may have misheard this one; but probably not); a tape recorder for Lastenia (preferably Anna's). And so on. Any credit Aguadiente won with Anna, for recognising that she was missing David, for going out and getting her headache pills, for his obvious affection for his pretty little daughter, evaporated for the moment on presentation of these demands. She had great difficulty in persuading him to take no for an answer. Jacoman would have been proud of her, she thought, as she heard herself discoursing eloquently, in Spanish, on the subject of limited resources; she even re-used Jacoman's image of a very small bottle, of resources, to fill a very large glass, of needs. Of course she would have carried it off with more dignity, if Lastenia hadn't giggled at her throughout; if she hadn't been tempted, her friendship with Lastenia being as good as it was, to giggle back.

But what she felt afterwards, quite strongly, was that Aguadiente and Jacoman deserved each other. Was there ever anyone else had roused in her simultaneously such exasperation and such pity?

In the summer of 1988, it became clear to Jacoman that he no longer had any choice. To stay on in Switzerland, at Bader-Kleitz, would have meant losing his children to Giselle and Canada. It was, as he said, no contest. At the same time – about this he was much more reticent – his leaving did have a certain professional advantage. He'd finally lost his minder; Taylor had been given no option but a job as Medical Director, Bader-Kleitz Caribbean. Though his successor, Dr Hicks (the man known in the company, Piet told Anna, gloomily, as 'Hicks the axeman') was not due to take up his appointment till October, Taylor left Switzerland in early July, not before he and Jacoman had caroused together over a final dinner. Had Jacoman himself hopes once of succeeding to Taylor's job? If so, had he believed himself a credible candidate? Indeed, *was* he regarded as a credible candidate? Neither Anna nor her husband could be sure about the former; once he knew he hadn't got the job, Jacoman denied all intention of going for it in the first place. At the same time he implied that he'd been sounded out quite seriously – did he want the job or didn't he? But as to the latter – in the light of Hicks' subsequent activities, in the light of what Piet claimed was the brief given to Hicks, on which he based his activities, Anna doubted if Jacoman had been in the running; at least not at this stage. Hicks was a minimalist; his whole career was minimalist. As Piet said, as various other Bader-Kleitz executives said, you could spend money in Bader-Kleitz if your department was making it; if it wasn't, they'd bring in an axeman like Hicks to clamp down on spending. Jacoman's department was not making money – Jacoman himself, by company standards, had been throwing money out of the window – how much, precisely, on the epilepsy project was not suspected by anyone till Hicks started investigating. Nor did Jacoman have allies in other departments who would help him recoup his position by taking on some aspects of his projects, as indeed happened later. Had the minderless, big-brotherless, empire-on-sand, too clever by half, Jacoman still been around then, maybe that would not have happened.

In the light of the reputation signified by the name 'axeman' – Hicks went from job to job, rarely staying long in any, always hand-in-glove with his marketing colleagues, above all past master at drawing in horns, closing down, rationalising efficiently, if not brutally – what *was* certain was that Jacoman knew life under Hicks would be more than difficult; neither of the Kerns could be entirely certain if Jacoman really was leaving Bader-Kleitz just for the sake of his children. Probably Jacoman couldn't be certain, either. Honest he might be in most respects, but honest with himself he was not always, as Giselle was well aware; she often, bitterly, accused him of lying to himself; creating illusionery labyrinths in his head, was how she put it.

'Just like your pictures, Giselle dear,' said Jacoman, a psychologically quite astute remark for him; he was, genuinely, suffering.

'Where do you think I get them from, Carter?' she answered.

She and Carter boxed and coxed all that summer; he would fly off to Canada, sounding out colleagues, looking for jobs and apartments (in Montreal at this point; the words separation, let alone divorce had not yet been mentioned; or rather Giselle had stopped mentioning them, because, Carter assumed, he'd agreed to return to Canada with her. He still drew the line at Quebec. Even Montreal would mean a crash course in French – 'How do you square the maple leaves, Giselle, with aspirations for a free Quebec?' he asked his wife, once, ironically, eyeing the Canadian flags, still dangling everywhere. She made no answer; French, she might be, but, as he suspected, she saw advantages in her command of the English language, in being at home in English Canada; not that she allowed herself to see it, she could delude herself quite as well as he could. Yet she too, now, was talking about Montreal as a base; in Quebec she'd heard art jobs were much harder to come by. Out of Jacoman's earshot she'd even been heard to murmur that if the perfect job came up she might, just, settle for Ottawa.)

While Jacoman was in Canada, Giselle stayed in Switzerland looking after her children. While he was in Switzerland, on the other hand, she would either be in England, visiting her beloved grandmother, who tried, vainly, to persuade her to stay in Europe – Giselle had not yet got round to telling the old lady how bad things were with Jacoman; or else she would be in Canada, also looking for jobs and apartments; evidence of the latter was one thing that started Jacoman wondering if, though he might not be losing his children, he might end up losing his wife. Not that Giselle said anything about it; he only knew of the decline in her enthusiasm for Quebec because she came home from Canada enthusing about

Montreal. Jacoman found it hard to imagine anyone enthusing about Montreal.

It was not till early July, well after the Kanterberg meeting, that he at last allowed himself to consider the possibility his marriage might, finally, be ending. He did not know for sure what he felt about it; was there relief, somewhere, at the prospect of not living with Giselle any longer? This had not stopped him feeling inordinately sad and edgy, long before he had clear evidence that she was not just dragging him back to Canada, but, actually, planning to leave him – all through the summer they continued to talk about jobs and schools and apartments like any wife and husband, indeed with rather less acrimony than they had been prone to. At the Kanterberg meeting, his friends, Anna and David, were aware of Jacoman's gloom and unease; but of course they did not know the meat of it – the possibility of Carter's leaving Switzerland, his likely failure to get Taylor's job, let alone the parlous state of his marriage were not things he felt like discussing, even with them. The oblique phonecalls seeking marital advice had ceased altogether. In return they respected his pride and silence, almost without knowing they were doing so; whatever they might have suspected, they went little further, even between themselves, than debating how Jacoman would get on in Bader-Kleitz after Taylor's now imminent departure.

In late August finally, Jacoman confronted his wife, demanded her precise intentions; this was just one week before she was due to finish packing up the house and leave for Canada with the children to stay, initially, with her father. He had the offer of a job by then; he had the offer of a rented apartment. He was urging Giselle to inspect it, when something about her face made him stop; yell at her, 'OK, Giselle; get down to the nitty-gritty.'

Anna and David could not believe it when Jacoman told them this story; that things could go so far between a husband and wife without anything being said; people whose whole lives were being taken apart, one way and another, who were about to be dumped with their children and possessions on another continent, even if it was the one they originally came from. (Giselle had not lived there for twelve years, Jacoman getting on fifteen.)

Giselle had taken up tapestry lately, transferring her own designs to canvas; 'Am I going to have to sit on the things now, Giselle?' Jacoman mocked her, quite kindly, watching her needle stab in and out at the heart of what would be a huge crimson rose, with a worm nesting at its centre – Giselle knew her William Blake, even if Carter didn't.

'No, Carter,' Giselle said; *'you're* not going to have to sit on them; you needn't worry.'

Here comes the bludgeon, thought Jacoman at this point. 'We are going back to Canada together, aren't we, Giselle?' he enquired.

Giselle said: 'No, I don't think so; no.' Stabbing her needle so furiously in and out, he had the impression that even she, for once, found this conversation difficult, if not painful.

'Stop that bloody sewing, can't you,' he shouted. But she would not; it enabled her to hide her face from him, he realised, he couldn't see her eyes – was she crying? – she just might have been crying – he could only see her mouth. He had never been so aware that in punishing him, or anyone, she punished herself also; punished herself even in her very triumph, even *because* of, her very triumph.

Her beauty these days was so very different from the way it had been. Above all her mouth showed it; he did not need to see her eyes. She'd had such a soft mouth when he first met her; a soft virgin's mouth – even though by then she was not one literally. She did not have a virgin's mouth any longer; it had hardened, turned, imperceptibly, downwards, Jacoman thought, staring at her angrily, the pain he felt the more piercing, making him the more angry, when he thought, suddenly, starkly, not quite – it's all my fault – but, at least – was it being married to me did it? He did not usually think in these terms; usually it was easier for him to blame Giselle for everything. He still blamed her; yet, there it

382

was, insidiously; is it being married to me did it? Smothering the thought as best he could, giving her even less quarter, he asked, 'What about the kids then? They'll live with me of course.'

'They'll live with me, of course, Carter,' Giselle said, just as if he hadn't spoken. 'I've paid the first quarter's rental on a house with a backyard for them to play in — and if you're willing, Carter, I've found a bilingual school for them, or rather Papa has found it.'

It was the 'backyard' dumbfounded Jacoman more than anything; that as much as anything convinced him that Giselle was not lying. Giselle might paint flowers and gardens, but she wanted nothing to do with tending them. In Basel Jacoman had done all that; her one role, horticulturally speaking, was to nurse her sometimes bizarre houseplants; Giselle's tongues, David nicknamed these when he saw them, on his very first visit to Basel, your bloody tongues, Giselle, Jacoman had mocked her with it since; almost the only way he dared to mock her. There they were under the window; and for the first time he saw the full irony of the fact that all the plants, small and large ones, some with flowers, some without, some dark-leaved and some paler, were one way or another tongue-shaped, thrust tongue-shaped leaves at him, in a few cases tongue-shaped flowers.

What piqued him even more, however, was the mention of Papa; he stopped feeling sorry for Giselle. 'But I thought we *had* chosen a school,' he said. 'I thought you liked it; I thought we'd entered them even; we fixed it.'

'Papa cancelled their entry. This is better. It's a private school,' she said.

'And who's paying the fees?' asked Jacoman.

'You are, of course, Carter,' she said. 'Papa's helping me draw up all the papers.'

'I thought you hated your father,' said Jacoman weakly, for the moment routed.

'Did you?' said Giselle. 'Well then you thought wrong, Carter.'

The sheer nerve of it all numbed Jacoman — and he hadn't even heard the worst of it; it also had him, almost, applauding. Now he came to think of it, it had been the sheer nerve, the cheek of this smooth-faced, innocent-looking girl that had attracted him in the first place, quite as much as her enigmatic beauty. Almost the first night they met, she had not only goaded three young men to jump into a lake from which the ice had barely melted, saying she would follow if they did, she had let them jump and then not followed, just linked arms with Jacoman and stood there laughing at them as they crawled out, teeth chattering. Perhaps Jacoman would have admired this less had he been one of the three young men; but he'd never much cared for cold water. 'You're the only one with sense,' she'd told him, going off in his car later.

Giselle's scheming this time was total; the rapprochement with her father, clearly, part of a master plan. He was seeing to everything, he was even giving Giselle an allowance to live on, till she could start selling her pictures or find some kind of art job. And all without reference to Jacoman, who had been searching for family apartments, who had got himself a job in Montreal, with its obligation to improve his French and so on; and all for nothing. She hadn't wanted to say anything till it was fixed properly, Giselle told him, through her tears. How to tell him such a story? she asked him – she was now quite definitely crying; and so to his horror was Jacoman himself. Taking her in his arms – even if he wanted to take her in his arms after the bludgeoning she'd given him – was out of the question; yet in the very midst of his baffled rage, her crying was too simple – artless by her standards – to be bearable. He hadn't known Giselle simply cry, with grief, for a long time, not since she'd given birth to their first child, Louis. And now he couldn't embrace her, couldn't be the tender-hearted Carter only seen otherwise by their children; because she had set this great monster between them, their final separation, as she had armoured herself with needles behind this monstrous tapestry of hers, this rose with the worm at the heart of it; her revenge, he didn't doubt; revenge for what, exactly? What was she doing sewing at this moment of all moments? he screamed inside himself. Only she wasn't sewing any longer. Any more than, for once, she was using tears as a weapon. She was just crying, crying, crying.

Jacoman went on crying also. They sat separately, at either end of the brocade sofa – currently set in Giselle's preferred position – crying instead of speaking; there was always something to stop them speaking. But this time it meant their end, truly, as if not only she but he had been tied up in some neat, maple-leaf stamped package, bar details to be sorted out – like when in future, how often, Jacoman would get to see his dearly beloved children (whom he was due to fetch, any moment, from the friend's house where they were all – even Louis for once – playing). He determined to drive a hard bargain. If Giselle expected it, if she wanted him to drive a hard bargain, never mind, for this once he would oblige her.

Pulling himself together after a while, he turned to stare at her defiantly. Whereupon she lifted her head at last, sniffed a bit, muttered something, rather primly, about her father – that it would be nice for their kids to have a real grandfather around after all these years. Could Jacoman believe what he was hearing?

'Is that supposed to make it up to them for not having their father around any more?' he yelled at her. 'Jesus, Giselle, how could you?'

Giselle pushed her hair right back, at this point, stared him full in the face her eyes red-rimmed, her cheeks still messed with tears. She finally coshed him. 'Oh by the way, Carter, did I mention it?' she said reproachfully. 'This house, this bilingual school Papa was clever enough to find, aren't in Montreal, after all; they're in Toronto.'

Chapter Seven

'Surely,' said David, calmly, surveying the gathering around yet another green baize table, convened this time to discuss the analysis, the writing up and the publication of all the material gathered (or in the case of the Locks to be gathered) in Kenya, Ecuador, Pakistan and Turkey; 'Surely none of us are going to scratch someone else's eyes out to get our names first on papers?'

That's what he thinks, thought Anna, looking at Charlene Lock, that's what he thinks; if she hadn't known before the kind of pressures that drove Charlene, her husband and their kind she knew now. The two red spots on Charlene's cheeks in a face otherwise whiter than ever, matched almost exactly the colour of her track suit – the manufacturers no doubt called it 'cerise'; a garment on her so unlikely Anna had to assume she'd thought it the only appropriate thing to wear in the Swiss ski resort where Jacoman was holding this meeting. Having just thumped her fist on the green baize table, Charlene was now thumping it for the second time, this time with the flat of her hand. It looked as if what should have been Jacoman's finest hour, the height of his showmanship – gathering up, orchestrating, conducting his entire team, neurologists, psychologists, anthropologists, Kenyans, Ecuadorians, Americans, Canadians, English, Pakistanis, Swiss, Dutch, Turks, and for some reason Anna never fathomed, a solitary Egyptian, over three days of non-stop meetings – was about to disintegrate in a welter of accusation and counter-accusation that Jacoman himself, sitting beside David at the head of the table, but somewhat distant from the proceedings – they had both noticed it – seemed incapable of stemming. What had happened to him? Anna thought. Her sudden despondency, not to say alarm was much more related to his defection than the behaviour of Charlene Lock; much more powerful than her surprise at seeing the Locks so ill at ease, as out of their element, as at the Barcelona conference they had seemed, in the workshop at least, to be not only in their own element, but even to generate it.

Charlene, as usual, was the touchstone. Milton, sitting beside her, flanked by the three other Franklinites, seemed quite unperturbed, despite nodding his agreement at his wife's angry insistence that they weren't going to do all this work and not be credited with it, for Heaven's sake; whatever the norms were in Europe, academically speaking, no way it would wash in the United States, no way there would be papers published without the names of the individual authors on them . . . (David and Jacoman were suggesting that all publications arising from this project were credited instead in the name of the group, ERGO, the acryonym for Epilepsy Research Group Organisation; they'd invented it between them to cover the group as a whole, precisely as a means of avoiding just such disputes, such jealousies.)

The Kenyans, Bennet, Meaki, and the distinguished-looking, expensive-bellied professor of gastro-enterology, who had taken over Falconer's job were sitting on the far side of the table from the Locks, flanked by herself and the psychologist, Vittoria. Anna saw that they were laughing at Charlene. Yet Milton Lock continued smiling at them, benignly. Anna couldn't make him out at all. Was that his line? she wondered. To play negative always to his wife's positive? Anyone might have thought he liked seeing his wife laughed at. Perhaps he actually did like seeing his wife laughed at; Anna's sudden flicker of sympathy for Charlene Lock – it was disconcerting how she had these flickers of sympathy for Milton Lock's wife, even if she couldn't like her; not least Charlene herself wouldn't let Anna like her – was dispelled almost at once in another glance at Charlene's face. Charlene was now scowling at Anna. The next moment, still looking across at her, she was whispering something to her nearest Franklin acolyte, the tall girl in the baseball cap. Probably it had nothing to do with Anna. But she felt threatened all the same – maybe she was meant to do so. Vittoria, meanwhile had passed her a note, on which was written in neat capitals, 'IS THIS THE ACADEMIC RAT RACE DO YOU THINK?' 'YES. AND THANK GOD I'M A MOUSE,' Anna wrote back, and felt better, but only temporarily, because when she said to David that evening that she didn't mind how her papers were credited, what was all the fuss, he turned round and told her not to be smug; of course it didn't mean anything to her, she wasn't an academic, her career didn't depend on these things, the way his did; the way the Locks did.

'Anyone would think you were on their side,' said Anna, aggrieved. 'Well I'm not,' said David. 'But I know what the issue is, which is more than you seem to, Anna, so please keep your mouth shut.'

(This exchange didn't augur well, perhaps, for the academic collaboration on which they were about to embark, she and David, when the full results of the anthropological surveys in Kenya and Ecuador came through. But as yet Anna had no forebodings; none whatever.)

Kanterberg being a ski resort, was up in the Swiss Alps; at every meeting in the conference room allotted to them, a huge wall of windows waited behind the Locks, the Franklinites, and the two Latin Americans (Aguadiente, uncharacteristically quite silent, even helpful; Anna could hardly bear to look at him these days; each time she saw his face, she thought of his son first, then her fears for her adolescent Ben; and Meyersdorf, who, with an air of unbelief, his eyebrows raised, translated for the rest of them Aguadiente's reasonable suggestions about how the disagreement could be resolved). From their side of the table, Anna, Vittoria, the Kenyans and Piet should, the whole time, have been able to gaze on mountains. But they did not gaze on mountains. They did not have so much as a single glimpse of them the whole three days. It was one thing she'd learned in these years, Anna thought, remembering the volcanoes in Ecuador; you should never expect to see mountains. Even if everything around you, roofs, walls, balconies, the very lie of streets, if the very trees and flowers and meadows spoke mountains, if you could feel the mountains in your head and lungs and bones, you should not expect to see them.

Yet in this case, what a perfect example they were of the pathetic fallacy. Everyone here, you could say, was wrapped in a fog of some kind, made up of their own expertise, their own nationality, their language, their fears, ambitions, professional jealousies; the mountains were shrouded out of sympathy. Of course. Everything was obfuscation.

That the Locks were coming here at all had been obfuscation; or rather had been disguised by Jacoman's obfuscation, which may or may not have been deliberate; Jacoman had always been cagey on this one, for reasons that might have had something to do with his friends the Kerns' feelings, but as much, probably, with his own scarcely admitted academic ambitions. Whatever the truth, it wasn't until barely a week before the meeting, when Stan Heins had called them from Franklin, that the Kerns learned the Locks would be attending. Stan Heins had been beside himself. He'd accused David and Anna of being hand in glove with the Locks, of having gone over to the enemy. It was he after all, who had introduced them to the Locks, this had led to nothing but trouble for him; the Locks accused him of stealing their EMICs, as good as, of handing them over to Anna. And here they were encouraging the Locks to work with Jacoman, and the Locks' acolytes also, why hadn't they recommended him, Stan, if they wanted someone from Franklin?

Anna, getting David's half of the conversation only, could not think what he was talking about – turning his back on her, waving her away, as if he wished she wasn't overhearing, he said first, angrily, 'They're not, Stan, I don't believe you.' And then insisted, 'But we did recommend you, Stan. This is nothing to do with us; it's all Jacoman's doing.'

'I don't think he believed me,' said David, ruefully, when he came off the phone and explained the situation to Anna. 'I think this may be the end of a beautiful friendship. What's Jacoman thinking of? Curse the bloody Locks.' He was, genuinely, upset, snapping at Anna when she tried to reassure him – insisting no, this was the end, their valued friendship with Stan Heins was kaput; over. Later he acknowledged that in Franklin, in any American university, the lack of academic tenure – Stan didn't have it, nor Charlene Lock – was the problem; that if Stan's fury, not to say jealousy, were due to such insecurities, he might, just, come round in the end. All the same David was pessimistic; he felt in some way so obscure even Anna could not quite fathom it, that it was their fault, or at least it was Anna's for insisting, backed up by him, on consulting Stan in the first place.

'Sometimes,' said Anna, stung by this, 'sometimes I think you are like a recording angel, David, you have a little black book in which you note down what you see as my sins, for final judgment. There's too much Jehovah in your genes, that's your trouble.'

'Would you rather I was a cheek-turning Christian then?' asked David. 'Would you prefer me to love the bloody Dreadlocks?'

'No,' said Anna. 'I'd just prefer you to love me. And not to think everything's my fault, always.'

All this agitation, however, had prevented them taking in one of the words used by Stan Heins; the word 'acolyte'. And though Jacoman himself rang the very next day and told David at last, not giving him a chance to expostulate, that he had invited the Locks to attend the meeting, he still had not mentioned, or at least had not made clear, that the Locks would not be coming alone. Thus, not until they got off the bus at Kanterberg itself, did David and Anna realise that the three total strangers sitting a few seats back, weren't anything to do with Bader-Kleitz or the Turkish or the Pakistani contingent; they were the Locks' post-doctorate juniors from the university of Franklin.

'Fuck,' said David. And went in search of Jacoman, leaving Anna to exchange awkward glances with a slightly shorter-haired Charlene, clad, this was the first time Anna set eyes on it, in her fearsomely red tracksuit. Not unlike the one worn by Nikki the day she and Jacoman had met, which had so become Nikki, it did not become Charlene. She was too thin perhaps; or too unbending; or too consciously regal in her bearing.

'Isn't this just a great place, Anna?' she said, smiling her icy smile in a way that suggested she really didn't mean it to be so icy. 'Wasn't it great of Carter to invite us? Milton and I can't wait to get ourselves up a mountain. We thought we'd have time for a short hike before the first meeting. Would you and David like to join us?

'Oh and by the way,' she added, before Anna'd had time to answer, making it clear that neither side needed take that invitation seriously, it was merely meant to show that cooperation was at least intended; for of course there was nothing to be served by them not cooperating with each other: 'Oh and by the way these are Drs —' and turning to the much younger academics standing ill at ease behind her, she reeled off three names, none of which Anna took in, though dutifully shaking hands with their owners, one male, and two females.

Jacoman, meanwhile, in the hotel foyer, his hair limp and lank, his skin the colour of chamois leather, was telling an angry David what wonderful people these were, what wonderful research they were proposing; and, incidentally, if Anna played her cards right, what a help they could be to her.

'Maybe,' David said. 'But shouldn't you have at least warned us? I'm in charge of the science here for a start; not you, Carter.'

'Didn't I warn you?' asked Jacoman. 'Didn't I? Sure, I warned you.'

But he had not warned them; having failed to warn them,

having seen their response to his failure, he tried a little damage limitation, during the dinner that first evening, to equally little avail. In all the time they'd worked together, this was the only time he and Anna came close to a serious row. It was supposed to be a party of sorts, a Swiss evening in the hotel bierkeller; along with sampling Swiss wine, Swiss beer, and either cheese fondue or cheese raclette (at least five minutes of their afternoon meeting had been spent listening to Jacoman's blonde German secretary explaining the difference between these two dishes, with interpretations in Spanish and Turkish) they were to be serenaded by accordion players, and so forth.

Anna, opting for fondue, was directed to a different table from Jacoman who'd opted for raclette. But she'd only been eating five minutes, long enough to decide that after all she didn't much like fondue, it was too sour, too rich at once, it cloyed in her mouth, her throat, when he appeared at her side and expelled Piet, her chosen neighbour, saying Hi Anna, well, how was she, he hadn't had a chance to talk to her yet; she'd given a *great* exposition at the meeting this afternoon, these days anyone would think she was a professional, they really would.

'Thank you, Carter,' said Anna, in such a tone that he accused her of being sarcastic; that got them off on a bad footing. For what he had actually come to talk about, it rapidly became clear – as if the flattery hadn't made it clear – was the Locks.

'Of course he didn't tell us about them on purpose,' David had said after Stan Heins' phonecall. 'He didn't want to rattle you. I mean medical anthropologists aren't any threat to *me*; he hasn't landed *me* with half the Franklin neurology department.'

'He knew I wasn't experienced, when he took me on,' Anna said. 'He didn't take the anthropology seriously the way he took the rest, I can see that now.'

'He takes it seriously *now*,' said David, 'too bloody seriously, if you ask me. Hence the Locks.'

'It might be helpful. If it had been anyone other than

the Locks . . .' said Anna.

Soon Carter, having looked round to check that none of the Franklin contingent was in earshot, was well into the subject. 'That great stuff about witchcraft you dug up,' he was saying enthusiastically, waving such a generous hand, he almost knocked one of the fast slumping candles onto the red-checked tablecloth, 'well, the Franklin people, by going right in there, looking at a small group of patients in much greater depth than you could within the parameters set by our big groups, Anna, they'll help you put all that into the cultural context.'

Anna had not, in fact, dug up, as he put it, much about witchcraft. She hadn't expected to, given the constraints – what Jacoman called 'the parameters' – under which they had been working all along. It was now she discovered exactly how far she and Jacoman had travelled since the beginning of this project, each of them in reverse directions. (Which had been the more thoroughly brainwashed, you could ask; Jacoman by the Locks, or her by the medical profession? Hearing herself speak in such ways amazed her.) 'That's all very well, all very fascinating, Carter, but how's it going to advance what we're doing? What we really need is stuff that's going to validate our questionnaires, give people clues to treatment objectives in future. How's understanding witchcraft going to help all that?'

Carter had hardly touched the plate of food he'd brought over with him; now he tore off a hunk of bread, dipped it into Anna's fondue on its heated cradle, took a large bite, then with his mouth full, waved a hand round at the rustic candlesticks, the alpine horns, cowbells, painted wooden plates and so forth with which they were surrounded; above a sudden burst of accordion music and yodelling he shouted, 'Bullshit, Anna. Bull*shit*. I've spent the past eight years hearing that kind of shit from Bader-Kleitz, "effective treatment proposals", etc., etc., etc., da, da, da, what we need now is academic acceptance, that's what the Franklin lot will give us.'

'OK, Carter; OK. But apart from that,' said Anna, 'we need publicity, noise, all the stuff you used to talk about putting epilepsy on the map – how can Franklin help?'

'You're so naïve, sometimes, Anna,' said Carter, sourly. He did not seem to be enjoying this argument for once, and nor was she. 'OK, you want publicity, you want aid programmes. But you're not going to get either, unless your academic credentials are bona fide.'

'OK, OK, Carter, I take your word for it; we actually need them. But you're sending all those Franklin people out to all those places – who's going to help them when they get there? I mean there's a lot of space out there, there's a lot of people, even if they did find the right houses, the right people, they can't just walk straight in there, someone's going to have to take them.'

'Lastenia can help them. Bennet can help them,' said Carter.

'Did you ask someone to sort that out, Carter? I mean there's . . .'

'The logistics are none of my business,' said Carter, dipping bread into fondue again, taking it out, dripping cheese all over the table before thrusting it into his mouth. 'I've got better things to do than channel information, Jesus, that's what this meeting's for, Anna.'

'Carter . . .'

'You ask your husband what . . .' he began.

Anna lost her temper almost. 'Shut up for a minute, Carter, let me speak.'

At which point Carter really did lose his temper, bellowing at her, 'Don't tell me to shut up, Anna. I know you mightn't like to remember it, but I'm the boss here. This is my show. If it wasn't for me you wouldn't be here blathering on about treatment objectives, just like the bloody sales manager.'

'Thanks for reminding me, Carter.' But she spoke quite quietly; partly because taken by such surprise, even shock at the anger in his voice; partly because she became aware now, taking a closer look at him, just how dreadful he looked; despite his red-checked shirt, the overall colour of the man was somewhere between grey and yellow. A moment before she'd been wondering how she could, ever, have been attracted to Dr Jacoman; now, in passing, she wanted to take him in her arms and hug him.

Carter turned morose thereafter. He gave up on the fondue, lit a cigarette, only half remembering to offer Anna one as he did so, stubbed it out almost at once; even a cigarette, it seemed, could do nothing for him this evening. 'You see all this crap, Anna,' he said at last, waving a hand once more at the painted plates, the alpine horns and cowbells, the carved chairs, the check tablecloths, the grotesque accretions of candlewax, like gnomes, on the wrought iron candle holders. 'This crap's what's wrong with Switzerland. This crap is what Switzerland thinks it is, along with Calvinism and cuckoo clocks. What hope's a Canadian Jew with a family motto taken from a play by a New York Jew got among that lot? So don't talk to me about treatment objectives, Anna, leave that to your husband. If I wanted someone who knew about treatment objectives, dear, I wouldn't have picked you, I'd have settled for –' here he pointed to one of the Franklin women, the very tall girl, very prim, flat-chested, with pale eyes and a sulky mouth, not seen so far without the faded red baseball cap proclaiming the Franklin Radicals ('a female baseball team?' suggested David) 'I'd have settled for someone like that.'

'I wonder why you didn't then,' said Anna; 'Why didn't you, Carter?' Whereupon he threw her an angry glance, said, 'You know why I didn't. But like I said, the way you're getting above yourself, Mrs Kern, I almost wish I had,' and left her.

David had not had a good evening either, trapped between Aguadiente on one side, Vittoria on the other. Aguadiente discussed the pros and cons of going back to his wife all evening; Vittoria, in between interpreting for Aguadiente had insisted on describing exactly, with actions, how you made a crab mousse, 'A Cajun crab mousse,' said David, morosely. 'Whatever that is.'

When Anna tried to report at least part of her conversation with Jacoman, he lost his temper entirely.

'That's it,' he said. 'That's it. Jacoman's done it this time. So he thinks the Locks will validate us academically does he, the cretin, tell that to my department, how could you even listen to him talking such rot, Anna? I tell you something Piet told me, what's more, that pair of clowns, the Locks, they don't trust any of us, they called up Franklin after the meeting this afternoon to check on me in the citation index. That's what they're like, you can see why Stan Heins hates them. They've bust up my friendship with him, they put their spies on to my academic record, and then Carter says they're the only ones will make us academically respectable. Listen to me, Anna. You're not listening to a word are you? If there's much more of it, I'm going.'

(This was the first time Anna had heard that there was such a thing as a citation index; that academics were judged not only on the number of papers they turned out, but on the number of times they got cited in other people's papers. Having made David explain it she laughed out loud. He said, tersely, this showed how naïve she was, it was no joke, professionally.)

Over the next day or two, even though she avoided them as far as possible, it became clear to Anna that the Locks and their acolytes grew ever more at sea. Whenever she came across them, they'd have their heads together in corners of the bar or lounge, looking suspiciously at all comers. Carter had overstated the case to them, too, in usual Jacoman fashion; nothing was as cut and dried as they seemed to be expecting, not least the dates and sites for their proposed research. At least *they* might have known or thought they knew, the dates and sites, but the Kenyans, the Ecuadorians, the Turks and the Pakistanis didn't know them; Anna's question as to whether Carter had consulted people on the ground in countries to which he proposed to send the Franklinites proved more to the point than she'd realised or he'd been prepared to acknowledge.

In consequence, the hitherto relatively silent figures of the Kenyans, the Pakistanis, the Turks, the solitary Egyptian – the chief contribution of the last three in particular had been to complain that everyone else spoke too fast – became somewhat less silent, at least between themselves, at the prospect of the proposed invasion by the Locks, or if not the Locks, by their acolytes.

The Kenyans, in particular, were disinclined to accept it.

Bennet said angrily to Anna, 'They just want to . . . we have worked all these years with these patients, we care what becomes of them. They just see them as material for academic papers,' or words to that effect; he spoke very quickly; Anna never could reproduce his accent; she still could not always understand it.

But if the Kenyans could not make out the Locks, the Locks were still less capable of reading the Kenyans. That same day Charlene Lock came up to Anna, and asked, of Bennet, 'Why's that man so jumpy? Hasn't he any confidence in himself?'

As a means of getting Anna's confidence – if it was that; she had the feeling it might be – it was not successful. On the other hand it confirmed what she was beginning to suspect. Watching Charlene visible in her cherry red – did she have two identical red tracksuits? – from one end of the foyer, the dining-room, the conference room, to the other, she decided this outfit had been chosen deliberately, to counteract the Snow Queen image; yet the way Charlene quenched the colour reinforced the Snow Queen image, rather. Watching her waylay this person or that, Anna saw what the confidence of the pair had disguised in the other places; that what had so got her back up in Oxford, Connecticut, and Barcelona might not so much be malevolence, or academic go-getting, was, just as likely, Charlene's lack of talent in engaging with anyone to whom she had no certain, defined connection. Given the Locks' growing unpopularity; given that they would all have to get together at some point, and that she wasn't going to help them achieve it, and Jacoman had lost all will to achieve it, Anna could have felt sorry for her; she didn't.

Anna Kern's diary. May 23rd.

Raining all day. Now everyone seems at odds with everyone. Last night I saw Charlene laying into the acolytes, not just full blast vocally, full blast of her icy eyes; I saw her laying into everyone, including her husband. I don't think the Americans are enjoying this any more than we are.

But if Charlene seems even angrier, Jacoman looks worse than ever. Outside meetings, he spends most of his time with Meyersdorf and sometimes, summoning him peremptorily, Piet. Piet reports gleefully, to me not Jacoman, that the Locks have been trying to subvert him, trying to pump him about Jacoman and us. Also that they have been muttering darkly about meetings with Gomez in Washington; about how Gomez now says he was cheated, that this should have been his project; and that any minute Piet was going to lose all credit for his work also. Given the way the Locks have ignored Piet before he tells them, 'Nothing doing.' Good for him.

May 24th. Raining again all day; still no mountains. This evening, finally, the prospect of writing up this stuff making me more and more anxious, I did what Jacoman keeps suggesting, bearded the Dreadlocks to ask for help; or rather I bearded Milton Lock, plus the three acolytes whose names I still haven't sorted out, except for the one in the baseball cap, Sharon Lambert, because she's obviously Charlene's chief disciple, they are always whispering together; maybe Sharon is one person who likes her; or maybe it's politic for Sharon to seem to like her.

There was no sign of Charlene. She was off having a swim, Milton said, she'd be in later. If I'm honest it was one reason I chose this moment to approach them. Milton still seemed so much the easier of the two. I still found myself liking the look of him, yet feeling I ought not to; with his wife it's the other way about entirely. I hate her; but I'm not so sure I ought to hate her.

It was a very informal meeting; we were all

sprawled on orange armchairs with leather arms, or, in my case, on the floor in the corner of the hotel foyer. And Milton, sprawled rather close to the pretty Franklinite, whose name I now remembered was Deborah, and who didn't seem to object, despite her lurking husband, was nice to me – too nice, I should have realised; he started by offering me his orange armchair – I declined it – and went on to a discussion of parametrics – doubtless he suspected my knowledge of parametrics was vestigial. He ended, 'You won't need anything like that, Anna (too right I wouldn't), just start with a few distributions, you can't go wrong with that.'

Then he said, more kindly than ever, 'Now, Anna, let's take this situation in the round; let's look at your project – which by the way I think you've done a great job on – let's look at it from the point of view of a naïve social researcher,' whereupon I say, deadpan, God help me, I was joking – how could I have been naïve enough not to realise that with this lot no one jokes? It's all too serious, a matter of academic life or death – 'But I *am* a naïve researcher.' He pretends not to have heard me, at least I think he's pretending; failing to take the hint, not seeing he thinks I mean it, I reiterate: 'But I *am* a naïve social researcher.' And in that moment, in horror, realise I've thrown myself open, just the way Jacoman and David were always warning me not to; by being too clever in this case – more like Jacoman who's always a bit too clever – not vice-versa.

'Of course I'm joking,' I added hastily, seeing Milton's look of benignly lethal triumph; too late. For of course, not believing me, he thinks he's got me. *Now* he can screw me.

And boy, did he screw me. Not overtly, of course; but the Franklinites knew, two of them even looked sorry for me; only the becapped Sharon looked smug, not to say pleased, as Milton proceeded to bombard me with statistical theory, pausing now and then for me to nod, or whatever; at the end he said, 'Of course this isn't my field, I leave all that stuff to Charlene. As far as these things go, Anna, I'm another naïve social researcher . . .'

On cue appeared Charlene, with wet hair, looking cross. The only compensation in this whole affair was seeing a crack for the first time in that unbreachable façade called Professor and Mrs Lock. Not only Milton moved, smartly, a foot further from the pretty Deborah; I recognised the same note in Charlene's voice as I've heard myself use with David and David with me, as she moaned out, 'Where the hell have you been, Milton? I thought we'd arranged to meet upstairs. I've been waiting for you, for ever, how could you do it to me?' And so on . . . For the first time, just for a minute, at least, she stopped being like the Snow Queen. She sounded like any other nagging spouse, myself included; tiresome but human.

For maybe she did have to wait for ever for Milton in a great many other senses, as well as this one. Seeing Milton's oh so patient, oh so patronizing look, I could not bear it.

'I'm sorry, Charlene,' I said, as humbly as I could. 'I just thought it was time we talked. Milton should have said you were waiting for him.'

'I should think he should,' she snapped back, still glaring at Milton. Then she turned to look at me.

'Isn't this desire to talk a bit late, Anna; shouldn't we all have got together the day we got here?' She'd stopped glaring at Milton; she glared at me, instead.

'Why didn't we then?' I asked, as sweetly as I was able.

'It's your show, Anna, it wasn't up to us,' the professor interjected. The acolytes, I noticed, were getting to their feet; in a moment they'd melted away; leaving me, to my horror, in sole possession, for the moment, of Professor and Doctor Lock; or rather, more accurately, Professor and Doctor Lock in sole possession of me. Will you walk into my parlour, says the spider to the fly; look into my eyes, look deep into my eyes, says the Snow Queen; and here I am in the Snow Queen's castle – clinging grimly to such images in face of the science with which they blind me. It's not

400

long before I forget all over again the Snow Queen's revelation of herself as human.

Actually they don't blind me for long. Having rubbished the kind of large-scale survey we've just done, and which they, back in 1986, back in Oxford, Connecticut, approved of; they add, kindly, 'but of course you didn't have much option in your set-up, Anna, you had to do it like that; but what we've come to the conclusion *is*' – and of course the conclusion they've come to is that small scale close-up in-depth interviews with a few patients – what Jacoman is prepared to pay *them* to do – is much the best method. There's a whole lot of talk now about what they call illness narratives; EM's don't get a look in, let alone EMICs.

In this way they also contrive to dash any real hopes I might have had – the only reason I bearded Milton – of help with my analysis. Instead what I get is peroration, from Charlene mostly, on what a terrible week they'd had, how Jacoman had misled them; they didn't realise it was all still so vague; they'd thought the arrangements he'd suggested to them had been finalised long ago. And so on. Here I can have some fellow feeling; given how often we too, David and I, have been dangled on the end of Jacoman's arrangements, only to have them withdrawn, or changed completely.

'And of course,' says Charlene, Milton nodding in agreement, scratching his boots – he is slumped across an armchair, like a cowboy on a horse, she sits primly upright, staring at me directly, 'and of course the worst of it, is how unwelcome we have been made to feel. *Everyone's* been so hostile.'

'You've been hostile, Anna,' adds Milton giving me yet another (un)kindly smile.

'I'm sorry,' I say, and manage not to add that this, too, was Jacoman's fault, for not warning us they were coming. Not that I need to; they're no fools. They know how threatening they are to me, exactly. Most of why they are so threatening is not their fault either, they

certainly didn't get all their degrees to make Anna
Kern feel inadequate.

'We've had a dreadful week, Anna,' says Charlene.
'Dr Gomez did warn us that Jacoman was like that.
He felt cheated, he felt that Jacoman had driven him
out of the work he started. To be honest we just
thought the guy had a chip on his shoulder. But after
this, the way Milton and I have been made to feel, we
can really believe the poor guy got a raw deal, can't we
Milton? We haven't enjoyed ourselves the slightest.'

'Nor have I,' I say truthfully; and, what the hell, I
think, what have I got to lose any longer; I ask
Charlene outright if she is prepared to help me in any
way to analyse my data. Knowing David's views on the
matter, I decide I'll square this with him later. But
actually I don't need to square it; after all this,
Charlene looks at me for a long while, I look back, less
intimidated, funnily enough, than I ever have been.
Gazing into her slaty eyes, maybe this time she has
managed to bewitch me, I almost think it would be
nice if we could work together in a friendly way, to
hell, I think, with Milton, to hell with David. But then
Charlene nods – as usual she blows it (it's pretty clear
to me by now she does this with everyone, one minute
pulls, the next pushes; I daresay she can't help it).
With a dismissive smile she hands me her card; Dr
Charlene Perkins Lock, it says, M.A. Ph.D.,
Department of Medicine, Franklin University. 'Sure,
Anna, honey, call me any time you like,' she says. Only
to add immediately that she is of course extremely
busy, with her own academic work, with this and that
academic woman's committee, implying, almost as an
afterthought, that for whatever help she gave me, she
would, of course, expect some kind of fee. The bitch.
The *bitch*. As for Milton, seeing him smirk at me, oh so
kindly, his dirty work well done, I hate him as much as
I hate her; more if anything; I hope the pay off for
what he gets her to do is that in private he really is
nagged rotten.

Charlene's hair was still wet from swimming I

noticed; the water somewhat dulled its blackness, making her look much older; much more tired; as I left them, I heard Milton say something I could not hear waving a hand towards her hair; instantly I heard her round on him. So maybe he does get nagged rotten. Maybe one day he'll leave her for some juicier, more amenable little student, like Deborah, he's just the type, and all too fanciable; he's such a cowboy; such a smooth bastard. Oh God, poor Charlene.

On the morning after, to the Kerns' glee, the Frankli-nites were routed on one front at least – by the only people they'd already noted as being able to stand up to them; that is the Kenyans, Bennet and his colleagues. This raised David's already high opinions of them. If it wasn't either Lock got routed directly, it was the next best thing – Charlene's acolyte, confidante up till then, Dr Sharon Lambert; she changed her earrings, daily, Anna noted, but not her jockey cap; 'Franklin Radicals continue to Rule OK,' said David. The lady herself, however, did not continue to do so. Indeed she looked so crestfallen, so depressed from now on, Anna could not but feel sorry for her. Since no one but she and the Kenyans were present at the fateful meeting, however, the only account of it available to the outside world came from the Kenyans. They said Dr Lambert had whined at length about her schedules – about how she'd set this coming vacation aside to do the work, and no, she couldn't just wait for instructions from the Kenyans as to when her visit would be most convenient for them, that wouldn't suit her at all, what about her schedules?

'Schedules, my *schedules*,' mimed Bennet in a high voice, a weird Kenyan version of an American accent, while describing the meeting to Anna, clowning it almost, in ways she had never imagined of him, as if exhilarated by being part of the Franklin routing. As if exhilarated by everything. For if Jacoman, this project, had changed anyone, Anna had been observing all week how it had changed Bennet. Or rather how it had changed his presentation of himself. Charlene's comments on him which might have seemed apt a year ago, now seemed, to Anna, imperceptive, not to say misguided. He talked of going to international meetings convened by the World Bank. He wore a leather jacket, an open-necked shirt to meetings instead of a suit. Today, the last day it had actually stopped raining, he walked up the path behind the hotel with Anna, wearing a large high peaked straw hat, tipped rakishly sideways. He made Aguadiente seem ill at ease – but then he was lucky enough to speak English. All the non-English speakers looked ill at ease this week, sidelined, Anna thought, by the imperialism of language. (Each time she spoke to Aguadiente, not only did he look ill at ease, not only did he agree with everything she told him, he shuffled and blushed like a schoolboy.)

According to Bennet, when asked, very politely, why she thought Kenya needed her, Dr Lambert had told the distinguished professor with his degrees from both Cambridge and Columbia that it was because he didn't know anything about medical anthropology, and she did. And that was that. This culturally sensitive anthropologist couldn't go to Kenya, now obviously, nor to Latin America – she couldn't speak Spanish – nor to Turkey – she didn't speak Turkish, and anyway, the Locks were going – nor to Pakistan – they wouldn't have a woman, or rather they wouldn't have *this* woman.

Of the remaining acolytes therefore, the man, Dr Birnbaum, was to go to Pakistan and the woman to Ecuador. (Aguadiente had no objection; she was very pretty. Alas, she had, too, a husband in tow.) The Locks as stated were going to Turkey; the only one who wasn't going anywhere, other than where she had been already, was Sharon Lambert, Franklin Radicals or no Franklin Radicals. 'Maybe it's a woman's football team?' said David, gleefully; adding even more gleefully, 'Next goal Charlene Lock, perhaps?' 'Don't be so bitchy,' said Anna, as astonished to find in herself a need to defend the woman, as she was to find in her husband such academic – Franklinite – sensitivities; not to say jealousies.

'Franklin one: London one. Wouldn't you say that was

the score, Anna?' David added, ignoring her.

'More like Nairobi one,' said Anna.

(It was the time, perhaps, for premonitions; intimations. One conversation with her husband, Anna recorded ashamedly. It was the second to last night, after the conversation with the Locks.

'Do I have to do the analysis?' she asked, in sudden panic. 'Isn't there anyone else?'

'Of course you have to do it; you took on the job,' said David.

'You encouraged me to,' protested Anna.

'More fool you to let me,' he said. 'More fool me, come to that.'

'I hate this place,' she said. 'I hate this whole thing. Why don't we just go home tomorrow? Why don't we go home and make love and get me pregnant, and forget it, every little bit?'

She regretted this at once. 'Is that how you see it?' he asked in a quiet voice. 'Is that how you see it? Us having a baby to get you out of something you've contracted to do, and now don't fancy? Or is it,' he looked at her in sudden understanding – she could see he meant it as a joke – but it didn't come out like a joke – 'is it that you've fallen out of love with Jacoman?')

On the last night of the Kanterberg event there was yet another dinner, in a castle beside a lake which, having descended the mountain in a 1930's train, they crossed by a pre-war – pre first war – motor boat, all mahogany and polished brass. It was more of the same, really, David thought; only the settings altered; what Anna called the big men went on as ever. Jacoman played host, as noisy as ever, but much more mechanical, not to say ghostly – ghastly – by his standards. As far as Jacoman ever flirted with anyone, David noticed, he flirted with Charlene – whenever that is, Charlene wasn't continuing her attempts at subversion among his colleagues, none of which Jacoman himself appeared to notice. Worst of all Dr Taylor appeared from nowhere – this was the first time Anna had met him. Within two weeks of leaving Basel, he'd come to congratulate everyone on their hard work; the usual story 'May I share with you . . .' and so on. As he orated, smiling blandly, making polite gestures with well manicured hands, David, eyeing his broad, almost simian shoulders, imagined plastic joints and pins shifting beneath the cloth of his expensive suit; still more than usual in such light, such a setting – they ate in the castle hall, lighted candles in iron sconces above enormous oak tables – he could see why Giselle Jacoman had dubbed this yet other cliché, Taylor, 'Action Man'.

Jacoman wasn't a cliché, though, even this gutted out, mechanical Jacoman; who could not let go, even now. When they got back to the hotel he insisted on David having a drink with him somewhere. Conscious of an early start next morning, David would have refused; only Jacoman looked so woe-begone, so bedraggled, by his standards – it had poured with rain on the return journey; Jacoman had waited outside for everyone to emerge from the coach – he did not have the heart to. But the way Jacoman then added there was something serious he had to talk to him about, he was suddenly too needled to take the thing lightly. It was late; he was very tired; he had hated that dinner; last night, what's more, he'd had his row with Anna, and had not been able to sleep. 'Now you mention it,' he said, frowning, 'I've got to talk seriously to you too, Carter; we've got to get some things clear about those Locks; or else. I warn you . . .'

The bar did not seem the appropriate place to discuss any of this. David took Jacoman up to his room, therefore. This meant banishing Anna, whom they found reading in the sitting area of the family suite they had been allotted, up the small flight of stairs to the bedroom. She was not pleased. David ignored the expression on her face, took a bottle of whisky and two tooth mugs from an otherwise empty provision cupboard, and sat himself and Jacoman down in the easy chairs ranged either side of a low table. Upstairs Anna could be heard banging about, much more noisily than necessary; this filled David with irritation but also guilt; how childish she could be, he thought, not willing at this moment to concede she might have a point; he had been very peremptory with her. Yet, he had a right, he thought, to be peremptory. At the same time, as he watched Jacoman bring papers, schedules out of a brief-case, something about this intimacy of jutting knees, of the light of the low lamp falling on a low table, glinting on Jacoman's spectacle rims, picking up the Baltic pallor of his hair, his eyes, reminded him of their very first meeting; a kind of nostalgia began driving away his anger.

But not for long. Because Jacoman's heart had been so in things then, in Jerusalem; whereas now, in Switzerland, they were not; he made the right noises only. Alongside everything he said, too, there seemed to be something lurking that he was not saying. After a while, David stopped expecting to hear it said. He also stopped picking up this point Jacoman made, or the other, about minor matters of organisation. He began to feel obliged to try and cheer Jacoman up; telling him how much they'd achieved on this project, how near they were to finishing it; they had the epidemiological results already; and in the beginning at least, they'd had only Jacoman to thank for it, it had all been due to his energy and enthusiasm. Which was fair enough. What with that and the whisky, Carter took on colour, after a while, unwound a little; whereas David altogether lost track of his rage about the Locks. When, even so, he tried to raise the subject of the Locks, Jacoman got up. 'Is there anything to eat in that icebox, over there, David?' he asked. 'This whisky's making me hungry.'

David's search of the refrigerator produced one packet of peanuts and two of crisps. On these Jacoman fell, distractedly, tipping his head back, dropping in handfuls, nuts first, then crisps. If there was an element of deliber-ation in this, even of performance, it didn't stop his actions seeming in more respects somnambulistic. 'What about the Locks, Carter?' David repeated. But all Jaco-man answered, as if it had nothing more to do with him, was no longer his problem – had David but known it, very shortly it wouldn't be his problem – was: 'What about the Locks? What about the Locks, David? What's the problem?' But the trace of anger in his voice faded immediately. He sat looking at David, a sleepwalker once again. David was reminded of music somehow; if the first meeting in Jerusalem had been like the beginning of the first movement of a symphony – presto, forte, con brio, now definitely, definitely, they were nearing the end of the second movement, a largo, an andante of the most melancholy kind. What about the third movement? David wondered, watching Jacoman move his papers from the table to the floor, and back to the table, lighting a cigarette, stubbing it out again immediately. Will it be jolly or frantic? Not jolly, surely; assuming there was, for him, a third movement? He'd stubbed out the cigarette with such finality, he might have been stubbing out himself if not the project; as if for him the piece was already well and truly over. Excellent diagnostician that he was, David could see it all, clearly. As he could tell it was no good, any longer, going on about the Locks. What he couldn't tell was the reason for what he understood. He had really no idea that for Jacoman it was now or never.

At one point Jacoman opened his mouth, hesitated; for a moment David had the impression he was at last to be told something important. But in the end all Carter gave him was some brief remark about his son, Louis. Then, taking another cigarette, he embarked on a story of his own childhood, making it clear as never before that he was the youngest in his family by quite some way, just like David. He then said something about his mother; then opened his mouth again, then shut it; David had the impression Giselle was about to be mentioned, or maybe Anna; but they were not mentioned. At this moment a moth started fluttering around the lamp, banging against it, sinking back, banging again, its wings frantically whirring – where it came in this semi-sealed room was by no means clear; where it found such furious, such useless energy was by no means clear; for all the weight of its body, it was such a flimsy looking thing. At times it subsided; sat quivering, its jewelled eyes gleaming, throwing a shadow twice its size. In one such pause Jacoman occupied himself by trying to catch it; in vain; once more the insect started uselessly fluttering and banging. But Jacoman did not stop trying to catch it. He lurched about so clumsily that after a while David could not bear to watch him any longer, he leaned over Jacoman, ran his hands across the surface of the shade, gathered up the frantic insect. How it fluttered in his hands; a buzz, almost audible, a tickle, subsiding like lost life; then stillness.

In some unexpected impulse, David held out his hands to Jacoman; opened his fingers enough for Jacoman to see their contents.

'Just put it out of the window, will you,' Jacoman said harshly. 'Jesus. Don't hurt it, David. What's it done to us?' David, astonished, did as he was asked. Afterwards, he slammed the window, loudly, as if this was the only means left to him to express his exasperation. He slammed it so loudly the sound woke Anna, assuming she'd ever been asleep. She appeared at the top of the stairs in her dressing-gown, her hair on end.

Jacoman looking up at her, said, 'Anna, you look beautiful.' Seeing her smile, a wave of rage overcame David; he said, 'Go back to bed, Anna.' Seemingly appalled at his ferocity, she did as he asked, meekly, thereby, had they but known it, bringing to end before it started the last chance of the Three Musketeers meeting, sinking their differences, let alone David's last chance of letting Jacoman know clearly his feelings about the Locks, not to mention Jacoman's intention of telling either of them about Giselle; about his impending departure. Jacoman, too, left shortly. In the morning, while David and Anna were hastily getting together the last remnants of their belongings before heading for the bus to take them to the airport, the two not-quite empty glasses, the half empty bottle of whisky still sat forlornly on the table, next to an ashtray full of Marlboro stubs; David could not remember Jacoman smoking so many; but he must have. The room stank.

Chapter Eight

Almost four months later, sitting on Giselle Jacoman's brocade sofa, along with a tatty copy of *The Plumed Serpent*, an even tattier copy of *The Weirdstone of Brisingaman*, three pieces of lego and an armless doll, Anna, to her horror, heard herself blurting out, 'Ben has – had – epilepsy.'

She had not intended to say it; she did not know why she did it; immediately she could not even bear to look at Jacoman; she fixed her eyes instead on Giselle's 'tongues' – her plants – how dry they looked and dusty – Carter had already told her he was leaving all these plants behind – and took another great swig of the liquor that she by now associated with late night drinking in the company of Carter; scotch.

She should not be here at all, really. She had agreed with Jacoman when he said that with Giselle already back in Canada, it was probably better if she stayed at an hotel during her visit to Bader-Kleitz. But, of course, he said, he'd like to take her out to dinner. They'd settled on the second night – the night before she had gone to visit Piet, his tall Dutch wife and his tall Dutch children. Jacoman had picked her up at the hotel, but then asked if she'd mind if they dropped by his house for him to change. It was more or less en route to the restaurant.

He'd offered her a drink then, while he went up to change, and she'd accepted. It was still daylight; the late sunlight sliding through the big window that looked onto the street picked up each rubbed spot on the sofa. It looked shabby. The whole room looked shabby; also dusty; also lonely and empty. Most of the ornaments and so forth had been cleared. Next week shippers were coming to pack up all the rest. Suddenly, not even knowing the whole story, not even knowing yet that he and Giselle were separating, Anna felt desperately sorry for Carter.

When Carter came downstairs he got himself a drink also. He sat facing her and she made some mention of his going to Canada, just for something to say – there was a sudden, quite new awkwardness between them; where-upon – to break the silence, perhaps – he had started to pour out the whole story. He did not cry; nothing like that. He was just so bleak, so brittle, she could hardly bear it. When he'd finished, he said, 'Well perhaps we'd better be going,' and poured them each a second drink.

Anna never could quite remember afterwards how it came about that they did not go to the restaurant; which of them it was suggested eating at Carter's. It ought to have been Carter; he'd have known the contents of the fridge, whether there was actually anything for them to eat. She remembered confessing to not being very hungry; at the same time she remembered Carter saying something about its being tiresome to go out. Maybe they spoke simultaneously. What was certain was that they found themselves in what had been Giselle's kitchen shortly after, being domestic together; Carter was open-ing a bottle of wine and making a salad dressing with the remains of Giselle's extra virgin cold pressed olive oil and Balsamic vinegar; Anna was beating up eggs for an omelette.

Anna got quite drunk; that was one problem. She was not feeling very happy either; the night before her coming to Basel, she and David had their first major argument over working on the statistics. When they had stopped talking about Jacoman's life, his broken marriage, Anna confessed her anxieties over doing the analysis, writing the papers.

Carter told her she didn't have to worry; she was bright; David would help her. He didn't seem interested particularly; she realised with a pang of loss how he had really lost them now; how totally he had cut himself off from the project.

And maybe that was it, really; why she found herself blurting it out about Ben. One excuse could be that when, red in the face with the agitation this caused her, she protested Jacoman's lack of interest towards his own creation, Jacoman, more perceptive than she'd given him credit for, said; 'Your degree of commitment to this thing, Anna, has always been amazing; was it all your husband? I sometimes have to be jealous of David.' And she then – what was it – the meal they'd made together, the drink, the intimacies Jacoman had been telling her about his marriage, about Giselle? – she then, in her turn, made her most intimate confession: 'Ben has – had – epilepsy.' Having gone so far, there was no point in hanging back thereafter; she told Jacoman the whole story.

Later; not that much later, she said she should be going. Having agreed he was not fit to drive her, Jacoman went off and called a taxi. Coming back from the telephone, however, he walked right over to Giselle's brocade sofa and pulled Anna to her feet; they stood holding hands, facing each other, looking at each other. And it could have happened then, easily; you can always tell taxis to go away, for a small consideration. But it did not happen. And if it *had* happened it would have been for all the wrong reasons; because Jacoman was miserable, because Anna liked talking to him; because she'd had a row with her husband; because she didn't like leaving Jacoman alone in this empty house with the ghosts of his wife and children. Perhaps, above all, because she had told Jacoman about Ben; and was thankful to have admitted it at last, even if it was her husband to whom she really wanted to admit it. She might have stayed with their friend, simply because she could not admit it to David.

The problem was; the reason why she didn't stay – Jacoman had almost but did not quite ask her to – was the same reason: her husband; also the fact that she didn't fancy Jacoman; not like that; she never had;

though at times, beguiled by his tongue she'd *thought* she fancied him. She didn't fancy his crooked teeth, she realised. Maybe when it came to it Jacoman didn't fancy her, either. Or maybe he felt too much loyalty to David, or was just too drunk, or too plain miserable. In other words there was no right reason for staying with him – maybe there would never have been a right reason for staying with him; except the project itself – the way it had swept them all along. At the same time it had always so exhausted them that at no time had there been energy left over for such a physical consummation, she realised. There wasn't enough energy left now, this evening. And besides, for Jacoman, there was no longer, seriously, a project. Did Jacoman, too, see either of those things? Certainly, though she could see him still considering the matter, he didn't actually ask her to stay. He just kissed her with a little more fervour than might have been proper for an about to be unmarried man with a married woman; but that was all. And then the doorbell rang. And then Anna went back to the hotel in the taxi and rang David to tell him she loved him; out of guilt, partly, that it was to Jacoman she'd told her secret; but she did love him. Next morning when she saw Jacoman, she had a hangover and he looked as if he did. He talked Bader-Kleitz to her; and that was that.

BOOK 3
Close Out

Chapter One

('Close *out*' was Hicks' terminology; though claiming to be just a technical expression for what was done – a more ruthless version of close down, *he* said – the sound 'out' being much harder, more clipped than the sound 'down', made it a phonetically as well as semantically more appropriate description of what he did, fitting both man and process.)

It was not that there were no hopes of some ongoing effects of all their work. Apart from the academic papers to be written, and with luck published, there was ERGO, the international research group Jacoman and David between them had proposed and partially set up, as a reference point, in due course a network, it was hoped, for Third World epilepsy research worldwide, if funding could be found for it. Nevertheless, as far as most of the patients were concerned, the international stage of the project was over; in Ecuador, those still inclined to fetch their drugs from the Medical Centres still kept supplied did so, but, short of individual initiative by individual health workers, no one checked up if patients kept coming, let alone checked if they took the drugs they'd collected. Nor, apart from the few picked by Franklinite Deborah for her intensive anthropological survey, were they faced with any more lists of questions. The new crop of rural doctors were as ignorant about epilepsy as the last had been before the project. As for the neurologists – they had all gone home; Aguadiente, for instance, to take up a practice he had abandoned for almost two years; whatever you say about Aguadiente, it cannot be denied that he was committed to the project, that he'd worked, as Jacoman would say, his ass off. He'd started agitating again about papers, about furthering his reputation. (His suspicious helpfulness and acquiescence during Kanterberg, turned out, as David and Jacoman feared, all too short lived. Not that this was Jacoman's problem any longer. But it was Piet's problem; it was David's.)

In Kenya, on the other hand, not only were the patients still treated at Dr Meaki's clinic, the male Franklin acolyte, Dr Birnbaum, was doing a useful study of compliance – that is, why those patients who did what they were told did so, why those who didn't do what they were told did not. Bennet and his colleagues in Nairobi were finishing off their reports, preparing an education campaign among doctors throughout the country, and trying to put the concept of the social marketing of Lenytol to a not entirely unsympathetic market manager. (Whenever they wanted help in all these areas they continued to call on David.)

The Locks were headed for Turkey; Dr Birnbaum was due, on leaving Kenya, to turn his attention to Pakistan. His colleague, the beautiful Deborah, plus husband, was busy interviewing Aguadiente in Quito, before heading for the Altiplano.

As for Anna Kern, now embarked on the analysis of her results; deep in computer printouts, lists of figures, percentages, chi squares, and so on, doing her best to pretend she was a scientist, her calculator always to hand, the burning question in *her* life became, what *is* science, exactly? Just a way of doing? A way of thinking? Or what?

In the course of this, round about December 1988, Anna and David were invited to dinner by Dr Denis Taylor; beside whom, of course, Carter, even in memory, appeared not only socially canny but modesty itself. To hear Taylor talk, for instance, you'd have thought he alone was responsible for the growing connections between the pharmaceutical industry and non-profit-making aid organisations. He'd chaired this committee, set up that trust, organised those conferences and so on. He was a one man Magic Marketplace, all by himself. Telling them of an ongoing wrangle with some female aid executive in Paris, to whom the idea of commercial sponsorship had come as such a shock that she'd said, 'Let me sit down,' when Taylor first suggested they worked together, also gave Taylor the excuse to flatter Anna in ways which would have been wholly familiar to Giselle after her dinner ten years before. 'You're a clever woman,' he said smiling at her, most kindly. 'But *she* wasn't. She was *not*.'

This was a few months after he left the company to become Medical Director, West Indies; he was only in London for a week. David had prevaricated at first, when Taylor called him. Anna, however, who for the purposes of the book she was supposed to write was interested in hearing what Taylor had to say about the epilepsy project, and even more curious as to what he might have to say about Carter Jacoman in the light of Jacoman's own recent resignation, pressed him to accept the invitation to dinner. What Anna hoped for was not, of course, why Taylor himself had invited them. 'He wants something,' said David, who made no bones about disliking Taylor intensely. 'And whatever it is, I won't want to give it to him. So what's the point?' In the end, however, Anna persuaded him. Or rather, David left replying so late, that Taylor assumed they had accepted.

There was no nonsense about Taylor taking them to a downmarket Indian restaurant, as he had Carter and Giselle ten years before. They went to a very new and expensive nouvelle cuisine one, specialising in, though not limiting itself to, vegetables and fish. The colour scheme was pale green and pale pink; the delicate tracery of leaves across the walls was hung with pink flowers like columbines. The pale green cloths on the off-white bamboo-look tables matched the pale green seats of the off-white bamboo-look chairs. Pink linen napkins folded into fans, stood on white porcelain crockery, each table was decorated by a stem vase containing a single freesia. Amid all this, burly, red-headed Denis Taylor in his checked shirt and expensive leather jacket loomed like a buffalo in a bird cage. He himself seemed to feel it could not contain him; the first thing he did was call for the freesia on their table to be taken away. Freesias made him sneeze, he said. He didn't, in fact, sneeze once all evening, despite the abundance of freesias elsewhere; but Anna remained conscious then and afterwards in relation to that dinner of the flower's pervasive, sweetly alien, scent; as also of the arias and ensembles from *Così Fan Tutte* with which they were serenaded from the beginning of the meal to the end. The exquisite melodies, the sometimes deep, tranquil feeling, seemed as inappropriate to this setting, to them, this meeting, as they did to the farcical cruelties that pervaded the opera itself, thought Anna. What went on between them, though, did not, as in some parts of the opera, merely mimic triviality, or lack of heart. Where the music there served to demonstrate the lie, here, rather, it underlined a truth.

Not that David's dislike of Taylor was not real enough; this was obvious to Anna as it most likely would not have been to anyone else, Carter excepted – he always claimed with some, if not total, accuracy to read David like a book. She, on the other hand, enjoyed herself somewhat. David's reluctance to exchange reminiscences of medical school with Denis Taylor, Denis Taylor's seeming desire to delay declaring his real reason for entertaining David, left her free to dig out of the man what she would, flattering him mercilessly the while, to her husband's distaste. The food was good, also; and in their case, by chance perhaps, just like the restaurant, green and pink; she, for instance, ate salmon (pink) in a sorrel sauce (green); David ordered lobster tails and a spinach salad (pink and green). Taylor insisted on having walnut oil on the salad of lamb's lettuce which accompanied his steak au poivre vert; the meat too was pink, not to say bloody – he demanded it rare. When David murmured something about mad cow disease, he just laughed, moving his leather elbows like a boxer as he cut vigorously at the meat, and told them the story of a Frenchwoman he knew who had filled vol-au-vents with calves brains and fed them to a neurologist colleague. 'Blow me,' said Taylor, 'if he didn't turn green when he found out what he'd been eating. Blow me if she wasn't surprised by his reaction. Talk about cultural misunderstandings,' (here he smiled at Anna, the anthropologist). 'This was long before BSE of course. Bovine spongiform encephalitis,' he pronounced, with gusto, taking another mouthful of rare beef.

Anna stole a look at David. He had not been able to help himself laughing at Taylor's story, but now his face was again deadpan. In a dark suit, straight from the hospital, his heavy lids were even heavier than usual; he looked washed-out and tired alongside the ruddy cheeked, suntanned Taylor. He continued to say very little. Anna found no difficulty in diverting Taylor back to the epilepsy project and Carter. What was much harder later was persuading him to stop, to get down to the purpose of this dinner, what he wanted of David, thus enabling them to escape. They couldn't stop him even by asking after his wife; they knew from Carter that she spent six months and more of the year in her native Australia (so much for him managing her and his job both, said Carter, to whom Taylor had made clear, often enough, that a good executive should manage his wife as efficiently as his job). He talked of her so blandly and affectionately he might have expected her to be back at his hotel when he got in; as if she hadn't attended tonight on account of a bad cold, or maybe theatre tickets for something she didn't want to miss. He talked about his two sons also, one at college in the United States, the other at boarding school in Australia. He even brought out photos. A healthy youth – as healthy as Taylor, but still more athletic – grinned at them from a surf-board in one photo. The other son wore a skin-tight purple and red ski suit and a purple and red hat; he carried a pair of skis on his shoulder. He looked like Superman, thought Anna.

Afterwards Taylor went back to the subject of epilepsy and so forth, though not before he'd interrupted himself briefly to choose a dessert; he did not seem at all put out by David and Anna's refusal to choose from the list of confections he insisted on reading out. He ordered *Tarte Tartin* for himself, as an afterthought, ignoring her protests, added fresh figs for Anna.

'Epilepsy was an ideal subject for us of course. Not least because you could spell it. If you have to get money from the States always present them with a disease they can spell. The head of the WHO himself told me that, and he should know. Also it's easier to have a disease which is off the political agenda. You don't want to tread on government toes in any part of the world if you can help it, by overlapping with some scheme of theirs. No government wants to tackle a chronic disease like epilepsy. So there we were.'

This, of course, was more or less the opposite of what Jacoman had said concerning both political agendas and chronic disease. When Anna pointed it out – here David kicked her under the table – Taylor laughed heartily and said Jacoman was a smart chap, but you always had to take what he said with a pinch of salt. And then he had launched into what he called a 'critique' of the man: how clever he was – too clever in such a company for his own good – but how disorganised; how Taylor'd had to groom him; teach him when to shut up in meetings – teach him not to drop his notes all over the place when he was making a presentation, the Swiss didn't trust that in an executive, any more than they trusted brilliance. He'd sent Jacoman to a good barber; he'd even told him to fix his teeth, but Jacoman hadn't listened to that. But then Jacoman rarely listened to anyone, didn't bring other people's ideas in, didn't delegate, and so forth. That was one of his problems. He didn't build a team. Didn't suffer fools gladly, which of course you had to sometimes in this world. Often he put people's backs up. Of course his wife had said to him, Taylor, once, 'You don't listen to people, Denis,' but he did listen; the thing was he wasn't interested in was what other people thought, what he was interested in was what they had to offer. And he would submit, this *was* what he listened for. Whereas Jacoman...

Taylor had almost finished his *Tarte Tartin* by now. Anna was digging her teeth into the pink-green flesh of her second fig. The third, slyly, she offered to David, who took it, held it in his hand a minute, then shook his head and handed it back. Anna did not eat it either. The fruit remained whole, still voluptuous, on a white dish. 'Did you know,' she said to Taylor, demurely, 'did you know, Denis, that the apple in Eden wasn't an apple at all, really, it was a fig?'

Taylor's red eyebrows shot up. His Euro-shrug – Anna giggled remembering Giselle's description – was intense. 'That's just the sort of information we need you anthropologists for,' he said, smiling at her. Only when the coffee came in its copper-framed cafetière did he turn, at last, to David. This, it was clear from his change of mode, his sudden briskness, his businesslike, man-to-man, yet at the same time almost deferential tones, was the real point of the evening. He wanted to pick David's brains he said, on some neurological drug trial in the West Indies where he was now medical director; he half suggested David himself should take part, but picking up his reluctance well before he had voiced it, turned his request adroitly, asked instead for the names of reliable colleagues who might be interested in working with him. David, reluctantly, gave him a name or two – Anna could imagine him calling up next day to apologise to the people concerned. He then offered, politely, a modicum of professional advice; warned of odd problems; of the odd logistical puzzle; suggested some solutions; all very succinct and very precise. Hard as Taylor tried to prolong the discussion, it lasted, at the most, twenty minutes.

When it was clear no more was forthcoming – David had begun looking at his watch – Taylor called for the bill, upon which he laid, carelessly, a gold American Express card; David at once leaned over and proffered two twenty-pound notes towards the cost of the meal. Anna was used to such arguments in restaurants. Out with friends, for instance, David was always reluctant to let them pay; at the very least he regarded it as a duty to argue the case, to Anna's embarrassment on occasions. Yet he did not usually attempt to pay his share of a business dinner. Whatever was he about? It was all pointless, of course, as well as embarrassing – Taylor seemed much more practised at this sort of thing than David. He simply handed the notes back, waving the waiter away with his gold card; the whole thing so polite as to be almost perfunctory. Anna was not reassured by the politeness. She was as relieved as David when Taylor refused the offer of a lift to his hotel, endured as best she could the kiss Taylor gave her outside the restaurant – David got away with having his hand shaken. Taylor smelt peppery rather; a smell of aftershave and tobacco; something like the colour of his foxy head.

'Christ,' exploded David as they drove away, 'Christ what an appalling evening. What an appalling man. The way you and he buttered each other up, Anna. How could you? How could someone behave like that when not only his wife's just left him, he's been demoted practically? Moved sideways, if you like. But Medical Director West Indies. Well.'

'If that is all true,' said Anna, 'and I'm not sure in fact his wife has left him altogether, if it is true, you could say the man was heroic. Being so cool.'

'Oh come on, Anna, he's much too thick-skinned to mind.'

'No one's that thick-skinned,' said Anna. '*No one*.' But they went on rowing about it most of the way home. David, of course, responded more or less as Giselle had nine years before, Anna thought, remembering one of Jacoman's stories as David proclaimed for the umpteenth time, 'The whole thing made me feel dirty.'

'Jacoman never made you feel dirty. Is that why you tried to pay for our part of the dinner? To purify yourself?' asked Anna. While David said bitterly, 'You love it, I can see, Anna. This whole thing's corrupted you. How could you?'

'OK. He's awful, in his way. But so what? He's so different from most of the people I come across, I can't help being intrigued.'

'Well, aren't you lucky,' said David, 'I have to deal with people like that all the time. I just don't want to have dinner with them that's all.'

'You sound like Prospero in *The Tempest*,' Anna said. 'When Miranda says "Oh brave new world." And he answers, "Tis new to *thee*." You sounded just like that.'

'Oh did I?' said David. 'But aren't you a bit too old for Miranda, sweetie?' Thereafter he fell into a gloomy silence, while she drove on, worrying whether he was right, whether she was corrupted a little, and whether it mattered. In other words whether corruption was inevitable if you lived in the world at all. In which case, what you had to be certain of was that you at least knew you were corrupted. Or corruptible. How complicated it all was. Remembering the way he had spat his last words out, she wished, also, miserably, it didn't lead to such a distance from her beloved husband. They seemed to be arguing constantly about things like this, these days, even more than they had in the beginning, as if the soul of their relationship, the heart of it lay within, not to mention all the answers to their differences and dissensions; whether drug companies were ethical organisations really, whether you could trust their attempts to reform themselves, whether social – responsible – marketing, so-called, was more than a gimmick, cynically designed to increase their profits. David thought so; despite all his research collaborations. Anna was inclined to give them at least the benefit of the doubt. On top of that, Anna's attempts at analysis of her results and writing them up were driving them both crazy. Never before had they, journalist and scientist, seemed to inhabit such different worlds.

Chapter Two

Anna Kern's notebook. SCIENCE. *Science at last, I think David would say. Let's start with a short scientific vocabulary; no definitions – I'm tired of definitions; whoever wants them can get out their own dictionary.*

Empirical
hypothesis
validation
methodology
data
randomize
phenomenological,
function,
dysfunction,
variable.
rigorous (as in 'the research was rigorously conducted')
robust (as in 'the test proved to be robust')
etc., etc., etc. . .

'Freudians, politicians and historians see almost no limits to what their pet theories can explain. Science, in contrast, is a strictly limited endeavour . . .' (Dr Steve Jones, Reith Lecturer.)

(NB. Anna. Where do medical anthropologists see themselves in all this?)

'Science is organised knowledge . . .' (Herbert Spencer.)

'Science is nothing but trained and organised common-sense, differing from the latter only as a veteran may differ from a raw recruit . . .' (Thomas Huxley.)

'Experiments are the only means of knowledge at our disposal; the rest is just poetry, imagination.' (Max Planck.)

'If therefore the organs of sense, ears, noses and tongue were removed, I believe that shape, quantity and motion (primary qualities) would remain but there be no more of (secondary qualities) smells, tastes and sounds. Thus, apart from the living creatures, I take these to be mere words.' (Galileo.)

'Physics and chemistry are already starting to become qualitative again, that is to account also for secondary qualities ... Mythical thought for its part is imprisoned in the ... experiences which it never tires of ordering ... But it also acts as liberator by its protest against the idea that anything can be meaningless.' (Levi-Strauss. The Savage Mind. p.22.)

'The completely unique individuality is too frequently ignored or forgotten by doctors ... Every intervention is an experiment, because the full nature of the patient is never known or understood. Medicine is an indeterminate art, however much scientists and the public would prefer it not to be.' (Philip Rhodes. 1985.)

'Scientific practice [is] ... a rule-governed ... craft of narrating the history of nature. Any scientific statements about the world depend intimately upon language; upon metaphor ... Scientific practice is above all a story-telling practice ...' (Donna Harraway. Primate Visions.)

(N.B. Anna: Jacoman's anecdote about the Pakistani doctor; about diagnosing epilepsy from the story – the history. N.B., also, assuming I do it, my writing the story of our project – of Jacoman; science as story with a vengeance).

The subjects about which Anna was supposed to produce scientific papers for both the Kenya and Ecuador studies were three in number, meaning six papers in all (other subjects were being followed up by local workers); namely: the degree of stigmatization of epileptic patients as revealed by her questionnaires (did people laugh at them, run away and so forth): the effects of epilepsy on the social and economic functioning of patients (did they have friends, spouses, jobs and so forth): patient attitude to, and their usage of, medical services, both scientific and indigenous (that is both doctors and *brujos*).

Given that it took her nearly nine months to analyse the appropriate figures from her questionnaires, pursue the necessary references and write the papers, given the profound effect on her marriage of these reluctant efforts, it might be appropriate, Anna thought, to set out these effects – and the conclusions to be drawn from them – in precisely the same form as that with which she was struggling; a form as alien to her as it was normal to her husband. Which was indeed the whole problem; C.P. Snow's two cultures, she thought, met head on these days on her desk, on her bookshelves; worse still they met head on in her marriage bed. Was it significant that Snow himself was a scientist, also, like David, married to a writer – a novelist, of course, in his case, not a journalist like Anna, but still a writer?

Anna Kern's notebook; October 1989. (N.B. Preliminary draft. Tables and references missing)

Summary
This paper looks at the effect on a couple's marriage of writing scientific papers together, where one has been educated within a scientific culture and one has not. Variables looked at which could constitute or influence this effect are the psychology of the protagonists, their age, their family situation, the status of the marriage at the time the study was carried out. The conclusion arrived at was that though the overall effects recognised were, in the short term, deleterious to the marriage, the couple's mutual affection, and a tendency exhibited by each of them to develop more sympathy and understanding towards the thinking of the other, or at least more understanding as to what constituted that thinking, offers a more hopeful prognosis for the future.

Introduction
In the course of the heated debates on education, recently, there has been an upsurge of interest in the theory of the two cultures advanced by the scientist and writer C. P. Snow (Snow 1947). His contention was that an education system which requires schoolchildren to specialise at an early age has led to a cultural divide between those who opt for the sciences and those who opt for the arts. Scientists, lacking all knowledge and understanding of the language, ideas and methods of history, literature

and philosophy, also lack understanding of how, intellectually, socially, politically, we have arrived at the world in which we live; arts specialists, correspondingly, lacking education in the methods and theories of the physical sciences, lack understanding of the processes which have made the natural world around them, that has led to the technology which they, too, take for granted, and on which, they too, rely. Thus these two cultures, literally, cannot understand each other – the scientist regards the arts graduate as a sloppy and woolly-headed ignoramus, the arts graduate the scientist as an inarticulate, incomprehensible, obsessional or 'nit-picking' (A. Kern et al 1988) philistine. At a professional level, there is not much cooperation, let alone understanding; at a social level the communication is by necessity superficial. The significance of this study is that it offers the rare conjunction of two people from either side of the cultural divide, not only locked into that 'most intimate of all situations, marriage', (XYZ 1962) but forced to work together, at close quarters, and attempting to make use of the special skills of the other's milieu without compromising their own.

Population

David Kern is a neurologist specialising in epilepsy, educated public school, Cambridge, Guy's Hospital Medical School, aged 39/40 at the time of the study, private interests jazz music and Victorian architecture; Anna Kern a journalist, aged 38, with a degree in English Literature from the University of Sussex, a diploma in Sociology from the University of London, a long term private interest in anthropology, but no formal training in science since dropping biology at the age of 13. At the time of the study they have been married seven years, a significant stage in married life; see *Seven Year Itch*. (??? 1955) Dr Kern is childless, despite a previous marriage. There is one son (aged 17) from Anna Kern's previous marriage. His imminent A levels (summer 1989) are another strain upon the couple; not least the son has been sufficiently influenced by his stepfather to specialise in science subjects, a matter of some bewilderment and even jealousy to his mother, in the husband's view. This has added to the differences between the couple. The matter of further children has been raised, initially by the male partner, more recently by the female; the lack of agreement is another stress within the marriage, both related to and resulting from the professional differences to be discussed. A further possible complication is the mutual but almost certainly unconsummated attraction between Mrs Kern and Dr Carter Jacoman, the progenitor of the project; though the husband had turned a blind eye to the implications of this relationship, a residual bitterness did tend to surface at this time. It should also be noted that throughout the period of the study, the husband is doing virtually two jobs to cover the absence of a colleague, is therefore particularly stressed and tired, leaving all domestic activities to his wife; who is, in her turn, frustrated by being unable to pursue her journalistic career, owing to her work on the papers, and in any case in some doubt as to how she wishes to pursue it, thereafter; in particular she is undecided as to one option, an account of the project itself, which Dr Jacoman is pressing her to write. Finally, it must be observed that Dr Kern's elderly father, now deceased, was on his deathbed at this time, much to the distress of his son. Mrs Kern (source – A. Kern: journals) was of the opinion, that one reason her husband took on the extra work – he could in the circumstances have refused it – was in order to avoid confronting the imminent demise of his father.

Further human input is provided: 1) by Dr Carter Jacoman, pharmaceutical company executive, initiator of the project (see above), friend of Dr Kern, friend and admirer of Mrs Kern, able to communicate the differing values of each protagonist to the other, on the occasions that he appears; is enabled to do so in part because of his relationship, (as yet unrevealed to Dr and Mrs Kern) with: 2. Ms Nikki Kaufton, confidante of Mrs Kern, a Californian recently, since summer 1988, much 'into' (for the use of this expression see DEF, 1968) the works of Walter Benjamin, works which she describes in long telephone calls to Mrs Kern. Latterly she has also started to quote Barthes' theories of obtuse meanings. ('Give me obvious meanings any day,' mutters Dr Kern. A reaction which will indicate that though Mrs Kern herself is both baffled and fascinated enough to go out and buy the works of these thinkers, all attempts to interest Dr Kern in them exacerbates the already frayed relationship between the couple.) Sample quotes from Walter Benjamin[1] may explain both the attraction to the arts specialist, in this case a journalist/story-teller, about, herself, to embark on a complex autobiographical narrative related to the scientific project at issue, and its lack of attraction to the scientifically, not to say empirically trained mind, unaccustomed to dealing with abstractions.

Study design/methodology

Informal open-ended interviews with both protagonists, Dr and Mrs Kern, were embarked on, also much briefer, rather more formally structured interviews with Dr Jacoman and Ms Kaufton. The evidence of the kind of writing both have engaged in was looked at, as was the writing engendered by the project (Mrs Kern's journal, in particular has yielded much useful material). Above all the researcher has been in a unique position to engage in extensive participant observation. The kind of events evaluated are arguments, productions, statements of intent/belief, signs of stress, headaches, minor infections, and so on. The following rating scales are used: the number of ailments/dissensions/etc., are compared with those before and after work was begun and subsequently completed.

Results

I.1 Marital Dissension Rate. The Marital Dissension Rate rose twofold in the course of the couple's collaboration; at the worst point it went up threefold, from one major row a fortnight, or so, before the collaboration, to one a week during it, at the worst point two a week on average. (Table 1). The rate of minor altercations, exchanges of words, went from weekly to daily at this time. (Table 1)

1. '(The story-teller) . . . has borrowed his/her authority from death . . . is the figure in which the righteous (wo)man encounters him/herself.' (Walter Benjamin 1969, gender annotations, Ms Kaufton 1989)
'Those for whom life has become transformed into writing . . . can only read the writing backwards. That is the only way in which they may encounter themselves, and only thus – by fleeing from the present – can they understand life.' (Benjamin 1973)

I.2 Most common subjects of arguments. (Table 2)

1. Statement by Dr Kern that Mrs Kern doesn't understand what's meant by science. (20%)

2. Statement by Mrs Kern that Dr Kern doesn't understand what is meant by sociology. (20%)

3. Accusation by Dr Kern that Mrs Kern's approach to her work is not only not rigorous, it's 'sloppy'. (10%)

4. Accusation by Mrs Kern that Dr Kern is a) 'nit-picking' or b) 'obsessional'. (10%)

5. Dr Kern's insistence that Mrs Kern rewrites her papers, on grounds, eg a) result section not set out scientifically, therefore totally incomprehensible, and/or b) discussion arrives at entirely different conclusion from that indicated by results, how can she justify this? (9%)

6. Mrs Kern's son Ben's insistence on going out on average four nights each week[2]. (6%)

7. Medicine isn't a science anyway. (Mrs Kern's suggestion. It's basically guesswork. Dr Kern agrees, to some extent; is unable to say so.) (3%)

8. Mrs Kern's increasing tendency to justify herself with anthropological theory/jargon; this Dr Kern takes as specific criticism of his practice.[3] (3%)

9. Phone calls from Ms Kaufton (2%) (this would be a much higher figure if Mrs Kern had not learned, quickly, to keep Ms Kaufton's views on Walter Benjamin to herself; indeed, as time went on, to keep the fact that Ms Kaufton had called her, to herself).

2. Dr Kern asserts a) this isn't how he got *his* 4 A's at A level; b) that a scientist in particular can't afford to lose so much worktime. Mrs Kern (who is also concerned; see journals; but won't admit it) asserts a) it's none of Dr Kern's business; b) she's delighted her son is not such a workaholic as her husband; c) as she's begun to learn what science really is she doesn't want Ben to be a scientist; d) in particular she doesn't want him to be a doctor, if you can *call* medicine science, she's beginning to wonder. (A. Kern. Journal. Dec 1988)

3. Sample argument: source, Mrs Kern's journal. Feb 3rd 1989. Subject under discussion the way Mrs Kern is proposing a quotation section in one of her papers, juxtaposing patient statements on their disease in Ecuador/Kenya, with those in other studies.

Dr Kern: 'But this is supposed to be scientific; that's much too impressionistic to be science. It's not proper data.'

10. Miscellaneous topics related to 'culture gap'. Eg Mrs Kern's tendency to seek symbolic meanings in faceless kachina dolls, disappearing lakes, invisible mountains/volcanoes; above all in snakes; eg Mrs Kern's fondness for overwrought similes/metaphors[4]. (7%)

11. Miscellaneous topics not related to medicine, science etc, (eg who left orange peel all over the kitchen, threw away as yet unread newspapers, etc., etc.) (5%)

12. Uncalled for references to Dr Jacoman by either party. (5%)

I.3. Physical manifestations of Major Arguments. (All, unless indicated, due to action by Mrs Kern, regardless of who initially precipitated the argument.) (Table 3)

Broken window in kitchen (1) (Mrs Kern threw a cup at Dr Kern).

Coffee stains on sitting-room sofa (2) (Mrs Kern threw coffee over Dr Kern).

Bowl of muesli rendered inedible by being thrown on floor (1).

Versions of papers torn up (4) (= 2 by Mrs Kern, 2 by Dr Kern).

Attempt (symbolic) to strangle Mrs Kern (1).

Kicks on shins of Dr Kern (2).

Minor thumps on shoulder of Dr Kern (3).

Nights spent back to back in bed without usual goodnight embrace of protagonists (8).

Proportion of arguments ending in physical action of some kind, as opposed to mere verbal activity. 10% (Table 2).

Mrs Kern: 'But in this sort of area what people say *is* the main data.'

Dr Kern (smiling): 'I'll go on with my little scientific things then and leave you to your large ones.'

Mrs Kern: 'But your little scientific things and what I'm doing with this aren't mutually exclusive; microcosms and macrocosms aren't mutually exclusive – they're not a dichotomy in other words, they're a continuum . . .'

Dr Kern (smiling no longer): 'Am I going to have the word "continuum" thrown at me, ad nauseam, from now on?'

4. Eg comparing the medical profession, for instance, on one occasion, 'to an Uranus, devouring its own children, all the trappings, obsessive hand-washing, neat white coats, dark suits, etc., merely disguise the bloodiness underneath'. Groan from Dr Kern. (Transcript of taped data.)

I.4 Physiological effects of arguments. a) Dr Kern. Headaches up 10%. Insomnia up 10%. Colds 1. Stomach upsets 2. b) Mrs Kern. Insomnia up 15%. Colds 2. Stomach upsets 3.

I.5 Psychological effects of arguments. a) Dr Kern, increasing depression, weariness and edginess; this exacerbates tendencies to have arguments. b) Mrs Kern. Mrs Kern having more time at her disposal attempts to sublimate her distress by trying out kinds of discourse she has never attempted before: fictional modes, that is. 'A Pharmaceutical Fairy Story', for instance, is about an elixir of life; in another story, 'Brains', a long-term, long-suffering medical wife, takes revenge on her husband and his colleagues by feeding them the organ which they work on, in the form of calves brains. In this account, based on an anecdote told by a pharmaceutical colleague, recorded in her journal (December 1988), and written in February 1989 at a time when pressure of work keeps her husband increasingly from home, she signifies her growing disaffection with scientific attitudes, in particular, and the medical profession in general.

II. Attitude changes. Some changes in attitude are detected and will be discussed.
II.1 Dr Kern. a) More positive attitude by Dr Kern to indigenous practitioners – moving from 'definitely not' in answer to question as to whether they have any value to 'possibly' in course of study. Report of a recent lecture by him on the epilepsy project also confirms this point[5]. b) Dr Kern has evinced interest lately (three confirmed

5. Dr Kern stated that in his view the influence of indigenous healers, etc., in local communities was such, medical doctors wishing to sell their skills could usefully start by making contacts with *brujos* and *curanderors*, witchdoctors etc., and explaining their methods to them. He also made much of the psychological benefit of local illness treatments, in dealing with the kinds of psychosomatic illness most commonly presented in the surgery of general practitioners, for which scientific medicine has no remedies. Recommending therapy by guinea-pig as practised in the High Andes, he commiserated with his audience for not having such treatments available in their practice. (At this point in the report it was mentioned, somewhat disapprovingly,

reports) in such alternative therapeutic techniques as massage and meditation as a means of relieving stress both in himself and in his patients. (He has not mentioned to his wife suggesting these techniques to his patients.) c) Despite the above, in 80% of recently observed interactions with his wife, he confronted her statements on environmental or health issues with such phrases as 'Nonsense!' (50%) 'Where's your evidence?' (30%) 'The papers always write rubbish about things like that.' (20%)[6]

II.2 Mrs Kern. a) Mrs Kern has taken to reading such journals as *New Scientist* and *Nature* – complaining of the latter, however, she does not understand the half of it. (A. Kern, Journal). She also examines the *British Medical Journal* each week for articles of interest to her. b) She has grown much more sceptical at the more glib pronouncements of politicians and journalists on social/scientific issues; eg phrases such as 'miracle cure' or statements such as, 'There's no such thing as society' ('What does she *mean* by *society*?' and so on). Or at attempts at re-engineering social structures, such as the National Health Service, without proper investigation, let alone pilot projects[7]. c) In one recently reported conversation with her husband she claimed to understand at last what her husband meant when he objected to her using in literary metaphor chaos theory, or the behaviour of atomic particles, on the grounds that, 'The beauty of science is precisely its precision; if you compare like with unlike, Anna, the way you're so prone to, you lose that precision, you lose the beauty also.' (Taped conversation. October 1988).

that Dr Kern is well known among his colleagues for his unusual sense of humour. Also that these days, unfortunately, the influence of his wife was suspected in his pronouncements on such issues.) (Reported *British Medical News* 6.6.89)
6. Dr Kern appears to react particularly unfavourably when the subject in question is one frequently aired in the press, not least because these are the very issues which most concern his wife. (See 'Hole in the Ozone Layer', 'Greenhouse Effect', 'Post traumatic Stress Disorder', 'Myalgic Encephalitis', 'Acid Rain', etc.)
7. Sample conversation, Dr Kern: 'But that sort of thing isn't science.' Mrs Kern: 'But that doesn't mean you can't use scientific method to examine alternatives . . .'

Discussion

Before these results are looked at in detail, it is necessary to confront the problem that the kind of sociological exercise engaged in here is not strictly scientific, or rather that its methods of investigation may be scientific, but that its data and conclusions fall into the area of 'soft' science; that is, there are too many variables in all cases, for a hypothesis to be proven logically and practically, leaving no room for doubts of any kind. Medicine in itself is an uncertain science (Rhodes 1985). Its practitioners are dealing daily with distressing human situations in which outcomes are rarely certain, owing to the genetic and biological singularity of every human organism. The still greater uncertainties offered by the sociological sciences might seem particularly threatening, therefore, to a medical specialist confronting daily uncertainties in matters of life and death; this could account for some of Dr Kern's unease at Mrs Kern's academic orientation. At the same time there is also some justification for Mrs Kern's unease at whether or not the information she has been in charge of gathering, and now, of analysing, is wholly susceptible to scientific, statistical method; whether indeed the truth of what she is seeking may well lie elsewhere. (Kern Journal: visit to Beatrice 1987). Her problem here is that she is insufficiently experienced to be able to justify this point, either academically or personally. Her sense that her data can be interpreted in different ways, that where, for instance, as in Kenya, figures quoted in her results section show patients complaining very little of psychological, social or economic dysfunction, this does not necessarily mean they are not disadvantaged, and that other evidence justifies this view – not least the evidence of her own experience in these places – leads directly to the criticism by her husband that her results and her discussion section bear very little relation to one another, that the second is not validated by the first and that this way of working is not 'scientific'. He also claims, with reason, that had her study been better designed and tested on the ground, some of these anomalies would not have risen in the first place. Mrs Kern is very aware of this. This feeds her uncertainties, and where these meet those of her husband dissension is almost certain. (GHI 1979.)

The study undertaken here suffers from some of the same disadvantages as that undertaken by Mrs Kern herself; not least the number of variables listed earlier in the paper. The problem of the 'seven year itch' for instance; Dr Kern's adolescent stepson; Dr Kern's overwork, and the consequent falling of all domestic problems on his wife's back; the expected demise of Dr Kern's father; the uncertainty as to whether they should produce a child, a decision that owing to the increasing age of the protagonists will have to be made shortly; Mrs Kern's half welcomed, half feared, attraction for Dr Jacoman. All these factors could be influencing marital disharmony, the culture gap merely the language – or 'signs' in which this disharmony is expressed. In which case, if this Culture Gap did not exist, the disharmony would merely choose another sign system by which to express itself. In such a reading, culture gap would not, of itself, be the root cause of Marital Disharmony.

On the other hand, the fact that ninety per cent of all arguments at this time relate to the different educational cultures of the protagonists, (Table 2), indicates that this division is not just an excuse for the expression of deeper, psychological differences between Dr and Mrs Kern, though it may indeed be used for such purposes. Other studies of marital crisis do not show polarisation round such issues. Although in the case of the stockbroker and accountant of LMN's study (1984) the subject of money is, as one might expect, a key symbolic issue, the proportion of arguments arising from it is less than fifty per cent. Similarly in PQR's study (1985) of a painter and his wife, a lawyer, the casualness of the painter infuriates his highly organised spouse, but it is not the central factor in the arguments between them; in this case dissension focusses round the close proximity of the wife's mother. The closest parallels with Dr and Mrs Kern can probably be found in ABC's monograph (1979) which though a little outdated raises some interesting issues round a case study of a scientist and writer for children – in this case the potentially adulterous relationship between the wife and one of her husband's colleagues is the central issue; but, as the writer makes clear, the cross cultural arguments which eventually break this marriage all relate back to the wife's admirer; it is these which make the threat implicit.

What is striking in the case of the Kern's marriage, on the other hand, is that there are few arguments relating even indirectly to Dr Jacoman. The sense of threat manifested in the arguments and imagery each raises to counter the 'bias' of the other relates entirely to the 'bias' felt, rather than to any kind of sexual guilt or jealousy. Mrs Kern's Uranus imagery of the medical profession is typical – and directed, it should be noticed, equally amongst her admirer and her husband. Dr Kern's reaction to this image is also typical – and takes Dr Jacoman, implicitly as an ally. ('Why do you always have to get at doctors?' or 'at scientists?') etc. etc. Mrs Kern is equally intimidated by her incapacity to defend herself against charges of being 'unscientific', 'having no evidence' etc; as the high proportion of rows/arguments in the aftermath of such statements show, and equally inclined to see Dr Jacoman as a threat in this respect. It is also significant that all serious tension between the couple relates to the period after Dr Jacoman has returned to Canada, after the relationship between him and Mrs Kern has come to an end, that is the period when the papers are being worked on.

Looking at the stress caused by the son's examinations, by the father's death, as opposed to the writing of the papers, it is marked that tension declines after the papers have been completed, shortly before the father's death. Similarly it does not rise markedly in the summer, despite the boy's problems with his examinations.

In conclusion, the evidence would suggest that the Culture Gap has caused considerable difficulties in this marriage, although the evidence of changing opinions in the proximity of the other spouse (Table 4) offers some hope of improvement. The removal of the immediate problem – that is the professional cooperation over the writing of scientific papers – also seems to have reduced the level of dissension, despite the ongoing nature of other problems. It is clear that, for this couple, marital harmony is unlikely to be achieved by their working together on such projects in the future. However it should not be forgotten that in some respects, as their shifting attitudes make clear, this difference can be and is a source of mutual stimulus and interest. The strong

residual affection for her husband, demonstrated by Mrs
Kern in the story 'Brains', otherwise a story of disaffection,
should also be noted. Here further hints of reconciliation
can be detected by the sensitive eye.

In due course, with trepidation, Anna Kern showed this
effort to her husband. (It was because she wanted to show
it to him, of course, she hadn't mentioned Ben's affliction
as a variable; it was far too serious a matter for her to
do so.)

'Well,' he said, sharply, 'well, Anna. You still don't
seem to have learned much, after all my efforts to teach
you. Some of your results section should be in your
discussion; your discussion appears to relate very little
to your results.' Then he was silent. After a while Anna
dared look at him, and saw mirrored on his face her own
uncertainty as to whether to laugh, cry, bang her on the
head, or simply lie down and die. To laugh seemed best
– not because he felt like laughing on one level, any more
than she did, it hadn't been funny at all; which was
another good reason to laugh. What else *could* you do? It
was so nearly tragic, so touch and go, so nip and tuck;
these two people who did genuinely love each other had
very nearly lost themselves in their marital heart of
darkness, estranged by dichotomies functioning within
each head if they but knew it, as well as between them;
Nikki's random quotes and chance juxtapositions against
David's careful progressions (hook to eye and eye to hook
till the pattern is demonstrated for all to see, not one link
missing); theory against empiricism, imagination against
reason, overt meanings against obtuse ones, chance
against decision, Dionysus against Apollo, romanticism
against classicism, poetry against science, writer logic
against doctor logic; and plain bloody-mindedness
against plain bloody-mindedness. In all those dichotomies, laughter was one of two continuums they had,
painfully, discovered; and the most accessible; love was
the other.

God knows how they discovered it; what saved them
was not sense or sensibility or imagination or reason. It

was not even love at that point; indeed what saved them divided them in the short term more than ever; Anna had feared for months it would be the deciding blow, for a while thought it was so. But it was not. Far from it, for all the interminably fatal sound when the word – the forbidden word – the one we try to pretend doesn't exist, that we try to stave off with pills and elixirs and potions is finally pronounced aloud. Death, in other words; lose your – whose? – life to save whose? life, theirs? . . . David's father. And then there was Ben.

Chapter Three

Anna Kern's 'scientific' paper over-stated some things of course; it was bound to, the way she felt when she wrote it. She did not, for instance, include a very significant conversation she had with Nikki Kaufton around that time, which might have indicated greater understanding of her husband's point of view than she let on. Relations with him then being what they were, she recorded the conversation in her journal, but did not report it to him till some time much later, when, reading her journal through, she came upon the relevant passage.

Anna Kern's journal. 1989

Nikki's suspiciously interested in epilepsy all of a sudden: what's she after? *(This interest was, of course, the result of Nikki's developing relationship with Dr Jacoman; Anna did not make this connection as yet.)* On the phone today she asked all kinds of questions, picked up particularly on one thing I said, about the tendency in the brain for one epileptic seizure to trigger off a tendency to have seizures. 'Oh,' she said, 'that sounds just like something else I heard. I had a friend with a hyperactive womb, that is she kept having miscarriages, because when she got pregnant her womb would start to contract, and one contraction would trigger off more contractions. In the end they had to stitch her cervix up to prevent it.' Nikki was very pleased with this analogy; so would I have been a year ago, but now I thought; I do see what she means, *but* I also see these are physically quite different processes; if you liken them in this way, you lose the particularity of the process in each case. Eureka! Would David be pleased with me, I thought . . . The only problem was I was quite unable to explain my objection to Nikki.

Even before Hicks the axeman arrived in Basel, things were changing. Once Taylor had left, Jacoman was occupied mainly in sorting out his own affairs and clearing his desk; that left Piet, and Piet was no match for the marketing men who instantly began moving in. While Jacoman and Taylor were in charge, David had never so much as met a marketing man. On his first trip to Basel thereafter, he reported meeting four, including the French anti-Semite, Dr Dumeuil, whom Anna had interviewed over lunch. One hour with this man left David fuming. If Dumeuil was to be involved in any subsequent epilepsy projects, he said, count me out. 'In any case,' he added, 'they all keep insisting that anything in the future will be marketing projects, that it's a matter of marketing strategy now, not medicine; what's marketing strategy got to do with me? I'm a neurologist. I'm not, absolutely *not*, a salesman for Bader-Kleitz.'

If such an immediate upturning of priorities – and personnel – was one indication that Jacoman had indeed, as Piet put it, built his empire upon sand, it was nothing to what followed the arrival of Dr Hicks. Had David not been in touch with Piet – Piet seeing David as his only ally, was continually on the phone to him – they couldn't have escaped knowing what Hicks was up to. For one thing he used David as a source of information – he would ring him during his clinics, to David's fury; asking, for instance, such questions as 'Who is Dr Birnbaum?' with an intonation David said sounded anti-Semitic even if it wasn't. 'I've had a bill for 10,000 dollars from a Dr Birnbaum, relating to his academic expenses; also to his travel expenses. I didn't know Bader-Kleitz was a travel agent, Dr Kern. And Dr Kern tell me, *who* is Dr Birnbaum, exactly?' ('Why didn't he ask Piet?' asked

David.) For another the letters and faxes came from everywhere, from places he knew Jacoman had been in contact with, and those he hadn't. From Barbados, Indonesia, the Philippines, India for instance, they read mostly on the lines of 'Dear David, [or Dr Kern; depending on how well the writer knew him]. I've had this curious letter from a Dr Hicks in Basel. As you know Dr Jacoman had agreed to finance our small epilepsy project, under the aegis of ERGO. He'd given me to believe the matter was all agreed on. But now Dr Hicks has written informing me . . . Could you tell me what's going on . . . what's happening?' And so forth. David did not know who to be angrier with on this score, Hicks or Jacoman; as he said it was nothing to do with him. Why *should* he be lumbered with the results of Jacoman's largesse and Hicks' brutal excisions? But he was lumbered. The Pakistani neurologist rang him from Karachi; the Turkish neurologist from Istanbul; the Professor who'd taken over Falconer's job rang from Nairobi.

There were some strange stories, also. The one about the Dreadlocks, for instance, in Turkey; had they really been confined in some hotel room – in Ankara was it? because their bill hadn't been paid, and the local company and Hicks would not agree who was to pay it? Piet swore it was so. Certainly the Locks were in Turkey that summer, they did do their work, just in time by the sound of it. Anna saw the paper they published two years later – much sooner than her papers. It was a very good paper; as medical anthropologists purely, she had nothing against them, far from it. This did not stop her hoping that this hotel story, and another that surfaced later (about the Locks being accused of spying for the CIA because some of the patients they questioned – or rather their families – worked in a munitions factory) were true, that they hadn't been made up by Piet; David always did say Piet was inclined to exaggerate. But.

During Hicks' holocaust, as he called it, Piet not only telephoned the Kerns frequently, he was always coming to London; he spent hours closeted with David discussing how to save this part of the ongoing project or that part;

he even consulted Anna sometimes, as to how best he could present a social programme to his bosses in market terms. But in the end the only projects that survived more or less intact were those set up in Kenya; which had less to do with Piet finally or even David, than with the Kenyans themselves; who made it clear to Hicks that it would not be politically good for Bader-Kleitz in their country, even to truncate, let alone axe, their various projects.

Hicks stopped asking 'Who is Doctor Birnbaum?' He accepted the *fait accompli* jovially enough; though letting it be understood as he did so that in the case of Kenya it had been precisely what he intended from the beginning.

Ecuador, of course, was a different matter altogether. Aguadiente chose this worst of all times to make problems. He claimed by letter, by telex, by telephone, that not a word of his, not a figure, must be altered in any way whatsoever – the papers he was involved with had to be sent for publication as he wrote them; if not it would be academic falsification. To Piet, privately, he stated that Dr Kern was a madman; that his temper was quite uncertain; that in Ecuador, once, Doctor Kern had gone so far as to assault him; he could produce witnesses to prove it. (This, again, might have been a flight of Piet's imagination; but was much more likely to have been Aguadiente's.)

None of which should have mattered much, it was standard; Aguadiente, as usual, the corpse in the foundations rather than evil – not even the exasperated David thought he was evil. As for his fellow neurologists in Quito they, too, were embarrassed by Aguadiente's excesses; they promised David to curb him. But it did matter; it both hardened Hicks' resolve, and recommended his procedures still more to his colleagues . . . what was the point of working with such madmen? was the implication. That was the problem of doing such projects in such countries; you couldn't rely on anyone; better just not do them; stick to simple drug trials and go no further. That was all such places – such practitioners – were fit for.

It did not help that two extremely polite but insistent letters arrived on Hicks' desk around this time from Gomez in Washington, mentioning his share in the beginning of the whole thing, and claiming an unpaid consultation fee also. David didn't doubt that the Locks had egged him on – whatever the Locks had got out of the project – their work in Turkey, for instance – it can't wholly have made up for their discomfiture at the Kanterberg meeting, let alone the unceremonious routing of Sharon Lambert. Hicks gave Gomez short shrift, of course. But it was one more nail in an ever more cut-price coffin.

The night David's father developed pneumonia, a day or two before he died, David and Anna had a bitter argument – maybe not quite the most bitter, but certainly the most absurd one ever – over the way each of them ate fish; fresh sardines in this case. Anna had been pleased to find sardines on sale, she had meant them as a treat; even, given their dissensions, as reconciliation. David had promised to come home early; or at least not late; for once he had done so but only to claim the whole kitchen, their whole small house now stank of fish. It was true; it did stink of fish; Anna didn't like it any more than he did. It was a long time since she'd grilled sardines; she had forgotten how persistent the smell was.

'At least they taste all right,' she said. But David was looking at her plate; 'Look at you,' he said. 'Just look at you.' She had a sardine in her hand, it was the easiest way to eat them, as he'd found, he, too, held a sardine between his fingers. But whereas she chewed at the thing awkwardly, bones and all, seeing no other way to do it – the evidence was on her plate, a jumble of remnants, heads, tails, the bones she hadn't eaten – he took the head in one hand, the tail in the other and neatly ate between them. On his plate lay a tidy pile of heads and tails linked by their backbones. 'Just as if Korky the cat had been at them,' said Anna.

She was laughing; it was a joke. David was laughing also; but he had not been reared on comics the way she

445

had, somehow the joke misfired and in doing so curdled; the fish in her mouth did not taste nice any longer, either. In these fish – these ways of eating – was everything that maddened him about her, everything that fed her paranoia, her rage concerning her husband. This was the first evening they'd eaten together all week. David's colleague was still ill, David still covering for him. The row turned on that as much as anything; also on the fact that most evenings David looked in on his father on his way from the hospital, delaying his home-coming still further.

'He doesn't even know you're there,' said Anna. 'And when he does, he doesn't recognise you.'

'Sonia knows I'm there; it's her I go for,' said David.

'Sonia thinks you're nuts,' said Anna. 'She said you look ridiculously tired, she doesn't need you every night. Why don't you just go home and have an early night, *she* says.' Anna had meant to broach this idea, what Sonia had said, gently; not like this, not jumping in (as usual, she thought sighing, would she never learn) where angels fear to tread. Sonia and she together had discus-sed how tired David looked; it was Sonia herself asked Anna to dissuade him from coming every night. Anna managed, at least, not to mention this collusion; God knows, she thought, seeing David's reaction to what she had said, God knows if she had done – would he have thrown the whole lot at her – instead of throwing it as he did, all the fish, eaten and uneaten, cooked and uncooked – there were a few still remaining – into the wastebin. She managed not to protest that she'd still been eating hers, that she was still hungry. But she might as well have protested, David behaved as if she had; he fright-ened her he was so angry. He didn't touch her yet. But she didn't trust him not to. What could she do – what could she say? – nothing. He looked at her his face black, pitchy, his hands out towards her – was he going to strangle her? – he certainly looked as if he would like to.

'Are there any limits to your selfishness?' he hissed finally, pelting the words at her as if they were stones.

At this moment the telephone rang; Sonia. Her father

was breathing very heavily; she thought he might have pneumonia: could David come straight over.

'You see,' said David, glaring at Anna. All the same she went straight out with him to the car, not even pausing to get a coat, any more than he did, and he did not try to stop her.

The old man was in bed in the bedroom, from which lately he had scarcely moved; bedsores had become another problem (Anna had helped Sonia shift him a time or two, once even, helped her replace the dressings, trying not to look meanwhile at what they covered). Having taken his stethoscope and listened to the old man's chest, David confirmed his sister's diagnosis; it wasn't hard. The old man's chest heaved painfully up and down, his lungs were bubbling; Anna herself could hear it.

'I give him twelve hours at the most,' said David. 'You could get Jarvis in (Jarvis was the GP) if you wanted a second opinion; this isn't my area after all. But is it worth it?'

'You'll get him antibiotics won't you?' asked Sonia, clasping her hands together; she looked distraught; Anna had not seen her hair on end before, but it was now. For once she was not wearing her squash-blossom necklace. 'Surely you'll treat him?'

Anna and David had discussed this matter once; David had said quite dispassionately – the way he always talked about his father's illness, when, that is, he talked about it at all – that with someone in the state his father was, even if it was your own father, the more if it was your own father, there was no point in prolonging a life, not with antibiotics, not with anything. Any doctor would say so. Anna had not of course discussed the matter with Sonia, but she knew David had done. As she also knew that she had agreed with his views on what should be done, or rather not done. Of course she had agreed; calm, rational, virtuous, Sonia.

But now she saw to her surprise and dismay that, when it came to it, Sonia did not agree with her brother any longer; on this matter, at least, she was not calm or rational any longer; she was clinging to her brother weeping, saying, 'No, David, no.' While David stood with his arms at his side looking both grief-stricken and bewildered. Saying, helplessly; 'But I thought we'd *agreed*, Sonia.'

Anna went up to him; she lifted his two arms and put them round Sonia, her husband looking at her meanwhile, as if he could not think what she was doing. But in a moment he was clinging to Sonia as she to him, in the way two people cling to each other who are not used to mutual physical contact. Sonia's sobs caused her back, all Anna could see of her, to heave more violently than ever; though the way she ground her face into her brother's breast partly muffled the sounds she was making, sounds as uneven in their way as those from the lungs of the insensate old man dying on the bed; small whimpering sounds; then sudden, painful burblings, gasps for breath. Looking from one to the other of the Kern family, Anna felt strongly that she was not a Kern except by name; that this was nothing to do with her, whatever; that she shouldn't be here, watching private family business. Turning away, raising her hands to her face as she did so, she smelt sardines; not only on her hands; on her bracelet, the silver snake bracelet that Sonia had given her; that she had worn daily ever since, as Sonia wore her bracelet also. The meal seemed of an age long past; at first she had to strain to remember why the bracelet, like her hands, still smelt of fish.

Perhaps Sonia, Sonia's reaction to all this was more distressing than anything; much more than the proximity of death itself; death itself seemed less mysterious, than Sonia's desire to prolong the moment of it. Going downstairs, putting on a kettle – what else was there for an outsider to do in such circumstances except put on a kettle? – Anna tried to shift her mind beyond what she had always taken for granted, that, dutiful daughter as Sonia was, willingly as she did her duty by her demented, aged father, she wouldn't have chosen to lead her life that way, she had given up a great deal to do so; that it was doing what she should do which sustained her, not the hard – often disgusting – Anna thought of the shit Sonia wiped from her father's backside, of the bedsores – rituals forced on her by doing her duty. But now she wondered; the way Sonia had been entreating her brother, it was almost as if she was saying – when he's gone – when I can't wipe the shit off him any more, empty his pee bottle, feed him, what's left for me? Or alternately, I love this old man; he is my baby. Let me keep him longer; as if she was saying; in this lies all my strength. Take it away, what's left but weakness? But if Sonia was weak – even selfish – surely it would be better now to let the old man die – whose strength could you rely on? Who would be left to pay attention, what's more who would be left to persuade you of the merits of paying attention?

The tea was soon made; Anna could not stay downstairs for ever. When she carried up the tray, she found that the brother and sister, sitting beside each other on the bed, had as if changed sides on the issue. As she came into the room David was saying; 'Of course we'll treat him, Sonia, if you feel like that. Though I can't promise you it'll make any difference. I really can't.' Whereupon Sonia, her face unrecognisably swollen and tear-stained, answered in a low voice, picking at the blanket, 'You're the doctor, David. If that's what you think. You're probably right. It would be cruel to treat him. It would be cruel to keep him alive any longer . . .'

But David wasn't listening to her; he was writing out a prescription; having done so, he tore it off the pad, and held it out to Anna, demanding she find the duty chemist and have it made up immediately; he and Sonia must stay here for the moment. 'Are you sure even a chemist could read that?' asked Anna, looking at a scrawl still more indecipherable than usual. She meant it kindly. David did not take it that way. It was the tear-stained Sonia came to her rescue, sounding if anything relieved to be able to take issue on anything so relatively trivial (marital disharmony, that is, not life or death).

Chapter Four

For a long time after his father died, Anna knew less than ever what David was thinking. He shut himself away; behind his work, inside his head. She asked him once or twice if he wanted to talk about his father; no, he said, he did not want to talk about his father; what was the point? Thus when she did once hear him on the telephone doing so, far from being glad, as she knew she should be, she was filled with a desperate pain and anger, because whoever he was talking to was not her, his wife, his Anna; because to her he would say nothing. Nor could she tell if she felt better or if she felt worse, when she discovered that the person on the end of the line, to whom David was speaking, was Carter Jacoman.

Not that David talked to her about anything much at this time. The only thing that could be said was that they had stopped shouting at each other.

Nor did Sonia talk to Anna; or to David or anyone. Anna had not seen her weep again, after her father's death, not even at the funeral; not even at the graveside, gazing down upon his coffin. Sonia had made all the arrangements, she was throughout both brisk and efficient. The hat she wore to the funeral was brisk and efficient; it was black, it had a peak – it was appalling. When Anna asked if there was anything she could do, she said no, nothing. If Anna tried to go around there, she forbade it more or less. Anna went round a few times anyway; finding Sonia always, it seemed to her, playing Bach preludes, no worse than usual, but certainly no better. She produced Earl Grey tea and biscuits just as she always had done, while they talked desultorily of this and that; Ben's A levels, for instance.

Indeed had it not been for Ben's A levels Anna might have tried to go round there more often; Ben revising at home, was more agitated about them than she'd expected, made it clear he wanted comfort and cups of coffee from his mother; made it clear for the first time in many years that he'd prefer her to stay around. And as usual, she could not deny him – suppose this was, finally, the issue that triggered off new seizures? On the other hand, his agitation, if not all the reasons for her agitation concerning it, was one thing about which she could talk to Sonia. Sonia, as always, gave her sensible advice. Not that Anna really needed sensible advice, even if Ben did. If anything she was glad to have Ben to fuss over; the united blankness of the Kern brother and sister left her no foothold, no handhold, emotionally speaking. By contrast Ben's tantrums, his frantic outpourings about how he was going to fail everything, seemed, or would have seemed, but for her fear of their leading to further seizures, something of a relief.

Sonia's advice sessions did not outlast the exams, however. Even before they started she got up and went. The first Anna knew of her intention to do so was when her sister-in-law appeared at her door with a good luck card for Ben, and asked Anna to present it at the appropriate moment; she would not be around to post it to him herself.

'Where are you going?' asked Anna, foolishly, taken aback.

'San Francisco,' said Sonia, matter-of-factly; 'or rather Mill Valley, Marin County; that's the place Nikki lives in isn't it? You will keep an eye on the house for me, Anna, won't you?'

'And when *are* you coming back?' asked Anna, more shocked than ever.

'When I'm ready,' said Sonia, giving her a peck on the cheek; she wouldn't hear of her brother or Anna taking her to the airport.

For ten days thereafter, she left them in silence. Then, around six one evening, Anna answered the phone to hear Sonia's voice; it sounded almost cheerful – brisk, she might have been, efficient, without emotion, but cheerful she had not sounded, in the three months since her father died. The overt reason for calling was to remind Anna to water her plants; as Anna had been doing. But then she said, her voice now much too jaunty to sound like Sonia; she was, unbelievably, giggling, 'You'll never guess who's here Anna, it's Carter Jacoman.'

Anna spoke to Nikki and Carter in turn thereafter; all of them were giggling; even on the end of the telephone, she felt like someone sober at a party where everyone else was drunk. Later she thought – she said to David – who didn't seem interested at first, then said 'Nonsense'; but it wasn't wholly nonsense – that in effect this meant, for the moment, that David and Anna Kern were left only with each other. They'd better like it, or lump it.

'The bloody woman's spent months spouting Walter Benjamin at me,' she said, 'and now she's gone and swallowed Sonia.'

'And Jacoman,' said David. 'To hell with Walter Benjamin. You spent two months quoting him at me.'

'Yes but I wasn't doing it and at the same time not telling you I was having an affair with another of your best friends.'

'I should hope not,' said David. He actually smiled, as he added, 'What on earth does Sonia see in your friend?' Since this was the nearest thing in months they'd had to a conversation, Anna hesitated – the reason Sonia liked Nikki, in her view, was too close to the reasons David didn't; and her husband still didn't like being described to his face. In the end she just said, 'Sonia likes Nikki because she's so un-English. She's so direct.'

'You mean crude?' said David.

'You could put it like that,' said Anna; 'but I don't think Sonia would. I'm not sure I would, either. Nothing's that simple.'

'Then what does Nikki see in Sonia?' asked David.

'The same as I see in Sonia, presumably,' said Anna.

'Sonia's the only one of us knows exactly where she's going.' She didn't know, she thought, hadn't known this, till she said it. The image of Sonia that had haunted her lately, Sonia begging, vainly it turned out, for her father's life to be prolonged by any means, did not look like assurance in the least. Just the same, the moment the words were out, she knew they were the right ones.

As for Nikki and Jacoman; they ought, of course, to have guessed what was happening; but they had been much too bound up in their own arguments, in the fading of David's father, to have picked up the hints Carter dropped, the one time they saw him, on his way through London for the company he now worked for. Anna, besides, became too angry with him to pick them up; mostly because she could not be angry with David. Over their dinner at the Bombay Brasserie – Carter adored the Bombay Brasserie, of course – he had told Carter how a patient of his had asked that to cut down side effects, his anti-convulsant – Lenytol as it happened – should be reformulated as an inhalant. The idea had intrigued David. When he told him it also intrigued Carter. While they discussed the idea at length, Anna sat fuming, not because she was bored by such a topic, on the contrary, after all her work she, too, liked to hear about such matters; because, just as they had used to with their Jewish jokes, both her husband and Jacoman excluded her by doing so.

At least, unlike the Jewish jokes, this was an insult she felt able to acknowledge. 'Why don't you tell *me* things like that?' she accused David later.

'For goodness sake, Anna. It's got nothing to do with you,' he said.

'You mean I'm not a doctor? That doesn't mean I'm not interested – not given the work I'm doing.'

'I've talked medicine all day. What makes you think I want to talk it all night?'

'You talked to Carter about it.'

'But Carter's a doctor.' He bit his lip and looked away from her here, a mannerism not unlike his sister's;

smiling wryly – she smiled as wryly back – he said, 'Go to bed, Anna.'

What should have given the game away, of course, was when Carter quoted Henry James at them on the subject of the English; he'd been teasing David in his usual way, for being more English than the English – didn't Jews always become more like the natives of their adopted country than the natives themselves?

'Hence your heavy Brooklyn accent, Carter?' said Anna.

'Whaddya mean, Anna Kern, my Brooklyn accent?' protested Carter; who, they noticed, seemed much more cheerful than when they had last seen him – this should have given them another clue; but did not – how fatally locked into themselves they were at this time. Carter, meanwhile, was not to be deflected; 'You know how Henry James described the English,' he said. 'An inexpressive and speechless race; perpendicular and unsociable.' That's you David, precisely; maybe not so much Anna,' he added, laughing.

Henry James of all people, that chronicler of social knowledge, being quoted by someone whose downfall, if you could so call it, had been fuelled by a tendency not to pay attention enough to the prompting of social knowledge, was indeed ironical – Anna was as sure as ever Carter had still not read him; but someone had to have been quoting Henry James to him; someone who liked quotations. (Truth to tell, Anna still suspected Nikki of not reading Henry James either, or at least not all the way through; *Portrait of a Lady*, on her bookshelf hadn't looked particularly well-thumbed. While she could have sworn that *The Wings of a Dove*, in a Folio edition, had never been opened. Even so hadn't Nikki once quoted that very same judgment?)

'Where's it come from, Carter, which book?' Anna asked him – Carter didn't know – another giveaway if she was looking for one; but she was not. All she did know was that talking to him, though pleasant, gave her no frisson. The project these days was not the only thing that had been lost in old ends and new beginnings. The

454

worst thing about this visit was that Jacoman, not knowing any better, referred in front of an astonished David to his stepson's epilepsy.

Chapter Five

Anna Kern's notebook; 1991.

The sociologist is someone who spends £50,000 discovering something everyone knew already . . .' (Robert Merton.)

'Can a man really be held accountable for his actions? His behaviour, even his character, is always in the merciless grip of the age . . .' (N. Mandlestam.)

'Group action takes the form of a fitting together of individual lines of action . . .' (Blumer.)

'. . . any sociology of system must be complemented by an account of how the social is constructed within the personal . . .' (Lee and Newby.)

'Social choices and meaning are always fixed in relation to group life as a whole . . .' (Lee and Newby.)

'I've seen many projects – one person's enthusiasm, filling a vacuum – it goes on for a bit – then other people start asking questions – the project folds or is closed. I see no end to processes like this . . .' (Bader-Kleitz executive on Jacoman project.)

Anna Kern's diary. 1991.

I spend a lot of time now, when Leo allows – God help us when babies start walking – pondering that vexed question; which fuelled the project most significantly, Carter himself, or the circumstances in which he found himself; *would* he have found himself in such circumstances, without the influence of many things, economic, social, political, commercial, going on elsewhere? Probably not. On the other hand, I can't imagine anyone else I met in that company doing what

he did. It's the central problem of sociology, of course –
to what extent can an individual influence society, to
what extent is an individual wholly driven, not to say
enabled, by it? Not only sociologists ask that question;
historians do and novelists also; what's War and Peace
but a prolonged meditation on whether Napoleon did or
was done to? – did he make history or did history make
him? Similarly, did Carter do, or was he done to, I ask
myself, inclined to suspect both; that without the
circumstance, as without Jacoman himself, we would
never have had a project. On the other hand Jacoman
himself was the product of all those other social forces
on him long before he got to Bader-Kleitz; in that sense
he wasn't a free agent either; bound by his family
ethos, by Canada, by the decades he'd lived through –
the sixties not least – oh yes, Carter Jacoman, eighties
man you might have yearned to be, but with that eager
not to say naïve embracing of freakdom what were you
but a sixties product? – bound, though you might not
admit this, by the long history of the Jewish race.

Well, that's the sociological story. But this does not
stop me clinging blindly to a concept of, no, more a
longing for, human autonomy, accountability, on some
level. Not only because, emotionally, philosophically, I
prefer looking at things that way; but also because the
story I am struggling to write for Jacoman – God
knows when I decided to do it – I don't think I did
decide; I just found myself doing it – has to have a
hero; Jacoman, of course, it's what he wanted. (If he
turns out to be more an anti-hero in the end, that's
because of him, not history; I can't help that.) But as a
hero he has to be accountable in some ways; I think he
was accountable; more than he will ever be again, I
suspect, poor Carter. 'Jacoman's finest hour,' David
called the project once; and though he was being
ironical, as usual, I think he might be right, in the
beginning of the thing, the way he stirred us all up, at
least. Certainly it suits my thinking: for the sake of my
story, if nothing else, I want Jacoman there in all his
glory – I don't think you can bind an audience to social

457

forces merely, even if Berthold Brecht thought you could. In that sense you could say that the conclusions I've arrived at – or rather cling to – are pragmatic mainly, working hypotheses you might say, by which I can direct my work, and with my work my future life.

I can't prove it either way of course; I've got no evidence, scientific or otherwise; but one thing I've learned over the past few years is just how much good work scientifically is based, always has been based, on unproven, unprovable hypotheses, despite all that talk of rigour and accuracy and so forth. If scientists, too, can be pragmatic, use ideas that happen to be at hand, that suit their methods, their theories, why can't I?

Carter had *his* working hypotheses, all right; take the Pakistani doctor, take 'attention should be paid'. But this didn't mean he always paid attention; he didn't pay enough attention to his wife, Giselle, I suspect for one thing; he didn't pay nearly enough attention to his simple duty to finish the project he started. It was Taylor said, wasn't it, that Carter wasn't good at finishing what he started; that his job in the beginning was to train him to finish things. In the light of our story Taylor didn't train him well enough, you could say.

The collapse of the project after he left it, might have been telling – that without him it was nothing – except it didn't collapse wholly; the pendulum swung back. David went on talking to executives of Bader-Kleitz for at least two years after Carter left, on just the same issues. Hicks the axeman has gone; Carter type work is going on but now it's all linked, as Piet suggested it would be, with Reiner's Third World department. In that sense Carter did, up to a point, get his ideas into the culture – that was how he would put it – not all of them were lost for ever. On the other hand this might be putting it too highly; I daresay Reiner himself would dispute it was Carter put such things into the culture. I daresay he'd say that it had as much to do with him, on the one hand, the Pharma Policy department on the other. Carter himself said to me once that in Bader-Kleitz decisions consisted of, 'various absolutely unsubstantiated opinions that happen to be floating around Basel'; but then I daresay most companies are like that if you look at them closely; that's what makes openings for people like Carter – what else could make openings for people like Carter?

Anna had never seen David look the way he did, after Jacoman had let out her secret. When they talked about it later – or rather Anna talked; David, relentless, made her – it was her having told Jacoman he appeared to mind more than anything. Yet in an odd kind of way it made things easier; he was able, picking up papers on his desk and putting them down again – they were talking in his workroom – to pour all his anger and agitation into that; thereby foreshortening the whole thing, making less apparent, less of an issue, the very fact Anna had kept the thing from him for so long. Even though this was the aspect made her feel more guilty than anything; his reaction to which she had feared above all things all these years.

'It's just as well,' he said grimly, 'it's just as well I've had so much experience, Anna, in the behaviour of families with epileptic children. What you're saying to me makes perfect sense. I've seen it all before; often. Even if I haven't seen it before in my own family.'

Anna repeated, 'That was the whole point, David. I was afraid you wouldn't want to see it in your own family. I was afraid you'd run a mile if you only knew. Ben was afraid you'd run a mile. He as good as said so.'

'*Ben* did?' said David. 'Why should he have minded if I had run a mile? All I was doing was stealing you from him.'

Now Anna shouted, 'You're so stupid, David. You've never understood have you, you've never bloody well wanted to understand how much Ben wanted me to marry you, you to be his father. That's the whole trouble.' For suddenly she saw, in some ways, it was the whole trouble. In some convoluted way she couldn't untangle, didn't want to, wouldn't be allowed to – David didn't talk of such things – it was even one reason why David had held back from fathering his own child – children. As if Ben stood in the way. Just as for her, her not telling David about the epilepsy had stood in the way. In the middle of all this argument and guilt and tears – she was crying – her strongest feeling now was relief that he did know. How could she have kept something so central to her from him all this time? The moment it was out in the open it seemed unbelievable, unbearable, idiotic; but it had happened.

David said very quietly, 'Even if I had known, Anna, I couldn't have rejected you, not then; it would have made me consider it, maybe; but no, I couldn't have.' After which, as if such an admission was too much for him altogether, he reverted – his voice was angry again now – he reduced the volume in mid sentence to stop it reaching Jacoman and Ben in the attic, two floors up (throughout this whole conversation, he'd been hissing at Anna to keep her voice down); 'Why the hell did you tell Jacoman; if you didn't tell me; how could you?'

They got no further than this, that evening. David went to bed, accusing her as he did so of washing their dirty linen in public; Anna's reminding him that such an attitude was hardly appropriate in someone who spent his life telling people that epilepsy wasn't 'dirty linen' – that is, it wasn't a stigma – merely made him angrier than ever. He brushed aside all Anna's prot-estations that she hadn't meant to; she'd been miserable – Jacoman had fed her too much whisky on her trip to Basel; and besides he'd been going away by then, what did it matter? She couldn't blame him for brushing them aside; it had been a terrible thing to do. It had been. The irony being that all the time she'd told Jacoman about it, it was David she had wanted to be there comforting her about it.

David, at his most implacable – Anna imagined his little black book out – the recording angel going tick, tick, tick – brushed that argument aside also. They got into bed in silence; lay back to back; Anna trying to hide the fact she was weeping. Next morning it was hard to say goodbye to Jacoman as if nothing had happened. As soon as he'd gone, as soon as Ben had gone, she burst out crying. She spent most of the day crying, thankful that Jacoman wasn't coming back that evening; nor, till much later, Ben for that matter.

David, however, came back from work early. From her bedroom, as she was trying, somewhat frenziedly, to tidy up the disorder she'd created in her misery, she heard him climbing the stairs.

But if there was still disorder, he didn't seem to notice it. He came into the bedroom, kissed her and held her. He said, 'Anna, I've been thinking . . .' Then he said nothing. Neither of them did. They just went downstairs, put on the kettle, made coffee; sitting either side of their kitchen table looking at each other now and again, then, hastily, looking away, they drank it.

And then there was the earthquake in San Francisco. It was after the San Francisco earthquake, that David made Anna pregnant. Anna, of course, had been worried about Nikki when the news came through. For days she had tried to ring her, with no success; no one could get through to San Francisco; most of the Americans in London were trying, and they weren't getting through, either.

Nikki had been sitting in a library it turned out, on the far side of the bay area from Mill Valley; the floor had buckled – imagine a marble floor just rolling like waves on the ocean, was how she put it, just imagine. She didn't tell Anna to imagine it, however. She told Sonia; she rang Sonia, not from Mill Valley, but from Montreal. That was Jacoman's doing. When Jacoman couldn't get through to San Francisco, he didn't then spend three more days trying to do so, like most people attempting to contact friends in the Bay Area, in Marin County, at that time; he got on a plane, and went down there, to see for himself. And having seen, even though Nikki's place was not affected in any way, he gathered her up and took her back with him to Montreal, promising to marry her as

461

soon as his divorce from Giselle came through; which it was going to. Giselle, he said, had finally defeated him; she'd gone in a big way into alternative medicine; he was having to take her to court to make sure his kids got antibiotics when they needed, instead of some homeopathic junk; no hope of reconciliation, not any longer, he didn't want one, not after the earthquake, not after he'd decided to marry Nikki. And no, he guessed Giselle wasn't happy about it. He guessed Giselle wasn't happy in any way, but then she never had been, she didn't know how to be; that was her tragedy. But it wasn't his problem any longer. (Poor Giselle, thought Anna, who'd liked Giselle when it came to it, thought her hard done by. David, without animosity, said she always did take the female's part.)

As for Nikki: Anna almost cried when Sonia rang to tell her what had or hadn't happened to her; why hadn't Nikki rung her herself? she wondered. But in fact there was good reason why Nikki rang Sonia; it was not that Nikki these days liked her sister-in-law better, or not entirely. They'd cooked up a plan between them – Sonia asked Anna and David to one of her Sunday lunches to tell them all about it. (Ben was not with them; despite his fuss, he'd passed his exams respectably, if not respectably enough for Cambridge, as David had warned. Next year he was going to read biology at the University of Warwick; at the moment he was in Australia, staying with Anna's brother.)

'It's like this,' said Sonia. 'I'm taking over Nikki's apartment in Mill Valley, for the next six months at least, to see how I get on. If I like it, I'll stay there. I shouldn't have any problems with the immigration authorities – gosh, I shouldn't do, I'm self-supporting (Sonia's father had, indeed, left her enough to live on), I don't need to get a work permit; though I might, eventually, try for a Green Card. Oh, and the other thing, if it all works out, I'll sell this house at once; you'll get your share of the money, David. I'll use my share, maybe, to set up some kind of business.' Looking at the stunned faces of her brother and sister-in-law, she added, 'I've always loved America, particularly out West. I spent six months there once, after I left Cambridge. I don't suppose you remember, David. You never do remember things like that.'

It explained the Hopi pot, the squash blossom necklace, about the provenance of which Sonia had always been vague when Anna asked her; as if, up till now, America had been her secret, kept close to herself, to warm her, over all the years of tending her demented father.

Sonia did not say what business she was proposing; but when in due course she went into partnership with another woman she met in San Francisco, it seemed obvious enough; they dealt in Indian and Mexican artifacts, things like Nikki's kachina dolls, for instance. (Nikki had never told Anna the reason for the one she had given her having no face. When she heard what Sonia was doing, almost Anna's first thought was, Sonia will know; now I can ask Sonia.)

Once, before the earthquake, when Sonia and Anna were having tea together, Sonia had asked, suddenly, in relation to nothing much, 'Are you and David planning to have children, Anna?'

Anna's tea went down the wrong way. When she had recovered herself a little, Sonia, not to be diverted, asked the question again. 'We haven't made up our minds,' said Anna, reluctantly; 'maybe one day,' she said. Whereupon Sonia stated briskly, as if she thought such a statement was very silly – this was blunt Sonia, the opposite of delicately probing Sonia – that it wasn't the sort of thing that could wait for ever – they'd better be careful they didn't put it off and off, and then find it was all too late. Anna here had the weird feeling that what Sonia was saying had nothing whatever to do with her, Anna; or even David; that they were simply instruments of something, something Sonia wanted in a way that was also quite dispassionate; quite altruistic. She wanted a replacement for her helpless Dad; a continuation of the family name, in the form of a niece or nephew, something that would be her, their, elixir of life as well as David and Anna's.

463

She dared tell David about the conversation – it seemed an easier way of broaching the subject than most. But then she wished she hadn't raised it. For when she put her theory about Sonia wanting a replacement for their father, he rounded on her, saying how could she be so cheap, so obvious, this was all pop psychology, of course Sonia did not want any such thing, how dare she make up such stories about her, she didn't know Sonia, how could she? (But his fury was a spent end, she felt, rather than the real thing, any longer. Why did she think that? She *did* think it; he was buying music manuscript on manuscript at this time, with the money left him by his father. He spent his evenings sorting them, trying to read them; or listening to music with the scores on his lap. More than anything Anna could do, it seemed to heal him; about that she had to be – she was – thankful.)

As for Nikki; after Sonia was set up in Mill Valley, Nikki took to ringing Anna again, as if nothing had changed. What Anna got for the next six months was twofold – and most of it, she suspected, the kind of thing that would have been hard to discuss with Sonia; who always made clear when she found a matter of no interest. There were Nikki's problems with her residents permit, with her work permit, for one thing, along with the hassles of commuting to Berkeley to finish off her teaching assignments, she'd managed to push them all into part of one semester but even so. Of course, once Carter's divorce came through, there'd be no problem.

The other thing was Carter himself. How wonderful he was, how wonderful living with him was – how Nikki had never known a man who did this to her, that and the other – fond as she was of them both – it was her knowing Carter of course, was one reason Nikki liked to talk to Anna about him, none of her Bay Area friends knew him, she always said – Anna sometimes felt like telling her to shut up; sometimes she did tell her to shut up. 'I guess I'm a loud mouth,' Nikki would say, almost apologetically, to Anna's surprise. 'You should tell me to shut up more often, Anna.' Anna wanted to shut her up on this matter, not least because she *did* know Carter; she could not bear to listen to such stuff; sometimes she even thought – she'd never thought to hear herself think it – that there was something definitely to be said, sometimes, for being English, for being what was it Henry James said, as quoted by Carter? 'Inexpressive and speechless?' For being 'perpendicular and unsociable' come to that, also; she *was* unsociable at the moment, if not perpendicular exactly. Just for the moment – if not for ever – she was content with wholly English, wholly private lives – by which she meant the company of her Jewish husband.

Sometimes, almost incidentally, Nikki made enquiries about what she called Anna's interesting condition. (Anna hadn't told her about this, but Sonia had.) To this she sometimes appended comments about how she herself was learning to be mommy to Jacoman's children every third weekend, how that wasn't easy; much more often she appended stories about how many teeth friends of hers lost with each pregnancy, how much of their hair had fallen out; what a state their bellies were in for ever afterwards, unless they used the services of a plastic surgeon, of course. 'You forget, Nikki,' said Anna sighing, 'this isn't the first time. Do shut up.'

Nikki ignored her. 'Pregnancy accelerates the ageing process, hon,' she went on, earnestly. 'Look, I got this great face cream, God knows what it's got in it, rhino horn, rattlesnake venom I shouldn't doubt; you name it; it makes Vitamin E cream and oil of Evening Primrose look sick, I promise you. Next time Carter comes to Europe, I'll get him to bring you some.'

It was after the San Francisco earthquake, after Anna's description of the floor buckling under Nikki like the ocean, that David brought Anna one weekend a Siamese kitten; they'd been discussing for some while whether or not to have a cat. That was the end then, she'd thought, sadly, at the same time almost resigned to what seemed the meaning of the kitten; for who really wanted nappies, the sleepless nights, the kindergarten, and so forth, all the flies not to say serpents in that particular ointment, on which she had dwelt with anguish from the beginning? If a kitten was to be their baby; if David had finally made up their minds for them; she thought grief, she thought relief in equal mixtures. Now she could get on with her work in peace, she thought; write Carter's book; do a degree in medical anthropology; whatever. So that was all right, wasn't it? The kitten meant, for sure, that in spite of everything David loved her.

Two days later however, he came into the bathroom while she was applying some brand of spermicide – made by Bader-Kleitz, oddly enough – to her Dutch cap, before inserting it inside her – how many times had she been tempted to leave it out, she thought; how dutiful she had been over the years since she had known him, with all her chemical precautions, how dutiful she would continue to be now; or so she thought. David looked at her, for a moment. 'It's not romantic exactly that thing, is it?' is what he said. Before she had time to answer he took the tube out of her hand and threw it into the waste-bin, saying, as he did so, 'Maybe that's one pharmaceutical product we can do without for the moment.' The Dutch cap, the little plastic case it came in, even the talc Anna shook over the cap each time, after she'd washed and dried it, followed the spermicide into the bin. Anna watched in amazement. But she did not try to rescue any of those things. She did not want to. It was called in both their cases, jumping in where angels fear to tread; as with joining a Jacoman project, it was perhaps, she thought, the only way to do it.

A week or so later, they reckoned – the evidence of course in such things was always shaky, at least when it came to the accurate calculations beloved of scientists – they finally managed what they'd decided. Anna whispered in David's ear – the Siamese kitten was asleep on their bed also – they had not meant to let it sleep on their bed, but then could not bear to hear it wailing – 'Siamese cats are dreadfully jealous. Do we know what we are doing?' He answered, 'Did you know a woman of your age is known in the trade as an elderly mother?' 'Sod you, sod your profession,' said Anna. 'Maybe I'd better just stick with the kitten.' 'Maybe it's too late for that,' said David.

'I'm not going to give up work to look after a baby,' said Anna. 'Who asked you to, even if it is too late?' said David.

(It was too late. Anna and David Kern's daughter was born by Caesarian section, in Queen Charlotte's hospital, Hammersmith, West London, almost exactly five years after Dr David Kern met Dr Carter Jacoman in Jerusalem, at a time when her mother had reached the almost exact half-way point of her book about Jacoman. She weighed three kilos fifty at birth, and was given the name Leonora, for David's father, Leopold. On Anna's insistence, her second name was Sonia.)

Chapter Six

The disappearing lake, by the way, came back. David Kern went to Kenya again on the social marketing programme that Hicks the axeman failed to axe, that, marketing project or not, Piet, somehow, contrived to keep the anti-Semite Dumeuil out of, and sat by the lake once again. That was his final trip relating to the project.

Thereafter though, as far as they could see, Bader-Kleitz, went on as ever, good and not so good in equal measure. It still did not have enough new drugs in the pipe-line. It still, like all pharmaceutical companies, was attacked for Third World marketing abuses, still sometimes had problems with Adverse Drug Reactions. One, very minor, executive wrote to David Kern when the results of the project first came out, to ask why their research hadn't proved that Lenytol really was much better than Phenobarbitone as an anti-convulsant. David wrote a very brief, polite, but also rude letter back.

So much for the pharmaceutical industry. But as for the people whose lives it had entered; as for Beatrice, for instance . . . as for all of the patients, come to that, in Ecuador as in Kenya; who knows – maybe their lives were better – maybe they weren't. It was a mystery; Anna would never know the endings to these stories, any more than they, the patients, could know, imagine, the endings to her own. Why should they want to know them, whether or not their lives were transformed or stayed the same? Anna and her kind had come, but now they were gone. And if, in one sense, the hopes and fears of all of

468

them, Anna, Anna's kind and the patients, were just the same, in another it should not be forgotten that the patients not only had more immediately to hope for, they also had a good deal more to fear. It was not that the pit mightn't open beneath Anna's feet, at any time; the path of insecurity for her, as for anyone else, was always there lurking beneath the surface – look at Ben. On the other hand, her husband wielded no stick, her roof and walls were watertight, the neighbours did not avoid her; where her next meal was coming from was always plain. In that sense she had it easy. Because of which, she had come to understand now, rather better than she had done earlier, that in other circumstances, in other places, unfamiliar people, even those suffering from, or affected by, a familiar disease, might see some things differently. (Children, for instance, remained in most places much easier to acquire than chickens.)

It did not mean, of course, that she was not curious about the other people. She not only looked for, she found, some sequels to some stories. Don Manuel Padilla, for one, had celebrated his freedom from seizures by impregnating another woman; Anna learned this from Lastenia, in the one letter she ever received from her colleague, its careful formality no measure of their friendship. (Don Manuel's first wife, his favourite, still forgave him, however.) Three children in Kenya went to school for the first time. A young man up in the Altiplano, though much improved, had a seizure while riding a horse, fell off and died, another died for no apparent reason, after a seizure. Two women and one man married; if the improvement in their health was a factor, it was not clear. As for the rest, at least those whom medication benefited; did life with pills and doctors prove to be worth more than money? Did having seizures solve all the other problems also? Get them a job, for instance, social acceptance, a Sony Walkman? Probably not; but being without seizures was something.

And Beatrice . . . ? Anna looked hard for Beatrice; at last found her name and number in one of Bennet's meticulous reports. 'Patient 037,' it said. 'This patient

469

dropped out of the study and went up to Lake Victoria, to find her family, she claimed, after her husband left her. Nothing further is known of her.'

No; nothing further. Which did not mean that Anna would forget her, ever, nor that she expected Beatrice to remember her – maybe Anna needed Beatrice more than Beatrice needed Anna. In the end whose fate can you know except your own? And not even that always – what was the quotation from Walter Benjamin Nikki was so fond of? – 'The storyteller takes his authority from death'? You can interpret this any way you choose, so long as you make no special claims to wisdom.

Nikki and Carter Jacoman only came to London together the once; that time when, seeing them at her dinner table, Anna's immediate impression had been that the relationship between them remained exactly as on the day they had first met.

Next day, however, talking to Nikki first, then Jacoman, changed her mind completely. According to this reading, the evening before had been an aberration; Jacoman, recounting old triumphs, old disasters, had been sucked back into the world he had shared with the two Kerns, not only briefly but misleadingly. Anna realised now that Nikki must have expected Jacoman to be sucked back; that her very garb had proclaimed her intention to maintain her foothold on difficult ground; shoulder pads, fish earrings and all. Which meant she had been – she must have been – apprehensive about it; good heavens. For so had Anna herself been apprehensive.

Next morning, however, Nikki, in blue jeans and a splendid, almost liquid looking golden smock, showed no sign of power dressing. Anna's baby, Leo, was in her highchair, spitting out cornflakes, but it was Jacoman, not Nikki, who insisted on helping feed her; every now and then he glanced at Nikki. Nikki, on the other hand, did not take her eyes off him – what was maternal in her gaze was not directed at the baby; her interest in the baby, she made clear, was entirely because Leo was

470

Anna's. Leo didn't care either way, she just wanted her breakfast. She also, to judge by the spitting, enjoyed her flirtation with Jacoman. Anna had never seen Jacoman truly flirtatious before, not with herself, not with the psychologist, Vittoria, certainly not with Charlene Lock, and not even with Nikki. But he was flirtatious with the Kerns' baby; watched hungrily by Nikki.

'Marriage I am into, and how, but not babies,' she told Anna later; her face in the light beneath the window looked older than it had used to, but softer. Anna was more certain than ever that Nikki's hair was redder than before; that her face had once more been lifted. It did not matter; Nikki, turning the figure of the smallest babushka doll from Leo's set over and over between her fingers, looked splendid in her golden smock; ageless – better than Anna had ever seen her. Yes, she could see Nikki was into marriage; and suddenly, fiercely grateful to Jacoman, glad for her friend, she forgave, well, mostly forgave, all the gushing phonecalls; almost forgave Nikki's desertion of her for Sonia, even when Nikki told her at length how Sonia was – flourishing, she said; Sonia had recently made a deal with some outfit in Toronto; she had taken the Jacomans to dinner at a very austere, very expensive Japanese restaurant. She, too, these days, flourished an American Express Gold Card. Sonia's on the climb all right; maybe it's Sonia is the Big Man these days, thought Anna.

'It's just as well I'm not into babies,' went on Nikki. 'All those kids of Carter's . . .' she made it sound as though Jacoman's children numbered not three merely, but a hundred. She then proceeded to talk about Louis, about Chantal, about Suzette, about how tiresome Giselle was over access, in much the same way as she used to discuss her wardrobe with Anna, asking her advice, her opinion. Anna had the impression that for Nikki, what she called 'playing mom', had worn thin very quickly; but this Nikki was not saying; any more than she spoke, though she looked, her irritation, when Leo started to demand Anna's intention so entirely it was plain Anna was scarcely listening to a word her friend said. Pointedly, Nikki took the whole babushka doll apart and put it together again, nesting each aproned, apple-cheeked grandmother in the base of the next size up, before screwing on the top half with what seemed like excessive effort. 'They're so cute these things,' she said. 'I just love them. Though my grandmother wasn't fat like that, they always remind me of her. Does Leo sleep any time, Anna?' (Leo was not screaming; but looked as if she might scream, any minute.) 'Or is she awake always?' No, Nikki was not into babies. At her age – she must be 48? 49? at least now, it was, as she said, just as well.

Throughout their conversation, far from inviting discussion of Jacoman, she almost repelled it. In the end, grudgingly, Leo asleep on Anna's lap at last, her thumb in her mouth, she answered some questions from Anna about Carter's new job; his third since leaving Bader-Kleitz; this latest one, Nikki said enthusiastically, was the one he'd always wanted. A conventional pharmaceutical job, for a Canada-based company, it didn't sound much different from the others; his only research project was a small one to do with Parkinson's Disease among ethnic minorities.

'And just guess who he has to deal with in Washington, over that,' said Nikki. 'That schmuck, you know the one used to be in Ecuador – Gomez? Carter says he hasn't changed, he's just as self-seeking as ever; and just as charming. And drives Carter just as crazy.'

Anna asked if Nikki herself was working. 'Oh, some,' said Nikki carelessly. Adding she had some classes lined up for the Fall, and she was planning a new book also. She was not going to let Carter be a full-time job, though he could be, if she wasn't careful, he really could, and that was not to mention his kids. She also had to catch up on her reading; one of the first things Carter ever bought her was the collected works of the two Bowles. She'd read Jane Bowles of course, always; but Paul was another matter. Wasn't he great, Anna? But so depressive; Conrad wasn't depressive; not like that.

'Carter always used to see himself as a character out of Paul Bowles,' ventured Anna, cautiously, aware by now that however Nikki herself might mock her husband, she wouldn't suffer the smallest hint of criticism of him from anyone else. Leo shifting a little, she lifted her against her shoulder, and with that for excuse, did not look Nikki in the face. This was why she did not realise immediately that Nikki was laughing; that, stretching herself luxuriously across the sofa, enveloping it, seemingly, she was laughing and laughing.

'You're so naïve, Anna,' she said, at last. 'You don't understand anything. You don't understand Carter. Carter something out of Paul Bowles? Oh Anna. How can anyone who doesn't hate himself, who isn't disgusted with himself through and through be a character out of Paul Bowles? Carter doesn't hate himself; he doesn't have nearly enough in the way of self-disgust. And besides he's not interested enough in evil. You mustn't forget, Anna, Jacoman's Canadian.'

Nikki, going on laughing, made it sound as if she knew what self-disgust was, what interest in evil was; she made it sound as normal and as self-indulgent and as much to be laughed at as stripping off on a nude beach; an hour in a self-awareness seminar; a meal at Chez Panisse. At the same time an unusually wild look in her eye evoked death in a desert; or the worst kind of tropical corruption in a tin shack in the Congo. But then she'd grown up reading the Book of Revelations; whereas Jacoman had grown up thinking of God as a dirty word. What odd liaisons, what odder marriages we make, thought Anna, how very odd. Was Nikki happy then in hers? Yes, well happier, anyway. And Jacoman? Jacoman?

'I did think that maybe he was more out of Jack London,' she ventured. But Nikki was gazing out of the window intently now; a man was walking past with a ladder and a dog. Leo had begun, noisily, to waken, pushing her feet, her head, against Anna's shoulder – 'She isn't about to puke, is she?' asked Nikki, uneasily, half turning back. When Anna laughed and shook her head, she did not look wholly reassured. All the same she stared at Anna quite hard and said, 'Did you know,

Anna, there's a coin in Canada known as a loonie. And can you guess why it is? Because it's got a loon, a rare kind of duck on it. Only Canadians,' she said, 'only Canadians would make a coin with a picture of a duck on it.'

They were sitting there again later, she and Nikki, in almost the same positions, though Leo was now asleep upstairs, and the Siamese cat curled up on the remaining chair, when Anna, very happy suddenly, found herself quoting to Nikki the phrase about African women being like the mooring to which families were attached; attempting in doing so, to convey, if only implicitly, her own perception of loss.

When Nikki, surprisingly, said nothing, just looked at her, quite benignly, Anna added, 'Of course the flip side is it's the mothers and the grandmothers take the girls to be circumcised.'

'And they call in the footbinders,' said Nikki. Then she said, 'It doesn't look like you ran too far from that model, Anna,' pointing to where the baby slept, above their heads.

'Did you?' asked Anna. 'You seemed to have settled for domesticity all right.'

'Didn't I earn the right to, Anna?' asked Nikki. 'It was about time. Whereas you . . . for instance, have you given up on science completely, hon? I don't notice you talking about epilepsy much these days; only about babies.'

'No,' said Anna, 'I've got some plans. I didn't give up entirely.' (In fact she was considering doing a part-time degree in Medical Anthropology – not that her husband called *that* science; he said she'd end up like the Locks if she wasn't careful; she'd do much better to go back to journalism. Anna said she wouldn't end up like the Locks, no more EMICs for her; she was thinking of a thesis on the medical profession. 'That's what I'm afraid of,' said David. One way and another it would be easier to stick with journalism – and babies; perhaps she would. Perhaps it was her tragedy, like Jacoman's to plunge in, then in the end to go no further.)

474

But all she said to Nikki was – if this was her let-out, she'd be by no means the first to use it – 'You can argue with social systems; you can argue with men. But you can't argue with biology – why *shouldn't* I want babies? To that extent how can I help letting biology define me, for the moment, at least? If you ask me,' she added, obscurely as far as Nikki was concerned, 'biology's the real corpse in the foundations.'

'Come on, Anna,' said Nikki, 'Oh come on. As far as that baby is concerned anyone can see you *like* letting biology define you.'

'Only as long as I choose to,' said Anna. 'And anyway what's it to you? And anyway,' she added, 'as far as Carter is concerned, don't you?'

'Oh Anna,' said Nikki. 'How cute that you're still so naïve. Oh Anna.'

In Anna's view, it was actually Nikki was naïve about such matters. But for now she just smiled at her friend.

A little while later Jacoman returned to find them sitting in contented silence. The afternoon sun pouring through the window bathed Nikki in its light; her hair, her golden smock, blazed brighter than ever. Seeing Carter's face as he saw her, there rose to Anna's mind quite spontaneously, the phrase, 'Mine eyes dazzle.' For Carter's eyes dazzled all right, looking at his wife – even if she was hardly the Duchess of Malfi – she certainly had not died young. But then Jacoman wasn't dying either, he wasn't fat, he preferred tomato juice to porter. Yet this did not stop Anna, going on with the quotation game, being reminded by him of the dying Falstaff – 'His nose was sharp as a pen, and a' babbled o'green fields.' For Jacoman's nose was sharp as a pen, especially now that his teeth had been fixed. And he certainly babbled, *how* he babbled, she thought, remembering him going on about Ecuador last night; about the routing of Aguadiente.

Jacoman's habits with paper hadn't changed, though. He was scattering Anna's manuscript to right and left. That was one of the things he'd come for. Anna, of course, had insisted on his reading every word she'd written; she didn't want to publish the book, and have her friends suing her for libel.

Jacoman did not seem insulted, however, or not much. Nikki wasn't in the book, fortunately, she had nothing to do with the project; if she had it might have been a different matter; as Anna well knew, she offended much more easily than her husband. But Jacoman wanted to be famous – whether this book would achieve it for him, wasn't clear, in fact most unlikely, but the prospect excited him, she could see; why should he care for the odd wart; he didn't, and that would be quite enough to silence Nikki. As if to acknowledge it, Nikki left the room at this point saying to Carter it was OK honey, she wouldn't be long she just had to go out a minute. What worried *him*, therefore, Nikki's husband – Anna hadn't anticipated this, but she could see why it did so, the moment he mentioned it; what worried *him* was that she hadn't made enough of their achievement. He proceeded at once to spell it out. In doing so, word by word, phrase by phrase, he put on his old glitter; in that way making clear the extent to which he had lost it, to which they had all lost it as far as the project was concerned. Research was a bit like marriage, she thought; all the mighty passion resides in its beginnings. But if, later, it was a question of getting on with it, of more or less kindly accommodations, it did not mean to say that the research, like the marriage, had not been worth undertaking. Some people had more stamina in one direction than in the other, she suspected, she hoped. What stamina, Jacoman, for instance, lacked in research projects, she prayed, looking at her friend, he'd find in himself for marriage; this marriage, at least.

(Upon which, suddenly, smelling Leo on herself she found herself smiling with pleasure. It was an example, she thought, of what Jacoman, once, would have called cognitive dissonance; on the one hand her friend, colleague and once possible lover talking of their work together, on the other the odour of her child; milk, baby powder, warm flesh, sweet baby urine. But it wasn't dissonance, really; for her, some of the time, now, it was all of a piece.)

'We did it, Anna,' Jacoman continued. 'We set up all those studies, in all those places, with all those people, we completed them every one, even in spite of people like Aguadiente.' 'And because of him,' murmured Anna. It was amazing how fond she was of Aguadiente, with hindsight; remembering the aspirins he brought her; his raised finger; his '*momento*, Carter'. He and Jacoman were alike in this, at least in the beginning. 'And hence one master passion in the breast/like Aaron's serpent swallows up the rest ...' she recited to herself – she couldn't remember where she'd read it, but it would do; the project had been for Jacoman, as for Aguadiente, a master passion.

'We surveyed 72,000 people, for God's sake, Anna.' Jacoman went on, his voice growing ever more animated; 'That's a major piece of epidemiology by anyone's standards; those results are going to be quoted when prevalence of epilepsy is looked at from here to kingdom come; it's not going to do any harm to your husband's academic reputation, I tell you, having that under his belt. And having organised treating all those people, in all those out of the way places; showing it could be done. In Kenya it's still being done, even in Ecuador epilepsy is on the map; it's getting to be on the map in Pakistan and Turkey; that's all due to us, Anna, all of it. And look at those other people your dear husband was telling me last night are screaming to join ERGO.' (Anna didn't point out that ERGO had no money; it staggered along; but for Piet Van Dyke, who'd left Bader-Kleitz now, but didn't mind doing the secretarial work, it would have collapsed long ago. But, it was true, people were always asking to join it.) 'There's a whole network we set up there, Anna. That's us. And look at all the papers being published; and being cited already. Haven't you got two papers coming out, Anna? Well then, did you achieve nothing?' (Anna did not point out that the papers were only appearing after considerable revisions by her husband. This was to be expected in her view. Though, given what Jacoman was pointing out, she did have some reason to be pleased with herself, she thought; she was pleased.) 'Compare yourself with the psychologists, for instance, there's Vittoria, not one paper so far, I'm told, as far as anyone can make out. And Vittoria's a professional, Anna.' (Meaning I'm not, thought Anna. Well, she wouldn't quibble. But bloody hell, if she hadn't been much of a professional in the beginning, she'd become one; she'd finished the thing, hadn't she? Which was more than could be said for Jacoman.)

Jacoman looked at her, now. 'Yeah, I know it wasn't your area, Anna. I know it was a lot to ask of you. But you did it. That's the thing, you did it. And it changed you, didn't it? Don't tell me it didn't change you.' He was pleading with her to acknowledge it, as if it was the only thing that mattered; that he had paid attention to her. He had changed her.

'What about the patients?' Anna asked. 'It was much more important you changed things for them. Do you think you did?'

'Well I think things pretty much changed for some of them,' said Carter. 'I hope it did; given the shitty lives some of them were leading, as you should know, Anna. It was your work showed that.'

'And if you'd only changed one person's epilepsy, one person's life for the better, would the whole thing still have been worth it?' asked Anna.

'Sure it would have been worth it. What's all that work, what's all that money against one person's happiness?' asked Jacoman rhetorically.

'Life is more important than money. . .' murmured Anna. She looked hard at Jacoman now. He had thrown one leg over the sofa arm, laid his head against the back of the sofa. With the sun behind him you could not see the colour of his eyes; what light there was in his hair was picked up by light. 'And if,' she went on, '*if* one person was better off, but two people worse off, would it still have been worth it?'

'Yes, Anna,' he said; 'you'd better believe it; it would still have been worth it.'

478

The plain fact was, that treated or untreated, David's father had been tough, tougher than expected. Having developed pneumonia, having been given antibiotics, to no avail, he still took two days more to die; and even then he waited till ten o'clock at night. All of them were present – Anna had not intended to be present; the time had dragged on so, that despite her having expected in the beginning that every minute would be his last, this slow decline, this uneven, ever weaker breathing, became in itself a way of life, going on for ever.

But of course it could not go on for ever. Anna and David had scarcely got home from sitting with Sonia; when she rang for David; again Anna drove him; she had meant to put her head inside the bedroom door only, to give Sonia a sisterly kiss, maybe, then leave them. But as they came into the room, Sonia turned and looked at her younger brother and raised a hand. 'Wait,' she said, 'he's going.'

Hardly knowing what she was doing, Anna took David's hand. And then she could not have gone even if she wanted to, he gripped it so tightly. He almost dragged her with him across the little room to the bed, to his father; there they were, all three of them, looking down upon him, upon this surprisingly small shell of a once quite big man, whom age and disease had both withered and shrunken.

The breaths were sighs rather than breaths now; for five minutes or so they kept on coming, more or less as they had been; but after that the gaps between the breaths grew longer and longer; sometimes the gap was so long you thought that was really the end of it – but still, for what? ten? fifteen? minutes, the breath, the little, almost inaudible, yet unmistakably living breath, renewed itself over and over.

The last one when it came was different, however; it could not be mistaken for anything other than what it was, a final renewal, an assertion of life as well as its surrender; a long deep sigh; thereafter stillness fell; and a waxen silence.

They stood all three of them together, hand-in-hand,

looking down at the envelope of flesh tucked into the bed so lovingly, so neatly. How big the nose looked, Anna was thinking; the way the cheeks had fallen away, it dominated the whole face. Sonia leaned down and closed the open eyes, as dark, Anna noted, as David's. And then – how did it happen – had Anna actually pushed her husband – however it happened, he took his sister in his arms, they clung to one another; for the second time in three days – two days ago was the first time Anna had seen brother and sister touch each other, let alone embrace – now they clung very nearly as people cling who do such things often. And one of them, Sonia was it? – yes, probably Sonia – reached out a hand to Anna and gathered her in, also; an act of generosity which amazed her, remembering it later. But nothing amazed her at this moment, death itself seemed like life itself, not frightening nor appalling, not beautiful, not even moving. It was no word; it was itself. Anna had not seen her own father die; she had not even seen his body. If she had seen it, maybe she would have felt then, also, the profound, absolute sense of reality she felt gazing down upon her husband's dead father, the arms of her husband and her sister-in-law about her.

Anna raised her hand to her face at last to wipe away the tears that were starting; her silver snake bracelet brushed against her nostrils; it still, she noticed, reeked of sardine a little. In her, ever after, thoughts of death could be, were, evoked by the smell of fish.

☐	The Queen of the Tambourine	Jane Gardam	£5.99
☐	The Summer After the Funeral	Jane Gardam	£4.99
☐	A Long Way From Verona	Jane Gardam	£5.99
☐	Showing the Flag	Jane Gardam	£4.99
☐	The Glass Curtain	Carlo Gébler	£5.99
☐	Life of a Drum	Carlo Gébler	£5.99
☐	Malachy and His Family	Carlo Gébler	£4.50
☐	White Boy Running	Christopher Hope	£4.99
☐	Invitation to the Married Life	Angela Huth	£5.99
☐	The Goldbug Variations	Richard Powers	£7.99

Abacus now offers an exciting range of quality titles by both established and new authors. All of the books in this series are available from:

Little, Brown and Company (UK) Limited,
P.O. Box 11,
Falmouth,
Cornwall TR10 9EN.

Alternatively you may fax your order to the above address.
Fax No. 0326 376423.

Payments can be made as follows: cheque, postal order (payable to Little, Brown and Company) or by credit cards, Visa/Access. Do not send cash or currency. UK customers and B.F.P.O. please allow £1.00 for postage and packing for the first book, plus 50p for the second book, plus 30p for each additional book up to a maximum charge of £3.00 (7 books plus).

Overseas customers including Ireland, please allow £2.00 for the first book plus £1.00 for the second book, plus 50p for each additional book.

NAME (Block Letters) ....

....

ADDRESS ....

....

....

☐ I enclose my remittance for _____

☐ I wish to pay by Access/Visa Card

Number ☐☐☐☐☐☐☐☐☐☐☐☐☐☐☐☐

Card Expiry Date ☐☐☐☐